D0052844

ECOTOPIA
EMERGING

ECOTOPIA EMERGING

Ernest Callenbach

Banyan Tree Books in association with Heyday
Berkeley, California

© 1981 by Ernest Callenbach

All rights reserved. No portion of this work may be reproduced or transmitted in any form or by any means, electronic or mechanical, including photocopying and recording, or by any information storage or retrieval system, without permission in writing from Heyday.

All characters and firms portrayed in this novel are fictitious. Any resemblance to actual persons or firms is entirely coincidental.

Library of Congress Cataloging-in-Publication Data:
Callenbach, Ernest.
        Ecotopia Emerging.
        I. Title.
PS3553.A42E3   813'.54   81-10821
ISBN 978-0-9604320-3-5 (paper)   AACR2

green press
INITIATIVE

Heyday Books is committed to preserving ancient forests and natural resources. We elected to print this title on 100% post consumer recycled paper, processed chlorine free. As a result, for this printing, we have saved:

14 Trees (40' tall and 6-8" diameter)
4 Million BTUs of Total Energy
1,342 Pounds of Greenhouse Gases
6,463 Gallons of Wastewater
392 Pounds of Solid Waste

Heyday Books made this paper choice because our printer, Thomson-Shore, Inc., is a member of Green Press Initiative, a nonprofit program dedicated to supporting authors, publishers, and suppliers in their efforts to reduce their use of fiber obtained from endangered forests.

For more information, visit www.greenpressinitiative.org

Environmental impact estimates were made using the Environmental Defense Paper Calculator. For more information visit: www.papercalculator.org.

Orders, inquiries, and correspondence should be addressed to:
Heyday
P. O. Box 9145
Berkeley, CA 94709
(510) 549-3564
Fax (510) 549-1889
www.heydaybooks.com

Printed in the
United States of America

10 9 8 7

For Christine
lover, partner, friend

ECO-   from the Greek *oikos* (household or home)

-TOPIA   from the Greek *topos* (place)

Lou Swift was strong, even though she was slender. Living in the tiny seaside town of Bolinas on the northern California coast meant spending a lot of time outdoors. Lou moved with an appealing springiness, as if her energy flowed from the tips of her toes right up through her whole body and out through her large grey eyes. Brown tousled hair curled around her delicate face. She had a bubbly laugh and a voice that was low and throaty, especially for someone only 17—it tended to draw attention to her, sometimes to her embarrassment. Partly for that reason she usually dressed casually and kept some rein on her natural playfulness. In fact her highschool classmates mostly thought of her as rather mysteriously engrossed in her scientific studies. On occasions when she started talking enthusiastically of how important it was to crack the photovoltaic problem, Lou noticed their attention wandered. So she didn't talk much at school about the research lab she had set up at Bolinas, where she had been doing solar cell work since her sophomore year.

Much of the time Lou lived in Bolinas with her father Roger, his second wife Carol, and her step-brother Mike, who was now 13. The Swift house was a sprawling hand-made place that Roger and Lou's mother Jan had built together when Lou was still a baby. In a tiny house at the back of the lot lived Demetrios, nicknamed Dimmy, an old friend of Carol and Roger's, and his four-year-old son Theo. They were really part of the family, and shared use of the kitchen and main living spaces, and most of the time they all ate together.

1

Lou enjoyed the isolation of Bolinas. The Bolinesians (as they had begun calling themselves) seemed to her lively and individualistic— they had a pioneering spirit. People somehow became more independent when they lived a 20-minute drive—along perilous rocky cliffs—from the nearest real town. But Lou also had the option of staying with Jan, who was a painter and now lived in the nearby town of Mill Valley, in a warehouse she and some friends had turned into studios and living space. Lou's high school was in Mill Valley too, so she could go to the warehouse after classes, laze around with Jan and her friends, and maybe stay overnight. Or she could go back to Bolinas on the school bus, and do some studying until Carol returned from the store where she worked most days. Lou usually got more done in Bolinas, despite some distractions from Mike.

On this particular late autumn Friday, Lou wanted to get back to Bolinas in a hurry because she had been putting together a new experiment. She hadn't yet told Roger about it. He taught science in a San Francisco high school, and they often talked about her work; but Lou had found some years back that she usually came up with better scientific ideas than Roger did. That had been a real shock at the time. Now she rather enjoyed it—she could always ask him for advice and background information, but he usually preferred just to supply the information and let her generate most of the ideas. They made a good team. Lou often had a faint smile on her face when she imagined showing Roger some new development. He was, she knew, terribly proud of her. When she had won her first statewide school science prize (it was for a solution to a mathematics puzzle, and the awards committee had called her work "most ingenious"), Roger had insisted on framing the certificate. And he had strongly encouraged her work in photovoltaics.

Whoever developed the first cheap, efficient, reliable solar cell would be contributing something extremely important for the future. Lou didn't think of herself as particularly arrogant; she just felt in her bones that there was some small yet tantalizing chance she could bring it off, when hundreds of highly paid scientists working in big laboratories couldn't. One of her mother's best paintings was called "A Cat Can Look at a King," and when Lou at age six asked what that meant (the picture showed a cat with huge, piercing eyes sitting in a tree) Jan said it was an old proverb to remind you never to stand in awe of anybody—no matter how rich or powerful.

Lou was certainly not in awe of the big laboratories. She followed

2

closely the developments they reported in the open scientific literature and picked up what gossip she could. Their published papers were careful and skillful, but they ran to pretty good *little* ideas. What was needed was one good *big* idea. But the firms that had first opened up the field had been bought by large corporations—mostly oil companies—who didn't seem terribly eager to make things happen fast. Perhaps Roger was right in thinking they wanted to protect as long as possible their dwindling markets for oil and uranium to fuel power plants. But even if that wasn't their basic game, she agreed with Roger that the companies wanted to develop a solar cell that was patentable and protectable, so that it could generate the same enormous profits that oil production had. Then they could pursue a strategy of pricing cells just slightly below the point at which they were competitive with power-company electricity, because that way the maximum profits could be milked from the two technologies over the longest possible period.

Lou knew this was the kind of thinking that was now taught in business schools. But she had never been near a business school, and considerations that bore purely on money as a criterion of human action struck her as immoral and irresponsible. She had a vision of people being able to capture the energy of the sun directly, wherever they lived, without hooking up to a utility's ugly overhead wires. If she could produce a really good solar cell, then household electricity in modest amounts could be generated without pollution, without huge centralized power plants, and especially without nuclear ones—existing generating plants would have plenty of capacity for industrial uses for many decades. And during that breathing period, electricity at competitive costs would become available from wind, geothermal, ocean thermal, and mini-hydro sources. The bitter debate about nuclear energy would be ended; people could stop worrying about its intolerable threats to the future, and get on with the transition to an altogether renewable-source energy system.

Lou hopped off the school bus and headed up the lane to the house. Seagulls glided by on the strong southeast wind, and the sky was covered with low, thick clouds. It looked like the first really big storm of the year. Damn, Lou thought, no sun worth anything for days! Still, she dropped her books and went out to her lab. Once it had been a two-car garage. Now it was full of equipment—metal frames, electronic gear, old cell rigs, machine tools. The little pickup truck that Roger and Carol shared with some neighbors had to be parked out-

3

side, next to Lou's furnace. Once Jan had gone through a ceramics period, before she started painting; this had been her kiln, and Lou had increased its heat capacity to deal with the silicon melting that her solar-cell work required. Out of it came the thin sheets of molten pure silicon that she had poured a few days before over two tightly stretched squares of carefully cleaned copper window screen.

Today she was working on a new doping combination which might enhance certain electron transfer mechanisms through the presence of minute quantities of various metal compounds. These were added by a doping gun, a device which operated in a vacuum chamber. Then she assembled the silicon squares into their mounting frames, soldered the connections, attached the pickup network of thin wires, and fitted over the whole assembly the glass cover that protected it from the weather. For a moment she debated whether to run a strip of sealer around the cracks. But the joints looked tight enough and it was beginning to get dark; she wanted to mount the units on the rack in the yard before she had to quit for the day.

On the edge of the sea cliff, facing south along the coast toward San Francisco, she had built a wooden frame of salvaged two-by-fours. On it she could clamp her experimental cells. Wires ran to meters protected in a little hut under the rack; when these were hooked up to the cells, she could get precise measurements of their output. A small device called a solarimeter registered the intensity of the sunlight and enabled her to calculate the efficiency of the different cells. The whole affair looked pretty weird and Roger sometimes called it "Lou's chicken roost." But it did what she wanted it to do. She clamped the new cells into place and plugged in their connecting wires.

Off to the west the sun was going down, and for a few moments its light broke out from under the clouds. Lou stared at it: a great fuchsia-colored ball of fire, our life-giving star, source of the energy that powered every biological process on the earth. As always, the sun's movement seemed surprisingly fast as it dropped behind the ocean horizon. It shrank to a thin, luminous strip, orange-gold, and then disappeared. Lou felt a twinge of loneliness when it had gone, and pulled her jacket tighter. It would begin to rain soon. She went into the house to wait for Carol and Roger to come home.

For four billion years the earth has moved in its steady course around the sun. The known history of human beings is little more than an eye-blink in that planetary lifetime. Yet, in their brief years upon the planet, humans evolved such astonishing capacities in hand and brain that they became a species which altered its own environment. Chimpanzees might build rude nests of greenery in the jungle and occupy them for a few days, but humans learned to pile shaped stones into protective walls and buildings. Antelopes might range for miles seeking lusher grass; humans learned to dig ditches and divert streams to their gardens.

Thus, little by little, this unique species discovered ways to overcome the ravages of predators and famine and disease. And once humans found ways to live together in towns and cities, their collective powers greatly increased; their populations multiplied. In Asia and the Middle East they built canals and aqueducts to irrigate vast realms and support elegant imperial courts. The Romans flung their roads, their laws and their armies over an empire stretching for thousands of miles. Many such great centers of civilization arose and flourished and then collapsed—in a majestic cycle almost as imposing as the earth's own seasonal rhythms.

Through these slow pre-industrial centuries the cultivation of new land gradually produced more food, and the impact of starvation and malnutrition lessened; nonetheless, humans continued to live in a rough balance with their fellow species. Only with the development of technological society, which ambitiously harnessed the energy in coal and oil, did human population soar. Then huge factory cities spread over whole counties and the scale of human activities, in engineering and in social organization, became overwhelming. By the time that European peoples designate in their calendars as the end of the twentieth century, the planet was home to over five billion humans. Like a plague of locusts, they seemed to have escaped all natural checks and were devouring everything in their path. Unlike any creatures ever seen on the earth, humans exterminated other species by the tens of thousands—either directly with guns, or indirectly by destroying habitats in forest and river and grassland.

But the population explosion of the industrial epoch also subjected humans themselves to new and unprecedented perils. Human activities—even the detonation of nuclear bombs—remained puny in comparison to the huge transfers of solar energy by winds and storms. Nonetheless, in certain critical respects humans had acquired the power

5

to diminish the earth's capacity to support life. Deserts were spreading because exploitative land ownership patterns drove desperate people to overgraze and defoliate the land. Cancer and degeneration of the gene pool through mutations were rising, consequences of human cleverness in producing new chemical compounds for agricultural, industrial or military use. The burning of immense quantities of coal and oil was steadily increasing the carbon dioxide content of the atmosphere; if this continued, a "greenhouse effect" would raise temperatures enough to melt the polar ice caps, inundate parts of many coastal cities, and make deserts of now fertile temperate agricultural areas. Nor was there any certainty that the process could be reversed; it might turn much of the earth's surface into a Mars-like wasteland.

One peril was still more threatening. Under the industrial mode of life, humans were subjugated in vast quarrelsome patriarchal nation-states. The rulers of these states were now armed with nuclear weapons so fearsome and so numerous that if they were used even in small part they would end modern civilization, at least in the northern hemisphere. Even more ominously, a nuclear war would affect the outer atmosphere in unpredictable ways; its protective layers might lose the critical ability to shield the earth from the lethal blaze of the sun's radiation.

Thus, paradoxically, the technological ingenuity which had enabled humans to proliferate into every habitable niche on the earth's surface had also begun to threaten the survival upon the planet of all plant and animal life—including the human species itself.

Vera Allwen had been a state senator for six years, and before that had served several terms in the state assembly. She was now about 52, and though she was an extremely vigorous and forthright person she had begun to take on a certain grandmotherly aspect. (She was in fact a grandmother, her daughter by a previous marriage having recently produced two children; now Vera was married to a mathematician, a quiet and retiring person, several years younger.) This did not deceive her enemies in the state government, however; they sensed that in this still male-dominated institution Vera constituted an undefinable threat. She knew how to mobilize political energies, and bills that she decided to oppose seldom reached the governor's desk. The people around her tended to be brilliant if perhaps a little erratic; but their ability to marshal new ideas, coupled with Vera's steady judgment, had made her office an increasingly respected force in state politics. She sat on important committees, and was the *de facto* leader of the several dozen young, dynamic women elected in response to the antifeminist backlash of the early eighties. Tireless, with an almost old-fashioned air of moral authority about her, Vera made people feel that when they worked with her they somehow became better human beings than they were without her.

On this rainy night Vera's husband had left their modest apartment to her and gone out. Vera was stirring spaghetti sauce and waiting for a dozen friends who were due to arrive for a monthly gathering. They would drink some wine, gossip, put their feet up around Vera's handsome Scandinavian wood stove, and lay schemes to improve the world. It was nice, tonight, to be the one who stayed home and cooked, and didn't have to go out in the downpour. Next time it would be someone else's turn.

Putting the sauce on a low flame, Vera sat down to skim through the paper again. There was an item in the business pages which had horrified her, and she wanted to check it again: an Eastern food chain had announced plans to phase out sales of all fresh vegetables and fruits. A pudgy-looking male executive was quoted as saying that public unwillingness to pay higher prices on fresh produce gave the corporation no choice. He added that the company's nutritionists assured "worried housewives" that they could still give their families balanced diets by the use of house-brand food-supplement pills. "The American diet," he said, "must change to reflect new space-age economic and technological priorities." The article concluded with speculations by a stock analyst that the company's new policy would boost first-quarter earnings by two percentage points; other companies would be driven to follow suit. Vera Allwen's solid, square jaw set defiantly. "No," she thought. "No, simply *no*."

She went to her refrigerator and began washing and cutting up vegetables for her salad: cucumbers, mushrooms, leafy red-edged lettuce, tomatoes, bright red and green peppers. Then into the dark hand-turned wooden salad bowl she added alfalfa sprouts and sunflower seeds. With her bare hands she tumbled the mixture about, feeling the damp crispness of the vegetables against her skin. Finally what had only been vague in her mind before crystallized in words:

7

"Not out here. We won't let them do it here. We've got to take our survival in our own hands."

The first guests to arrive were Penny Fox and Gail Kramer, two of Vera's legislative colleagues. Penny was blonde and athletic and had a skier's winter suntan; she looked like a former debutante, which in fact she was. But she had also been a river rafting guide and had first gotten involved in state politics through struggles over preserving white water. Gail, who was small and intense, had come up through the city's Democratic Party ranks. Vera poured some wine for them and waved her clipping under their noses, and they too were aghast. Next Marianne Macy appeared, a freckled, rather disheveled woman with a well-worn hiking pack on her back. She lived a nomadic life as an organizer of community gardens, and she gave Vera's salad a professional inspection. She was followed by a couple named Jim and Jeanie Ferguson; Jeanie was an architect and Jim was a contractor and carpenter. They now specialized in lovely hand-made buildings, but in earlier times Jim had been a lawyer and labor organizer; he had once served a term on the city council.

The spaghetti sauce filled the apartment with the aroma of oregano and garlic and tomato, and people began taking hopeful stirs at the pot as they refilled their glasses. When the door next opened five people stomped in together, laughing. Pauline Sauvageot was a magazine editor with a radical publication headquartered in the city, and had been a political reporter for many years. Irene Cook had grown up with Pauline in Philadelphia; she taught biology at the University in Berkeley, and wrote poems in feminist magazines.

With them was another legislator, Fran Tuttweiler, about Vera's age, and two young biologists who had become environmental consultants and agitators, Bill Beckerson and Becky Tauber; their rapid-fire fact-laden testimony before legislative committees had earned them the nickname "The Beck and Becky Show." "I think we can throw in the spaghetti," Vera said. "We're just missing Henry." Henry Engelsdorf, one of Vera's oldest and most trusted friends, was often late. It was hard for him to tear himself away from people, and Vera knew he had been invited to another house for drinks on his way over. She forgave him, as she always did, and brought the water to a boil. Then great handfuls of pasta, freshly made in a nearby North Beach place, got tossed in. People took turns stirring, while others assembled plates and silverware and napkins. They passed around Vera's horrifying news story. Then finally everything was ready and they fell to,

8

with another round of wine to wash it all down. As was usual with this group, the conversation was lively, sometimes raucous. People told cautionary tales about absurd things that had happened in their political or personal lives since the last meeting. They satirized their opponents in the struggles they were involved in. They made little private plans to help each other in various ways over the weeks ahead. All went convivially as usual, until Vera picked up her clipping again.

"You know," she said, "this thing makes me realize that we can't just take this kind of non-survival behavior any more. We have to find some way of fighting it politically. But I don't know how we should go about it."

Six voices started to speak at once, but as the discussion sorted itself out it became clear that most of the people in the room had privately begun to feel it was time to try building a new political party. As Vera's three gallons of California wine steadily disappeared, a rudimentary consensus arose about the nature of a new party that would satisfy them—and might thus satisfy others. It would be dedicated to defending the biological welfare of the species, evaluating all political and economic actions by their long-run prospects for ensuring stable survival on the earth. It would be highly democratic and decentralized, with chapters in every neighborhood, and it would seek to transcend traditional left-right divisions in hopes of creating a new sense of community and of shared biological and social destiny. It would mobilize people's feelings of vulnerability and helplessness against pollution, cancer, noise, corruption, waste; it would help them take charge of their own fates. It would unlock the dismal paralysis of recent American politics. It would win.

Since the seventies, the Western economy had been heavily dependent on oil—particularly Middle Eastern oil. Because of American domination of the territories around the Persian Gulf, this oil had been available for several decades at extremely low prices compared to coal and other energy sources. When effective steps were initiated by the OPEC nations to drive the price of oil upward, the initial shock had taken both Western governments and corporations by surprise. They reacted with confusion and a variety of ineffective plans.

The conservative political tide which had swept the United States in the eighties had also pushed federal energy policies in suicidal direc-

9

tions. Vast sums were dispensed to subsidize synthetic fuel production even though such fuels would be, by the time they finally came on the market, more costly than renewable biomass alternatives and would cause additional cost burdens through air and water pollution damage. New missiles and other armaments were put into production, weakening the economy but adding to the public impression that American might could always preserve access to the Gulf oil fields. Federal funds shored up failing automobile corporations—which had proved unable to compete with Japanese firms in producing gas-efficient cars—instead of diverting them toward production of buses, trains, and other low-energy means of transportation. At a time when even utility executives recognized that nuclear energy was becoming economically unviable, the federal government slashed its budget for solar energy and conservation measures and put the money into nuclear development.

The government's only significantly realistic action was price decontrol, which allowed oil companies to raise prices further, generating almost incalculable profits. Higher prices drastically penalized the poor, who drove old cars and lived in badly insulated houses, but they did cut down on public gasoline and oil consumption. Most American politicians, however, continued to believe that reliance upon oil must continue and that increased drilling in the United States and in areas within its immediate sphere of influence (such as Mexico) would somehow provide so much new oil that prices would fall. Support for this belief could be found in the history of other industries, where increased demand had often led to increased production.

But oil was not an ordinary industry. Along with agriculture—which some thought could be made productive enough, through the application of ever more chemicals, to pay for oil imports—the oil industry had become the foundation of all social activity. And it depended upon a resource which, however much of it might remain to be discovered, was getting steadily more expensive to produce. Deeper wells took more complex drilling equipment, better crews, used more drilling and pumping energy. Wells offshore or in the Arctic required sophisticated drilling rigs and extraction technology; transporting their oil required expensive pipelines and often posed difficult ecological and political problems.

Oil prices, then, would ultimately continue to rise until energy consumers developed other, competing sources they could turn to, thus providing a real check. But this idea was so unpalatable, and its consequences so drastic, that it was literally unthinkable both to politicians

10

and to most of the citizenry at large. So a widespread national flight *from reality occurred, in which numerous alternatives to oil were considered and rejected. After all, it was felt, oil might be getting more expensive, but it was there; the alternatives were untried. Moreover, because the alternatives were at the moment slightly more expensive than oil, excuses could be found to reject them on hardheaded economic grounds—ignoring the fact that they would soon be cheaper since they relied on such "free," inexhaustible sources as the wind, the earth's geothermal heat, or ocean thermal differentials. Alternatives to oil for transportation purposes, such as burnable oils produced by desert plants, or alcohol fermented from sugar cane, grain, or agricultural wastes, were similarly discarded. Instead, officials fell back on a naive faith that the oil companies, if "unleashed," would somehow revive the good old days of cheap gasoline.*

Thus, like a lumbering dinosaur unable to face the fact that the climate had changed, daydreaming of the better pasturage of yesteryear, oil-hungry America lurched toward some unseen economic catastrophe.

All during the night the storm grew in intensity. Seabirds and flocks of migrating ducks huddled together, heads under wings in the downpour, in the sheltered waters of Bolinas Lagoon. On Bolinas Reef the flashing light was obscured by the wind-blown spray thrown up from a thousand waves breaking on submerged rocks, where many a ship had gone aground. The rain pummeled the thick grasses and scrubby trees of Bolinas mesa, and the field mice hid deep in their burrows. Wind and rain beat on the big south-facing windows of the Swift house. In the middle of the night Carol, awakened by an intermittent noise under the distant roar of surf and the surge of wind around the house, got up and found the roof had sprung a leak. She put out a pan to catch the drip and crept back under the down quilt beside Roger, who had not heard a thing. In the morning she'd have to get up on the roof with her patching compound again.

Along almost a thousand miles of California and Oregon coast, the storm pounded the shore. In the great sweep of geological time, that coast was heaving upward, with a slowness inconceivable to humankind. But the storm's short-term action was to grind it away, and people who had built too close to the fragile sea cliffs sometimes lost

11

half their houses on a night like this. The Swift house now stood back some 20 yards from the current drop-off of the cliff edge. When Roger and Jan built the house there had been a road running in front of it; now the road had mostly dropped away and there was only a footpath. Craftily, Roger had calculated that if the house stood for a hundred years (an unusual achievement for an American house) it would still not quite be undermined; the house and the cliff under it would collapse, he estimated, at about the same time.

On this night, with the wind strong out of the south, the huge swells crashing in off the Pacific sometimes threw spray fifty feet high, when a particular wave hit a particular rock formation just right. The wind then carried the salty spray up the cliff face and some of it swept on over the edge of the level mesa; old cypresses standing there showed the stunted shapes that resulted from being long subjected to this process. Lou's solar cell array, mounted to catch the southern sun at maximum exposure, also caught the wind-blown sea spray. The wind shook her mounting rack and finally worked loose a supporting two-by-four; the resulting strain twisted open small cracks in the frames of two of Lou's cells. Gradually, through the night, salty water seeped through the cracks. In one of the cells, the seal at the bottom proved tight, and the cell cavity slowly filled up with a film of water. Because the leads to Lou's meters ran out the top, the cell did not short-circuit. It shook in the blasts of wind and hung there on its rack till morning came.

The most advanced nuclear plant in the entire United States was situated a few miles outside the Seattle city limits. It had been given the name "Puget 1" since it was located on the shores of the Northwest's great inland sea, Puget Sound. In the seven years of its operation, a number of stainless steel pipes within the immense containment sphere of Puget 1 had developed imperceptible cracks.

The reactor, which had ended up costing three billion dollars, was operated by Great Northwestern Power, which in turn was controlled by a multinational corporation with operations in England, South Africa, West Germany and other parts of the United States. Great Northwestern's finances had been severely strained by the construction of Puget 1 and by surprisingly intense resistance by the public to the electricity price rises the company had demanded as a result.

12

Influenced by new cost-accounting systems worked out by a group of environmental lawyers, the state public utilities commission (formerly the company's staunch ally) had allowed only about half of the requested rate boosts. And to make matters still worse, the public had responded to even this compromise rate rise by further insulation of houses, adoption of solar heating, and diminished use of electric lights and appliances. Industry, seeking to control its costs, also deployed many energy-saving measures. Thus total per capita electricity use, instead of climbing steeply ever upward as utility and government experts had always predicted, followed a gently slumping curve downward.

To maintain its profit rate and keep its investors' capital, Great Northwestern had only one option available: cut back on its payroll and thus on operations and maintenance costs. In the last full inspection of Puget 1's emergency core-cooling system, X-ray technicians had noticed faint lines that might be incipient cracks, or then again just welding shadows. The supervising inspector had determined that the lines were welding shadows. "You boys don't know what you're talking about," he said when his men questioned this judgment. "I've seen thousands of these things. None of 'em ever blew yet."

All the same, as he drove home that night, the chief inspector had a clammy feeling at the back of his neck when he thought about one particular X-ray sheet. He had heard stories of other plants where inspectors had relabeled last year's sheets and stuck them in the files. His boss, after all, had told him corners might have to be cut. He was just doing his job. And besides, he had taken pains when he moved to Seattle to locate his family well upwind from the reactor site.

When Lou got up in the morning it was still raining. She added some wood to the stove, made herself a banana-and-egg milkshake, and started coffee for Roger and Carol. She emptied the drip pan Carol had set out, pulled the cord that lifted the insulation shutter from the rooftop solar water heater, and put her homework papers in order. Then she threw on a slicker and went out, tossing the previous day's kitchen scraps into the compost bin that stood near her cell array.

It was still windy, and as she approached the rack she saw the wind-loosened two-by-four, and the sagging row of cells. No damage, really, but she would have to take all the delicate cells off before she could do any heavy hammering to repair the rack. It would be a miserable job in the wet—she might as well wait till the rain stopped and things dried off. She opened the little door of the instrument hut and peered in to see if any damage had occurred there. Everything seemed all right; the meters were dry. Then she noticed that one of the switches that were on each cell's circuit had been jiggled closed by the wind's shaking of the rack. Normally she opened these switches every evening, cutting off the cells from the battery they were connected to as their charging load. Damn, she thought. With all that salt spray around, something is probably shorted out. She threw all the switches closed, and ran her eyes along the row of meters. As she expected, in today's grey-sky conditions they all read zero.

Except the last one. It was *not* at zero. It was well up on its scale, indicating an output far beyond the best she had achieved on such days previously.

Lou stared at it. This was the meter for one of the new cells she had installed yesterday. Could the meter be defective, she wondered? She tapped the meter face lightly, then opened the circuit switch. The needle dropped to zero, but returned to its previous reading when she closed the switch again. Lou stood bolt upright and leaped around the rack to look at the new cell. Her mind was doing lightning calculations, transforming the meter's arbitrary markings into power output figures. Unless something peculiar was going on, this new cell's output was about tenfold beyond anything that anybody had come up with yet!

The cell looked wet but intact. Then, as Lou examined it more closely, she saw a thin line running across the glass near the top. The inside of the cell, she realized, was practically full of water. Then why hadn't it shorted out? Well, evidently the positive lead had stayed dry. The negative lead, connected to the pickup grid that was covered with water, could be wet without changing anything, so long as the positive lead wasn't grounded in some way.

What had happened? Lou's heart was beating with excitement. She pulled out her notepad, but realized it was useless in the rain; she'd have to write it all down later. She made a mental list of crucial observations. First, by covering the cell, she ascertained that it *was* a photo-electric effect: when the cell received no light, it gave no current. Then, systematically eliminating other factors, she centered on the probability that something about the water getting into the cell

14

had increased its output. She examined the other cells; several of them were wet too, yet their meters rested at the bottom of the scale. But how could water produce that kind of effect? Rain was basically distilled water and thus generally inactive though it picked up some pollution as it fell through the atmosphere. She would have to do a chemical assay of the fluid in the cell—which by now must be a messy mixture of the water that leaked in, traces of her new doping compound, and God knows what else. A few drops of it seemed to be oozing out of the cell frame. She put her finger under it and caught a drop. Knowing a scientist should not do such things, she tasted it.

It was salty.

She looked out over the sea, still rough. "So it could be partly sea spray," she said to herself. Carefully, so as not to cause further leaking of the cell, she unclamped it from the rack, took it into her lab, and emptied the liquid into a clean container. It was Saturday, but when Roger got up, and she told him what had happened, she was sure he would drive her and the sample to the analysis lab in town.

Since the beginning of the war-production drive of 1940-1945, which transformed the United States into the greatest industrial machine the earth had yet seen, chemists had been developing new substances at an astonishing pace. Once they learned the basic techniques of hooking and unhooking atoms their imaginations seemed unlimited. They played with shiny colored balls that represented atoms, building them into beautiful, complex new molecules; then, first in laboratories and later in immense plants that resembled oil refineries, they produced the actual compounds.

Many of these new materials had extraordinarily interesting properties. Some of them could kill insects; these were manufactured by the millions of tons, and given names like DDT or 2-4D. Some were useful as drugs, though they had unsuspected side-effects of nausea, headaches, sweating, gastric upsets, circulatory disorders. Some were glue-like and hardened as strong as steel, but could be molded into infinitely varied shapes. Some could be made into thin, almost weightless transparent films. Some could be used in foods as preservatives, flavorizers, tenderizers, or to make foods stiffer or creamier. Some were dyes, widely used in foods, clothing, plastics. Some were capable of foaming up and then hardening into spongy or rigid forms.

15

They appeared in paints and varnishes, they were made into bottles and pan-coatings and phonograph records. They were eaten and drunk, sprayed and powdered, applied in a thousand ways upon the landscape and all the creatures who inhabited it. By the end of the seventies there was no human activity in all the United States, from contraception to the management of terminal disease, carried out free of materials that had not existed on the face of the earth forty years earlier. This, it was widely believed, was a testimonial to humankind's improvements on nature. People clamored for the new wonder products, and could no longer imagine living without them.

Especially during manufacture, but also for weeks or months later, some of the new compounds gave off some of their molecules into the surrounding air, which thus became permeated with strangely penetrating smells. Children and animals attempted to evade these smells, but tens of millions of adults were exposed to them regularly—on their jobs in industrial plants or on farms, in their houses, on the roads, and in the streets. Through the lungs, and also through food and water, the new molecules entered into human bodies. What they did there, aside from causing an occasional headache or bout of nausea, nobody then regarded as important.

About thirty years after the great boom in chemical production began, American public health officials and doctors realized that the nation was experiencing an alarming new rise in the incidence of cancer. Some attempted to explain this by saying that modern sanitation and medicine enabled people to live longer, and that when they lived longer they just naturally fell prey to diseases like cancer. Others noted the rise in certain cancers due to cigarette smoking, or the taking of popular drugs that had been insufficiently tested, or dietary factors. Research was hampered by the fact that there were so many different types of cancers, and many of them took twenty years or so to develop. Increasingly, however, people of all ages were suffering from the disease—with more than one in every four Americans becoming victims.

Through the endless ingenuity of chemists about a thousand new chemicals per year were introduced into the environment; the total reached well past 80,000, of which almost 35,000 were officially classified as known or potential hazards to human health. After many citizen protests, the federal government had begun a program of testing these substances to determine how severe were the dangers they posed. But it was estimated that, at the budget allotted, this testing program would not catch up for a hundred years—if then.

Meanwhile, pesticides were being impregnated into upholstery and carpets and building materials. They were sprayed or painted onto buildings by insect and rodent exterminators. Pesticides and herbicides were sprayed in parks and public buildings and buses and on gardens and golf courses. They were sprayed along roadsides, where they drifted onto nearby houses. Highly toxic materials called PCBs were dispersed throughout the land as insulation material in millions of electric-pole transformers and capacitors, television sets, fluorescent light fixtures, and industrial equipment; whenever these leaked or exploded or were tossed into dumps, the oily persistent liquid diffused over nearby earth, automobiles or people. Agricultural pesticides and herbicides were sprayed from airplanes and helicopters; combined with fertilizers, they were used to soak seeds before planting. Each year, in the western states alone, hundreds of millions of pounds of carcinogenic and mutagenic compounds were distributed. Toxic substances in quantities large enough to require destruction of poultry and eggs ended up in the food supplies of 17 states; in the East and Midwest, many lakes and streams were closed to fishing because of dangerous chemical concentrations.

Researchers hoping to find a viral cause for cancer were reluctantly driven to the conclusion that, though some virus process might be involved, the precipitating causes of cancer were something like 80 per cent environmental. People were doing it to themselves. But this was not a message that most Americans were then prepared to hear; it went largely unreported and undiscussed, and the cancer rates continued rising. Chemistry graduates continued to receive lucrative job offers before they even stepped off campus. People went on breathing air that was known to be dangerous to their health, drinking water known to be contaminated, eating pesticide- and additive-laden foods, and concentrating their attention on making money in order (as they imagined it) to survive.

Like the Elephant's Child in Kipling's fable, Lou had always been insatiably curious. And like the Elephant's Child she got into a certain amount of trouble as a consequence, though the trouble usually seemed outweighed by the long-range benefits. In any case, that was the way she was. Jan and Roger, in Lou's earliest years, had encouraged her explorations. When she was first learning to crawl, they let her crawl off the edge of their bed and tumble the fifteen inches to pillows they placed on the floor nearby, so she learned about falling. They let her play with fire quite literally, watching her but allowing her to burn her fingers with matches. And they had also put no restrictions in her way when she discovered the pleasurable potentials of her body; later, of course, they instructed her that many people felt these pleasures should be enjoyed only behind closed doors. In her heart Lou thought this was somehow silly—but if it was the way the game was played, she could go along with it.

Sometimes, though, she was careless. One winter Friday afternoon when she was 16 a particularly heavy rain had begun, and she had decided to spend the weekend in town. When she got to Jan's studio nobody was there, and she found a note from Jan to one of her housemates saying she wouldn't be back till evening. Lou built herself a fire in the stove and turned on some music. The big common room—used for cooking, eating and socializing—was a friendly, cluttered place, full of pieces of old furniture and art works in various stages of completion or abandonment. The old warehouse roof, though it was insulated by now, still had a metal covering, and the rain added a soft background noise. There wouldn't be anyone around for several hours; she'd catch up on some reading. She slouched on a big old overstuffed sofa by the stove. After a while her jeans felt tight and she unzipped them. That was better. It felt even better when she slipped her hand down inside, and she explored how it felt when she didn't quite pay total attention either to the reading or to her fingers' quiet fondling. Still, she noticed that the fondling tended to get more interesting and the reading less.

Suddenly she became aware that someone had come in from the entrance hallway and was looking across at her. It was one of Jan's painter friends, Jeffrey. He had a reassuring smile on his face. Lou wondered if she should pull her hand out of her jeans, but decided that would be even more awkward.

"Hello, Lou," he said. "Don't be embarrassed—we all do it, you know! Sorry to surprise you—Jan gave me a key so I could drop by and get a turkey into the oven. Big feed tonight—you going to stay?"

Lou nodded. "Yeah. Too rainy to go out to Bolinas." Jeffrey came over and sat on the arm of the couch. He was rather delicately built, wore his hair a little longer than most men, and had a beautiful, androgynous face. Lou's curiosity had not yet managed to decipher if Jeffrey was gay, or what; she had sometimes wondered if he was a lover of Gary, the only man who currently shared the warehouse. But

18

then on other occasions Jeffrey was very affectionate toward Jan's former housemate Marcia, who occasionally bought one of his paintings.

Jeffrey put his hand on Lou's arm. It felt warm and gentle. He looked at her carefully and kindly, with that same twinkly reassuring smile, as if they now shared a beautiful secret. Lou smiled back, and Jeffrey moved his hand down Lou's arm, very slowly, stopping to wiggle it playfully under the elastic of her underpants. His fingers felt tingly, and she stretched herself out so there was more room for them. Jeffrey slid down onto the counch alongside her, put his other arm around her, and kissed her.

Well, she thought, he certainly isn't *just* gay! She extracted her own arm and put it around him. His body was lithe and felt marvellous— she squirmed against him. He moved beautifully, she realized—not like the highschool guys who just liked to paw your breasts and crawl around over you like you were some kind of obstacle course. It was more like dancing, even though they were wedged onto this rather narrow couch.

Lou stopped kissing him for a moment. "Aren't we supposed to *talk* about this first?" she asked.

Jeffrey slid his fingers up under Lou's shirt. "Nobody's supposed to do anything," he replied. "This is liberated territory. What do you *want* to do?" His fingertips touched her breast so delicately that Lou shivered with pleasure.

"Oh, more, more!" she said happily, and hugged him.

"All right," he said. "But first we'd better deal with that damned turkey." So they extricated themselves and hastily prepared the bird and stuck it into the oven.

"What about the stuffing?" asked Lou.

"We'll get to that in a while," said Jeffrey, leading her back to the rug in front of the stove and spreading out a big woolly blanket. "Come here, little love," he said, kneeling down gracefully, "and play with me." So they rolled around on the rug, puppy-like and laughing. They crawled on top of one another and wriggled deliciously. They kissed and licked. Lou was delighted to find that Jeffrey simply enjoyed whatever they were doing; he wasn't in a hurry like the guys she had made out with at parties or in cars. They gradually took off their clothes, and she was delighted at the things he knew how to do with her. "Jeff," she cried out joyfully, "why didn't anybody tell me it could be so much better than masturbation!"

19

"There's more," he said. "There's always more, sweet Lou!" Then he somehow produced a condom and they were coupled. How lucky she was, Lou thought, to be doing this with trustable Jeffrey and not somebody who thought making love was like playing football— plunging toward the goal line. "Show me, Jeff," she whispered. "Show me *everything!*"

And so they had many more trysts at the warehouse. To Lou's relief, Jan approved of the affair. Looking back on her own life, Jan wished she had had an older lover who could have taught her about sex; so she was pleased at Lou's good fortune. She liked and trusted Jeff; she also knew that he had had a child earlier, and then a vasectomy, so she didn't have to worry about Lou getting pregnant.

The relationship had lasted about a year. Jan initially feared it might get too serious for Lou, but she also watched for signs that Jeff was getting really attached to Lou. Once he admitted to Jan, "Well, if Lou was eight or ten years older, I'd be in real trouble!" But he had stayed loose about it, perhaps deliberately—he kept on living in San Francisco, where he had other lovers. And then Lou, mysteriously, had begun to feel ready to end it. For one thing, she wanted to spend more time at her lab work in Bolinas. And she felt that perhaps she had learned what she could from Jeff, delightful as he was. She found herself having frequent twinges of desire for other men, and wondered where her curiosity would lead her next.

As things turned out, it led her into a relationship with a young musician named David Vandermeer, who had graduated two years before and was spending most of his time with a band he had started. He was as interested in his music as Lou was in her science, and this seemed to suit them both. She taught him some of the things she had learned with Jeff. They had wonderful times together, but made sure they both had plenty of time for work.

On Monday Lou took her checkbook along to school. She still had about ten thousand dollars of the inheritance left to her by her grandfather Thomas. Something of an inventor in his day, he had lived in the East. So Lou had not seen too much of him; but on his visits he had always encouraged her interest in science. The money he left her had been designated "for expenses in connection with research and development work." Lou managed it cautiously, hoping to stretch it through her college years. This particular lab test would cost several hundred dollars, but chromatography was something she couldn't do herself.

After classes she walked briskly across town to the lab. It had not been easy to keep her mind on French irregular verbs and the causes of the American Civil War. She rushed in the lab door, which closed with a swish of pressurized air behind her. They had the report ready, and Lou ran her eye down the print-out. She had dug up in the school library a list of the chemical components of seawater—they had surprised her by being so numerous. So she had that list to compare with the print-out. What she was looking for was something anomalous, some compound not normally found either in her doping mixture or in seawater—some clue to the magic ingredient in her new cell!

There was nothing new on the print-out. Her mysterious liquid was just rain and ordinary seawater, with its dozens of chlorides and bromides.

On the other hand, she realized, what was so wrong with that? In fact, in a certain way, what could be better? After all, wasn't she trying to build a solar cell that could be made from common materials by almost anybody? The silicon in her kiln came from sand, after all. Now she would have to do a series of elimination experiments to discover what component of the seawater was producing the extraordinary rise in output of her cell. And of course—Lou had a sudden sinking feeling in her stomach—she'd have to check further to make sure there wasn't some chemical reaction going on which mimicked a photo-electric effect—though that might be nice enough in its own way. There were many puzzles still to figure out, and she would push on until she solved them.

Since the waning of the last ice age—some fifteen thousand years ago—a green strip had lain along the Pacific coast. Cut off from the dry, desolate continental interior by the steep Sierra and Cascade ranges, this favored region received ample rainfall which sustained an abundance of plant and animal inhabitants. Because of its geographic isolation, the region came to boast many species found nowhere else. Unimaginably vast stands of redwoods, tallest trees on earth, covered the damp coastal mountains from Santa Cruz northward into Oregon, where they gave way to luxuriant stands of cedar. In the Sierra grew the

21

giant sequoias, not so tall as the redwoods but the most massive trees ever known. Mixed stands of fir, cedar and pine blanketed most of the cooler sites in the region, and drier areas supported thick-growing, fire-blackened chaparral or open oak-dotted grasslands. In the spring a stupendous profusion of wildflowers covered the slopes, from the mountain rocks and meadows down the foothills to the great marshes of the interior valleys. Salmon swam in the rivers by the millions, and along the coast shellfish abounded. Inland there were great herds of antelope and elk; grizzlies prowled the foothill coverts.

Into this temperate and abundant land the first known human inhabitants—moving down the continent from the Bering land-bridge—came with bows and arrows which enabled them to hunt even the great mammals. Their descendants settled into a quiet existence, coming to understand and respect the creatures and the places of the region; they knew how all sustained all. The black oaks and blue oaks and tanbark oaks provided acorns for animals and Indians—rich in protein, fat, and starch. Sturdy pines gave their oil-rich nuts. The hills were graced with delicate wild iris and edible bulbs. Tule rushes choked the lakes and streams, providing flour from their tubers and canoe-making material from their stalks. There were plants whose berries had medicinal properties, or whose juices would stun fish or hold arrow feathers to the shaft. The soap plant gave a delicate lather for washing. The arrowhead plant sprang from potato-like tubers that could be baked in slow campfires or pit-ovens. Grasses and aspen roots gave fibers for basketry and nets and snares and ropes. Manzanita in its dozens of species—its stem wood hard and mysteriously red-barked—gave bright berries good for a soothing tea.

Intensely localized peoples, the Indian inhabitants lived in small, peaceful tribelets, each occupying its own watershed. They knew their environments with an intimacy unfathomable to urban people, but this knowledge was limited to their own tiny territories. Then in 1805 Lewis and Clark were sent by Jefferson to explore the upper reaches of the newly acquired Missouri watershed. They crossed over to the basin of the mighty Columbia—greatest river of the Pacific coast. After wintering at its mouth, on their return trip they took with them detailed observations of plant and animal life which gave the first basis for systematic understanding of the biology of the coastal region.

Much later, in 1877, a professor named Thomas Porter would publish one of the first botanical maps of the United States. On it he defined what he called The Pacific Region. Its southern extremity was the ridge

22

line of the Tehachapis, extending to the sea at Point Conception. Encompassing the valleys of the San Joaquin and Sacramento, it ran north to take in the fertile Willamette valley and the low-lying areas around Puget Sound. Whether from scientific caution or diplomatic tact, Porter broke off his map at the Canadian border, though the plants themselves defined his Pacific Region as continuing several hundred miles further along the northwest coast. In more recent times, scientific refinements would adjust the boundaries here and there, and a new name, Oregonian Bioregion, would come into use.

Nonetheless, the underlying biological unity of the area would endure—despite the coming of what white-skinned humans called civilization, which imported alien grasses and trees and animals from other regions, indeed other countries. The whites occupied the land unthinkingly. They drove the original occupants into extinction or into virtually uninhabitable reservations. They divided the land according to boundaries (often laid out on random lines of latitude and longitude) which had little correspondence to biological or even social reality. Thus Washington citizens on the north bank of the Columbia increasingly went across to Oregon for the necessities or pleasures that only a city like Portland could provide. Small mountain communities near the northern border in California felt more akin to neighbor towns a few miles away in Oregon than they did to their own state capital of Sacramento, 200 miles distant and engrossed in its farm-economy affairs; and Los Angeles might as well have been on another planet. People who lived in Truckee or other small towns east of the forbidding Sierra passes, often cut off by winter snows, felt themselves allied with Nevada rather than with California. And patterns of agricultural and retail trade, determined more by population levels and freight rates than by political allegiances, evolved without reference to state lines.

Bearing small relation to official school-taught geography, the economic and social organism of the society developed a definite shape of its own. Railroads (and in the East, canals) provided its circulatory system. Like stomach, brain, or fat deposits, its major cities digested raw materials, provided direction and guidance, and stored capital reserves for expansion or hard times.

But in its vastness, the country never became altogether one organism. Beneath the smooth unified surface, under the patriotic rhetoric of national holidays, lurked persistent regional customs, attitudes, and loyalties. The South, denied autonomy, built a political party machine that would use its conservative bloc veto power for a *hundred years to thwart development of the industrial North into a progressive democracy. New England rested on its intellectual and industrial achievements, regarding the rest of the country as somewhat underdeveloped. The agricultural Midwest, finding itself cut off from the centers of financial power, developed an isolationist disdain for the complexities of coastal culture and the entanglements of international politics.*

Despite such differences, however, most of these regions were interlocked by dense transportation and communication networks. It was only the Pacific coast, isolated by immense distances and rugged topography, which constituted a separate socioeconomic system. It imported goods by ship around the Horn when it could, or made do with what it had. Even after the transcontinental railroad came, the infant economy of the West remained largely separate. While the rest of the continent alternately baked or froze, the green strip along the Pacific grew into an empire apart.

Allan Munton was 68 years old and somewhat shrunken in body; like a snake, he moved only when there was some important reason to do so. But he also retained his powers of coiling and striking, and was still the operating chief of the U.S. Metals conglomerate. Today he was reviewing a policy memorandum from his top managers which recommended the closing of another steel mill in Indiana. USM had long since ceased being merely a steel company; the profit centers of the corporation now lay in construction, in real estate, in chemicals, in the supplying of rare metals, in shipbuilding work for the government. But steel was still close to Munton's heart. The capital liberated by closing this mill would be diverted into a joint venture with an Indonesian company whose technology was more advanced; there would still be steel rolled with the USM mark on it. All the same, it was sad to close the old place down. His father had built it, and it had generated many a dollar in its day.

In fact USM engineers had earlier developed plans to re-equip the Indiana plant with a new generation of machinery, incorporating pollution-control devices that would make the plant more efficient and thus actually save money, as well as comply with the few remaining government controls. But at the moment the market was weak and, as Munton's canny subordinates had pointed out, closing the plant would have subsidiary advantages. It would teach the union a lesson. Accountants could squeeze tax savings out of the closing, and best of all it could be portrayed in the press as a consequence of the hamstringing effect of government pollution regulations.

Munton was a dour man, seldom given to shows of emotion, and never of enthusiasm. But as he initialled his tiny, precise "OK" on the document, he permitted a slight smile to cross his face. "How easy it is to get away with these things," he thought.

Vera Allwen was in New Orleans for a conference on state government problems. Arriving early, she walked around downtown and discovered that New Orleans, like San Francisco, was small enough to have a human scale. It also had enough remaining tradition of open-air socializing that its street life, at least in the old sections, was still vibrant and interesting.

When she returned to her hotel, Vera realized with a touch of surprise that she was afraid to drink the water. She turned on the faucet and ran a glass full. Held up in the sunlight, it looked innocuous enough. And the smell indicated little more chlorine than her native San Francisco water. She sniffed it again. Was there some other smell too, not quite masked by the chlorine? She knew perfectly well what the water actually contained: industrial wastes like trichloroethylene, toluene, carbon tetrachloride, vinyl chloride, PCBs—many of them known carcinogens. Her nose might be translating this knowledge into a sensation. But then again—what *can* you trust, after all, if not your nose? There were things that were dangerous even though they had no smell (like carbon monoxide) but on the whole, Vera reflected, it was a sane rule that if something smelled funny you should stay away from it.

By now she was getting distinctly thirsty. She disliked the feeling of being controlled by situations. She hated soft drinks, which were available in a hallway dispenser—and anyway they were doubtless made with local water. It was too early for wine or beer. This was ridiculous! And yet, she knew, polluted water threatened tens of millions of people who lived in Chicago and Detroit and Cleveland and Cincinnati and St. Louis and other midland cities whose water supplies came from the rivers or the Great Lakes—all heavily contaminated from agricultural pesticide and fertilizer and herbicide run-off as well as industrial discharges. The water in these cities had been known to be unfit for human consumption ten years earlier. Why had the citizens not risen up in righteous rage and insisted on activated carbon filtration? Why had the federal government not required it?

Vera knew why. It wasn't just callous stupidity, though there was plenty of that too. It wasn't even necessarily willful blindness to the fact that needless cancer deaths hurt the nation economically as well as humanly. Cleaning up our drinking water was just not worth the trouble. Politicians couldn't see enough mileage in it. Most voters would rather not think about the problem, just hoping it wouldn't get *them*. Bureaucrats couldn't agree on priorities. Business couldn't figure how to make it profitable. Labor didn't see it as an issue. The press couldn't figure how to make it sell newspapers. Drink now, die later, Vera thought bitterly.

And yet a few people would somehow turn up who *did* care. On their own time, sacrificing income and sometimes reputations, they would dig up the research information, find a few friends in the political structure, mount a campaign, do the publicity, do the organizing, do the endless writing and phoning, find the funds, convince the bureaucrats, galvanize even the most hidebound engineers. In the end, the water would be drinkable again. And the doughty campaigners would move on to deal with some other outrage—as the ancient Quaker phrase put it, "telling truth to power."

Vera looked at the faucet, and thought of hanging a little sign on it: Drink at Your Own Risk. Then she went down to the hotel's liquor shop and bought two cartons of bottled water. Normally she regarded bottled water as a snobbish extravagance but this, she thought wryly, was an emergency!

Yet of course it was merely blind luck that the problem was not so severe in the Northwest. The largest cities there drew their water from mountain sources. The natural water cycle, acting as a giant distilling system, dropped rain and snow on the mountains in a relatively pure state—and reservoirs captured the streams at high elevations, before they could be polluted by farm area run-off.

But when Vera returned home, she looked into the situation and discovered it was worse than she had thought. The major cities were all right. But 40 percent of the people lived in small cities and towns which drew their water from wells or local reservoirs threatened by nitrate fertilizer and pesticide and herbicide contamination. To pro-

26

tect their water, these people would have to organize politically, and the new party could help them do it. Vera had heard of inexpensive do-it-yourself kits people could use to test their own soil and water for pollutants. What would happen if these were made available on a massive scale?

One of the reasons Lou was interested in David Vandermeer was that she envied musicians their nonverbal ways of playing together. She felt she could not really understand anything unless she could visualize it concretely, or perhaps put it into an equation. But David and his band operated on what seemed to her strange unspoken wavelengths, picking up cues from each other with unbelievable agility. Sometimes Lou thought they must literally have better ears. At any rate it was fascinating to watch and listen, so Lou often dropped around after school to a teen-age club called The Belfry where David and his band played, and where they did their rehearsing. He and his friends were slowly developing a style for themselves. It wasn't exactly rock, it wasn't blues, it wasn't jazz, it wasn't country, though it had elements of all those. But they had begun to make their style work coherently and it became steadily more assured, and sometimes more savage. David wrote some of the material, and a lot was also written by Ellen, who played guitar and sang; she was sardonic but warmhearted, and she and Lou had gradually become good friends.

Today as Lou approached the locked stage door she could hear amplified music within. She waited a few minutes until it paused, then banged and kicked loudly on the door. After a bit it opened a crack. Two beady eyes peered out. "Hi Jer," she said. "It's me."

"Oh, yeah, come on in, we're workin'."

"Okay," said Lou. "I'll sit around and listen."

The interior of The Belfry was painted flat black, and it smelled of ancient deposits of sweat and cigarette and marijuana smoke. The group had turned on some bare bulbs above the stage area, but otherwise the room was gloomy. It had the bare, tawdry look that entertainment places have when they are empty of people. The band stretched, and broke up to chat with Lou for a few minutes.

"What you up to?" Ellen asked.

"Mainly working on those solar cells," Lou replied. "I seem to have hit on something that really works. But I can't figure out why."

"Well, that'll keep you out of trouble for a bit. You always have to have an *explanation!*" Ellen looked at Lou affectionately.

"Oh, come on," said David, "you want her to go off and leave us?" He came over and hugged Lou. "Want to hear our new one?"

"Sure—what is it, that love song, the torchy one?"

"Nah, this one's political." He looked down, a bit uncertainly. "Paul and I got this idea, about pollution. It's kind of bitter. Anyway we're working on it."

Lou looked at him. "—You don't like the feel of it?"

"Well, I dunno. I can't tell quite where the energy is, in it. But it's *bad*, you know?"

"Downright beastly," said Paul, in a fake British-rocker accent. David gave his hair a yank.

"All right, let's do it," he said. "The only part we're really happy with so far is the refrain. It goes—" David took up his guitar and picked out the first few bars of melody. Jer, who was the drummer, got the rhythm going, Ellen came in with the bass, and they were off, David leaning up close to the microphone, his face suddenly intent and angry. The chords were dissonant, tense, the rhythm was skewed. David faked some of the verse words, "Ta-ta ta dum, ta dum ta-ta," and then the group swung into the chorus:

So step right up for your chemical swill,

If cancer don't get ya, a heart attack will! (Oh yeah!)

They stopped abruptly, looking for Lou's reaction. "Jesus," she said, "you're getting pretty tough, aren't you?"

"Is that good?" asked David.

"I guess I don't know. But I *like* it. It made my foot go. It's music. Which is more than I say about some of your stuff, like that awful number you were working on last time."

"Okay, you were probably right—we've dropped that one. For a while."

Lou looked at them. "I have the funny feeling that people are going to like this new one. It's like those things in the middle ages. They beat themselves with whips—you know, flagellation? Beat yourself with music! That's strong stuff."

"Wow," said Paul. "The Chemical Flagellation Blues!"

"Fuck you," said David happily. "How about just calling it 'Enough'?"

"What do you mean, enough," said Jer, waking up a little.

"No, dummy, the *title* would be 'Enough.' As in 'Enough already.'

28

Now about that C major to A flat. That needs to be *nastier*—how about going to A flat minor?"

Lou wandered off to make herself some tea in the kitchen area. It was dilapidated but homey too; it bore the marks of recent and forthcoming life happening there. David and his group, she could feel, were slowly but surely growing into a good, solid band. They had even thought up a nice musically punning name: Sharp & Natural. People liked to dance to their music; people paid attention to the words. Already, around the band there hovered a faint halo of incipient success. A guy from the city had dropped by one evening and listened, and offered to be their manager. Maybe later, they told him. For now, they were too busy developing their music. Also, they had the feeling that a manager would want them to stop giving free concerts in parks and otherwise spreading their music around.

Riding the public enthusiasm for clean air and clean water which had moved Congress during the seventies to enact major environmental protection measures, the Environmental Protection Agency had early scored substantial victories. An immense program of improved sewage processing facilities—welcomed by construction interests as well as the public—helped to lower pollution of streams and rivers. (It did not, however, address the ultimate necessity of removing industrial wastes—toxic metals, dangerous chemicals—from sewage sludge, so it could be recycled back onto the land and thus sustain a permanent agriculture.) Air quality standards helped to reduce the burden of certain pollutants, though auto smog in major cities remained severe, and the auto industry secured delays and exemptions in exhaust pollution abatement.

Other industries also proved recalcitrant. Illegal night-time dumping of toxic compounds was commonplace; EPA regulations designed to track dangerous substances from their creation to final disposal proved easy to circumvent. Many large corporations making steel and paper and chemicals found it cheaper to flout environmental laws and pay the insignificant fines that resulted, rather than to clean up their operations. Then, during the early eighties, Congress's support of environmental protections waned—despite the fact that a substantial majority of Americans remained stubbornly in strong support of them, even at considerable financial cost. The EPA thus gradually ceased to be the champion of a clean environment and promoter of public health and welfare; instead, it became a weathervane responding to which way the winds of Washington pressure blew. Good people continued to work within its programs, but their efforts were more frequently countermanded by higher levels of the administration—more concerned with budget-cutting or rewarding powerful political contributors than with the death and destruction being wreaked upon the people.

In some cases the EPA's lethargy became literally farcical. When it finally got ready to issue hazardous-waste regulations (two and a half years behind its Congressional deadline), an official ceremony was planned to take place at a notorious chemical dump in New Jersey. However, the dump exploded before the ceremony could be held, with 55-gallon drums hurled through the air amid a spectacular fire which sent a cloud of dangerous fumes over adjacent counties. Release of the rules was then blocked for some days by budget officials who feared suits from the chemical industry. As if to remind mortals that nature will not indefinitely allow herself to be mocked, the dump exploded twice again in succeeding weeks.

In the usual Washington style, the agency acted mainly when compelled to—usually through lawsuits brought by environmental groups, who were able to prove it was derelict in its duties. At other times only massive citizen outrage could bring action. Thus, in the forested areas of the Northwest, women who lived in small towns surrounded by timberlands sprayed with the herbicide 2,4,5-T noticed a dismaying rise in the number of miscarriages, deformed fetuses, and birth defects, along with an increase in various chronic kidney and other diseases. The women and their doctors went to the media with horrifying photographs; anti-spraying groups spread throughout the lumber country. Finally EPA agreed to put a temporary ban on 2,4,5-T spraying.

However, the timber and chemical companies fought back ferociously. One chemical firm argued that traces of toxic dioxin in the forests did not come from 2,4,5-T at all, but from forest fires. In any case, other sprays were available—perhaps safer, or perhaps more dangerous. And so spray helicopters resumed their runs, and people's suspicion of federal inaction settled into despair or defiance.

One morning Lou awoke much too early, well before dawn. She pulled the covers tighter and tried to go back to sleep, but her head had already begun turning over hypotheses about the cell. After a bit she gave up, got dressed, and went out to her cell array. There was nothing she particularly had to do there; she just felt like checking up on things. Everybody else was still asleep—even Theo, who usually awoke at dawn.

Strips of cloud ran north to south, and off to the east, over the soft, rounded ridges, a few of these strips were turning faintly rosy. Lou went back into the house, got her heavy parka and a square of blackened glass, and bundled up in a lawn chair to watch the dawn. Maybe, she hoped, the sun would bestow a new idea on her this morning.

Slowly, the pinkish sky tones gave way to lemony yellows. To the north there were a few more rounded clouds that were high enough to be already in full sunlight; they gleamed white against the pale sky. The hills were no longer just silhouettes; Lou could make out the edges of forested areas, and to the south an occasional house. But westward over the Pacific the cloud strips lay closer together, a deep dark blue, almost black.

Lou heard the kitchen door open and looked around. It was Mike, yawning sleepily. "What you doing out so early?" he asked.

"Nothing," Lou replied. "Woke up and couldn't get back to sleep. So I came out and checked the cells."

"And—?"

"Nothing. It's all okay."

Mike rubbed an eye. "So why not go back to bed? You have to keep watch to make sure the sun comes up?"

Lou turned on him. "Come here, little brother," she said. "Sit down—I've got to tell you a thing or two!"

Mike slid another chair close to hers and sat down. Lou went on, "You think I'm a bit cracked about all this sun stuff, don't you?" Mike drew back as if to say "Awwww," but Lou pushed right on. "Well, maybe you ought to think a little more about the sun. Look up there—see where it's brightest, where the edge is going to show in a minute or two? Okay, now you just listen while we watch. First off, *you* would not be here if it wasn't for the sun! In fact the *earth* would not be here: if the sun's gravity didn't hold it in place, it would just fly off through the universe somewhere! And this body of yours—" (here she poked a finger at Mike's stomach) "—would never have

31

come into existence because none of our ancestors all the way back to single-celled creatures could have come into being without sunlight. And the water you drink and that waters the crops you eat would still be seawater and too salty if the sun didn't evaporate it into the air, and then cause the winds to blow that drive storms onto the coast so that the rain can fall."

She looked around. "There's hardly anything in sight that doesn't owe its shape and its being to the sun. The broccoli and cabbage in the garden, of course. And look at those clouds—what got all that water vapor up into the air? And what do you think gives clouds that puffy shape? It's warm air rising—and you know what warms it? —Right! Why do those trees have leaves or needles instead of just being knobby or something? Because a leaf and branch structure gives the tree about an acre of photosynthetic area to pick up solar energy with, that's why!" Lou could tell that Mike was getting a little impatient with the lecture. Maybe she was overdoing it. Besides, a faint brilliant slice of light had edged over the hills. It was very thin, yet it was blindingly bright. "Don't look directly at it," she cautioned Mike, handling him the little square of glass. "It may be 93 million miles away, but it can still blind you."

They watched in silence for a few minutes. The sun's disc slowly crept upward, as if straining to be free of the horizon. For an instant Lou had a queasy feeling in her stomach as she momentarily felt geophysical reality touch her: she was only an almost invisibly tiny being on the earth's huge crust, which was being whirled majestically eastward as the earth revolved. Unimaginably heavy with the molten matter at its core, the earth turned, transporting Lou and all the creatures westward of her into the sun's light, to bless them with another day of warmth.

Mike was looking eagerly out to sea, hoping to catch a glimpse of the Farallon Islands as the sun first lit them up against dark sky. Lou didn't know whether he had really understood anything at all of what she felt, but she wanted to say a bit more to him anyway. "What it comes down to, Mikey, is that the sun provides our only real *income* to the planet. We can use it by photosynthesis, by dams that utilize the water cycle, by fermentation, by my cells if I can get them to work! But that's all we've got coming in. All the oil and gas comes from what the sun did hundreds of millions of years ago, and it'll be gone soon. So the sun is our future, if we have one. And that makes me feel—well, sort of grateful, I guess. That's one of the main reasons

I work at the cells so hard—kind of wanting to do something in return, you know?"

Mike smiled at her and gave her a pat on her parka sleeve. "C'mon," he said, "let's make some breakfast. Then we can eat it out here with the sun on the back of our necks!"

In the weeks after the rainy night meeting at Vera Allwen's, the people who had been there began to think of themselves as a coherent political group. Vera chivvied them together, sometimes all at once and sometimes in small groups with narrower purposes. She flung herself into the new enterprise with contagious enthusiasm. "If you're going to do it, *do* it!" she said. In formal and informal gatherings they started seriously working out a program.

Some people recommended finding ways to coordinate existing groups into a larger entity that could become a party, a sort of alliance. Vera, however, argued for something new. "It's time to start afresh," she said. "Do any of you in this room really have any enthusiasm for yet another regrouping of the old tribes?" She looked around. "I didn't think so! All right then, it's a new game. Let's invent rules we feel comfortable with, so that it seems truly worth playing! We have to convey a *dream*, a vision, of something new. And it had better seem new to *us*, or we'll have no hope of getting others to listen."

And so the group sought a shared vision they could hope to transmit to the people at large: a vision of a society that would take long-term care of its natural resources the way a responsible farmer takes care of productive fields. A society that would protect members of the human species but also all others. A society that would arrange its institutions to encourage people to respect each other and work with each other, rather than working against each other. A society that recognized the unbearable fearfulness of uncontrolled hazards to life—whether they were nuclear or chemical. In short, a society that would feel safe and free, a society that an uprooted, exploited people could learn to call home.

Vera's initial impulse was to paint a vivid picture of this new, sustainable, livable world. "We have to seize the moral initiative," she said. "The rightwingers mustn't be left a monopoly on that. If the new party can create a coherent and powerful vision of a fair, *moral* way to live in this country, people who feel confused and cynical will respond."

But how, she was asked, will we convince them this is any different from the alleged new deals of previous parties?

"It will only work," said Vera, "if it *is* different. If we were offering the same stuff that the Democrats and Republicans have been offering, of course the people would rightly reject it. They've been through that. They saw that the Democrats had no real answers, so they threw them out. Now they've seen that the Republicans really had only the same answers, except in a more visibly exploitative form, and it worked even worse. We can lump these two old parties together as the Money Party, which is what they really are, and become the second party ourselves. But only if what we are proposing really *is* an alternative! We must not compromise or trim our sails. Otherwise we'd be failing in our historical function. We might win, but we would have lost—that kind of success is really failure. It isn't even worth trying. No fun!"

When Vera spoke like this, her eyes shone and she seemed to be speaking to the heart of everyone. Dedicated, sure, she radiated a simple kind of human goodness. Many politicians are smart, many are tough, many are wily. Vera seemed by contrast plain, quiet, with a clear, sturdy common sense. People trusted her. And so her conviction that the new party must make a strongly moral appeal won out over more cynical proposals to play upon people's fears. But how could they dramatize their position, put it into a form that could be taken into the public political arena?

Someone suggested the Bill of Rights as a model—after all, it provides ten basic rules for civil society. Ten good basic rules for ecological and political sanity could also be devised. Then someone pointed out that both the Bill of Rights and the Ten Commandments were in the negative. If you prohibited the right things, people were free to do everything else. Maybe it was legalistic, maybe it was patriarchal, but it seemed to work. So how about ten no-nos appropriate to our age in the same way the commandments were to the time of Moses, or the Bill of Rights to the newly independent colonies? Like those earlier codes, the new one might often be broken; but it would set standards that people could share and aspire to.

The very fact that it would be so difficult to formulate a simple, high-impact group of commandments proved exciting, and after a few more meetings a strong consensus developed for making the attempt.

34

So a process of proposing and winnowing began. Drafting subcommittees worked to compress and organize ideas into compact, memorable phrasing. An ambitious mass-media campaign was planned.

It proved relatively easy to work out the first directly survival-oriented items on what became known as the "No More!" list. (To each item a paragraph of explanation was to be appended, showing how the party proposed to gradually implement these goals.)

> *No extinction of other species.*
> *No nuclear weapons or nuclear plants.*
> *No manufacturing of carcinogenic (cancer-causing) or*
> *mutagenic (mutation-causing) substances.*
> *No adulterants in foods.*

To make clear the party's fundamental commitment to human equality, the next item read:

> *No discrimination by reason of sex, race, age, religion,*
> *or ethnic origin.*

But then more agonizing questions had to be addressed. The private automobile system of transportation was the most costly, in energy and dollar terms, that the world had ever seen. It was causing a potentially fatal hemorrhage of dollars from the American economy, and no technical fix was going to stop it. Only withdrawal from dependence on the automobile offered a possible long-run solution. Yet the American people were still massively addicted to automobiles, and for many of them an automobile was an absolute necessity since there were no other ways to get to work or supermarket. Few Americans had had the eye-opening experience of car-free environments in parts of European cities or in the pedestrian malls that had been created in a few American cities; cars were kept from dominating the landscape only on college campuses, and few people yet realized they could serve as a model for how entire central cities should be laid out.

Was a compromise possible? Could some formulation indicate the ultimate necessity of phasing out private cars in favor of buses, taxis, streetcars, subways, bicycles, mopeds, carpools, while making it clear that it would take decades to rebuild the cities in compact form so that transportation needs would be greatly decreased? In the end, clarity won out: better to state the goal bluntly rather than to obscure and weaken it by qualifications. And so the item finally read:

> *No private cars.*

With that critical problem behind them, the drafters moved on to the other major technological artifact of American society, television. Here strong voices advocated total abolition, on the grounds that TV is physiologically deleterious, socially and politically centralizing (and thus authoritarian), aesthetically ugly, and a dangerously hypnotic substitute reality. Others argued that it was microwave-broadcast commercial TV which was the problem, and that a cable system, capable of two-way communication, could be turned to democratic political and cultural purposes if it was taken out of the hands of the advertisers. Though the more purist thinkers had prevailed on the car question, here the consensus in the end went to the formulation:

No advertiser-controlled or broadcast television.

Turning to problems of economic organization, which they realized would dominate human relationships in a future society no matter what ecological principles it might adopt, the drafters sought ways to embody their support of employee-owned and -controlled companies. But they found that more consensus existed on another aspect of economic organization—the need to curb personal irresponsibility by corporate officials, who used the corporation as a legal shield and thus could not be convicted of wrongdoing even when they deliberately manufactured deadly or defective products. Although some argued it was a throwback to indefensibly small-scale enterprise, there was strong support for:

No limited-liability corporations.

And once that had been settled, the form of personal responsibility desired in organizations was expressed by the companion formulation:

No absentee ownership or control—one employee, one vote.

Through this prohibition, the democratic principles that at least in theory governed political life would be extended to economic life. This brought the total "no-nos" to nine. General sentiment demanded a round ten. There was considerable feeling behind an item on air pollution, but since all combustion processes (except the virtually "clean" burning of hydrogen) produce some pollution, no compact formulation could be arrived at. Another proposal was to institute a prohibition against government secrecy. But in the end it seemed most important to confront another underlying, fundamental problem, from which so many others stemmed, and so the final item was:

No growth in population.

Various ideas for a name for the new party had been floating through the group's discussions since the beginnings, but they had put off a final decision. Sometimes they thought of calling it simply the New Party, or the People Party. But the underlying concern was for biological survival—for taking seriously the idea that the species should learn to survive on the earth in harmony with the rest of the biosphere. So the name Survivalist Party was proposed.

"But wait a minute," someone objected. "What about those gun-freaks a few years back who called themselves survivalists. The ones who bought gold coins and stocked up food in mountain cabins and waited for Armageddon with their sixpacks."

"Well," said Vera, "we could consider them heretics—they got the gospel twisted. They suffered from violent fantasies that you defend yourself against social breakdown by having lots of firepower. It was never true, of course. Under the Nazis in World War II, when the social order really did break down, the people who survived were the people with friends—support networks. Power grows out of social cohesion, not the barrel of a gun. You're only as strong as the people who will come to your aid."

"I agree," said Henry Engelsdorf. "Some people may be a little confused in the beginning, but they'll figure it out. It's crucial to keep our focus on biology, and 'survival' is a good term to do that. Nobody's going to visualize *us* going around with submachine guns. Let's not give up a good name just because it was besmirched for a while by a few gun nuts!"

The core group that had formulated the basic program for the party now became a sort of sponsoring body. Vera, joined only by Henry from the original party founders, now moved to begin building a working staff. Initially they were met with much skepticism. Some prospective allies argued that the successes of the environmental movement in the seventies had come because it had outflanked party divisions and gained broad support in many quarters. Others quickly pointed out the many obstacles the two existing parties had managed to place in the electoral paths of third parties. To this Vera had a simple response: such obstacles are effective against *weak* attempts at another party. If Survivalist ideas really caught on, however, they would be easily overcome; they were tactical problems, not hopeless impediments. Vera had a way of mobilizing people's faith; she often shook their easy cynicism, and some of them joined the campaign.

An early and critical convert was Maggie Glennon, who became Vera's chief of staff. Maggie had been involved in union organizing and in anti-nuclear campaigns. She was hot-tempered and hard-driving. Her body carried a lot of tension. Now in her forties, she could have been a success in business, but had chosen politics as her arena. She had a knack for setting priorities, focusing political energy at critical points at critical times. She seemed to need only about four hours of sleep a night, and burned men out in brief, intense affairs; then sometimes she would turn to women for solace. She had been married once, but it didn't fit in with her work. Now she shared a house with two other women and a man—old friends. Tall, lean, with striking curly red hair and blue-green eyes, she could be overwhelmingly persuasive in meetings. Compared to Vera, Maggie was more attuned to pure organizational, structural power, and was less concerned with the personal and moral.

Henry provided a counterpoise to Maggie's intensity. Sometimes Vera thought of Henry as the court jester. He was small, witty, with a rather lumpy body but large, expressive mouth and eyes, and skimpy straight hair brushed across his head from side to side. In party discussions it was sometimes Henry's role to bring things back down to earth with a joke. Though most others in the first weeks of the new party did not realize this, Henry also had an unusually direct feeling for human needs, and it was this even above his dedication to ecological sanity which endeared him to Vera. Maggie might propose some abstractly brilliant, dangerous strategy; it was Vera and Henry who would cleave to the human side of the issue. Yet he and Maggie were great friends and sometimes Henry pretended to be smitten with her—though, as Vera and only a few others knew, he was actually gay, and lived quietly with a longterm lover.

Another source of early strength was Nick Ballard, who became Maggie's associate. Nick had been in the civil-rights movement (he was black) and had links to the old San Francisco power structure and to the labor movement. Sensitized by the discovery that a host of building materials that carpenters and other construction trades people were exposed to daily were saturated with carcinogenic chemicals, Nick had been one of the first to realize the potential of a new coalition—between labor, whose members suffered most from both work-place and residential-area pollution, and middle-class environmentalists whose political skills had accomplished so much with so little. A stocky, solid person, he was more down-to-earth and compromising than Maggie. He had earlier worked in Vera's office in Sacramento, and on her election campaigns. Maggie relied on him as a reality-check. Nick had been married several times; now he lived in a big apartment with four other people. Like all of the original Survivalist crew, he was in the habit of working irregular and long hours. None of them made much distinction between work and private life. Whatever would happen to the Survivalist Party, it *was* their life.

Perhaps it was this sense of identification with their work that made it easy for the initial group to accept a 32-year-old biologist, Raye Dutra, as their chief scientific person. Raye had married an architect but had no children; she was in the habit of putting in days on end in her lab. When Raye first joined the Survivalist cause, people wondered how she could spend so much time apparently just mooning around. Gradually they discovered that when Raye sat motionless in a corner she was actually thinking hard. She had a jumpy mind that sometimes seemed to bounce completely off every available wall— but in the process would come up with interesting connections nobody else had thought of. And she somehow managed to read more than any of them.

Gradually, through intricate networks of personal and political connections, the original Survivalists recruited people to their cause—some as open supporters, some as silent sympathizers, and some who would watch and wait, and perhaps help later. They went to union leaders who had begun to realize the magnitude of environmental assaults on their members; they went to enlightened corporate planners. They attended endless meetings, spent long hours on the telephone, cultivated key people whose opinions swayed others. They distributed unsettling information about ecological problems and proposed ingenious, bold modes of dealing with them. Little by little, they gave many people in the region a sense that new and better ways of running the society might be possible. And so new lines of contact and communication were laid down among hundreds and later thousands of people. Like a jellyfish that is almost invisibly transparent yet sucks in nutrients, propels itself, and trails its tentacles at a surprising distance, the new party grew in the turgid political waters of the region. As Raye put it, there was a niche waiting to be filled, and they would fill it.

In the heavily populated and industrialized areas of Southern California, pollution from cars, factories and refineries concentrated in the stagnant atmosphere as smog. It stunted citrus and pine trees, rotted rubber tires, attacked the paint on buildings, and produced irritation of

eyes, lungs and other sensitive parts of the human organism. On days of particularly heavy smog, school children were kept indoors so their breathing intake of pollutants would be minimized. On such days, when visibility was reduced to well under a mile, hospitals reported a rise in patient intake (including mental cases) and suicides were significantly more frequent. But most people merely cursed and grumbled and suffered headaches and other mysterious symptoms without connecting them with the smog.

In the great industrial belt running from Chicago eastward, prevailing air movements did not accumulate pollutants in this way, but the output of pollutants was even more immense. The state of Ohio had one of the largest concentrations of coal-fired power plants in the world, and more were planned. Indeed Ohio produced twice the sulfur dioxide emissions of New York, New Jersey and all of New England combined. But Ohio's emissions did not remain in Ohio. Instead, both gaseous sulfur emissions and tiny jagged-edge particles so light they could float on air currents were carried east and northeast across other states and on into Canada, for hundreds of miles. Sometimes they were even transported entirely across the Atlantic. But generally, because rainfall is frequent throughout the year in that region, the pollutants descended to the earth as rain.

Sometimes this rain was more acid than vinegar. It raised the acidity of soils, already dangerously high because of artificial fertilization practices. It caused metabolic disturbances in plants, so that crop outputs fell—oats, spinach, soybeans and white pine suffered measurable injury even when the acid rain came from air considered clean by official standards of the time. The acid rain fell directly on lakes and streams, and was collected by their surrounding watersheds. In the pristine Adirondack mountains, hundreds of miles from major industrial areas, 90 percent of the lakes above 2,000 feet were so acid that all their fish had died.

Air quality regulations were written in such a way that a polluting corporation could (if it bothered to obey the regulations at all) build a higher smokestack and obtain waivers permitting the discharge of four times more sulfur compounds. Like the tendency to ignore effects downstream when factories spewed liquid pollution into rivers, such policies merely displaced a problem instead of solving it. Emissions were more widely dispersed, but even then they were so massive that they reduced visibility through most of the industrialized East, sometimes as much as in the dim-outs caused by Los Angeles smog.

40

In the seventies, attempts to curb coal-burning plant emissions had been made, but because of the oil crisis the federal government began encouraging greater coal use. In the eighties, pollution regulations were relaxed or removed, and sulfur and particulate emissions rose substantially. Everywhere the acid rain and acid particles in the air steadily leached at anything made of limestone or marble. Even the stones in great buildings had begun to weather noticeably—visible signs of the unseen enemy lurking in the air that people relied upon to support life.

Whitey Whitehead was a country boy, originally out of central Pennsylvania. He had escaped the teen-age doldrums by going into the army at a tender age, and saw action as a helicopter pilot in Vietnam, where he flew strafing missions, search-and-destroy landing missions, transport missions, and anything else he could get assigned to. After Vietnam he ended up in San Francisco and at first he thought he could get a job as a pilot for the metropolitan area helicopter service. But those jobs were tied up by pilots with more seniority. Then the company went bust. Whitey was neither surprised nor greatly displeased; ferrying business types from airport to suburb wasn't his idea of fun. He drifted north, finding he could get jobs doing agricultural spraying from the companies that were eliminating their old biplanes in favor of copters. It was easy work. Unlike Vietnam, you never got shot at, and you could let your fantasies run. Was that little patch of orchard a VC hideout? Zoom over it, let them think you hadn't seen 'em, then suddenly veer backward, zap 'em with that old 2,4,5-T! After all, it *was* Agent Orange. Some of it, for a while, had been straight out of the military surplus barrel.

Whitey had settled in southwest Oregon, finally, because there was almost always work for the Forest Service or private timber companies. He got himself a trailer outside Myrtle Grove. It wasn't the fanciest part of town—mostly trailers, with an occasional old rickety house. Most of the people were loggers or handymen or construction workers—good folks, but not much in the way of money. Whitey felt comfortable there. They didn't have any goddamn hippies or artsy-fartsy types. People chopped their own wood, fixed their own cars, and made their own livings.

The Fir-Aid Company that Whitey worked for was in the business of spraying herbicides to kill young broad-leafed trees and thus "release" the profitable Douglas fir planted by the timber companies in clear-cut areas. Some people, Whitey knew, thought clear-cutting was a mistake. They moaned over photographs of clear-cut areas, they worried their soft little asses off about erosion, and damage to the forest floor, and the dangers of mono-cropping if some kind of insect or disease came along that just happened to love Doug fir. The way Whitey and his friends thought, these folks were assholes. If they ever got out in a forest and tried to cut timber, they'd soon see why you had to chop down everything in sight. Sure, it involved waste. Sure, in time it might even wreck the forest floor's fertility. But what the hell could *they* do about it? If all your competitors are clear-cutting every piece of timberland they can get their hands on, are you supposed to go back to using oxen or something, to harvest only the older ripe trees? Or get a goddamn blimp and haul logs out on cables, like some nut had suggested?

And once you clearcut, are you going to go out there with an axe to kill off the broadleaf stuff? There *were* a few people willing to do that—those weirdo Hoedads—but they were hardly human: live in tents, share all their money, decide what to do by some kind of group-think. Plenty of groping too—men and women all mixed up together in their camps, not married, nothing, just goddamn free-lovers! No wonder they work harder and faster than other people—tree-freaks, dopers. Some of the women have arms like wrestlers. And the worst of it is, a lot of them are college kids, middle-class kids, who could live perfectly normal lives if they wanted to.

When such thoughts hit him as he flew spray runs, Whitey sometimes made double passes, pretending he was strafing a Hoedad encampment. Then later, back at the trailer, he would jerk off, imagining that he was raping a gorgeous Hoedad woman.

From the eighties onward the business mentality triumphed. A professionalized management elite had fought off regulation of almost every kind. To maximize profit rates, basic production industries unable to compete with lower-wage facilities in Korea or Taiwan were closed down. Their workers were pushed (along with most women workers) into service industries with low pay, weak unions, and low productivity. The real average wages of Americans slowly declined, but most people attributed this puzzling fact merely to inflation. Resent-

ment fed absenteeism, waste, even purposeful sabotage. Meanwhile, corporate profits flowed into non-productive tax-loss investments or were exported abroad. A global web of interlinked corporations controlled governments, commanded private armies, and enjoyed the sympathies of American diplomatic and intelligence operatives.

The rule of the corporate masters was not a benevolent one, and economic self-congratulation in the elite media concealed widespread, potentially explosive social unrest. Welfare expenditures had been cut ruthlessly and a quarter of the population now lived at or below the meager official poverty line, with millions among them totally destitute. Conditions of life were deteriorating steadily, especially for the mass of working people. Workplace standards for noise, dust and chemical exposure were eliminated, and compensation for job-connected injuries and death was made more difficult to obtain. The industrial accident rate was rising rapidly, and vast numbers of workers were utterly without union protection against dangerous work assignments. Auto and truck emission regulations had been scrapped, and metropolitan air quality was rapidly worsening. Auto safety standards and speed limits, which had cut fatalities and damage repair rates, were dropped. Regulations guarding drinking water supplies against chemical contamination had been by-passed. The federal agency which had formerly made occasional feeble efforts to protect consumers against products that would burn, maim or cause cancer was first weakened and then destroyed. Agencies which had, for a time, offered poor people help in securing legal representation were disbanded, and so they found themselves defenseless against fraud and exploitation; their anger became more chaotic and diffuse. And if exploitation, corruption, bribery and larceny of the public purse were routinely committed by so many of the rich, then the poor felt entitled to their own kinds of thievery. Thus the hijacking of cargoes, the diversion of supplies, the private appropriation of corporate goods, the expectation of kickbacks spread throughout the society. When fire, flood or blackout struck, massive looting followed and even martial law could not contain it. Burglary and assault, committed by the cynical as well as the desperate, rose in frequency and viciousness. In many major cities, people had openly begun to flaunt weapons on the streets.

Any social system that hopes to last for long has to command the voluntary loyalty of the vast mass of its citizens, who must be convinced that the ways of the society are legitimate. Under the impact of the economic stringency of the eighties, what was left of American

43

middle-class social cohesion dwindled. Tax evasion became a national sport, and organized tax revolts broke out frequently. Barter, a means of evading sales taxes as well as recycling unused goods, spread widely even among the prosperous. Attempts to revive the military draft were met with determined middle-class resistance. Aside from the Air Force, which was richly provided with expensive weaponry (sometimes of doubtful combat durability) the military became largely a mercenary operation, its ground troops mainly poor people of minority races, whose political allegiance to the ruling elite was increasingly doubtful.

Thus American society, as seen through the establishment media, might give the appearance of being under the stern power of the elite and its institutions—the police, Congress, the bureaucracy, and the armed forces. But people who drew their information more directly from experience, and especially a few journalists who had contacts ranging down into the lower levels of society, knew that social decay had reached an advanced stage, indeed only a short distance from a silent, undeclared civil war. Vast numbers of people had nothing more to lose, and still greater numbers felt that they were losing what little they had. Slowly, unrecognized by those in power, the feeling spread that something was terribly wrong.

In most of the country, the result was growing chaos and despair. Only on the West Coast did a coherent set of political alternatives begin to become visible as new ideas that might fill this political vacuum.

Lou's plan since she had begun working on the solar-cell problem had been that if she came up with something she would simply put it in the public domain, so anybody in the world could use it freely. Roger, however, had suspicions that it might not be so easy, and now that she *had* discovered something, he felt they should get a more precise legal fix on the situation. Roger turned up a patent lawyer named Zack who was supposed to be a good guy; he had worked with a friend of Dimmy's on the patenting of a game. It turned out that his consultation fee was stiff, but Roger said he would pay for it.

Still Lou resisted. "But Roger," she said, "I haven't even been able to make any more cells work the way that first one does. I can't really claim I can replicate the experiment yet! So it's ridiculous to talk to anybody about it." And even when the replication problem was solved, she would only be beginning with the *real* problem. Lou suspected that ions from the seawater were working their way into the silicon structure—possibly penetrating fairly far, like some of her doping substances. But what would they do there, deep in the silicon lattice? To make matters more complicated, surface physics was still an under-developed field—important things could be going on merely at the silicon surface. And she had little idea what might happen if some of the sea salts formed compounds with the silicon. There was even the possibility that rain water, which could have leaked into the cell first and might have been slightly acid (even here in untouched Bolinas!) could have caused some chemical reaction within the cell, whose by-products were responsible for the high current output. All these possibilities would have to be explored, and most of them eliminated, by further experiments.

Roger, Lou could tell, was just very nervous about the whole thing. He felt he needed some kind of consultation; being totally in the dark about protecting the invention was too anxiety-producing. Finally Lou agreed to go see Zack, though she felt uncomfortable about the visit; the fewer people who knew about her work, the better! Then it turned out that Zack's law office was in downtown San Francisco next door to the Omni Oil building. Neither Lou nor Roger had any idea of how far they could count on an attorney's discretion in a case where very large amounts of money might be at stake. But Zack turned out to look reassuring; his tie was pulled loose at the collar, his desk was piled with books, and he propped his feet up on the desk to talk with them.

Lou started by describing her discovery in general terms, and her wish to have the new cell help provide renewable-source electricity for the world at the lowest possible cost. Zack replied by telling about the patenting process—how complex it was, how precarious, and how costly. And licensing negotiations, once the patent application had been filed, would also be time-consuming, and might require tens of thousands of dollars before anyone was authorized to manufacture and sell the invention. Perhaps a corporation would have to be formed to raise funds for such expenses and to make possible various legal and financial maneuvers.

When all that had been done, he concluded, Lou could license her cell to whomever she pleased, on any terms she felt like: a million a year, a dollar a year.

Lou felt confused and frustrated. She had hoped a lawyer would come up with something simple but secure. Irritatedly, she asked,

45

"Could I license it for nothing a year?"

Zack frowned. "Unwise," he said. "It's best if there is an exchange."

"I'd be getting a lot of gratification out of it!"

Zack inspected Lou with disbelief. "As your attorney, I could never advise you to forego substantial income."

"Well," said Lou, "there must be other ways."

There was a silence. Roger said, "Is this drawn-out patenting procedure the only way to avoid somebody else patenting the process, or are there other alternatives? Warren said you were an ingenious person. Are there other possibilities that could protect the invention and get it quickly into public use?"

After a pause Zack said, "I suppose you might want to consider *public disclosure*." He made it sound vaguely obscene, and added, "But I certainly couldn't recommend that."

"Well, what is it?" asked Roger.

"There are several possibilities. The best is to publish it—do an article in *Popular Mechanics*, say. Or you can put the invention on sale. Or put it in public use in some way. Or several of the above. In any case you would disclose the practical steps that are being used."

Lou sat up at full attention. "Does that mean you disclose the actual physics of the process?"

"No," said the attorney. "It means you describe exactly how it is done. You give the recipe, as if you were describing how to make a pie. You don't explain the chemistry of the crust. You say exactly what is done, and what the result is—so much current under such-and-such conditions, and so on."

Roger too was concentrating hard. "And this prevents somebody else from coming along and patenting *part* of it—by figuring out exactly how the recipe makes the crust flaky, so to speak?"

"In principle, yes. If a lot of money was at stake, of course efforts might be made to develop a slightly different recipe that *could* be patented. Someone else might come up with a significant and nonobvious improvement." Zack looked pained at the thought. "That is one of the reasons why I would not recommend the disclosure route. You would probably ultimately encounter legal problems there too. And as a lawyer I like to encounter problems on the most favorable possible terrain."

Roger looked at Lou. "I can understand that," he said. "But our overriding concerns are speed and also expense." He shrugged. "I'm a schoolteacher, you know."

46

"Well," replied Zack, "patent attorneys generally work on a fee basis. It is not cheap, I admit. Though we could work out a delayed schedule of payments, perhaps. If you're willing to go the normal patenting route."

"And if we went the public-disclosure route?" asked Lou.

The lawyer folded his hands on his desk. "Then you could just pay me for a couple of hours consultation to make sure the publication is in proper form, that's all. And kiss the potential income goodbye." He turned to Roger. "Look, Mr. Swift," he said, "I appreciate your idealism, but if this cell does what Lou says, it could generate a *great* deal of income, which you could put to many good uses."

"Like lawyer's fees," put in Lou, with a wicked little grin.

Roger was shocked—Lou could tell by the way he sniffed his breath in sharply—but he said nothing. Lou's voice dropped into its throatiest register. "It's *my* invention, you know."

"Pardon me if I offended you," said Zack, trying to regain his ground. "Most of the people who come through this office are itching to *make* money, not to give it away, so I really find it hard to appreciate your position."

"Yeah, well, I suppose so." Lou looked over at her father. "I've been told it's arrogant to try to change history. But I'd just like to have people free to use this thing without some corporation sucking profits out of it. Is that too much to ask? The sun belongs to us all, right?"

"Okay," said Zack with a sigh. "I guess you know what you're doing. But here are some protective steps you can take right now, before you decide whether to go the patent route or the public-disclosure route. Write yourself a letter describing the invention and mail it to yourself registered mail, and keep it unopened in a safe-deposit box. Also, before you mail the letter, explain it to a couple of people you have absolute trust in, but who aren't relatives and are not financially involved with you in any way. Make sure they all really understand the process. Get them to sign the letter at a notary's. Then they could swear in court if need be that you divulged the invention to them by such-and-such a date."

"There could be a great deal at stake here," said Roger. "You can understand that we have a certain amount of anxiety about it. I assume we can count on you to keep the existence of this invention confidential?"

Zack had heard this question many times before and had a practiced if not altogether convincing answer ready. "The ethics of the patent attorney profession are subject to intense mutual scrutiny, believe me. If any of us ever pulled any fast ones, we'd be out in the cold very quickly. It just wouldn't be worth it. We're in this business for the long haul, you know. Individual cases come and go. Little ones, big ones. Don't worry about it."

All the same, Lou and Roger went home with feelings of apprehension. What would it take in the way of possible pay-off to make such an attorney forget about his devotion to the profession's ethics? If the control of Lou's cell could, as they suspected, be worth literally billions of dollars, an energy corporation could afford to pay a great deal to get it. Precautions were clearly in order.

In the days after they visited Zack, Roger was depressed and preoccupied. One afternoon he seemed to have come to some sort of decision and announced, "Lou, I guess I have to explain a few things to you. May sound a little crazy—but I want to make sure you really know what you're doing."

"That sounds ominous," said Lou. "What are you talking about, anyway?"

"Well, c'mon, sit down, this is going to take a while." Roger was tall, but he moved crisply; Lou had always thought of him as terribly elegant. He poured himself a glass of wine and sat down in an old hand-carved rocker by the big side window. This was, Lou knew, where he liked to sit for serious talking. When you sat there, you looked out over the mesa toward the west; in the afternoon it was sunny and warm.

Lou sat on some big cushions on the floor. She did a few stretches while Roger got organized. He always envied her limberness. "All right, prop up that sillyputty body of yours," he said, "and listen closely."

Lou sat up. Roger liked to kid around, but she could tell this was important. "First of all," he began, "I don't think we've ever really talked about the impact this cell of yours could have on the utility companies of this country. These outfits are in big trouble, Lou. They have dug themselves into a stupendous financial hole with nuclear plants, and they are having trouble getting the public utility commissions to bail them out by jacking up rates when the facilities are sitting unused."

"Thirty-five percent back-up when only 15 is required."

"Yeah," said Roger. "You got it. They planned all these damn things back in the sixties when it looked like electric demand would shoot up forever. Of course it didn't, as any fool could have guessed."

"Did they really think they could keep prices constant?"

"They probably just hoped everything else would go up equally fast, and that nobody would ever give solar a thought. At any rate, they are now hooked in to these giant nuclear jobs."

"Which aren't running half the time."

"Well, from the power company viewpoint it would help if they were down even more, so that they could justify building something new."

"Dad, you're being ridiculous. Why don't they just shut them down altogether and forget about it, if that's true?"

"Daughter, you are naive. Power companies do not basically make money by selling power. They make money by getting into debt."

"Oh, come on!"

"No, here's why. The PUCs allow utilities a fixed rate of profit on investment, right?"

"Okay."

"So if they add a billion dollars worth of investment, they get an additional percentage of that, right? The PUCs allow them to set rates so they come out with a fixed profit."

"Sounds like a guaranteed annual income for corporations!"

"That's precisely what it is. But of course they don't want to look any more ridiculous than necessary. They want us to think they're our last line of defense against the oncoming dark, the congealing of our blood—"

"Yeah, Roger, I know, but what does this have to do with my solar cells?"

"You are going to make them look a lot more ridiculous, for one thing. Second, if a roof covered with your cells can generate enough power to run even just a stereo and the light bulbs and a refrigerator, it will cause a great many people to unhook from the power company lines entirely. Their *rate base* will shrink, Lou. Do you see what that would mean?"

"Sure, it sounds wonderful! A lot of people won't have to bother with electric bills at all."

"Yes, but those who remain hooked up will then have to carry the whole enormous load of providing a guaranteed profit for the company. Their rates will maybe double. The political impact of that is going to be devastating, and the companies know it. *Now* do you see

49

why I'm worried? General Motors put spies on Ralph Nader just because he had found out their Corvair had a little tendency to turn over at corners!"

Lou considered this. She dimly remembered hearing about Nader. It was a David-versus-Goliath tale. Nader had sued, revealed the GM plot, and gained a nationwide following in his consumer crusade. By the time Lou became conscious of him, he seemed almost an Establishment figure—far away in Washington, doing struggle in a ritual power ballet with sluggish bureaucrats and corrupt corporations. But if Roger was right—well, her cell *would* hurt the power companies a lot more than cancelling the Corvair hurt GM.

She felt the beginning of a slow chill creeping up the back of her neck. Only once before had Lou felt that chill. When she was out camping, at maybe age ten, she woke up in the night and heard a wild animal creeping near her sleeping bag. She hadn't known whether to scream for help or keep silent and hope whatever it was would go away. She heard faint rustlings in the underbrush and imagined she heard breathing; she strained through the dark to make out the gleam of feral eyes. And then, slowly, slowly, whatever it was *had* gone away, and after a while it was dawn. She had learned then the panic of being hunted. Were there hunters, at this very moment, laying devious plans to thwart the distribution of her beautiful discovery, or even to do her some dreadful personal harm?

"Roger," she said, "you scare me. I hadn't really thought—"

"It scares *me*, too. We've got to be very careful, Lou. This is not fun and games."

"Well, what do you think I should do? You're my father, give me some advice! It sure sounds like I could use some."

"All right. I think it's crucial to get this idea under real legal protection. We can scrape up the money for the patent route somehow. Once that's done, they'll figure it's just a question of buying you out. Even a high price would be well worth it to them. And of course . . . "

Roger's voice trailed off, and he got a strange, almost sad expression on his face. "What, Dad?"

"Well, Lou, you know if they were dealing with somebody like me, they'd probably work up to a price I would take. But luckily, you're not me."

"Roger! You know that all along I've been planning to just publish this thing and let anybody use it who wants to! I'll be damned if I'll let some corporation get hold of it and put it away out of sight!"

"Yes, I know that, and I admire you for it. You're right. I just worry about you, that's all."

"Well, what could happen that would be so awful, after all? Suppose there *are* these corporations who don't want my idea spread around. Suppose they know they won't be able to buy it. What are they really going to do, kill me?"

To Lou's astonishment, Roger looked around suspiciously. "Lou," he said quietly, "that is exactly what I worry about. You think of these people just as businessmen, mere money-grubbers keeping busy buying cheap and selling dear. Lou, they are *criminals*. You have to have a killer instinct to get to the top of those outfits. Once you get there, you have to keep it." Roger heaved a great sigh. "My beloved daughter," he said ruefully, "we live in a dangerous society. If you threaten powerful interests, they will threaten you back. Can you see that? This discovery of yours means you're in the big leagues!"

Lou assimilated this notion for a while. Then she jumped up and began pacing around the room. "Okay," she said, "if this is the big leagues, we can't afford any errors, can we? The problem is that if we try to go the patent route, we need to know the actual physics of the thing, and I'm a long way from cracking *that*, you know!" Her voice trembled a little. "We couldn't even do the public-disclosure route until I get reliable replication."

"Well," said Roger, "let's put off the decision then and see how the time factor works out. If you can build some more working cells, and if we could teach other people how to do it, that would accomplish two things—the idea couldn't be stolen and put away in a vault, because actual people would know how to do it, and it would form the basis for the public-disclosure process." Roger sighed again. "I'm just not going to be able to relax about it for a while, I guess. But I did hear about another attorney. Friend of your uncle Andy's, and supposed to be a radical. Maybe he'll have some new ideas."

Vera Allwen had long been fascinated by anthropology, which seemed to her to offer endless insights about how people might adapt to new and more ecologically sensible ways of living. She had also looked into an obscure branch of sociology called group theory. Most of the people who wrote in these fields seemed to her hopelessly academic, but by reading between the lines of their work she could

51

sometimes discern practical ideas that were interesting. She had come to believe, for instance, that the natural size of effective human groups was less than 20 people. In organizing Survivalist functions, therefore, she tried to ensure that whenever anything serious had to be done the number of people involved was under 20. "Beyond that," she was fond of saying, "you're into a mass meeting. Nobody really talks to anybody else, just to the crowd. And nobody listens."

But Vera's principle had other consequences too. It was only in small groups that people could easily feel at home. If you forced them into large offices or factories, they somehow or other always managed to divide themselves up into comfortable-sized informal groups in which individual characters and needs and potentials could be dealt with. And since these often half-conscious groupings were the real sources of social energy, Survivalist organizers should tap them and shape them, not go against them. Survivalists were urging experiments with ways to provide replacements for the dwindling nuclear family by living in larger groups of various kinds; they were organizing neighborhood political groups; they were working with people setting up employee-owned enterprises. In all these activities, as well as in organizing their own offices, Vera pushed her colleagues to adhere to the small-groups idea and then find ways to coordinate and interconnect the groups.

Vera was also fond of homey little rituals. The sharing of food had always seemed to her an essential feature of truly solid "tribal" groupings. And it was through her influence that Survivalist meetings often took the form of potluck suppers. The group would eat together, socialize, and then after a decent interval of conviviality, they would get down to assessing how far they had come and how far they yet had to go.

FURTHER DECONTROLS NECESSARY
TO FOSTER ECONOMIC GROWTH,
PRESIDENTIAL COMMISSION SAYS

Washington, Jan. 21 (WPI). Despite relaxation of many environmental controls in the early eighties, remaining regulations on air, water and foodstuff pollution still put unreasonable burdens on economic development and hurt America's international economic position.

This is the chief conclusion of a new report released today by the President's Commission on Renewed Progress. The blue-ribbon group has been studying relationships between industrial development and pollution for almost a year. Its membership is mainly industrial leaders and economists, together with a number of research scientists. Often referred to as the Munton Commission, the group is headed by Alan Munton, chairman of the board of the U.S. Metals Corporation.

The Commission's findings suggest that a significant breakthrough in the nation's declining productivity and international trade balance can only be achieved through new degrees of sacrifice. A planned relaxation of remaining controls on sulfur emissions into the atmosphere, pollutant discharges into waterways, dumping of toxic chemicals, and auto emission levels could add as much as two percent to the annual economic growth rate, Commission economists predict. This would probably return America to the lead in the industrial competition with Japan and Germany.

The report takes the unusual step of recommending that the public health toll of such relaxation should be accepted as an essential national risk. It proposes a new concept, "permissible deaths," which would be used in evaluating decontrol steps. "People die in any event," the report's conclusion argues. "While Americans certainly deserve a cleaner environment in the future, they must have a healthy economy *now*. And since the former cannot be achieved without the latter, rational priorities must ensure that industry's health take first place." Elaborate tables are included in appendixes of the report, giving estimates of the rise in deaths from cancer and other health problems that would occur under the new policy. The report's conclusion emphasizes that, since cancer takes many years to develop, most of these additional deaths would not actually occur for several decades, and a commission staff member stated that this fact should make such deaths more politically acceptable. "We have tried to think some unthinkable thoughts which have to be dealt with if the nation is to regain its position as Number One," he declared. "That was what the President asked us to do."

One of the Commission's principal arguments is that attempts to improve the American environment through restrictions on American businesses simply cause them to move operations to countries where lower wages prevail and governments don't worry about pollution. "No modern business," Munton stated at a press conference today, "can accept lowered financial returns when realistic alternatives for more profitable operations are available elsewhere. To do so would violate elementary business principles and expose a corporation to a disastrous loss of capital investment. The nation must choose between free productivity and continuing pettifogging interference from well-meaning but unrealistic bureaucrats."

The Munton report contains a minority statement by Dr. Simon Saroff, a biologist at Rockefeller University. Saroff criticizes the report for ignoring long-term cost considerations, such as increased medical costs, declining agricultural output, productivity lost through illness, and indirect damages to the family and social structure. "The report," he charges, "is in fact a prescription for ultimate biological and social catastrophe." Saroff also noted that the report's impact would be severest on the congested and already heavily polluted industrial areas of the Northeast. "The newer and richer areas of the Sunbelt and West can 'afford' some remaining degree of protection, and we have already seen states like California installing their own regulations to protect workers when federal efforts have withered," he writes. "But who is going to protect the workers of the East? Are they going to be offered up as productive sacrifices to the corporations' appetites for profit?"

President Maynard, in issuing the Munton report today, called it "a searching examination of painful and far-reaching issues, which will be useful in the preparation of new legislation by my administration. We expect members of the Congress to study it carefully." But Senator Burbank Forbes (R., Oregon), a persistent critic of industry attempts to avoid pollution controls, released a statement condemning the report. "It is becoming clearer and clearer," he said, "that this administration will stop at nothing in its drive to make life safer for business and more dangerous for the people. First we saw the dismantling of the remains of federal occupational health programs. Then we saw the repeal of the windfall profits tax on oil, which was intended to develop cleaner and healthier sources of energy. Then came the elimination of pollution regulations on energy-producing installations, and the ensuing steep rise in atmospheric pollution and acid rain. Now we are told that we must not only suffer for the salvation of the corporations, we must be ready to die for them!"

However, most initial political reactions to the Munton report have been cautious. When queried, senators and Congressmembers have replied that they needed more time to study the details of the report's recommendations.

Jamie and Mary McBride lived in the Oregon woods near Myrtle Grove. They had come up from San Francisco with the savings from four years of hard labor and living poor. Jamie, a big, muscular person, had worked as a welder, always looking for jobs with plenty of overtime; Mary, who was small and slight, had done office work and waitressing. They had bought 20 acres, about half timber, right up against a National Forest boundary, and were happy that their privacy would be secure on that side anyway. They spent their first six months building their house out of poles they and their friends cut and shaved and hauled, plus scrap lumber and windows and doors they picked up here and there. Jamie had taken some courses at night while they were still in the city and now he had a half-time job fixing trucks. Mary helped out in the co-op food store and once in a while she got in a day as a substitute teacher. They also had an enormous garden, more than an acre, and canned or froze what they couldn't eat or trade. A small clear creek emerged from the National Forest and ran through their property, so they had plenty of water. Gradually their little homestead took on a settled and comfortable look. They no longer worked 12-hour days, and began to think of having their first child.

None of Jamie's family had ever owned a gun, but he discovered that almost everybody who lived in the country had a deer rifle, so he bought one too. Jamie had not been in the army, and he didn't know how to use firearms; he had to get a friend to give him some lessons. To his surprise, he had found that he was a crack shot. But the intense noise of the gun offended his ears, and the terrible damage to targets he practiced on gave him an aversion to the whole idea of shooting. Some of his friends believed that meat you killed yourself, since it had been obtained in a more or less fair struggle, was okay to eat. Others, who came from old-fashioned small-town families, simply felt that "getting your deer" was part of the yearly ritual of life. But Jamie was never comfortable about joining their hunting parties, and he spoke for a while of getting rid of the rifle—much to the amusement of his older neighbors especially, for whom a household gun was as obvious a necessity as a hatchet. In the end he kept it, hanging it on a couple of spikes over the front door in the traditional rural way, with the ammunition in a cupboard nearby. Mary didn't much like it there, but sometimes she did worry about bikers or other intruders. Jamie offered to teach her to shoot. When she held the gun in her hands, however, she disliked the metallic, dangerous feel of it. "I'd rather take my chances," she said.

Vera Allwen did a great deal of speaking. She addressed consumer groups, business groups, political groups, and student groups, outlining Survivalist ideas in terms she tried to keep plain and simple.

"People sometimes ask, Why do you Survivalists make all this fuss about energy? Aren't there other things that are really more important? We're all for energy conservation, they say. But what's new about that?

"I'm glad that most of us are for energy conservation nowadays; only a few years ago there were lots of people who denied that we had an energy problem at all. We have come a long way. But we have not yet focused on where we still have to go if we want to be assured of a stable, non-inflationary, reliable energy system that will serve us over the decades to come. And that is what the Survivalist Party is trying to bring about. We want to learn to live within our energy income. Only through energy self-sufficiency can we escape dependence on erratic and costly foreign energy supplies, and the threats of war that they bring with them. Energy self-reliance will bring us peace—and freedom from creeping militarization.

"For a long time, it was believed that there were infinite resources of fossil fuels—coal, gas and oil. In the period after World War II, indeed, oil was so cheap that engineers and consumers practically ignored how much it cost, or how much we were using. Now we have entered a period of relative scarcity when these energy resources are costing us more every day. There is a great deal of fossil fuel still underground, accumulated over 500 million years of earth's history. But we have used up the easiest parts to reach, and the cost of extracting the remainder is rising. It is particularly expensive in the case of oil—of which we use immense quantities because of our overwhelming desires to drive around in private automobiles.

"The conventional vision of the old political parties is that we must concentrate on developing fossil fuel resources, no matter what the cost in money, pollution, depletion of scarce water supplies, or distortion of our industrial system. But whatever is done about synfuels from coal, new uses of coal, or new findings of oil and gas, these forms of energy are bound to cost relatively more and more as time goes on. (This is not true, as I will explain in a moment, for renewable energy.) If we continue to rely on fossil fuels, we will be forced to pay relatively more and more of our incomes, personal and national, for energy—leaving us less and less for food, housing, health, education, and our other necessities. We might in this way remain energy-rich, for a time, but we will grow poorer in everything else. And the day of reckoning, the day when we must finally turn toward living within our solar income, will only be put off; and we will be weaker when that time comes.

"The Survivalist Party has developed an alternate vision. We do not like this hard path to economic decline and despair. We believe that the time to make a fundamental and permanent change in our energy policies is now, before it is forced upon us by circumstances. We can no longer put false hope in technologies such as nuclear fission and fusion, with their bankrupting costs, their vampire-like drains on the national treasury, their health-threatening and enormously expensive 'accidents,' their unreliability and their low rate of net energy output. We must recognize what our permanent soft-path energy resources really are, and learn to live within them.

"All renewable energy on the earth comes from the sun, directly as radiation and heat, or indirectly through photosynthesis that gives us wood to burn, food to fuel our bodies, or winds to run our windmills. This solar input is a fixed quantity, year following year without end. So it puts an outer limit on humankind's expansion: even forgetting about human impacts which are rapidly turning more of earth's precious agricultural land into desert, we have access only to a fixed amount of solar energy and thus to a fixed maximum of agricultural production. We have not yet reached the theoretical maximum possible agricultural production for the planet, but we are not terribly far from the practical limits. Already we know that the diversion of agricultural crops to alcohol production for auto fuel is reducing the amount of food produced. The world is being forced—not in ten years, but today—to choose between feeding people and feeding cars.

"The fixed input of solar energy thus means that earth can only

57

support a few more people, even at the subsistence levels common to more than half its current population, and that we probably have far too many aboard Spaceship Earth for a comfortable long-term voyage. If we do not voluntarily reduce our numbers, famine will begin to reduce them for us; indeed it already does in many areas of the world.

"The fixed solar input also gives us a kind of economic measuring stick for energy expenditures. So long as fossil fuels were cheaper than solar energy utilization, short-run economic wisdom said to use them up first. But our reluctance to develop solar in a dynamic and determined way has meant that oil prices have had room to rise even further. In the end, the price of competing energy is the only real limit on oil prices. The faster we deploy a permanent solar technology, therefore, the more insurance we will obtain against further oil price hikes—and against disruption of our foreign supplies, and also against the likelihood of our being unable to develop solar energy fast enough when we really need it desperately.

"We know how much sunlight we receive. We also know roughly how much geothermal energy we can obtain from steam in the earth on a sustainable basis. Our objective, if we want to stop being kicked around by our energy problems, must be to develop balanced ways of using this sunlight to heat our buildings, generate electricity, and grow our crops. If we do these things, we will need fossil fuels only for industrial purposes and for the manufacture of plastics, and oil prices will stop rising. We can thus achieve a stable energy pricing system, and one which does not cause us to run up staggering foreign oil payments. We must stop taking on debt that we will have no way to repay except by giving the country away to OPEC.

"The Survivalist vision is that we can do this, and we can even do it rather easily—*if* we have the will. The technology exists, for example, to harness the winds, which are driven by differences in solar input on different parts of the earth. A wind generator never runs out of fuel, and nobody can raise the price of the wind. So long as we keep it repaired, a wind machine goes on generating electricity forever. The technology also exists to extract energy from temperature gradients between cool seawater in the depths and warm seawater at the surface; here again, we will never run out of seawater. And these processes of extracting electricity from natural, solar-driven processes do not affect the over-all heat balance of the planet. They cannot lead, like the large-scale consumption of fossil fuels or the large-scale application of nuclear or satellite-powered energy, toward a catastrophic heating up of the earth's atmosphere. They are energy technologies we can live with, indefinitely, and pass on to our children's children with a clear conscience.

"Morcover, it seems altogether probable that new advances in photovoltaic cells—devices that generate household electricity merely by lying in the sun on your roof—will soon make it possible to greatly diminish our overall demand for power-company electricity. Within 15 or 20 years, therefore, we could produce all the electricity we presently use—which is much more than we really need, if we adopted sensible conservation measures—*entirely from renewable sources*. They will be safe, secure, and less expensive than fossil-fuel sources.

"This is a major part of the Survivalist vision. We also see that these sources of electricity could displace some liquid fuels used for transportation, since electric vehicles are already practical for many local applications. In our compact, energy-efficient future cities that Survivalists are planning, vehicle propulsion will be partly by electrical and partly by alcohol power.

"The Survivalist vision is also against waste. We advocate recycling and re-use of materials, to minimize damage to the environment. But we are also against *economic* waste. The massive American armaments program is not dangerous only because it stimulates an arms race which increasingly jeopardizes our citizens. It also diverts a large proportion of our available capital, our best brains and our most efficient productive resources into the manufacture of useless things which can only be shot off into space, blown up, or thrown away as obsolete. Our arms manufacturers have thrived; our civilian industries have decayed. Countries like Germany and Japan, which spend only a small fraction of what we spend on arms, have put their industrial strength to much more effective uses. We Survivalists are planning to devote American resources to producing useful, productive, safe things that Americans really need: better housing, a new energy-efficient transportation system, a network of human-scale neighborhood medical clinics located where you can reach them easily, modernized factories that can produce goods without burdening us with pollution and that can provide a decent work environment for the people who spend half their waking lives there. We cannot accept a society that builds enormous surpluses of highly accurate ballistic missiles but finds it impossible to run a decent city transportation system.

"A billion dollars of military spending creates only 45,000 jobs. Survivalists would spend that billion on health, where it would create 85,000 jobs and also improve our national productivity—or on construction of transportation facilities, where it would create 70,000 jobs and cut down our energy consumption. By such decisions, made in the light of our basic criterion of long-term survival, we would also build up the facilities we need to be reasonably competitive with other countries.

"But our objective's not competition in itself. Our objective is self-reliance, the knowledge that we have managed our energy supplies, our agricultural base, our transportation system, our population levels, so that they can be sustained on a stable basis as long as humans can see ahead.

"We have heard much foolish and frightening talk in recent years about the supposed necessity for America to recapture its dominant role as Number One in manufacturing. We are being asked to make heavy sacrifices to reach that goal. The time has come for a new perspective on this question—a perspective from a longer-range view. In the 19th century it was Great Britain that dominated the industrial world through its industries and its empire; then we took over that role. But such domination remains a 19th-century idea, founded on the false notion that natural resources are infinite. In the 21st century, the nation that is truly Number One will be the nation that first learns to live on a stable-state basis within the sustainable resources of the planet. It is *that* nation whose future will be truly secure. Here at the end of the 20th century, we need to look ahead, not backwards. The 20th century will be seen, someday, as a transition between the old ways and the new. Let us strive to be Number One, then, in meeting this new challenge, not an outdated one. We have had enough of expansionist crises and folly. We must seek a new goal: to live modestly and cooperatively and in freedom within the resources of our beautiful planet and within the energy budget set for us by that lovely star, our sun. This is a noble goal, one that our species can be proud to achieve. We invite you to join us in the Survivalist Party to work for it."

The city of Berkeley, California, had experimented in the seventies with a plan for diverting through traffic around certain residential neighborhoods. However, since the plan had not been accompanied by improvements in bus services or other public transportation facilities, it merely increased congestion and pollution on the major arteries surrounding these lucky neighborhoods. As a result, the city was bitterly polarized on the issue; the traffic barricades only survived by a narrow referendum majority. And irate drivers continued to vandalize the wooden barriers, sometimes even ramming them.

However, as the years went by, the greater quiet, safety for children, and fresher air within the barricaded neighborhoods was widely noticed. More frequent bus service and cheaper taxi service was gradually provided, and the growth of neighborhood shopping centers cut down the amount of cross-town traffic. A network of "slow streets" with bumps to slow cars to around 15 miles per hour had been instituted, giving bicyclists and people using slow vehicles (wheel chairs and little electric cars) safe routes through the city. Nonetheless, residents of two Berkeley neighborhoods petitioned the city council to turn their streets into narrow cul-de-sacs where cars would park end-on to the curbs and would have to share the street, at a walking pace, with pedestrians and children.

The plan was closely modeled on successful Dutch practices but it was rejected by the council, which feared a repetition of the barriers controversy. In the weeks that followed, the residents of one of the neighborhoods fumed, argued, then plotted and prepared. And one fine night they turned out en masse and, working all night with a great burst of shared energy, built a masonry wall across one end of their street, planted trees and bushes along it, removed all non-resident cars and parked their own inside white stripes they painted on the alphalt. When morning came they sat on their stoops with their coffee or tea and waited. Some people went off to work. A few visitors arrived and duly parked in the vacant spots. At about ten o'clock a police car finally passed the walled-off end of the street, paused, then drove on—the officer in it probably assuming that the traffic department was trying some experiment he hadn't heard of yet.

In fact it was not until three days later, when a city streets department truck crew' happened to drive past, that the dastardly deed was discovered. Police visited the block, and everyone from greybeards to tiny tots told them that the wall had always been there, and they had no idea who had built it. The police, who in Berkeley wear long mustaches and rather luxurious hair, were amused, but duly made their reports. Court orders were filed; the street department laid plans to bulldoze the wall. It was rumored that the county D.A. was not at all amused, and planned prosecutions.

At this point the neighbors, who by now loved their protective wall passionately, realized they had to wage a do-or-die political struggle. They organized visits to the street by journalists, TV crews, and block organizations from many other parts of the city. They managed to get almost all the members of the city council to come and take a look. They provided safety statistics and readings of sound levels, and a poetic neighborhood petition signed by all the residents. They made an elaborate and ingenious but legally hopeless argument defending their "direct citizen volunteer construction plan" as a response to city council budgetary stinginess.

Most of the press and media coverage of the case was surprisingly favorable, though editors worried over the precedent-setting danger of citizens taking their neighborhood welfare into their own hands—especially in the dark of night. "Vigilante Progress?" was the headline of one ambivalent editorial. In the end the city council, rather embarrassed by the whole affair, passed an ordinance that gave official blessing to this particular street-closing and also defined a procedure that residents of other streets could follow in debating, designing and building their own street patterns. The D.A. dropped plans for prosecution, and to celebrate this announcement the neighbors— this time acting on strictly legal lines—secured a proper city permit and closed their street entirely for a Sunday afternoon block party. Small children added flowers to the planting box that ran along the top of the new wall. Bigger children dug holes for more trees, and the adults beamed at each other and lifted each other off the ground in great bear-hugs, and joked about renaming it "Wall Street."

BIOLOGIST CONDEMNS MUNTON
COMMISSION "WHITEWASH"

New York, Jan. 22 (WPI). Dr. Simon Saroff of Rockefeller University has attacked the recent Munton Report as "fallacious, shortsighted, and self-destructive." In a statement even more sharply worded than his minority report included in the Munton document, Saroff today said that if the Munton proposals are followed, the deterioration of the environment—which was slowed and even in a few areas reversed in past decades—would resume pellmell.

"We do not even know the real extent of the damage," he said.

"We do know that chemicals in the biosphere are causing cancer, sterility, mutations, genetic deformities in fetuses, and probably a generally higher level of a host of illnesses. We know that sulfur emissions are causing acid rain which, along with auto smog, cost hundreds of millions of dollars in immediate or indirect agricultural damage each year. We know that smog also causes costly damage to rubber, trees, and human tissue. The problem is that the Munton people have an easy time calculating industrial profit rates, while people trying to calculate pollution damage have to rely on approximations. But by any reasonable test, pollution controls restrain damages a lot more than they restrain profits. In other words, their cost/benefit ratio is highly *positive*. They ought to be continued, and indeed strengthened."

Questioned about Saroff's remarks, Alan Munton, chairman of the board of U.S. Metals, said Dr. Saroff had been a disruptive and uncooperative member of the Commission, and that he doubted anything Saroff said would have any constructive value. "Our report lays out the real alternatives pretty plainly," he said. "We have to get rid of these costly, cumbersome controls and let American industry do the job it knows how to do: produce the goods. Sure it has costs. But you can't make omelettes without breaking eggs."

When Roger came back from his visit to Dana, the second lawyer, he seemed even more worried, and called an immediate family conference "to discuss our security problems." Carol and Mike and Dimmy joined Lou at the big round dining table, somewhat alarmed at Roger's mood. Even Theo could tell something was up; he came and crawled onto Dimmy's lap to listen.

"Well," Roger began, "Dana basically says that until you really know how the cell works, the public-disclosure thing isn't much use. If some big company hears about the general idea they'll put their lab to work on it, find out the crucial ingredient in the salts, and patent it. Even if your disclosure could be documented as prior, it's too *broad*, Dana says."

Lou frowned. "So then they'd be able to make people pay to use the process?"

"Exactly. It would be in their power. Just as if you had had nothing to do with it. So when they hear you've got something—and they will, through that attorney or somehow—we can be sure they'll start snooping around trying to find out what you're up to."

There was a silence. The little group felt alone and isolated. Finally Lou spoke up.

"So we have to be sure nobody comes around here and finds out anything crucial."

"Anything at all, if possible," said Roger. "So we're going to have to not leave the house unguarded at any time. That's going to mean bringing a couple of neighbors in on it."

"I can promise to be here daytimes two days a week," put in Dimmy, "when I'm not at the museum."

"I'll talk to Cindy," said Carol. "I'm sure she could take the morning shift on the other days. And Ed's designing a new boat, so he could probably bring his drafting stuff over and take the afternoons, for a couple of weeks anyway."

"Another thing," said Roger, "is that we have to assume the phones are tapped, and the house may be bugged for sound."

"Aw, Dad," said Mike, "how could anybody get in to do that?"

"They don't *have* to get in anymore," replied Roger. "They can point a laser device at a big window that vibrates with the air inside the house—like when you talk. Then they pick up the vibrations. They can be miles away, even."

Lou laughed. "What are we supposed to do, write each other notes?"

To her amazement, Roger dropped his voice to a whisper. "Not a bad idea, for anything connected with your work, Lou. Let's just make a rule: no science talk in the house! We can go out on the beach where we can see whether anybody's around."

"And what am I supposed to do with my notebooks? Write 'em in code, like Leonardo da Vinci? —Actually, maybe that's not a bad idea!"

"No, it's a terrible idea," said Roger. "These people have cryptographers who could just read out any cipher we could construct." He frowned and began whispering again. "I think actually you're going to have to keep it mostly in your head. And I can take notes, every day or so, and stick them in our bank safe-deposit box. But you'd better use some kind of code too, just in case!"

Carol looked unhappy. "This is really paranoid-making," she said. "Roger, do you really think spies are going to be creeping around out here? I mean, it's so exposed, and Bolinas people don't exactly ignore strangers!"

Roger looked unhappy too, but there was a flush in his cheeks and a kind of excitement in his voice—part fear, part defiance, part determination, part guile. "I wish I *didn't* think they'd do almost anything," he said slowly. "But you've got to realize that our Lou, here, is on to something that could cost these people billions upon billions of dollars in lost profits. If they really realize what's going on out here—well, I wouldn't put it past them to wipe out all of Bolinas if they could think of some way to do it!"

Lou shuddered. "Oh, Daddy, you're being melodramatic."

"I *hope* I am. But we're in this perilous period, Lou. —How long do you guess it's going to take to really crack the thing? I know that's a dumb question, but I had to ask it."

"I really don't know. All the ideas I've had so far have blanked out. There must be something going on that's totally obvious, but I don't see it. —I'm sorry," she added, feeling like crying. "I didn't want to cause all this trouble!"

Roger and Carol moved over to her side of the table and put their arms around her. "Hey, it's okay," said Carol. "We're all in this together, remember?" She gave Lou some affectionate massage strokes on her shoulders. "You don't have to hold all that tension up there, all by yourself!"

Lou broke into fullblown tears, her head on the table. "Oh, thank you," she blubbered. "But you know, it may take months—I don't know, maybe years! I just don't seem to be able to *get* it."

"You'll get it all right," said Mike. He looked across the table at Lou. "We all know you will. So does David."

"David?" sniffed Lou.

"Sure. One time he was kidding around out here with me, and he said, 'Know the most interesting thing about your sister?' And I thought he was going to say, well, you know, so I just laughed. Then he said, 'No, really, it's that she doesn't know how *good* she is.'"

News about the Survivalist Party trickled through society in unpredictable, irregular paths and caught the attention of people from many different backgrounds. One day a contractor named John Forbes dropped in to see Vera Allwen. He had heard, he said, that the Party was coming out with some new ideas about the car problem, and he wanted to tell his story. Vera gave him some coffee and listened.

A few years earlier, Forbes had been making plans to build 42 houses on a piece of almost level land he had managed to buy near Mt. Diablo, east of San Francisco Bay. Because of land costs, he had been forced to adapt his original luxurious design to a partial condominium pattern—at considerable trouble in dealing with the county building and zoning departments, who still hoped large single-family homes could be sold in that area at a profit. (They even argued that he could afford the costs of adding sewage-treatment capacity and putting in streetlights.) But as Forbes had found, suburban housing prices were beginning to soften. People who didn't absolutely crave a suburban life-style were beginning to think of living closer to their jobs in town. Forbes and his fellow developers had countered by including in their sales booklets information on bus lines and the possibilities of carpools. Still, there was no denying it: suburban living was becoming relatively more expensive and difficult. What with heavy gasoline outlays and higher heating losses, it consumed about six times as much energy per person as living in town apartments. It was cheap oil that had enabled people to flee deteriorating cities instead of putting their shoulders to the civic wheel and rebuilding them. Cheap oil had also enabled farmers pushed off their land by suburban development to operate further away, trucking their produce to city markets. But now cheap oil was a thing of the past.

Forbes had not really seen what was happening, he said, until a group of young people from the Salinas Valley, an agricultural area a hundred miles to the south, approached him about buying his land. He was still negotiating over his 42 units with the county and wasn't eager to sell. But transportation costs had become such a factor in their business that they wanted to establish their vegetable-growing operation closer to the population centers they served. And they were willing to pay about ten percent more for the land than Forbes had paid for it—which was about all the profit he could hope for even if he did finally get his plans approved. So one day, he told Vera, he drove out and looked at the site, carrying his development plan rolled under his arm. He could envision his rambling condominiums there, full of people happy in their new suburban paradise. But it wasn't going to happen. When everything was added up, the tomato farmers could use that land more effectively than he could. They would put up their greenhouses and their packing shed. Growing tomatoes, he reflected, had become what was called "the highest possible use" of that land.

As he had walked back to his pickup truck, Forbes realized he had had a kind of revelation. From now on, he saw, the great flood tide of suburban sprawl would begin to ebb. Though of course many things would continue to be built in suburban towns, the premium would be on compact clustering of buildings, on the use of rich-soil areas for agricultural production, on keeping travel distances short, on access to public transportation. In the end the only real answer to the transportation energy problem would be to arrange things so less transportation was needed.

This understanding had seemed alien to Forbes's developer friends and competitors. They thought the 'energy crisis' would soon pass—through the development of synthetic fuels or some other technological solution. When Forbes had begun to concentrate his activities on building and remodelling and adding to existing buildings near shopping malls and other centers of activity, they thought he had lost his drive; and he did not enlighten them about the growing amounts of money he was making at it. He knew perfectly well that something new was going on, but he had no one to talk to about it.

Thus, when he had heard that the Survivalist Party had a vision of compact, energy-conserving minicities, he figured he should find out more; maybe he could be useful. One line from a news story had stuck in his head. "We should hardly be surprised," Vera was quoted as saying, "if we pave over our richest farmland for housing tracts and then find that food prices rise. And there is an answer: tax development on flat farmland more heavily than in hill areas."

So John Forbes and Vera Allwen talked for a long time. Forbes thought that in the vast spread-out suburbs, central points like transit stops and shopping centers would become city centers. As car travel became more expensive, condominiums and offices and then apartment buildings would locate close by. Residential areas in between these centers, formerly considered especially desirable locations, would be affordable only by the very wealthy and much of the land would return to agricultural uses. The new patterns Forbes saw seemed welcome to Vera because they fit in with the ideas she had been developing—of a dispersed city built upon strong neighborhoods, compact, well defined and self-reliant, each one offering its inhabitants the basic necessities: dwellings, workplaces and stores. These neighborhoods—each containing around ten thousand people—would be small enough that the residents could get around to most things they did daily either by foot or bicycle. The streets

67

would be reclaimed for human beings instead of only providing runways for automobiles. There would be many little squares and parks where people would see each other, talk, deal with community problems. Such mini-cities, Vera knew, would be enormously more energy-efficient than existing cities. They would also be more democratic and a lot more pleasant to live in. With their centers connected by a network of fast trains or streetcars, they would form interrelated constellations that could support the traditional glories of urban life: the kind of art, science, music and literature that compact cities had given us in the past. (The sole art form of the suburb, she liked to say, was the neon sign.)

The decline of the automobile would, in fact, necessitate a wholesale rebuilding of American communities. What Forbes had understood only as brutal economic necessity, Vera saw as civic virtue. So John Forbes joined the Survivalist Party on the spot, promising to help work out its land-use and development policies.

As he returned home, Forbes had another revelation. Passing a tract cheaply built for an easy market right after World War II, he foresaw its already dilapidated houses being bulldozed away. But the land was not then covered with condominiums. Instead it was replanted to fruit and nut trees, which had covered it only 50 years before. The car had conquered—but not for long.

Toward the end of the seventies a public-opinion-polling organization had asked a novel question of a chosen sample of Americans: would they like to work in an employee-owned and employee-controlled company?

This was during a seemingly conservative period, not marked by frequent strikes or political conflicts. Commonsense would have predicted confidently that a negligible fraction of the citizens would answer positively. Even in Europe, where the revolutionary events of 1968 in France had produced inspiring models of self-management in industry, the idea of workers' control was still new. In the United States, only a few medium-sized companies were in fact worker-owned, along with somewhat more numerous small ones, especially in the Northwest. The question was not even on the fringes of the official national political agenda, as served up by the media.

However, some two thirds of Americans polled answered Yes. The pollsters, puzzled, rechecked their data—and found them free of statistical sampling error, interview or question-format bias, and the other usual perils of opinion research. There it was: a monumental mystery. Nobody could explain it, and few tried.

Nonetheless, in the dark hours before dawn, it sometimes haunted the wakeful hours of a few thoughtful corporation executives, who sensed in it some vague premonition of coming danger. And a few people interested in fundamental social change pondered it also—wondering if this great unknown and unexplored social force might be tapped to move American society in bold new directions. Meanwhile, the feelings revealed by the poll lay in the minds of more than a hundred million Americans, like a bomb whose fuse could be ignited at any time—but only by certain as yet unspecifiable events.

When Vera Allwen and her friends had originally conceived the Survivalist Party they envisioned it as a national organization. Getting deeper into their organizing work, however, they found it difficult to achieve a broad meeting of minds with people in most other regions. There were individual sympathizers everywhere, and sizable concentrations of them in places like New England. But in the elections as the century closed, most of the country had moved steadily toward a more conservative and anti-environmental stance. It was only in Washington, Oregon and northern California that the Munton report had been considered a genocidal outrage, and in those areas strong environmental measures continued to be backed by the voters. Anti-nuclear initiatives had passed handsomely in Washington and Oregon while being defeated elsewhere. Representatives with generally people-oriented positions continued to be elected in the Northwest while business-oriented candidates swept into office in most other areas. And it was only in the Northwest that Survivalist ideas were getting a warm reception from large numbers of people.

These diverging trends forced themselves upon the Survivalists' attention. But nobody among the original organizers relished the idea of becoming a regional party. Maggie Glennon actually hated it. "It'll mean isolation and eventual defeat for our ideas," she said. "We could totally control three states, or at least two and a half, and still get *nowhere* in Congress." "That's being all-or-nothing," said Henry Engelsdorf. "In politics you have to bite off whatever you can, and chew it. Then you go back for a bigger bite. You can't sit back and not eat at all just because you're not sure you'll get the whole pie!"

"Henry, we're not talking pies, we're talking votes. Forty votes in Congress is a *joke*. You bargain for crumbs."

Vera put in mildly, "Well, we all know regionalism is on the upswing—has been for five years now. As the transportation patterns go, so goes the political consciousness. Maybe people in other parts of the country really want their *own* regional agendas, and our ideas don't fit?"

Maggie looked furious. "Listen, the problems are the same *everywhere*—the ecological ones, the economic ones, the political ones. You all know that! And we happen to be putting forward valid answers to them. They aren't *western* answers, for Christ's sake. And you couldn't put them into effect just in the West. You'd be swamped, dragged down into the pit by the rest of the country."

"I'm not sure of that," said Vera. "To the extent there *is* growing economic and cultural regionalism, you could do a lot of things. Let's get specific: as a first step we could go for a nuclear-free Northwest. Let the rest of the country follow our example later."

"Sure, but I'm talking about legislative power, not just single issues. Anti-nuclear isn't worth a damn just by itself. —I take that back, it's worth a lot, but nowhere near enough. We have to aim at passing national legislation, or we're dead. That's the real ball game."

"But Maggie," Henry said, "that game may be closed to us, at least in any realistic time frame. We're evidently facing a situation where we have to invent a new game. You may be right that the issues are the same everywhere, but if people only *see* them out here, then here is where our work lies."

Maggie's red hair bristled. "I am not in this to create a little ecologically favored enclave here on the West Coast! If that's what it comes down to, well, I've got better things to do."

Maggie marched off. Vera and Henry shrugged at each other.

"Well, Henry," asked Vera, "so you really think we have to go it alone?"

"Yeah. Maggie knows it too. She'll come around."

"But what about her argument? How can we keep from being dragged into the morass?" Vera sighed. "It's enough to make you believe countries can have a death-wish! If something doesn't work, they try twice as much of it. If somebody proposes something really different, they laugh at it."

Henry was looking off into the distance. After a moment he said, "Maybe we could do some kind of regional thing, a little like the

70

TVA—a super-state structure. Congress might see it as a way to get the environmental movement off their backs. Experimental ecological programs, city decentralization experiments, regional transportation . . . "

Vera had fastened her attention on Henry. "My God, Henry, that's fiendish! Get federal *sanction* for regionalization—"

"—with an implicit *quid pro quo* that if they let us alone we confine our organizing and experimenting to this region, where our ideas seem to be welcome. No special favors—just give the regional authority block grants, pro rata. Do it four years, let us hang ourselves." Henry folded his hands in satisfaction.

Vera looked at him with her patient smile. "The Pacific Ecological Authority. Green-PEA?"

Maggie came back and stuck a letter in front of Vera: her resignation. Vera barely glanced at it. "Maggie, don't be ridiculous. Henry has just had a very interesting idea. Now sit down and listen to this."

Late on an evening in February, Otto Hunt drove home in distress from a Redding city council meeting. His elaborate plan to build a $6 million incinerator to dispose of the city's garbage had just been shot down.

Otto, like the good engineer he had been trained to be, had thought of *everything*. He had designed the firebox, he had designed the flues, the feed machinery, ingenious devices to extract ash. He had calculated flow rates and oxygen capacity. He had even worked out a novel dumping ramp so that city trucks would have a minimum hesitation time as they unloaded.

This beautiful plan had been defeated. And by an unholy coalition of a renegade economist from the local college, two uppity housewives, and a well organized bunch of dreamers from some new confederation of eco-freaks operating out of San Francisco called the Survivalist Party, which had just established a branch in town. What did any of them know about burning garbage? Zero! Otto Hunt knew everything there was to know about burning garbage—its physics, its costs, down to the last mil. They had beaten him by trickery, by changing the rules of the game—and the council members had gone along with them. They had talked about a full analysis of energy flow, and future energy cost projections, and the possibilities of turning the waste stream into compost, or recycling half of it, or squashing garbage to produce burnable oils, for God's sake.

They had proposed ridiculous limitations on his pollution output, and groaned and wailed about scrubbers for the stack, and what they could and couldn't do, and how much they would cost, and what to do with the toxic sludge they produced. Petty details! Then they had somehow convinced a majority of the council that their panacea, "source reduction," was a feasible alternative. They had the amazing faith that free Americans could be persuaded to throw kitchen scraps into compost heaps and paper and cardboard packaging into fireplaces. And, on the basis of pitifully limited experience with recycling pickups, they argued that spending city money to go around and collect newspaper, metal cans and glass bottles could be turned into a paying proposition.

Otto knew better. Americans were slobs. A majority of them barely had the brains to come inside when it started to rain. You couldn't even keep them from simply dropping their garbage as they walked down the street, or dumping it out of car windows as they drove. How the hell could you expect them to separate it into three-part recycling bins? The poor saps were lucky to find their mouths with their forks half the time. Well, the city could try this noble experiment. It would be a disaster. In two years they'd be crawling back, crying for his incinerator—anything to get rid of the stuff! But by then Otto Hunt would be gone. There was a city in New Jersey that wanted him. Back there they didn't coddle nitwits, and certainly didn't elect them to city councils. They knew that to get progress, you had to suffer a little. They'd love his incinerator.

"Vera," said Henry, "I hope you don't mind, I've asked two Indian people to come to the staff meeting tonight. I think we all ought to hear what they have to say—I met them the other day at an Indian affairs conference, and it's powerful stuff. One's John Hanley, a Mohawk, and the other's a hotshot young lawyer, Ramona Dukane—part Navajo, part Chickasaw, I think. Anyway she's been working to stop uranium mining on the reservations."

"What do they want to talk about?"

"Actually they didn't want to talk about anything. I gather Indians don't make a habit of going around telling whites what they ought to do. But they're curious about our position. There seem to be some interesting parallels."

Meetings among the Survivalists always involved circular arrangements of chairs, and they had just finished shoving things into place when the two Indians arrived. John was a quiet, solid man wearing a checked shirt; he moved slowly and gave the impression of having a great deal of power inside him somewhere. Ramona was highstrung and sharp-eyed; she wore her hair in a braid, but aside from broad cheekbones that was the only thing noticeably "Indian" about either of them.

They took places in the circle and waited comfortably to see what would happen. Henry welcomed them to the group and explained that these meetings were to give the opportunity for people to be together, to share ideas and feelings as well as to make plans and report on developments. He explained why he had thought it would be a good idea for the group to hear what they had to say. John thanked him for the welcome, but he did not speak for a few moments. He seemed almost to be waiting for the spirits of the people in the room to come to rest. Vera had the feeling he might have waited for hours if that was what it took. In time, it was Ramona who got things going. "Henry told us the other day about some of your ideas. I told him they sounded like Indian ideas in certain ways. Particularly the notion that we must treat the earth with respect if we want to survive here. To tell the truth, I was surprised that white political people were thinking in that spiritual way. Indians are used to being called unrealistic and backward for holding to such ideas."

"I'm not sure how deeply spiritual it is with us," replied Vera. "With us it began out of very practical considerations. Terrible things are being done to our land and water and air. They damage us, even if indirectly."

Now John spoke, slowly and deliberately. "To Indians, every part of the creation is alive. To rip open the earth for uranium, or to destroy the salmon runs or ruin the forests is a direct hurt, from which all creatures suffer. Now there's a scientific term for it—disrupting the biosphere. Indians have always considered this wrong. For thousands of years. We have known it in our bones, even if we had no scientific theory for it."

"There's something else," said Ramona, "that interests me a lot. Henry says you are also proposing new ideas about how political groups ought to operate—small, democratic, consensus-based. And I

73

wanted to remind you that Indian political ideas were important in this country's history once before—and they might be again now."

"You mean Franklin?" asked Henry.

"Yes. —Does everybody know about that?"

"No," said Vera. "You mean Benjamin Franklin?"

"It's been established by historians that Franklin was friendly with a number of Indian leaders from the Iroquois federation. The Iroquois had a democratic federation since before Magna Carta, but the idea had never arisen in European cultures. So when Franklin and the other colonial thinkers started talking revolution and the creation of a new kind of country, they didn't want to fall into the centralized pattern of the British monarchy, and they didn't want to revert to the local scale of Athenian democracy—"

"So federalism was an Indian idea?" interrupted Vera, astonished.

"And an Indian practice," said Ramona. "Indians also practiced internal democracy within the tribes. Indian decision-making has always been done by consensus, including the selection of chiefs. Their powers, by the way, were very limited, and that may have given Franklin some ideas too. Anyway, you can see why it interested us to hear you were working with ways to avoid just straight majority-vote procedures."

"We come at it from group theory," said Vera. "Getting to a consensus can be slow, but it's more solid. In the end it generates more social energy. And it *feels* better."

John nodded. "To Indians, it is as if all persons are members of one family. It is necessary to hear each other truly. Each has the right to speak, to be understood, so that when a decision is made, all will honor it in their hearts." There was a pause, and in the Survivalist group little warm glances went from person to person: this was how they tried to operate, though they didn't always succeed. Then John went on. "Now I would like to speak to you of some other things. It is not good for people to divide themselves up against each other in senseless ways. But if you have holy traditions, you will not have to fight over everything every day; people will know what needs to be done. Now we have to have lawyers like Ramona here to fight for us, but Indians do not like endless lawsuits and sharp dealing. In the old days we didn't have to use all our energy defending our 'property.' We had plenty of time for dancing and music and talk and poems and singing. When we awoke in the morning we had time to pay attention

74

to our dreams, which we knew were more important than punching a time clock in a factory.

"So even though Indians have been killed and sent away to strange schools and pushed back into tiny corners of this continent, we have kept alive in our culture the sense of what it means to live in harmony with the earth, sharing it with the four-footed creatures, with the birds, with the million grasses that all bow to the same wind.

"We know what it is to have different ideas and to live within a society that seems bent on self-destruction." Looking at Ramona, he added, "We have had to learn self-defense, so we can go into white courts and seek redress against broken treaties—so we can regain our independent status as nations and build an Indian society that cannot be destroyed by white greed. But we have also remembered to trust to prophecy."

Here John's eyes closed and his face became calm; he suddenly seemed much older. Ramona, Vera noticed, had crossed her arms and was looking at John expectantly. "I am pleased to see white brothers and sisters taking thought about how to treat our common mother the earth. I see you learning hard lessons: how to survive against heavy odds, how to endure because your ideas are good. I see you listening to the wisdom of the eagle, of the bear, of the wolf, and learning to read again what is written in the rocks and the trees and the clouds. Then you will feel at home again on the earth. Then the earth will no longer be only something to be exploited—it will be part of you, and you will treat it with respect.

"But I see you suffering for your devotion to the earth. I see many people despising you, and laughing at you, and calling you names. I see them trying to cast you out—to get rid of your ideas, which will fill them with uneasiness and guilt. You will have long marches with many tears. But you will fight bravely because you are people who know the truth.

"In time I see this struggle revealing to you a great secret—that you have become a new people, with a new language and a new way of understanding, even if you speak with English words. Then you will find yourselves living on a kind of reservation too, and you will learn why it is that Indians insist on being recognized as sovereign peoples, so that they can care for even a small part of the earth in the way the great spirit intended—as a sign to the others that one day all humans must learn again what has been forgotten."

75

John opened his eyes and reached out to the people on either side. A circle of hands soon linked the whole group into a circle, and for a long time nobody said anything; they just sat quietly, looking ahead in their own ways to what the future might bring.

Dimmy's little house in the Swift backyard literally measured ten feet square. But he had organized its interior with the neatness and efficiency of a boat, so there was actually room for everything that he and Theo needed. A small bed platform occupied the otherwise wasted space above the sink and food preparation counter. Dimmy slept on a Japanese-style mat which could be rolled up and stored during the day. He had a worktable which folded back against the wall when it wasn't being used. Ingenious shelves held dishes, glasses, silverware.

Theo was four; every morning Dimmy got him up and they ate breakfast together. Then, on his way to his job at the museum, Dimmy dropped Theo off at the child-care center. Luckily Dimmy's job had flexible hours; if Theo got sick, he could take a day or two off and do some work at home. He had also set up cooperative exchanges with neighbors who had small children too, to provide for emergencies, and of course the Swifts often helped out. Theo was an adorable child, very small and delicate compared to Dimmy, with deep dark eyes. Lou liked Theo; he was a snuggly creature, and having him around gave a certain sense of the ongoing generations—after all, both she and Mike were getting on toward grown-up status. Theo was the new person, the unknown one, whose destiny was as yet almost totally unknowable.

Lou was also touched by Dimmy's devotion to Theo. A year and a half after Theo's birth, his mother had died. Dimmy didn't talk about it much, but Lou had gathered from Roger and Carol that she had been a moody, passionate woman and, perhaps because of her illness (she had a brain tumor), not very good with Theo. After her death the in-laws had tried to get Theo away from Dimmy, saying he was really their responsibility. But Dimmy had hung on, blindly, through the first impossible months. Then he had moved into a group house where there were several other single parents, and that arrangement had worked for more than a year. But when the Swifts told him their cottage was going to be available he jumped at the chance despite the

76

miniature scale of the place. He loved Bolinas and the idea of Theo growing up there, close to the sea, with the great open expanses of the mesa to roam around on, greatly appealed to him.

There was plenty for Theo to do around the Swift household. Mike was a mechanical sort—he and his friends were always building something. They didn't mind having Theo around as a junior helper on their go-carts and treehouses and subterranean hideouts. Dimmy and Theo ate with the Swifts except for breakfasts and they pitched in with the food preparation and clean-up. (It surprised Lou how much a four-year-old could actually do around the house if he was seriously expected to do it.) They had their own section of the vegetable garden, and Dimmy built a sandbox in one corner of the yard. Often, when Lou was working in her garage-laboratory, she would see Theo and some little friend playing in the yard. They were under strict orders never to touch her cell array or its meter hut, but just in case, Lou had put a lock on the hut's door—she never underestimated the power of curiosity.

From an airplane above an American city, the only human activity visible was the movement of cars. (For some years now cars had outnumbered people in many areas.) With the blind determination of ants, the cars crept about on their prescribed paths, halting mysteriously as if to sniff at something, then moving on. They streamed rapidly on straightaways and hesitated or gathered in clumps at junctions. Sometimes, where a number of paths converged, they jammed in so tightly together that they looked like a mass of beetles covering the earth, and they seemed unable to move at all.

From a closer view, the movement and noise of cars dominated the urban landscape. No location remained untouched by the roar of motors, the grinding of gears, the hiss of tires and airstream wind, the petulant bleat of horns. In human minds routes and the vehicles that connected them often seemed more compelling than the places the routes supposedly served. Automobiles dominated human beings and their economy like an occupying mechanical army. At any given moment, a vast part of the population was busy manufacturing or repairing cars, or servicing cars through highway and street work, gas stations, police forces and courts, licensing and taxing bodies, insurance companies, hospitals, morgues and mausoleums. Everything consid-

ered, the automobile consumed well over an eighth of all the productive capacity of the American economy, and many individuals spent a quarter of their income on their cars.

Moreover, average Americans spent about ten percent of their waking time in cars, and for some the percentage was far higher. Such people were subjected to heavy health risks from breathing so much exhaust-contaminated air, and their bodies were flabby from lack of exercise. Aside from working and watching television, riding in cars was the most regular and familiar waking activity of human beings in this sector of the planet. They rolled in their millions along freeways and turnpikes, they sped down boulevards, they wended their way through residential neighborhoods, they went in spurts of stop and go through endless suburban sprawl. At any given moment, more than one in every fifty drivers was drunk or loaded on drugs. The total deaths from accidents since cars were invented now approached two and a half million, but the fact that the weekly death rate was only around a thousand (plus another couple of thousand maimed) was regarded as a sign of the competence of American drivers, whose accident rate per mile driven was far below that of most other industrialized countries.

Drivers thought of their vehicles merely as convenient (though increasingly expensive) machines to convey them from place to place. But cars inevitably functioned also as parts of the biosphere. In each one, a powerful internal combustion engine turned over insatiably, gulping in several gallons of gas per hour, mixing it with large quantities of air, and expelling the polluted air exhausts, like one long, continuous, carcinogenic fart. So markedly did the voracious cars out-breathe humans that there was no particle of air in metropolitan areas that had not previously passed through the cylinders of at least one car, and bore in the noxious gases and particulates that it carried the traces of that passage.

❧

It was now the beginning of March, and Lou had worked for several months on an exhausting series of repeated attempts to replicate her original findings: that is, to do deliberately and repeatably in new cells what had happened by accident in the original one. She would set up a similar cell, carefully giving it a leaky seal. She would spray seawater at it with a plant sprayer. She would let it sit overnight and in the morning she looked at the meter in the little instrument hut.

Its needle always sat stubbornly at the low end of the scale. Something was not working.

Laboriously, in varying sequences, Lou retraced her steps. She re-did the doping; she tested for the possible presence of lucky contaminants in the kiln. She checked the doping compound for impurities. She obtained copper screening substrates from the same supplier. But the new cells refused to do anything unusual, while the original cell sat there beside them, maddeningly continuing its incredible output.

They looked the same. They had been built in the same way. Was there some small forgotten difference in what she had done? For the hundredth time Lou went over all the steps. Disgusted, she gave one of the legs of the cell rack a good kick. It shook a bit, and Lou felt ashamed of her temper; after all, it wasn't the cells' fault! She opened the instrument hut to see if the kick had dislodged anything in there.

One of the switches had fallen closed, and suddenly Lou remembered that on the gusty morning when she first discovered the unusual output reading a switch had also fallen closed during the night. But was it *that* switch's cell that had the high output?

Her mind went into high gear again. If the battery was at all charged—which it was—closing that switch, once the cell had salty water in it, would have set an electrolytic reaction in process. It would create chlorine, it would create sodium hydroxide, but it would also create a bunch of other compounds. And some of them could easily diffuse into the silicon! Then in the morning, when the sun began shining again, one of these mysterious compounds enabled the cell's output to multiply.

Lou was shaking with excitement. So it *was* partly chemical! That would be a reason nobody else would have tried it. They were working on one-step processes, but nature did it in two steps! She felt as if her brain was spinning in her head, a gyroscope suddenly set to a new course. All right—she would do it all over, this time with the switch closed for a few hours while there was a cover over the cell to keep out sunlight. Everything else just the same as before. "Wait till Roger hears about *this*!" she thought.

This time, when she allowed the electrolytic process to go on for between five and six hours. she got almost the original extraordinary results. The output wasn't ten times up, it was maybe eight. A little disappointed, she built another series of cells, running them electrolytically for different periods.

Lou took Roger out to the cell array and explained, in whispers, her new theory. At first he didn't want to believe it. "Too complicated," he said with a frown. But when Lou showed him the new cell, quietly giving almost the same reading as the first accidental one, he was convinced. "My God," he said. "That must be it, then!" He looked at Lou with a strange new look. "You've done it, daughter!" Then he began capering around the cell rack like a madman, hopping up and down and laughing, and coming back to hug her, and going over to the new cells and patting them, until Lou began to think he was going completely out of his mind. But in a bit he calmed down.

"All right," he said finally, "now we have something that's firm enough to publish. Who knows what the exact mechanism is, but this is clear and definite and simple—and it *is* do-it-yourself!"

"Were you worried?" asked Lou, with her throaty chuckle.

"Yeah. I thought it might be something really exotic that would replicate only in some kind of high-tech conditions."

Lou went over and peered at the new cells. "I wish I knew what's going on in there," she said. "I just realized I'm going to feel kind of—well, ashamed, if we publish without knowing how it really works."

Roger looked alarmed. "You'll still be the one who discovered it. It'll be known as the Swift Effect, even if somebody else finally figures out the steps of the mechanism."

"I suppose so." Lou stared sullenly at the cells. "But I want to figure it out, too."

"Look, Lou, now we can build a bunch of them and give them to people, and teach some other people how to do it. Then it's under public disclosure and it'll be safe. We don't want to prolong this state of danger and uncertainty!"

Lou looked sad. "I suppose not." Then she said, "Isn't there some way we could *sort of* publish it—enough to fulfill the legal requirements but not really draw the corporations' attention to it? I'm still worried there's some way they could figure out to steal it."

"I doubt it. We heard the alternatives. We can go the public-disclosure route, or lay out ten grand and patent it. Which also takes longer and means trusting lawyers. I think we should do it quick, Lou."

It always made Lou nervous when she saw that Roger was fearful, and it was contagious even though she had no real way to evaluate the situation. Was Roger being paranoid? There was the safety of the idea to think about, and then the question of personal safety. It was tempting to think of holding off the publication just a few more weeks, maybe a couple of months. Then, with luck, she could make the truly beautiful splash she had often envisioned: a clean, mind-blowing paper that would simply settle the business once and for all! What risks, Lou wondered, was she really willing to take in hopes of that?

In Washington, amid the grandiose architecture of a capital deliberately built to resemble that of imperial Rome, presidents came and went. After one assassination in the sixties and several later attempts, they were seldom seen directly by the populace they governed. Instead, they made themselves visible to the nation from time to time through brief presidential addresses and other official televised appearances. The media, through well-known news personalities, then analyzed what the president had said, or seemed to say, and what it might mean. August grey-haired senators and eager young members of the House alike watched these programs for clues on the backstage maneuvering by which legislation moved to the floor of Congress and won or lost — or was blocked in execution even though it won, or was implemented by regulation even though it lost. The press, more leisured and independent than the networks, and occasionally willing to dig for scandal, generally confined itself to polite analysis of the proceedings — seeking trendy labels for the chaos of events.

This media-transmitted dance had its stately attractions. In principle, the enormous power of the executive branch — capable of destroying civilization through a nuclear exchange, or waging undeclared wars so expensive as to bankrupt the economy, or interfering in trade to the ruination of whole industries — was held in check by the legislative branch, controller of the tax-revenue purse strings. In actuality, however, the interconnections between the government's two branches and the several thousand people who owned and controlled the commanding industrial power centers were so intimate that the whole operated as one organism. True enough, there were continual conflicts over policies that might favor one group over another or upset applecarts with powerful owners. These conflicts agitated the participants but were regarded as insignificant by the vast mass of the people. To them, sitting at their television sets in Portland or Wichita or Atlanta, the media dance qualified as mild entertainment, hardly as exciting as a football

*game and seldom compelling enough to motivate a trip all the way to
the polls on election day. On TV, most leaders somehow looked small
and petty. They wore too much make-up, and argued about formulas
and catch-phrases; their eyes skittered nervously across the tele-
prompters. You wouldn't want to trust them with your life,
certainly—but didn't somebody's hand have to be on the red-alert telephone?*

*Thus the number of voters had dropped until public offices of the
greatest importance, including the presidency itself, were being filled
through the voting support of only a quarter of the adult population.
Upon the distracted and precarious consent of this small group the
business of the republic was transacted, involving decisions that would
determine the fate of whole generations.*

*Naturally enough, this situation dismayed part of the citizenry. They
saw the nation stumbling this way and that, buffeted by international
forces and paralyzed by internal political blockages. In their different
ways, they began to opt out. The better-off who had managed to move
to the suburbs disavowed the agonizing problems of the cities. They
voted for tax cuts that reduced public services and withdrew financial
powers from local governments. They bought guns and began to hoard
food and gold coins against a currency collapse, and many of them
seemed almost to relish the idea of a war over the oil fields of the Middle East.*

*But another group of citizens, most numerous in the Northwest,
drew different conclusions. The surreal state of the national life made
them seek a new kind of moral grounding for their lives. So they re-
treated far beyond the suburbs to the real country. There they hoped to
restore a sense of fundamental reality. To learn "where they were" they
studied the geography and geology and botany and history of the
places in which they lived. In this process, they hoped, they could see
how the region could best support them; and if they truly knew their
region, perhaps they could defend it against the national madness.*

*Building small but lovely and often innovative houses with their own
hands, they lived on city savings until they learned subsistence agriculture, or the growing of marijuana as a cash crop, or found jobs in
nearby towns. They began, in a way new to most late-twentieth-century
Americans, to consider themselves settled and permanent inhabitants
of their region—responsible for it, and for passing it on unimpaired to
their children, so that the land might support their descendants unto the
seventh generation. When they could not see having their lively chil-*

dren subjected to the lockstep curriculum prescribed by the state, they founded their own cooperative schools. They became crafty gardeners, alert to variations in soil and moisture and sun. They rehabilitated or replanted orchards let go to ruin, and relearned old methods of drying fruit in the sun instead of with expensive gas dryers. They started cooperative natural food stores and handicraft sales outlets. They planted trees; they cleared underbrush, doing with their labor what fires had once been left to do. They mobilized politically and fought off developers, highwaymen, miners. They sought out the places of early Indian habitations and, sitting on great rocks next to old acorn-grinding holes, they found comfort in knowing that humans had once lived in these spots in balance with the natural order. And so little by little, year after year, their children grew up—knowing the plants and the insects and the fishes and the angles of the sun, knowing the natural stages of creeks and rivers, feeling at home on the land, occupying it not for profit but for sustenance and survival.

One day in April Lou got a note from a young man, Bert Luckman, who had been a couple of years ahead of her in high school. He had heard about her cell work from Ellen and David. He had some ideas about it, and wondered if he could come over some time.

Lou arranged to meet him at Jan's one day after school. She realized she did remember him; he was a lanky, distracted type, and she had seen him once through a doorway at school, in what looked like a meeting of the chess club. And he had written literary pieces in the school paper.

"Come on in," said Lou. "This is my mother's place. I live here part of the time. My lab's in Bolinas, though."

Bert ambled in and looked around. "I like it," he announced. Then, seeing the kitchen alcove, "You got anything to eat?"

Lou laughed. "Sure," she said. "Cheese and crackers? Fruit?"

"Wonderful!" said Bert. As they munched on the snacks, he told Lou that since he got out of school he had been writing for local papers and magazines, but lately had gotten more involved in the Survivalist Party. "You know about that?" he asked.

Lou did, in a general way. Roger and Carol and Dimmy had gone to a few meetings and come back intrigued; they planned to join soon. And Lou had heard the name Vera Allwen. The party sounded like a good thing, but up till now rather abstract and distant. "You're the first live Survivalist I've met," she confessed.

Bert wiggled his ears at her. "We can all do that," he said. "It terrifies the polluters—they think we're from outer space. No, seriously, I'll tell you all about that another time." Bert licked his fingers and bit into an apple. "What I want to know about now is this cell of yours. It sounds like it might be, uh, let's say the first great technological breakthrough of the Survivalist era."

He asked Lou some basic questions about the cell and nodded more and more enthusiastically at her answers. Then he launched into a long, fanciful diatribe which convinced Lou that he was either quite crazy or some kind of genius. When he talked his eyes shot around this way and that, as if looking for the ideal listener. He saw Lou's cell as a new paradigm for techno-social innovation; he saw it giving the people confidence in their own powers again; he saw it unifying the country's rooftop architecture as red tile had once done for Mediterranean cities; he saw it spawning small, decentralized supplier industries; he saw a corps of young people sailing from country to country teaching cell-production workshops from Lapland to Patagonia; he saw the cell taking its place in powering videophone electronic communication webs that would make it less necessary to move bodies from place to place for work and business purposes, thus loosening the throttlehold of the automobile on the economy and liberating entire new patterns of social and psychological energy. He saw it as the master metaphor ("You must mean mistress?" interrupted Lou, but Bert rushed on) for an entire next stage of eco-civilization. What pyramids were to the Egyptians or the Aztecs, or the railroad or warship to imperial Britain, or the airconditioned skyscraper to urbanizing America, Lou's cell would be to the new society it would make possible. It would be its very heart and crystal consciousness, the absolute apotheosis of energy with *no moving parts! totally silent!* "Why," he gasped, "it's almost as beautiful as photosynthesis itself!"

Lou grinned. "Gosh," she said, "I thought I was just making this little cell. But maybe I think I see what you mean. Sort of." She looked at Bert, who was still, she could tell, buzzing in his head with ideas; his eyes hadn't had a chance to settle down yet. "But you said you had some concrete ideas about what should be *done* with it?"

Well, yes, he did. Bert outlined his vision of how the Survivalists should start a network of teacher-practitioners, each one holding classes in neighborhoods so residents could learn to help each other

84

with frame construction and wiring, and then fanning out to other neighborhoods in a network of mutual support and self-education and hands-on experience which, he figured, would bring the cells more quickly, more cheaply and more reliably to more dwellings than any centrally directed mobilization program conceivably could.

"All right," Lou said finally. "I think we should try it. It turns out anyway that to protect the idea legally, we need to get a bunch of people using the cells as fast as possible, and then write up the process somewhere. So what you want to do fits in very well with that."

"I'll start on it tonight! I'll—"

"The only thing is, I don't have too much time for the organizing work because I'm still working out the mechanism."

Bert's face fell. "But if it works, why not let that wait till later?"

"I'm not really sure. I just can't let go of it. Rigor and elegance, I suppose."

"Well, we'll make a great team. You do the physics, I'll do the organizing. Build a dozen working cells. Pass 'em out and teach people how to teach others how to build more. Make up some written materials and get 'em in magazines. And then look ahead to the big push. Assess the materials situation. Get the Survivalist Party to make it an official program."

"Yeah, that sounds good. We ought to get going on all that."

Bert's eyes shone. "Okay. Great. In fact, stupendous!" Awkwardly, and almost landing both of them on the floor, he gave Lou a hug and rushed out.

Lou sat thinking about the episode, wondering whether Bert really *was* a little crazy. After a few moments Jan called from her room. "Hey, Loulou—there's a draft through here—?"

Bert, in his excitement, had forgotten to close the door.

The first major achievement of the Survivalist Party came in the spring, in the critical area of housing. During recent decades real estate prices in the cities had climbed beyond the reach of all but the upper-middle class. New urban construction had been producing chiefly office buildings and boutique complexes. The traditional real estate market mechanisms could not produce living space at reasonable prices. Thus in San Francisco, whose downtown was filled with dozens of proud new skyscrapers, the people who worked in those skyscrapers could not afford to live in the city; unwillingly, they jammed into commuter buses and lived in outlying bedroom suburbs.

The Survivalists made a bold bid to reverse this pattern. They started an initiative campaign for a measure to force the builders of office structures to simultaneously construct nearby living space for the employees the offices would house. For each new desk to be filled, there would have to be new apartment space within walking distance, rentable at a rate the desk occupant could afford. This plan, the Survivalists argued, would halt the decline of San Francisco's population. It would make those who profited from downtown development responsible for meeting residential needs as well. It would give ordinary people who worked in the city a stake in the city's future, and in their neighborhoods. It would generate more construction jobs since corporations planning skyscraper offices would also have to build skyscraper apartments. It would greatly decrease the energy consumption of the people working in the skyscrapers since they could now dispense with private automobiles.

This proposal met strenuous opposition from the building interests, who threatened to cease building office space. It proved, however, to be an issue around which the Survivalists could construct a solid coalition of environmentalists and union people, of ethnic voters determined to revitalize the city without turning it into a sterile upper-middle enclave, of people hoping to keep the city habitable for families with children. It drew support from many downtown employees itching to find some way to move into the city. The measure indeed proved to have so much popular appeal that the city council, hoping to take the issue away from the Survivalists, enacted it before the election came.

Suddenly the Survivalists found themselves no longer a fringe organization, but a power in San Francisco politics. Cultivating new alliances, Vera and her colleagues began developing new and daring plans for solar installation and insulation programs that would generate vast numbers of new jobs.

One day in May, while Jamie was working in town, Mary McBride was building an extension of their chicken run. They had about a dozen hens but had decided that while they were at it they might as well add a few. It was no more trouble and little more expense since the chickens mostly ate kitchen and garden scraps. They could barter the extra eggs for goats' milk or something else that one of their neighbors had in surplus. Such little exchanges always enriched your life—you got more variety in your diet, ate fresher food than you could find in stores, avoided the cash economy with its incessant tax drain, and helped out your friends. Besides, delivering and picking up stuff gave the chance for neighborly visits, which were a precious part of country life.

The clap-clap-clap noise of a helicopter in the distance made Mary uncomfortable. Normally their environment was deliciously quiet; you could even hear the babble of the creek from their bedroom. So Mary was startled by the copter sound, like a deer who hears the click of a hunter's rifle safety catch. She turned her head and localized the sound source—somewhere over the first ridge to the southeast, coming closer. Damn spraying, she thought, and went back to tacking on chickenwire.

The wind that morning was moderate, from almost due east. It was warm and sunny. As the noise of the copter grew louder, Mary looked up. Suddenly she saw it, gleaming in the sun, approaching, with a long, graceful cloud of herbicide streaming out from its spray boom. It was much nearer to the Forest boundary than any spray copter had ever come before. "My God," she thought, "it's coming over onto our land!" She sprang up and began waving, with a pushing motion, hoping to get the pilot to steer away. But the copter swooped onward implacably, and even seemed to veer to pass nearer her, like some venomous creature spewing its poison. The spray cloud settled slowly toward the forest, but in the wind conditions of that day it also drifted as it sank. Mary, threatening the copter with clenched fist, became aware of tiny droplets settling on her face, stinging her eyes, acrid in her nostrils. She realized she should try not to breathe it in. Holding her breath she ran westward past the house, down the lane until she couldn't hold it any more. Then she exhaled violently, gulped air, and began to cry. Her stomach knotted, she felt faint, and she went down on her knees and began to throw up.

In the weeks that followed Mary suffered mysterious headaches and occurrences of nausea. Jamie at first did not have them, and in their talks about the matter they tended to blame Mary's symptoms on the emotional upset of being sprayed. When Jamie got them too, however, they thought about other possible causes. They took a sample of their drinking water, which they drew from the creek just as it

87

emerged from the Forest, and had it analyzed; small amounts of 2,4,5-T were found in it. They also had household dust analyzed, with the same result—after which they started hauling in water from another source and thoroughly washed all the interior surfaces of their little house. Neither of them, however, felt much improvement in their condition, and they snapped at each other in situations where, earlier, they might have made little loving jokes.

Vera Allwen was becoming popular as a speaker, and community cable television channels had begun to broadcast her talks. Vera always spoke in a homey, low-key style and she felt comfortable with the presence of cameras. And of course she welcomed the chance to bring the Survivalist vision before larger numbers of people.

"Tonight," began Vera in one of her TV speeches, "I want to talk with you about the relationship between economic statistics and real-life experience. Many of us tend to get frightened by official-sounding economists, who will tell you that unless our Gross National Product keeps going up we must be in terrible trouble. These economists often disagree violently among themselves about what is actually going on in our economy, but most of them get cold chills at the prospect of a society that simply runs along steadily at roughly the same level and provides enough for all. That idea probably sounds pretty sensible to you (it certainly does to me) but to economists trained in the expansionist past it raises terrors of being 'second-rate,' which they equate with total worthlessness. They seem to feel that if you stop having ever-accelerating growth, somebody else who happens to have it at the moment must be somehow better than you are.

"This kind of doomsday thinking never bothers to ask whether further growth would do anybody any good, or what harm it might cause. It's a kind of blackmail thinking, which assumes that human beings are created to serve the Gross National Product, as if it were God.

"We in the Survivalist Party think the economy should be made to serve the people, not the other way round. Our quality of life does not depend merely on the amount of goods we have access to. It depends on whether those goods are worthy of buying—whether our food, for instance, is free of dangerous additives and growth hormones. It depends on a web of social relationships that link us to each other—

88

whether those relationships are hostile and competitive, or harmonious and caring. It depends on our safety in the streets and our safety in breathing our air and drinking our water. All these are 'goods' that cannot be bought.

"Nor does the Gross National Product measure only truly useful goods. A car crash, for instance, which destroys one car and requires the production of another, increases the GNP. So do medical-care expenditures for people who get cancer from chemicals.

"So we have to look carefully at this old idea that a high level of goods-consumption is necessarily a good thing. People will tell you that we in the Survivalist Party are willing to accept a drop in the American standard of living, as measured by the GNP. Well, that accusation, I'm happy to tell you, is perfectly true. If we can find ways to improve our quality of life and at the same time decrease our GNP, we think that would be a fine thing. As a matter of fact, much of our planning toward a decent future is intended to accomplish precisely that. Nor are we worried about the small drop in productivity that has been occurring naturally; much of that drop has occurred because of subsidies and distortions introduced into our economy by special-interest groups, and policy changes we are proposing will make our economy more efficient and productive, as well as more just and fair.

"But the Survivalist perspective in these areas is not limited to merely economic questions. In the global picture, Americans have been consuming far more than our reasonable share of the resources in materials and energy which exist on the earth—40 percent of them, though we have only six percent of the people. But we have been enormously wasteful in this consumption, and as by-products of it we have created grave problems of waste and pollution and disease. We Survivalists want to stop fouling our own nest. We want to live, in our wonderful section of the earth, as a good farmer lives on the land— preserving its fertility, guarding its soil against erosion, making sure it will remain productive for the generations to come. If we take care of it, it will produce plenty of food for us, in partnership with the rain and the sun. But you can't accomplish that with short-term economic calculations only. It takes a long-range view of the future. It takes a determination to keep what is fundamental and essential—our biological welfare and survival—really foremost in our planning, and not to let ourselves be panicked by economists.

"Some of them will cry out with alarm that as other nations have grown economically and politically stronger, our grip on the world's resources is no longer so tight. They worry about this like the kid on the block who got his growth first and turned into a bully, and then noticed that some of the other kids were catching up. They tell us we must struggle to regain our dominant position, no matter what the cost. We Survivalists think this goal is misplaced and self-defeating. It puts things backwards.

"We believe the proper approach is to decide how we want to live and then arrange our economic house accordingly. If we decide to distribute our available goods more fairly among ourselves, for instance, our society will be happier and healthier and less crime-ridden. If we decide to reduce the 'insults,' as they're called, that our polluted and socially decayed environment inflicts on us, we can live better, even if it means that our total statistical consumption of goods drops.

"Let me give a couple of examples of ways where improving the quality of our lives and diminishing the GNP go hand in hand. Police expenses are counted as a part of the GNP. Because we live in a society filled with desperately poor people, and people who become criminal because their lives have been rendered senseless by the competitiveness and alienation of our society, we hire far more police per capita than other countries, and spend far more on jails. If we rebuild the social fabric so that we support each other instead of undermining each other; if we develop new family patterns within which we can all feel secure and needed; if we have confidence that the rewards of life are being divided justly among all the people, then we will have less crime, and fewer police, and a better life. But since our police expenditures will be smaller, we will also have a *smaller* GNP. Who should complain about that?

"Or let's talk about diet. The money we presently spend on expensive fatty meats, and high-fat cheeses, and sugar-loaded soft drinks counts as part of the GNP—a very substantial part of it. And so of course do the medical expenses this diet brings on us. If we ate a diet based on nutritive and inexpensive grains, vegetables and soybean curd, with meat and fish used mainly for flavoring rather than for bulk, we would greatly decrease our food outlays, improve our health, and trim our medical budget. But we would also be decreasing our GNP.

"A smaller GNP, in other words, can mean a *better* life, personally and psychologically and socially. So we should not panic that our rate of growth has slowed. A stable-state society gives us the long-

90

neglected opportunity to redirect our economic expenditures so that we are a healthier and happier people through the very process of consuming less. We should never be frightened by numbers; we should be frightened only by things that we can see and feel and smell and know directly. *We* are the only judges of the real quality of our lives, not economists sitting in government offices somewhere.

"So we Survivalists try to look around us in the real world and decide what things are truly contributing to our welfare. Those are the things our government policies should foster. And then look around for those things which are merely of statistical importance. Those are the things we can do without. Please join us in the process of deciding which are which!

"This is Vera Allwen of the Survivalist Party. Goodnight."

"Hey Lou," said Mike. "Got something peculiar to tell you. Have a minute?"

Lou had just come back from Jan's and was anxious to get to some studying she had put off. But Mike looked puzzled and a little worried. He had sprained his hand a few days earlier and they had been putting comfrey poultices on it, by the advice of an herbalist friend. "More trouble with your hand?" Lou asked. She didn't really need another dose of his adolescent anguish. Still, he was her "little" brother.

"No—it's there was this guy this afternoon. Drove past the corner in a big new car, sort of cruised by. I noticed it 'cause he came by again, a few minutes later, real slow. You know, not like somebody trying to find a house or something, just *looking*."

"What's so funny about that? Sounds like some dumb tourist to me—wanted to see naked hippies or something."

"That's what I thought at first, too. So I didn't pay much attention. But then—well, maybe 15 minutes later, I happened to look out the bathroom window. He had his car parked down at the corner, and he had gotten out, with a pair of binoculars around his neck. So I thought, oh, he's a birdwatcher. And he did look out over the lagoon, and then out toward the reef."

"Well, sounds like your mystery is solved."

"You're wrong. Because I stood there at the window taking a pee and watching, and you know what he did? He looked out to sea for a

91

bit, and then he'd kind of swing around on his heel just for a sec, with his binocs still up, till he was looking toward the house. It was kind of spooky. And you know what he was pointing the binocs at? Your cells!"

Lou's mouth went dry. "Why didn't you go out and ask him what he wanted?" she said. "Or Dimmy could have—why didn't you ask him?"

"Well, the guy was wearing this double-breasted suit—I dunno, I just thought maybe it was better not to let him know he's been seen."

"You think he was some kind of a spy?"

Mike shifted uneasily. "Well, who knows? He sure did act funny."

Lou's heart sank. She hated this conspiratorial stuff that Roger had set her off on. Why couldn't she just do her research in peace, and after she had it all figured out decide what to do with it? Who could this phony birdwatcher be, anyway? Should she take steps to conceal her cells from prying eyes? Or set up dummies for them to look at, and do her real work on the roof? It was a dismal series of questions.

"Mike," she said, "thanks for being so observant. I don't know what it means. Have to see what Roger thinks when he gets home."

"Sure. At any rate I'll be around tomorrow to see if he comes back. I can't really write with this hand so I'm going to stay home—play hookey."

"Mike, you lunatic, why don't you just level with Carol and Roger—they'd let you stay home once in a while."

"I guess I just like the excitement."

"Well, it looks like somebody is cooking some up for us. Keep your eyes open."

"Sure will, sis. Hey, you help me with my math a little tonight?"

"Not tonight. I got this new idea about the cell mechanism while I was dreaming off in English class."

The Raussen Chemical Corporation maintained a hazardous waste landfill in the hills back of a heavily industrialized California city called, appropriately enough, Pittsburg. The dump was actually within the borders of the town of Oak Creek (population 700), whose inhabitants had for many years accepted its existence as a fact of life—and Raussen's taxes as a welcome contribution to the town's treasury.

Recently, however, some Oak Creek people had discovered that trucks carrying polychlorinated biphenyls were using the dump. By this time, after the Michigan disaster when PCBs got into cattle feed and poisoned much of the state's beef supply, the hazards of PCBs were widely known. The Oak Creekers quickly became alarmed. They feared that seepage from the landfill might work its way into the creek, in which children played on hot summer days, and into the town's drinking water well. They also feared leaks from the big trucks that rolled through their main street—they could see the town becoming totally uninhabitable if one of those tankers should have a wreck.

One afternoon a startled truck driver was confronted, as he approached Oak Creek, by a mob of residents blocking the road. Some had guns; one old woman held up an awkwardly printed sign which read, NO PCB POISONS FOR OAK CREEK. The trucker turned around and drove off. Next day the county police appeared and were sufficiently impressed with the determination of the Oak Creek people to call in the state public health department. Their analyses seemed to indicate that the landfill was well designed and posed little risk to the inhabitants. The sheriff's office put the town officials on notice that their citizens must not obstruct passage of the trucks.

A few days after that, a PCB truck again headed for the dump. It passed through the quiet, tree-lined streets of Oak Creek without incident, but as it approached the dump site, the driver saw that a road crew was digging a culvert across the road. "Hey," he yelled from his cab, "when you gonna have that covered over so I can get through?"

The people in the ditch leaned on their shovels. "Can't really say," one of them replied. "This ain't a county road, you know. Just us Oak Creek folks working on it. Might take a long time."

"What do you mean, a long time—be finished tomorrow?"

A man in the big ditch grinned. "Aw, no, nothing like that. Maybe a couple of weeks, maybe a couple months. You better find some place else to haul that stuff."

In the weeks and months that followed, Raussen sued the town; the town sued Raussen and the county. Legal briefs and counterbriefs flew back and forth. Town attorneys employed their best delaying tactics; Oak Creekers occasionally went out and threw a few shovelsful of dirt out of the culvert excavation.

The evidence against PCBs continued to mount. Congress had, in its Toxic Substances Control Act of 1976, ordered the EPA to ban PCBs, but it was not until mid-1979 that the agency acted, and even then its regulations exempted most uses of the dangerous substances. By then, some 440 million pounds of PCBs had been distributed throughout the environment.

But from that date onward, no more trucks got through to the Oak Creek dump.

Lou was so consumed with her work on the solar cells that she didn't see much of her friends, even David. Occasionally they would take a weekend walk in the country, or climb up to some isolated hilltop and make love. It was always such a wonderful experience that she'd resolve not to let so much time go by until next time. But then she would get busy again. As Lou had predicted, Sharp & Natural had quite a success with "Chemical Blues," as they finally called it, and the rest of their work seemed to be catching on too. Offers were coming in to play in clubs as far away as Sacramento and Santa Cruz, and sometimes Lou went along to hear them. One evening they were playing in Berkeley at a place called Spooney's. A friendly club, its physical structure seemed permeated by the music that had been played there by Jerry Garcia and other great musicians of earlier years. Sharp & Natural had appeared there a few months earlier, so they felt at home and played very well. The crowd was electrically enthusiastic. Lou and some other friends of the band sat at a front table. Also in the audience was a suave-looking man in carefully informal clothes, checking out the act; he was Art Metzger, on business for Cosmos Records. He'd heard Sharp & Natural was a promising group. But he wasn't expecting their curious combination of talk and music. Between songs they had an act that was almost like a stand-up comedian routine. Sometimes they based their patter on newspapers, which were rich in ridiculous stories. Lou thought Ellen, with her sharp tongue, was especially good at using these. "Says here," she would begin, waving her paper, "they have a new plan to save us from air pollution. Isn't that *nice?*" (Apprehensive giggles.) "Yeah, it really sounds wonderful. At last a solution that doesn't involve government interference with the god-given rights of cars. Ready for it? Okay, here it is: *breathe less!*" (Guffaws.) "Yeah, wonderful. Somebody has discovered you can really cut your risk of lung cancer if only you wouldn't keep taking those (panting) *deep breaths*—" More unsettl-

94

ing still, the group got the audience involved in responses, almost like slogans at a political rally. "Goddamn cheerleaders," said Art to his companions. He had an instinctive dislike for mixing music and politics. Still, he had to admit they were good at it.

After finishing their last number of the set, Sharp & Natural didn't disappear backstage, but laid down their instruments and began to mingle with the audience, each one going to a different table and chatting a while with the people there, sometimes sitting down for a bit. Art couldn't tell what was said at these encounters, but the members of the band seemed to be good at bridging over from their magical status in the lights up front to sweatily human status among the audience. As far as he could tell they were looking for feedback, and they were certainly getting it—a lot of hugs and smiles, but also considered reactions and suggestions. Somebody even wrote something down on paper for one of them, and handed it over. With most bands, you'd figure it was the phone number of a groupie or a new dope source. With these kids, Art sensed it might be an item for a new lyric. Something about this band was, well, *serious*. It made Art uncomfortable.

Nonetheless, when an opportunity offered he sauntered up and said, "Hi, I'm Art Metzger from Cosmos. I've heard lots of good things about your group. Thought maybe you'd like to talk about cutting a record with us. You going to take a break sometime?"

"How about after the next set," said David. "Come on backstage." Then, hesitating, he added, "But maybe you already know—we have some doubts about recording our music."

"Okay, I'd be glad to hear 'em. No promises, just some friendly talk."

"Sure. See you later."

At the end of the set the band played a new number they called "Midnight." The words were loose, allusive, about the dying of light, the long dark of the world and the soul, the feeling of coming to the worst of things and having no faith in the dawn. The melodic line was looping, intricate, allowing for interesting variations. The band played with it, embroidered it, seemed about to let it go, then did it again—toying with the music and the crowd's expectations, obviously enjoying themselves hugely. When the piece came to a crashing yet somehow melancholy finish, the applause was not the hysterical energy that crowds give to the ordinary strong rock climax, but slower, more heart-felt.

Metzger, coming backstage, was clearly impressed. "I'm not going

95

to kid you, that was terrific," he began. "You're ready to record, no question about it!"

"Thanks," said Ellen, wiping off some sweat. The group members smiled at each other—they knew they had indeed been playing well. They lay back and waited to see what Metzger would say. Lou sat on an old couch along the wall and watched.

Art hesitated. Something told him that his usual means of courting a new group would be self-defeating here. These kids weren't going to be terribly interested in hearing stories of the big-time musical life. He wasn't even sure they used drugs, though he didn't know anybody their age who didn't at least smoke a little grass. So he began by asking how much material they had so far. It turned out there were about 20 of their own songs that they were really happy with and a few more they were working on.

"Plenty to choose from," said Art. "Or maybe scatter in a couple of things by other people."

"We don't play other people's music," said Ellen flatly. "Let 'em play theirs and we'll play ours."

"I can understand that feeling—I *admire* that." Art could see this was going to be difficult. Their stuff was good, no doubt of that, but still, who the hell ever heard of Sharp & Natural? He needed something buyers would recognize. "Anyway," he said, "we could come back to that later, if we had to."

"Well, listen," said David diffidently, "you know you haven't really gotten the picture from our side, I don't think. We're kind of against recording at all." He looked down at the floor, shyly.

"What do you mean, against recording? You don't feel you're ready?"

"No, we want to play live, for real people, so we can talk to them, get to them."

"Well, for Christ's sake, you get to real people through records—and the radio play you get from records—but you get to about a hundred times *more* people. And make about a hundred times more *money*!"

"Yeah, we know that," said David stubbornly. "But that isn't what we're trying to do."

"Tell me more."

The members of the band looked at each other and at Lou. Then Ellen spoke up. "We don't like to separate the music from the rest of—well, we don't want to be just rock stars, up there, you know, separated from the people listening. We want them to think of us as friends. They *are* our friends. We've got to be able to talk to them."

"So you're going to deprive everybody else in the world from hearing your music? That sounds like sixties bullshit to me—free concerts and all that."

"Well," said Ellen, "if that's what they did in the sixties, maybe they had some good ideas. Actually, we're getting set to do a lot more road work. Portland, Eugene, maybe Seattle."

"Well, that'll tighten everything up, that's fine. We could do a contract that wouldn't push you—do some recording when you get back."

David put in, "No, it isn't that. It really is the principle of the thing. We just don't like records."

Art had learned to control his temper when dealing with these young musicians, but he sometimes allowed himself a little sarcasm. "Then what is all that eight-track recording gear you've got running out there?"

"That's so we can really study what we've been doing," Ellen replied. "We want to be sure we get the right balance, don't wipe out the words the way a lot of groups do."

David added, "And it's a way of saving it too. If we broke up or something, we wouldn't want the music to disappear."

"So you *are* thinking of records someday!"

"We don't rule it out absolutely. But the tapes are more like a scrapbook. Helps us keep track of what we've done."

Art sighed. "All right, I begin to get you. So I'll just stay in touch. Maybe send you a rough contract you could think about, one of these days. You know where to find me when you get ready." He smiled and went back to his table.

The band members looked at each other. They had heard rumors that the record companies were becoming aware of them, and had wondered when the first overture would come. They were perfectly serious in their position, even though they knew Metzger would suspect it was just a way of angling for a better contract. Still, the attention was flattering; it confirmed their feeling that they *were* getting pretty good.

"I don't think he knew what hit him," said Lou, and laughed. They all chuckled a moment. "Okay," said David, "there are people waiting out there."

Henry's idea for a regional ecological authority had kept Maggie from bolting, but when it was proposed around Washington by legislators and lobbyists sympathetic to the Survivalist cause it encountered only disinterest or outright hostility. With the national economy in chronic trouble, who wanted to hear about beautiful plans for environmental reform? A half dozen major corporations were on the verge of bankruptcy. Rebel forces were making headway in Central and South America. Budgetary constraints had forced decay and even shutdowns in rapid transit service in Eastern and Midwestern cities, making people even more dependent on automobiles. People in cold areas were being punished by heating-fuel increases to the point where freezing to death in one's own apartment was no longer newsworthy. The huge financial drain to pay for energy was in effect taxing the older areas of the country to favor development in the sunbelt. Washington politicians had things more pressing to worry about than the Northwest and its ecological manias.

However, the regional element in Henry's idea did not die with its rejection on the federal level. Instead, the Survivalists began to focus their attention on the state and municipal governments of Washington, Oregon and California. They developed analyses of problems in transportation, energy, water, pollution, recycling, population—which all pointed toward the practical virtues of a regional approach. They held regional conferences and issued regional publications. Little by little, new bonds and alliances grew up across state lines among politicians and bureaucrats as well as within the Survivalist Party itself.

Experiments with intensive bicycle transportation and sun-rights ordinances in Davis, California, began to be adopted by Eugene in Oregon and Seattle in Washington. Portland and Seattle, which were the first two American cities to develop energy-conservation plans based on widespread citizen participation (and thus with real bite) became models for San Francisco and San Jose to the south— impressed by the fact that Portland had reduced its energy consumption by 40 percent. A region-wide program of waterfront protection and rehabilitation was begun, and lessons learned in beginning to turn the banks of the meandering Willamette between Eugene and Portland into a river-long park were put to use in reclaiming the Napa river, formerly so polluted that even touching its water was dangerous.

But the most striking and controversial result of Green-PEA, as the interstate compact that was worked out was indeed called, concerned cars. The first car-free zone in the region had been created in Portland some years earlier: a mall running entirely through the downtown area, which was given free and frequent bus service, with elegant glasscovered kiosks to shelter waiting passengers from the rain; these even boasted telephone booths. Merchants discovered that downtown business volume increased significantly. So did bicycle riding, and many stores began to provide bike racks.

This successful pattern was now passed on through Green-PEA to other cities, and special car-free zones were established in many congested downtown areas. Pedestrians felt so happy about the new system that they jeered at cars which happened to venture onto the prohibited streets. Gradually curbs were removed so that the whole space between buildings was one flat paved area, irregularly planted with trees, bushes, flowers. Fountains, benches, newsstand kiosks and other amenities were scattered about. A few taxis and delivery trucks navigated carefully among the pedestrians and bicyclists.

While Marissa D'Amato was in junior high she had gotten invited to the Sierra on a week-long camping trip. The experience of the high, open country had exhilarated her so much that she had gradually inveigled her family into trying it too. Her father Angelo and her mother Laura, intensely social people, liked camping only when a large group was involved, so each summer the family (augmented by four or five friends or relatives) would cross the hot central valley and head for the cool of the mountains. They would drive in for miles over dirt roads to remote trailheads. There, backpacks heavy with the supplies they'd need for ten days, they set out along foot trails to small lakes fed by snow-melt and tiny mountain streams. Finding a grove of trees for daytime shade, they set up their base camp.

Then followed long days of sleeping, fishing, simplified cooking, lazy talk in which the pressures of urban life seemed far away and insignificant. Marissa loved this stripped-down existence. She wore the same hiking pants and grimy shirt day after day. She grew accustomed to swimming in chilly alpine lakes, followed by baking herself on glacier-smoothed rocks. She enjoyed the sensual feel of the mountain air, neither warm nor cool but just right, blowing gently over her skin. There were subtle smells, sounds, sights surrounding her; she was much more conscious of the sky, by night and by day, than she ever was in the city. This life, she felt, gave a kind of standard by which to judge supposedly "normal" living. Thus she enjoyed the fact that here Angelo did much of the food preparation; Laura, who was fascinated by topographic maps and liked to walk, organized day hikes. There was something about living in the wilds, where even a sprained ankle would be a genuine emergency, that made Marissa alert and tested her sense of self-preservation. Rattlesnakes and coyotes shared the territory with bears and conceivably even a mountain lion. And whereas in the city Marissa could go for days with little consciousness of any species save her own, in the mountains she was visibly surrounded by deer and chickadees and woodpeckers and gophers and butterflies and flies and mosquitoes and beetles—a thousand species all coexisting within a few feet of her campsite.

She noticed too that the so-called necessities of life looked different in the Sierra. If you had to carry everything you needed, you pared it down to the real essentials: food, a shelter against thunderstorms, sleeping gear, a minimum of clothes, cooking equipment, first-aid supplies, maybe a special book or two. That sufficed—it had to. There was a satisfaction in this enforced austerity. For the rest, you improvised, or went without. And you survived, on your own know-how and common sense, not because a supermarket happened to be handy.

Marissa began to do some serious nature study. She bought identification guide books and began learning species names. More and more, she became fascinated with the way different species found their ecological niches and established themselves. One day she and her older brother Ben went off on a hike to the east. The family camp that year was a bit above 7,000 feet, so before long they were approaching timberline. As they went up, Marissa could see how the trees fought to climb the inhospitable granite walls; she could even see the process in its different stages.

First, in a crevice where melting snow run-off had deposited fine gravel that stayed damp, a pine seedling would sprout from a seed dropped there by a squirrel. Its rootlets, with acid-excreting tips to eat their way into rock, would gain a foothold. Blown at by fierce winds, scorched by summer sun, submerged in hard-packed winter snow, the tiny tree would cling to its crack and prosper.

In a few years it would be big enough to deposit needles around its base; the needles would decompose, providing more soil both for the

100

tree itself and for other plants that might try to establish themselves in the neighborhood. Thus a pine three or four feet high might have around it a half dozen dwarfed manzanitas. As the years pass, the soil-covered area expands. Another tree, growing up nearby, offers new shelter against wind and storm. The plant community, alone in the alpine desolation, begins to offer mutual support to its members. In thirty years, a tiny tree-bordered meadow might nestle in a hollow where only rocks once were. Worms, mice, birds, insects and soil microbes would by now have colonized this little new world.

To Marissa the pines, only a few feet high but twisted and bent by heavy snow, were especially touching. As she passed them, she would give their needles a friendly stroke and wish them luck; they needed it. Ben didn't have much patience for Marissa's devotion; if she dawdled he would look back at her gloweringly from up the trail. What Ben wanted was to get to the summit. They pushed on, up toward a saddle between two peaks. The wind increased and it was cooler; they were well over 8,000 feet now. Finally, scrabbling on bare rock for the last half mile, they came to the top.

No haze obscured the view that day. They could see far out to the west, where the mountains dropped off into rounded foothills. North and south, the mighty barrier of the Sierra range extended for hundreds of miles, peak over beyond peak, with passes so high and craggy as to be impenetrable by roads; only here and there were places where, after enormous effort, a highway or railroad had been pushed through. At their feet was the steep eastern escarpment of the range, dropping off several thousand feet in only a couple of miles.

They found a rock ledge sheltered from the wind and sat down for a snack and a drink from their canteen. Ben pointed to the north. "See that promontory? If you had a gun emplacement there, nobody and nothing could get up this mountain. And look over southward—same thing."

Marissa was startled. "Who would you want to keep out? That's just Nevada over there."

"Everybody," said Ben abruptly. "This is the border—right up here along the summit line. Back of us is *our* country. It's green, it's reasonably sensible. Out there is the enemy—the desert crazies, the destroyers. Gamblers and land-rapers. Atom-bomb test grounds. MX missile territory. They should *stay* there, and leave us alone!"

"Well," said Marissa, "it's still part of the United States. You can't just write it off."

Ben looked at her fiercely. "I'm not so sure about that," he said.

Lou got up rather nervous one morning in June. She had received a call several days before from somebody who said he was Professor Phillip Gleason from the physics department at the University of California. He had heard she was a promising student, and since he was going to be in Marin on Saturday, could he drop by and talk about her possibly coming to study physics at Berkeley? Lou was flattered and flustered by the call, and said of course. She had actually been admitted to the University's campus at Santa Cruz, which had a strong natural resources program, but it couldn't hurt to talk to this person. She vaguely knew about Gleason—he was one of the department's younger shining lights, and had done some rather ingenious work. She couldn't remember if it had military implications. She also knew that physics departments were hurting for good students; these days the brightest people tended to go into biology. She felt almost like a star athlete or something. What, she wondered, were they prepared to offer—a car and a job weeding the campus? And what about the government aspects? Physics tended to be classified, secret work, highly dependent on federal money, and a lot of it had to do with weapons development. A while back, she remembered, it was revealed that certain Berkeley physics people had evidently had CIA connections. Gleason hadn't been there then, but still, she wondered. It would be a curious interview!

After breakfast Roger and Carol went off to see some friends. "Just don't sign anything, hon," were Roger's parting words. Lou ate breakfast and tried to breathe deeply. Then she went out to the garage and checked a few things. She had lost track of time when she heard a car pull up outside.

It was a silver Porsche, and as Gleason got out she saw he was handsome, blond, bright-eyed—quite a dashing figure. She offered her hand and he shook it warmly. "I'm certainly pleased to meet you," he said. "We've heard good things about you through the grapevine."

"Hope it wasn't just my father's friends," said Lou modestly. "That sort of gives me an unfair advantage."

"No, not at all," Gleason said quickly. "I've heard about you from a couple of people."

102

"Come in," said Lou. "Can I give you a cup of coffee?"

"That'd be terrific. —Wonderful place you live in, here!" They went into the house, where Gleason peered around curiously at everything, including pieces of paper on tables. He moved nicely, Lou noticed, and was obviously very observant—which was not something she would say of every physicist she had met. He was even vaguely sexy, she decided; must be 27 or 28. Lou put some homemade bread and jam on the table and fixed them both a slice. Gleason settled over his coffee and began quizzing her about her high school studies and future plans.

"Actually," she said, "I've been thinking of Santa Cruz. In fact they've accepted me there."

"Well," said Gleason, "I don't mean to run down another campus, but I think you'd be wasting yourself there. It's just not very high-powered in technical fields, you know. There are some good people, of course, but—well, when you come down to it, compared to Berkeley or Cal Tech it's just a little school in the trees. And Berkeley's closer to home, which your parents might like. With your grades, we could get your application switched over to Berkeley easily enough."

Lou was feeling better. The man seemed reasonably human. He was taking a good deal of trouble on her account, after all. He looked at her.

"I hear you've been doing some really interesting work on solar cells. Would you tell me about that?"

"Yes, I have been working on photovoltaics. How'd you hear about that?"

There was perhaps the tiniest missed beat before Gleason replied. "One of your teachers mentioned it. Said you have a whole experimental rig out here, and may be onto something important."

"Mr. Hartstine?"

"That sounds like it. I guess that rack outside is where you do your experiments?"

"Yes, mostly. I'm in the great doping compounds sweepstakes game. But I may have stumbled onto something new. Can't really tell yet—I'm still running tests on it."

"Can you show me your set-up?"

Lou was not sure of the scientific etiquette. She believed in openness and trust. Still, you heard these awful stories about people using other people's ideas as springboards and leaping ahead of them. Where was the line between paranoid concealment and stupid overtrustingness? She would have to play by ear, but decided not to tell him too much.

"Okay. Want a little more coffee first?"

"Just a drop." Lou poured it into his cup, and thought she saw him looking at her bare arm as she did so. At this moment Mike, who had been in and out of the room several times while they talked, came over to the table.

"Uh, sis, I've got to take off, but could I talk to you for a minute first?"

"Sure, what is it?"

"It's sort of private—come in here a sec."

They went into a bedroom and Mike closed the door. "God, what's so secret?" Lou asked.

"Who is that guy, anyway?" said Mike, half whispering.

"Some physics professor from Berkeley. Wants me to enroll over there, work in his lab."

"You sure? Is he on the level?"

"What do you mean? I've heard of him, he's really a physics prof."

"Well, I don't know. He looks like a narc or something to me. You know, super-slick?"

"Oh, Mike, that's just what people like that have to look like. To get their grants and all that. Don't hold it against him."

"Well, sis, watch your step, that's all."

"Okay, thanks. I know you're not trying to freak me or anything."

"No way. Just keeping my eyes open, like you said. Or my nose."

Mike wriggled his nose as if he smelled something rank, and opened the door. "See you later," he said, and left.

Lou could see that Gleason had not been pleased by the interruption. "Teen-age crisis?" he inquired.

"No, no real problem. We have a family life that's a bit bizarre sometimes."

"Your mother not around?"

"She lives over in town. She and Roger—that's my father—are good friends but they didn't want to live together any more."

"Oh, dear, I'm sorry to hear that!" Lou watched with some amazement as Gleason put out his hand and laid it over hers.

"Why?" she said. "There's nothing to be sorry about." But she left her hand there, beginning to wonder just what this handsome professor was up to. He patted her hand, then took his away.

"Well, I just meant it must be difficult not to live in a normal home." Lou knew it would take a long time to explain to him why her life was really perfectly satisfactory, and decided not to bother. "Let's go look at the cells," she said. Thinking fast, she led him outside. She knew he would not be able to tell what she was doing just from looking at the cell array, so she was in command of the situation. She decided simply to explain the general principles of her doping work and not mention anything about the seawater or the two-stage process. So she bounded around, showing how the cells were set up, how they were connected to the meters. She felt like she was on television, being stared at.

"May I see your metering rig?" Gleason asked.

"Oh, damn, I don't know what I've done with the key," Lou lied. "It's just a row of microammeters, right off the shelf." Gleason's face seemed to fall microscopically, so she added another lie. "None of them is working right now anyway."

Then she led him to the garage and showed him her workbench. He peered closely at her bottles—rows and rows of doping agents. A fantasy ran through Lou's mind that he was a Bionic Man, taking pictures of the labels with his eyes. Of course there was no bottle labeled "seawater," so she let him look as long as he liked. Then she showed him the kiln where she made the cells. "My idea," she said, "is to find a way of doing photovoltaics so they can be made with common materials and without too much in the way of fancy machinery. Not an electronic mousetrap, just a better mechanical one."

"Yeah, but you're not going to get much output that way," Gleason said.

"Maybe not so much, but maybe enough," Lou replied carefully. "If it was cheap enough and easy enough, people could afford to make lots of it."

"—People?"

"Sure, I want a process that anybody can do, like I said. Do-it-yourself electricity."

"Oh. I didn't know what you meant. —You're a remarkable person, you know?"

Lou straightened up and looked at him. "Why?"

"Everybody I know working on solar cells is trying to find something that's *difficult* to do, and patentable, so they can get rich. I like that youthful idealism of yours. In fact I just like you." They were facing each other, and Gleason reached out his hands and put them on Lou's shoulders. "If I wasn't trying to get you to be my student, I'd give you a hug."

Lou smiled. He really *was* cute, and when he put his hands on her

105

shoulders they felt good. Maybe he wasn't quite on the level, but still—a tiny trickle of energy ran through her body. "I'm not your student yet. And I'm going to do biology instead of physics anyhow." She smiled again, feeling very daring and grown-up.

"Tell you what," she said, "let's take a walk down the beach, it's really such a nice day. Do you have to be anywhere right away?"

"No," he said. "I've got hours."

"Okay, come on," Lou said. They headed off along the beach toward the reef, now exposed at low tide. Lou rolled up her jeans and leaped around on the rocks, looking for tidepool creatures, very lithe and athletic, as if her beloved sun had somehow energized her body. Gleason did his best to keep up, but he was wearing fancy shoes and couldn't follow into the wet places where she was willing to wade with her sneakers.

"Why don't you take those shoes off?" Lou said finally. "Water feels great on the feet!"

"I can see that," he said, and rather awkwardly took his shoes off.

"Put 'em over there behind that log," Lou suggested. "We can pick 'em up on the way back."

"No thanks, I'd better carry them," he said. "They're my favorites."

"They *are*? God, where do you live?"

"In Berkeley."

"Well, now you're in Bolinas, and the natives here hardly wear shoes at all!" She jumped around in a parody of savage dance. The sea breeze had rumpled Gleason's hair a little, and it blew his clothes against his body so that, walking over the sand, he began to look more attractive. Lou came over to him. "How old are you, anyway, Herr Doktor Professor Gleason, may I ask?"

"Twenty-six."

"Not too bad. Not far past the peak. Scientifically speaking. Anyway I've always liked older men."

She ran off down the beach. They had rounded the point, and in the distance was a hut built out of driftwood logs, set back against the cliff. Pains had been taken with it: pilings had been dug into the sand as foundation so that except in very high tides or extremely stormy weather it would have a dry floor. Old tarpaper had been tacked to the sloping roof to keep out the rain.

"Welcome to our little hideout," said Lou, and popped inside.

Gleason stuck his head in the door. "Real cozy," he said. "What do you do out here, anyway?"

106

"A bunch of us built it together. For making out in, of course! Don't they teach you anything in physics? Come on in!"

Gleason climbed through the little doorway, his shoulder bumping against Lou's. Running on the beach had made her feel sexy and a little reckless. She felt pleasant tingles of excitement in her body. For a moment she wondered if maybe the only way to find out what this handsome professor was really up to was to get affectionate with him. She could easily fantasize it. There was a delightful bulge in his pants. She could imagine rolling around with him on the floor of the little shack . . .

"Hey," she said, "I just remembered I have a joint in my pocket. We can get a little loaded and really talk, you know?"

Gleason sat up straight and looked out the door with a peculiar expression on his face. "Well, I—look, Lou, how old are *you*?"

"Eighteen, and never been kissed. No, look, it's practically legal, don't worry about it!" Jesus, did he think she was propositioning him?

"I don't know—anybody might come along the beach, find us smoking—"

"People out here sometimes see couples getting it on in this thing. Doesn't bother anybody."

"Well, I know pot's no big legal deal now, but smoking it *outdoors*, I guess—" He shook his head.

Lou was dumbfounded. Could this gorgeous hunk of man be as odd as he was acting? Lou had been around important people through her father, and they *all* smoked dope, practically. How come this guy was so rigid about it? Was he scared by it in some weird way? Or by *her*? The thought seemed amazing; she wouldn't have thought she'd be scary to a grasshopper. Maybe older men—past the great divide of 21—really did worry about the age gap! Or maybe—well, what *would* a CIA professor think about dope? A little flash of anger crossed her mind, and she blurted out, "Don't you physicists know how to have any fun?"

Gleason sat up rigidly now. His previously strained face turned brutally angry. "Listen, kid. I can see I've got to set you straight on some things. I don't know where you get this smart-ass stuff. Research in this country is serious business. You apparently haven't got the foggiest idea what you're getting into. I come over here and offer you a neat deal. You bullshit me about really wanting to do biology. You kid around and end up trying to get me stoned. Well, remember, I'm still Professor Gleason to you. If you want to get into Berkeley, or

107

any other decent school, you've got to do some serious work on your *attitude*."

Lou couldn't believe this was happening. She looked out the front of the hut: the waves were still rolling onto the beach, the wind was blowing, the sun was shining, and this madman or spook was lecturing her about her attitude! She said nothing, but edged around a little so that if he went completely bonkers she could leap out the window.

"Now you had better just tell me what you have really been up to with those cell experiments. Everything in those bottles has been tried before, and doesn't work. So what have you done that *does* work?"

Lou looked at him defiantly. "I don't understand why you think I am obliged to tell you *anything*," she said. God, to think that a few moments earlier she had been tempted to clutch on to that nicely muscled body of his!

"You had better think about that pretty carefully. Some people in this world are very anxious to make sure that nobody else gets a good solar cell process before they do. Anybody who looks like a serious competitor could get onto some important enemies lists."

"That sounds like a threat."

"*I'*m not threatening you. I'm offering to team up with you, work with you! But there are other people in the world who know about you, and they're not so sweet and gentle as I am."

"They'll put detectives on me? Steal my idea?"

"Aha, so you *have* found something!"

"Sure. I told you that."

"And you're crazy enough to think of going it alone?"

Lou looked him over. Maybe, she thought, she had begun actually to hate this handsome, heartless man who brought the predatory outside world onto her beautiful seaswept beach. She would run his expensive car into the corrosive waters of the Pacific! She would put dogshit in his delicate Italian shoes! She would spit on his next careful little paper!

"No," she said, playing her high card. "Not alone. The cell is in practical operation all over—lots of people are using it. Ever hear of 'public disclosure'?"

Gleason asked in a tight, tense voice, "How many people are using it?"

"Let's see. We set it up like a telephone tree. Each one teaches three others, helps them build it. By now it's about three to the fifth power—say 243 people?"

108

Lou saw Gleason's face pale. "Damn you, damn you!" he said. Lou braced for an attack. She knew some good crotch-kick disablement moves, even the eyeball-punch-out maneuver—such things wcrc taught to young women in high school these days. But Gleason crawled out of the hut and tramped off down the beach.

Lou crept out herself and did a few deep bends in the stiffening breeze. "Welcome to higher education," she said to herself. Then she headed up the canyon, taking the shortcut home. That way she could be there before Gleason and make sure he didn't mess up her cells. The game, she realized, had gotten even more serious, and the cold chill was in the back of her neck again.

Ken, Kathy, Kurt, and Karen were all in their twenties and all living in a common household in Eugene, Oregon. For a while Kcn and Karen had been a couple, though not very seriously; they had rented a big house and brought Kathy and Kurt into it. They all got along well and, by working at odd jobs around town, managed to survive quite handily. Since they really enjoyed each other's company, in time they began looking for some way to make a living together. They thought of starting a health-food restaurant, but Eugene had enough of those. Kathy and Kurt both had some experience remodeling houses but weren't particularly enthusiastic about more redoing of kitchens or adding on of bedrooms.

One day in a coffeehouse Ken and Kathy ran into a man named Karl, and since having names starting with K was a sort of comic bond among the members of the household, they started joking about inviting him to live with them. Karl was much older, about 55, but he had a beard and sparkly eyes and Kathy thought he was pretty handsome. It turned out that he was living as a carpenter, in fact had done it for years. And lately he had taken on a couple of insulation jobs. He was thinking of finding a regular partner instead of just making do with pick-up help when he needed it.

This made Ken and Kathy listen more carefully. They invited him to the house for supper that night to explore the possibilities. Like half the population of Eugene, the four K's were ecology enthusiasts, and as the evening wore on they began to work out a plan to specialize in energy-conservation remodeling. Karl knew the small contracting business and could train the others. Kathy and Karen felt that working in construction would be a feminist achievement. Ken

109

had some background in advertising—he could get the word out.

For a while they joked about calling themselves "The OK Konstruction Kompany," but settled on "Sunny Side Solar Remodeling." They developed a standard treatment that would work on most houses: a greenhouse or big doubleglazed windows (with summer overhangs) along the south walls, heavy insulation in attic, walls and floor, thermosyphon water heaters. They would insulate hot-water piping and hot-air ducts. They would provide either hinged shutters or insulating shades to cover windows at night. With an incense stick, they would survey the whole house for air leaks and then caulk cracks, fix leaky chimney dampers, and install or re-do weatherstripping around doors and windows. On demand they would also install heat-pumps, wood stoves, and sophisticated active solar systems.

By this time many people in Eugene had responded to ecological persuasion and rising gas and electric costs by various conservation measures. Some turned the lights off more carefully, kept their thermostats lower in the winter months, insulated their ceilings, turned off furnace or heater pilot lights in the summer. But usually such steps were taken piecemeal. Ken's publicity for Sunny Side emphasized that a household could deal with its energy problems all in one fell swoop. It made financing simpler. It gave people a satisfying, coherent plan to do right and save money besides. The basic treatment generally cut a house's energy consumption by at least a third; it would pay off in eight or ten years, and sooner if energy prices rose as most people expected.

In a few months the pressure of business grew so much that the Sunny Side group found themselves working ten-hour days. They began looking for ways to ease up. They could adopt a "normal" business structure and expand—have a manager, a sales person, and hire more employees. This didn't much appeal to any of the five K's; it would take the fun out of the operation. But they found what seemed a reasonable alternative: on each job, they would hire an apprentice. After doing a couple of houses, these apprentices would be able to go off and start their own firms. The idea could spread, without having an organization try to control it.

From its beginnings the Survivalist Party displayed unusual ingenuity in securing news coverage in both print media and television. After a few months the party began to issue the normal press releases

110

and brochures and background papers that any political group relied on. But it also developed a knack for creating dramatic events that constituted "news" and somehow also managed to educate people for the cause. To emphasize the need for separated bike-lanes the party mobilized a thousand cyclists to pedal four abreast through the downtowns of major cities. To increase feelings of neighborhood solidarity it sponsored street fairs, with blocks closed to traffic and the residents enjoying communal beer, potluck food, volleyball, and peaceful chatting on the street with their neighbors. When levees failed, or transportation systems broke down, or pollution scandals were uncovered, Survivalists were there with detailed and incisive plans for making sure the disasters were not repeated. When budgets were presented, Survivalists made dramatic counterproposals. To emphasize their principle of direct personal accountability, they issued "Crimes Against Nature" awards to individuals who committed especially gross offenses against the environment and their fellow human beings; these, it turned out, brought very unwelcome attention to the politicians and business executives who received them. A popular Survivalist-oriented new magazine called *Better Times* was growing rapidly in circulation. But the party still needed a way to reach large masses of people directly, and it began exploring the possibilities of television channels transmitted by cable—which would ultimately equip them for two-way communication. Religious groups had been acquiring such channels for years, but no political group had tried it.

The attempt seemed well worth making if only because, almost by accident, it was discovered that Vera Allwen was a formidable television personality. All her speeches were now covered by TV cameras, and through her appearances on talk shows and at Survivalist events covered by TV news she was steadily becoming better known throughout the region. Maggie Glennon first realized Vera's appeal when she had accompanied her to a studio for an appearance and had seen the switchboard light up after she talked, with dozens of people calling to ask "Who was *that*?" But it was Henry who most strongly pushed the idea of acquiring a channel, especially after an experimental broadcast on a commercial station at astronomical charges proved that Vera could hold a sizeable audience. Henry talked about the role of Franklin D. Roosevelt's series of radio "fireside chats" in carrying through the reforms of the New Deal, and he envisioned a regular series of broadcasts called "Visits with Vera." The idea was for Vera to establish herself as a new kind of public figure by delivering homey little fables without direct political relevance to candidates or policies; more particular things could be dealt with later. It was crucial to make it clear through Vera that the Survivalist Party intended to be a moral force, not just a new political grouping. It had to appeal to people personally and concretely if it was to by-pass their usual cynicism about the political process.

Vera talked straight at the camera in her friendly, warm, almost grandmotherly fashion. She took the viewer into her confidence. She sometimes told wry jokes, but she was never frivolous. As she and Henry conceived it, she was trying to make citizenship relevant again—to show people why their relationships with the social fabric were in fact matters of life and death. And wherever she could, she invented parables to get her underlying points across.

"Hello. I'm Vera Allwen, and I want to tell you a story. Once upon a time, I have heard, there was a country entirely made up of lazy people. At first they were just ordinarily lazy. If they had the chance they would always sit down rather than stand up. And if they could get somebody else to serve their food, they'd prefer that to dishing it out for themselves. But they were also an ingenious people, and they soon realized that (since slavery had gone out of fashion) they could build machines to serve them. They invented machines to wash their dishes, and dry their hair, and stir their batters, and saw their wood, and dig their holes. Slowly, decade by decade, they grew lazier and lazier. After somebody invented a machine called an automobile, their laziness increased by a great leap. They began to be so lazy that the idea of walking a block to buy a pack of cigarettes fatigued them terribly, and they would drive to the corner in their cars. They also invented a machine called a television to amuse themselves. Generally they watched television in a half-sitting, half-lying slump, and they designed sofas to make this slumping position as comfortable as possible. Soon the lazy people learned that if you bought prefabricated meals called TV dinners you could even eat in this TV slump and hardly have to move at all for an entire evening. Even their mouths grew lazy, since they didn't talk much when they were occupied watching television—and most of them watched it all evening long. And their eyes too grew lazy, since watching television they just focused their eyes on the screen and didn't have to move them around to look at things, the way we do in real life.

"These lazy people soon grew fat because they almost never got any active exercise. They died of heart attacks in great numbers and had many other diseases caused by their lazy habits. But they didn't care; they thought this was natural, and it just made them want to be lazier still. If anybody mentioned their terrible health statistics, they told them to go away and peddle their bad news someplace else.

"In time a brilliantly lazy inventor contrived the ultimate machine for lazy people. It was a large egg-shaped wheeled vehicle, just big enough to hold one person, made out of clear plastic. It had a slump-shaped seat in it, and it was called a 'char' because it was half chair and half car. It had an electric motor of the kind that had first been used in motorized wheelchairs. Now the lazy people didn't have to use their legs at all, and could still get around quite well, even in bad weather, using ramps and curb breaks and elevators originally designed for handicapped people. The chars were equipped with individual television sets and microwave ovens that could heat up a TV dinner. They had chemical potties under the seat so you didn't even need to go looking for a toilet. There was a radio intercom so you could talk to people nearby encased in their own chars, and a stereo system could play you Mozart or rock. A computer console connected you to the central communication grid.

"These chars came in many brilliant colors and you could get them with airconditioning and many optional chrome-plated accessories. They soon became immensely popular. After a while it was rare to see anybody on the streets or in stores or offices who was actually walking. Little prehensile tools were added to the chars, which people could manipulate from inside so they could continue to perform necessary tasks. And the lazy people felt that, at last, they had achieved the kind of life which the universe owed them. They were very happy.

"For a while. Because it soon turned out that there were drawbacks to the system. Deprived of exercise, their legs withered, and in time the lazy people found themselves unable to extricate themselves from the chars. Thus they never touched each other, and never developed physical bonds of confidence and trust, or fell in love, or indeed even expressed any lust; and so they produced no children. When they got sick, others were unwilling to get out of their chars to help them— they were all now too totally lazy and selfish. Indeed they hardly ever helped each other at all, and sometimes they would get so provoked at each other that they would ram their chars into each other until one of them tipped over, or cracked like an egg, and its driver would lie there on the ground, kicking feebly with withered legs, like a little baby.

"Now if anybody criticized the char way of living, the lazy people were furious and pointed out that they had achieved the highest level of civilization the world had ever seen and they were not about to give it up. But their laziness had made them weak, and when they started dying off in large numbers their neighbors began to take notice. Just to the north of the lazy people's country lived a barbarian people who survived mostly on nuts and berries and wild game. Their technology was pretty much limited to horses and fur coats and log cabins, but they spent most of their time outdoors and they were tough and strong. They passed many hours singing, and dancing, and making love, and playing rough games with their children. Sometimes they got into fights and punched each other, and then made up, and swore eternal friendship. They understood plants and animals, and they had never seen a TV dinner.

"One day a roving band of these barbarians galloped through part of the lazy people's country (which, they noticed, had quite a lot of nuts and berries) and saw what bad shape the lazy people were in. In a clumsy but friendly way, the barbarians tried to drag a few of the lazy people out of their chars, but they fell over helplessly as soon as they were on their feet, and protested loudly, and tried to creep back into their chars where they felt safe. The barbarians laughed at this spectacle, and since they were not called barbarians for nothing, they began to push the chars off cliffs and into rivers just for the fun of it. Soon their barbarian friends came to join them, and in a few days there were no lazy people left alive at all.

"This story happened long ago, in the old days. But there are new lazy people now, and new barbarians. What we need to do is learn from this history, so we do not repeat it.

"You might have some fun retelling this story to friends or family, in your own way.

"I'm Vera Allwen. Goodbye until our next visit, next week."

Larry had never liked working for other people. He was good with his hands, so sometimes he had worked in repair shops, but sooner or later he would have a falling-out with the boss. Then he'd move on to another place but the same thing would happen. It got him down. So

114

he had begun to build up a little sideline of his own: salvaging car batteries, melting down their lead, and selling it.

It was miserable work but it paid off, and Larry was tough. At first he just melted the lead in his oven, in an old shed he rented in an abandoned section of the industrial district of Oakland. Then he got sick from the fumes and a doctor told him he was in real danger. So he quit for a year until his blood test showed his lead levels down again. Then he did some reading, and built himself a bag house—a structure over his melting apparatus, full of burlap bag filters, with a big fan to suck the fumes up through it. He kept the operation quiet, though, because he was afraid the air-pollution inspectors would close him down. He just sold his lead quietly to small outfits—sinker manufacturers, for instance—who didn't ask any questions.

One day a man who said his name was Ben came by Larry's house and said he had heard Larry had lead to sell.

"Yeah, I have lead," said Larry. "How much you want?"

"I need it in bricks—can you do that?"

"I suppose so—I'd have to make molds for it, so it'd cost you."

"I could bring you the molds."

"Okay. How much you gonna want?"

"A couple of thousand bricks."

"Holy Mother! That's a lot of batteries!"

"I know. Could you do it in two months?"

"Probably. But to get that much lead I'm gonna have to hustle. It'll cost more than just picking them up at the junkers, you know. Have to go out in the valley, probably. Maybe even to LA."

"Well, you think you can do it?"

"Yeah, but let's talk money. I'd need twenty percent over my usual price. —What you doing with all these bricks, anyway?"

"I have this industrial lab and we're going into some new work with radioactive chemicals. Don't want to take any chances with it!" Ben fished out a business card which read "Sierra Testing Services—Chemical, Radiological, Biological Assays."

"Okay," said Larry. "I'll make your bricks."

"I also want to make something very clear," said Ben, and he looked at Larry in a way that suddenly seemed ominous. "This new process we're working on is very competitive, so we don't want any other labs or companies to know we're doing it. We don't want you blabbing around about selling us lead, understand? No matter who asks."

"No problem," said Larry, wondering what he had blundered into. "Nobody pays any attention to me anyway. I just sell a little lead, keep quiet—" He shrugged his shoulders defensively, and smiled.

Ben did not smile. "We'll pick up the bricks in small lots, every week, and pay you cash. Let's say Sunday evenings about eight o'clock?"

They shook hands on the deal.

As full summer arrived Marissa D'Amato began to feel sick of the city, resentful of how few trees there were on the city streets. She made a weekend visit northward, staying with friends and family contacts, people who had moved back to the land. She spent her time helping them clean up a stretch of river in which they were trying to reestablish the salmon runs—destroyed by pollution and over-fishing and the erosion that followed careless lumbering. It was hard, exhausting, yet exhilarating work. Marissa discovered that she loved it. She went back up the next weekend, cutting a day of school. The people she met were also involved in struggles over clearcutting, and herbicide spraying, and political reorganization. Some of them lived by doing carpentry or raising sheep. A former professor ran a vegetarian restaurant and had gotten elected to the county board of supervisors. One group was working toward a bold experiment with the idea that government representatives should be chosen by lot rather than elected—claiming it gave a truer representation of the people's needs and views than the current system, which favored the rich, the male, the noisy, and the well-organized.

Marissa found this kind of active country life fascinating. In midsummer she moved north, joining a group of young people who did contract work in the forests, in the style the Hoedads had pioneered in Oregon. They camped out, shared food, entertained each other around campfires in the evening. They cleared brush, removed logs from streambeds, salvaged sawlogs, thinned young trees, did erosion-control work. This backbreaking labor made Marissa's body grow thinner and more muscular. She had always been sturdy; now her endurance improved and her sense of her own physical strength became a real pleasure. She learned to handle chainsaws, tractors, trucks, the dangerous gear used to haul logs out of tangled forests.

She also studied the ways of trees: what they liked and didn't like in

116

climate and soil and drainage, how they coped with the thousand varying conditions that a stand of forest presented. Set by fate in a fixed spot, they somehow endured, living out their tranquil, slow-paced years. Sometimes, as she walked through the woods, the murmur of wind in the top branches sounded to her like a gentle, chanted conversation, and she would join in, with her human voice, singing without words. She touched trees, a friend said once, as if they had feelings. "How do we know they *don't?*" Marissa shot back.

Little by little, she began to feel that she had some special kinship with trees, as if they were a class of fellow beings without whom the world would be a bleak place indeed. She didn't exactly worship trees, as she heard the druids of the dark ages had done. But she felt, more and more, that trees partook of some mysterious earth spirit in which she too shared. These thoughts seemed odd to most people, so she usually kept them to herself. But she took to establishing little special places, almost shrines, near trees she was particularly fond of. One of these hideaways was actually inside the partly burned-out trunk of a huge redwood; it made a sort of cave. There she would sometimes sit, perhaps smoke a little grass, and enjoy the feeling that she and the trees were members of one single life-force, swelling up out of the earth, interconnected quite literally yet also magically through the atmosphere that linked them: trees exhaled the oxygen she needed and inhaled the carbon dioxide her breathing gave off. At such times Marissa felt supremely happy and contented, and when she came back into camp the others would notice a quiet radiance from her. "Here comes our tree witch!" they would say, and smile at her.

One evening when Marissa had returned from such a meditation the group sat around the fire discussing the sins of the Forest Service. A federal law called the Multiple-Use Sustained Yield Act supposedly compelled the Service to allow timber companies to cut trees in national forests only as fast as new trees can grow. However, the Service was under heavy lumber company pressure and its bureaucracy early devised ways to circumvent this law. In recent decades cut had exceeded growth by at least 20 percent. Moreover, in some parts of the country the Service literally subsidized the extraction of trees on remote, steep land, giving away lumber for far less than the cost of regrowing it. Here in the Northwest, where the virgin growth forests were nearly annihilated, the situation would soon be the same. The national forests, theoretically preserved forever for the enjoyment of the people, were being mined out—with the connivance of the agency charged with protecting them.

As usual, the group discussion was lively, full of trenchant criticism and painfully funny anecdotes about Forest Service wrongdoing. When a lull came, a slender and shy young man named Everett, who usually said very little, spoke up. "I've been sitting here thinking," he said, "that we're enjoying this negative stuff too much." Even in the dim firelight the others could see him blushing, but he unfolded his legs to a new position and went on. "It's easy and fun to condemn the Forest Service, but—well, how do we know we'd do it better if *we* were in charge?"

The group was outraged. Of course they would do it better! They were out here in the forests, caring for them; those Forest Service people were sitting in their offices with their calculators, figuring deficit timber sales!

"Yes," said Everett, "sure, but they're not stupid or malicious people. How do we really *know* we could organize this forest on a sustained-yield basis?"

Somebody asked, "What do you mean—if we ran it for Weyerhauser? Like one of those pulpwood plantations in Georgia?"

"No," replied Everett, "just suppose we owned it, and had to run it for ourselves. What would we actually do?"

There was an immediate babble of voices, all making proposals. How to truly estimate the allowable, renewable, sustainable cut. How to do selective logging so that the older, larger trees got harvested and the younger ones could go on growing. How to minimize erosion from roads and skid trails. How to handle mixed stands so that the presence of different species would keep down insect infestation and disease. How to produce seedlings for replanting. How to organize a permanent camp to live in while they did all these things. How to make sure the logs were not sent off to Japan. And also how to rotate the work, how to divide up the profits (if there were any).

This intense discussion went on for several hours, with Marissa in the thick of it. Finally it tapered off. The group customarily rose at dawn for a hearty breakfast and an early start to work; it was time for bed. Marissa looked around at the faces of these people with whom she had worked so hard. "I want to thank Everett," she said. "His questions started us thinking new and important thoughts." Everett shrank back away from the firelight, blushing again. Marissa went on, "And I'd like to say this: if we want our own forest badly enough,

118

sooner or later we can get it! We ought to go on with this planning and be ready when our chance comes. It isn't just talk."

The group split up, heading for their tents. Marissa went over to Everett and put her arm around him. "Come with me," she said.

Vera had serious doubts about relying too much on television. When she talked with Henry about these feelings, he urged her to incorporate them into a broadcast—a sort of confession. It might have useful effects, he thought. In her next broadcast Vera followed his advice:

"Tonight I want to talk with you about television. I'm a little embarrassed to say 'talk with you,' actually, because of course as TV now exists, I'm the one who gets to talk—you can only listen. The TV system we have now is a one-way street, and a narrow one at that. People who control TV stations get to decide what you can see—*you* can only decide whether to watch it or turn it off.

"In the Survivalist Party we're trying to think about how our world should be run to be a comfortable and friendly and democratic place. We don't really like the way TV now operates, with all that control at centralized spots, and in the hands of a small number of rich and powerful people. So we've begun asking if it isn't possible to use television so that you *can* talk back. And the reports from our engineers are highly intriguing.

"As you know, more and more American homes are being equipped with cable. You may think that the only thing cable does is give you more channels and better reception, but cable has other potentialities. The nicest one, we think, is that it is capable of two-way operation. That is, you could have a little TV camera on top of your set, and if I said something outrageous, or asked for your opinion on something, you could activate that camera and call up the central TV station—sort of like call-ins on the radio. Then I, and everybody viewing the channel would see you as well as hear your voice. We could have public debates carried on by video, in other words.

"Now obviously there would have to be ground-rules to ensure fairness. The Survivalist Party is already setting up some experiments to see how different ground-rules would work out in practice. If, for example, I stopped talking now and asked you a question about some public issue—a heavier tax on gasoline to promote oil conservation, let's say—a hundred viewers might dial in at once. So who gets to talk? We don't want somebody sitting here censoring the calls, or maybe picking out callers who will be favorable to one side of a question. But it's easy to have a minicomputer pick out callers at random. That means you would have the same chance of being heard as everybody else—which certainly isn't true of our newspapers and magazines, much less existing TV! That way we would not only be fair, we'd also get a more reliable sampling of what people actually are thinking.

"Then there's the problem of how long you could talk. Programs can't go on forever, so we'd have to establish some maximum time, maybe three minutes. When your time was up, you'd be cut off.

"This kind of use of cable would give us a modern equivalent for the original town meetings of colonial days or the democracy of ancient Greece. It would be especially useful for communities that aren't too large—maybe under fifty thousand altogether—which still offer people the chance to know each other. With cable, we would learn to have our public debates electronically, instead of in the town square or cafes.

"Admittedly, having any kind of machine come between people is not an ideal situation. It's usually a much richer experience to actually spend time with a friend rather than just to talk over the phone. And video images, always a little fuzzy and artificial, never give us the full impact of another human being's presence in the same room. So we must guard against thinking that talking with each other over a future video system can substitute for the real thing. We're sociable animals, we human beings. We like to touch each other, to play with direct eye contact, to hug or shove or make gestures with our bodies or our hands. For our most important experiences, we need to be with other people, not just with electronic images of them. But suppose we develop richer interpersonal lives, with closer direct contact in our families, and in our neighborhoods, and on our jobs. Then we could stop relying on commercial TV to kill our precious time, and begin using new forms of TV as interactive communication—not just passive staring. Using TV in that way could *extend* our humanity, not diminish it.

"I've been doing these evening programs for a while, now, and those of you who watch regularly know that I enjoy it, and we know that you enjoy it. It's good to be together, even in this one-way fashion. But it isn't enough.

"So the Survivalist Party is going into the television business. We are acquiring a channel of our own, and in a week or two my talks will be sent out over channel 33 instead of this one. But there will be a difference, because we're going to do an experiment. We're giving TV cameras to a couple of hundred households in our cable area, and we're going to invite people to do what I've just been talking about—call in and talk with me. Maybe we'll talk about how we can defend ourselves against polluters, or how we can deal with our transportation and energy problems, or how we can improve our health. If you're interested in getting in on this experiment, phone your neighborhood Survivalist Party office and ask. It should be fun, and it's never been tried before. Here is a *real* chance to be the first on your block—in fact the first in the world! I'll have more details next week."

Not long after the visit from Gleason, Lou got a phone call one afternoon from a Mr. Thomas Barber. He had a gruff, slow way of talking, as if he was thinking carefully of alternatives before pronouncing each word. After making sure that Lou was indeed the Lou Swift who was working on photovoltaic cells, Barber explained that he was in the legal department of Omni Oil, and that the corporation now had an extensive photovoltaic energy research program.

"Mmmm," said Lou.

"I understand," Barber went on, "that you have been doing some extremely interesting work. We are always on the lookout for new developments, so I thought we should have a meeting to discuss the possibilities."

"What kind of possibilities?"

"That remains to be seen," replied Barber. "Omni might be able to implement your discovery—if you really have something economically feasible—on a very large scale. You would of course participate in that."

"You mean Omni would hire me?"

"If that seemed the right thing to do, of course. But I mainly had in mind a profit participation. A royalty."

Lou grimaced, but decided to play another round or so. "Omni would take over the invention and market it?"

"Yes indeed. You wouldn't have to do a thing, once it proved out. You could soon be a very rich young lady."

Lou's first impulse was to remind Barber that she was a young *woman*, but she stuck to business. "Omni would control the patent rights, so nobody could use the process except by paying you?"

"Essentially, yes. We might or might not license it to other corporations."

"Depending on the profit possibilities?" asked Lou.

"My, my!" said Barber. "You *are* a bright young person! When could you come in and see me? I can tell that we have plenty to talk about."

"You're wrong about that, Mr. Barber," said Lou. "Frankly, I wouldn't license my discovery—if I really have one, that is—to any oil company."

There was a pause on the other end of the line; evidently Barber was startled. "Does this mean," he finally asked, "that you've had an offer from some other kind of company? I'm sure Omni would be able to meet any other offer. At least let's get together and talk about it."

"Put it this way," said Lou. "There are about four billion people on this planet who might be interested in a good, cheap, do-it-yourself photovolt—"

"Did you say 'do-it-yourself'?" interrupted Barber.

"Yeah, sure. That's what it's all about!" To her surprise, Lou found her voice was quavering. "Look, Mr. Barber. I am not in this thing for money. I am trying to do something for humanity. Can you understand that?"

Barber uttered something muffled that sounded like "Jesus Christ!" Then he came back on the line in his usual calm voice. "I certainly *can* understand it," he said. "And I really do think we must have a meeting. Omni can help you bring about what you want."

"No," said Lou.

"No meeting?"

"No nothing. Just forget about it."

"That won't be easy to do, if you're really onto something."

"Well, that's your problem. Now goodbye." Lou hung up, her hand shaking.

❧

The publication of the Survivalist Party's "No More!" manifesto, predictably, had been largely ignored at first by the national news media. Here and there, however, reporters had read the press re-

122

leases and speculated if something might come of it. A few of them had filed noncommittal stories, noting that the new party was apparently an attempt to weld together elements of the anti-nuclear movement, the ecological movement, the union movement, and the anti-war movement. As one political reporter had put it, "It seems doubtful, given the grinding pressures that have made American politics increasingly divisive in recent years, that this novel attempt to build a forward-looking new political consensus has much chance of success." Others pointed out that Vera Allwen and her associates had significant influence only on the West Coast and predicted little chance of her ideas making headway elsewhere.

Before a year had gone by, however, Survivalist meetings up and down the coast were regularly drawing substantial numbers of people. Discussion of the manifesto intrigued many who were accustomed to party platforms only as compromise documents. Whenever Vera or her chief co-workers appeared at mass meetings, impressive crowds turned up. Nick Ballard's efforts to build an alliance with the labor movement were paying off: the Survivalists could not be accused of being "elitists" and their programs always had beneficial employment-creating features.

The conservative swing that had begun in the late seventies was now widely discredited; the continuing inflation, the general feeling of paralysis in national politics, the continuing bad news about health dangers from chemicals and radiation, and a growing sense that the country was not coping with its energy problems all led many people toward an edgy impatience with accepted ideas. Whatever had been tried so far, they felt, was not working. Perhaps these Survivalists had something worth listening to?

Faced with this surge of public interest, the Survivalists debated what to do next. Clearly there was momentum here that needed to be directed—but in which direction? They temporized, but found they needed larger and larger halls for the crowds that kept coming to hear their speakers. And when speakers made specific proposals, audience response seemed especially warm—even, paradoxically, on the notion of cutting back on the private automobile, when the audience had mostly arrived at the event in cars. Vera and her colleagues were forced to conclude that something was snapping in the American devotion to cars. Indeed at some meetings they had the distinct and uncomfortable feeling that they were actually *behind* their constituents—that people were willing to go further than the Survivalists were proposing, and in directions they would not have predicted. This generated a kind of exhilaration but it also made them nervous, and they redoubled their efforts to have ample discussion sessions at large meetings, to break all large groups down into small, face-to-face sessions where individual views could be heard, and later assessed.

Most of these meetings did not receive news coverage—after all, they posed no threat of violence or disorder, as did a ghetto uprising or the picketing of a nuclear plant, and hence they had little "news" impact. But they did begin to be noticed by rather inquisitive persons who seemed to be FBI or intelligence agents. And their meetings were also scrutinized by some people in the established political parties who were aware of how shallow their own public base was, and so were eager to thwart any competing efforts to mobilize public sentiment. A few mainline politicians—usually Vera's enemies from Sacramento—began to snipe at the Survivalist document, calling it "simplistic" and "unrealistic." These attacks *were* reported by the media and hence alerted many people, who would otherwise not have heard of it, to the fact that the manifesto was being debated.

A political reporter from San Francisco, Mel Sealey, finally proposed to his editor at a national magazine to do a full-scale story on the Survivalists. He obtained interviews with Vera and other leaders. He spoke with people at meetings, in Survivalist neighborhood groups, and on the streets. Gradually he grasped that something important was going on, and it made his hair stand on end. But how to angle the story? Allwen and her cohorts were not crazies—they were experienced, skillful political people, most of them, and they talked quietly but persuasively. Somehow, they were getting people to listen to ideas that would have been laughed at a year or two earlier. Ideas that were *still*, in Sealey's opinion, laughable.

He would, therefore, portray the Survivalists as irresponsible dreamers. They had taken leave of the gritty reality of American life and begun to fantasize about a brave new world of ecological sanity. They had committed the mortal sin of politicians: taking ideas seriously. And where did these ideas lead? Obviously, toward a life that would be totally unacceptable to the American people. A life without private cars—unthinkable! A life without nuclear power or nuclear missiles—grotesque! A life without food preservatives and additives—impossible! With gusto and sarcasm Sealey sketched out the ultimate scenario implied by the Survivalist manifesto. And at the

124

end of his article, grinning at the hash he felt he had made of the document, he wrote: "We lack only a convenient name for this pie-in-the-sky new world that Allwen & Co. are peddling up and down the Pacific Coast. Maybe they should simply call it 'Ecotopia,' and let the rest of us get back to dealing with reality."

Sealey's article was widely lauded in the East as the proper treatment for disposing of what must after all be just another inexplicable California cult. Vera and her friends, however, regarded the article as a sign that they were being seen as important enough to warrant a major attack. And they were amused by the "Ecotopia" label. Indeed Vera adopted it for one of her speeches, in which she answered the magazine by speaking on what ordinary daily life might be like in an Ecotopian future. Some days later, she was surprised to notice a bumper sticker that read "Ecotopia Now!" And not long after, a short novel titled *Ecotopia* was published. Where Vera had only sketchily suggested what a future ecologically sane way of living might be like, the novel provided reassuringly minute details—technological, political, cultural. In the guise of a report by an Eastern journalist, it assumed that the Northwest had seceded from the union and, early in the new century, is being visited by a cynical East Coast reporter—rather like Sealey, in fact.

The reporter pokes around the new country, looking for flaws. But in doing so he gives a complete account of Ecotopian life. He describes the pesticide-free, stable-state Ecotopian system of agriculture and sewage, in which almost all nutrients are recycled back onto the land. He notes the Ecotopian love for wood and natural cotton and wool fibers. He rides fast magnetic-suspension trains and describes the energy-efficient Ecotopian land-use and transportation patterns. He studies Ecotopian cable television, which is an extension of the voting system, and the common use of videophones for business purposes. With astonishment he discovers that worker ownership is the universal form of economic enterprises in Ecotopia, and that Ecotopians have revived the extended family as their basic living arrangement. He learns of their sophisticated biosource plastics industry, which produces biodegradable plastics used for many things (including prefabricated houses) formerly made of wood or metal. He studies their energy system, which relies upon wind, biomass, geothermal, and ocean-thermal sources. He criticizes Ecotopian customs, like the ritual war games, which seem to him inexplicable reversions to savagery, and he is upset by the direct, independent ways of

125

Ecotopian women—who dominate the governing Survivalist Party. But in the end his cynicism wavers; he falls in love with an Ecotopian woman and decides to stay in the new country.

The novel had a surprising impact, even on readers with little political or environmental consciousness. Something about its specific descriptions of everyday Ecotopian life gave readers hope that a healthier, less stressful, more biologically comfortable way of living could indeed come about. The technology for a survival-oriented, stable-state, human-scale society already existed. The problem was to generate the political will to bring it about.

This, of course, was where the real-life Survivalist Party came in. Many people who read the novel had come to feel little but distrust for the leaders of traditional political parties. They flocked to Survivalist meetings. Vera Allwen, who rather enjoyed the novel's playful portrayal of her as mother of her country but did not wish to have the Party totally identified with the novel, set Raye Dutra and her crew to work preparing an official pamphlet called *The Survivalist Way to Ecotopia*. Like the novel, this document sold rapidly. And when Vera said in a speech that if the rest of the country persisted in its ecological follies, "we westerners may be forced to build Ecotopia by ourselves," she was answered by thunderous applause.

Barber's phone call had activated all Lou's anxieties, and she asked Roger to crawl up onto the house's flat roof with her to see what could be done about moving her cell array up there, where it would be safe from phony bird-watchers and other unwelcome observers. There would have to be a walkway, racks, fences. "Is it solid enough?" Lou asked. "Sure," said Roger. "Remember when we were putting in the solar hot water? We checked out the load capacity then."

Lou remembered, all right—it had been a great event, when she was about ten. Roger believed in turning big jobs into parties, and this one had been particularly nice. He had scrounged around for a big piece of double-pane glass, and fiberglass insulation batts, and an old hot-water tank, and some discarded lumber from building jobs. Then he invited over a couple of neighbors and a few friends and they all set to work. Dimmy had been there, bringing a huge pot of chili. Roger had decided a simple "bread box" pre-heater was the most

126

efficient way to go. But it still involved a lot of decisions. Lou helped to mark wood for cutting and drilling. There was a lot of back-and-forth about the best way to do everything, but somehow it all worked out right, in fact better than any of them could have managed alone.

Since then, the heater had faithfully done its job, cutting the Swifts' gas consumption by more than a half. Lou hoped this was a good omen for her cells. "We can put a platform over on the other corner," she suggested, "with a little permanent ladder. And then a low fence around the cell rack."

"Okay," said Roger, "let's get Mike and Carol out here." The Swifts were experienced at working together and quickly built a platform ten feet square. In the middle they put Lou's chickenroost. Then Mike, who was becoming an electronics nut, mounted infrared burglar detection beams at strategic points, connected to alarms in the house which he had earlier installed for detection equipment on the garage doors.

Roger surveyed their handiwork with satisfaction. "Well, that'll give 'em some trouble," he said. "But I worry about that ladder. Shouldn't we have made that detachable—keep it in the garage except when you need to get up there?"

"Oh, Dad, that'd mean dragging it out every day. Besides, I have an idea about that ladder.

"It falls backward if somebody climbs it?"

"No, better. You'll see."

Lou grinned, but Roger was not amused. "Listen, Loulou. I'm getting sick of the pressure. Let's publish, for God's sake! It works. Bert has people using it. Every day gives those people more chance to move in."

"I know! Don't keep bugging me about it! I think I've narrowed it down now. Please, Roger—I want it to be perfect. Give me a little more time!"

The organizers of the Survivalist Party knew the dangers of preaching only to the converted. Instead, they concentrated on ways to turn the converted into preachers too. And so Survivalist ideas about education gave a new sense of possibilities to enterprising teachers. Survivalist worker-ownership ideas found a startlingly wide and deep response among people who worked in factories, stores, warehouses,

127

offices. And the Survivalists reached out also to religious groups, seeking to mobilize their sense of concern for the human condition, to dramatize the plight and the possibilities that faced society after a hundred years of heedless and irresponsible industrial exploitation. Sometimes they did this with standard doctrinal appeals to Christian stewardship, but sometimes also with a new sense of poetry. There were even Survivalists who spoke with the fervor of evangelists. Their meetings gradually acquired a name: Vision Bringing, from the ancient idea that where there is no vision, the people perish.

"Now, O my sisters and brothers, let us speak of Original Sin.

"There are many sins we commit today; we know what they are. But let us think far back, beyond our ancestors, to the time of Adam and Eve. Let us not take that story too literally—insulting as it is, to both women and men, to imagine that man was created first, and then woman created as an afterthought. But let us return in our minds to the Garden of Eden, the original paradise. The place in which, at first, no human beings were, but instead creatures something like us, creatures with infinite slowness growing bigger brains, more useful thumbs, creatures finally learning to speak, to sing, to be human!" ("Hallelujah!" came the audience's response.)

"The Garden, then, the place in which the new human beings needed to wear no clothes, for the tropical air was balmy. The place where ripe sweet fruit dropped from the trees, where fish and shellfish were abundant in the warm rivers and seas. The place where all beings lived in a terrible and beautiful harmony, each one eating and being eaten in turn, to the glory of life!" ("Amen, sister!")

"For it was not the eating that was the Original Sin. All creatures were created as eaters. Even the lowliest worms and grasses in the Garden, each had its own food—organisms and substances proper and ready for each to eat. As day followed day and moon followed moon, the insects fed upon the flowers, the birds fed upon the insects, animals fed upon birds' eggs, and the rich decayed remains of dead birds and animals went back into the soil to fertilize the growth of new plants and flowers. All this was the great circle of life, my beloved friends—fearful and strange, but it was the law of the Garden.

"And human beings too lived within this holy circle. They wandered about gathering fruits by day, but when night fell they cowered in their caves until the tigers came, and sometimes their young were devoured as they played in the sun. Disease microbes thrived in their stagnant waterpots, and sometimes the parasites would grow in their

128

bellies until they died. And lo, their average age at death was 25 years. So their populations of small bands stretched thinly over the land, only eating what the Garden made ready to be eaten. They upset the great natural order of the Garden no more than a leopard or a snail.

"And so things went, O sisters and brothers, for more generations than the people could count. They hunted and gathered and fished in the ways their parents handed down, and the great earth in its majesty ceaselessly circled the warming sun, which gave light, made the plants to surge up from the earth, caused water to evaporate and then return as blessed rain." ("Hallelujah!")

"Thus things stood in the Garden for two million years after human beings first appeared. And all those thousands of generations came and went, and things remained the same. Those, O sisters and brothers, were the generations before the Fall, when all creatures and beings lived together upon the earth in equality. For some were strong in one way, but weak in another. Each had suitable gifts, of strength or guile or agility, fitting it to eat some other creatures, and each was eaten when its time came. The cycle endlessly turned. If we were there we would have thought that things would go on thus forever without cease—and without sin." ("Amen!")

"But then, O sisters and brothers, a great and terrible thing happened. We do not know exactly how it happened, or who did it. But instead of wandering about in the Garden, gathering food where they could find it, perhaps occasionally planting a little patch of yams but then moving on, humans discovered that they could plant and cultivate fields year after year. This sounds innocent enough, does it not? Who could blame them, who could call this quiet, industrious, cautious, productive change the Original Sin? But verily I say unto you, *this was the root of Evil*, this was truly the Devil's work. For consider what happened next. The people began to study the seeds of plants to select the best ones, so that next year's crop might be larger and stronger. They improved the soil so that it could produce more grain, and they began to regard land as private propety, valuable and to be kept from others. Moreover, this productive land could grow more grain than they could use, so they could trade it to other people—for salt, or shells, or furs.

"Some believe that it was women, caring for their babies in settled campsites, who thus invented agriculture, and that understanding crop plants constituted the Tree of Knowledge, and that when Eve in

129

the Bible story offered Adam the apple, she was entrapping him into agricultural society, the life of exploiting the Garden. At any rate, when men stopped hunting and gathering, and began settled agriculture, they soon developed Sin! They learned clubs, and then armies, to defend their fields and the market cities that grew up among the fields. They learned government, to tax the fields and support bigger armies, police, roads, temples and priesthoods. They learned fortifications, and metals and poisons. They also learned dietary and public health precautions. And lo, their numbers increased. They invented gods who told them to go forth and multiply, and subdue all the creatures among whom they had once lived in peace. They domesticated animals for power and developed machines like windmills to harness the forces of nature; they turned the Garden into a Factory. Their numbers rose unto the fifth and tenth powers over those of the tiny tribelets that had inhabited the Garden, and their cities and the filth they produced overran the rivers and the atmosphere. Until by our times, O my people, no square foot of earth anywhere, no matter how remote, was left unpolluted by our plutonium, our chemicals. And our interference in the circle of being had no limits. We killed off the wolves so we could graze sheep unhindered, then wondered why coyotes came to take their place. We chopped down the forests, then complained of floods and erosion. We developed chemical poisons for insects, then could not see why these chemicals also poisoned us—or why the fast-breeding insects soon developed resistance to them, while we did not.

"Now you may ask, O sisters and brothers, can we escape this blind pattern of Sin? Can we go back to the days before the Fall, the days in the Garden, and live again in peace and harmony with all beings? No, I must in sorrow say to you that we cannot. We have learned too much that we cannot forget. We have crossed over the fateful line from innocence. And also we have forgotten all those things that people knew when they still lived in the Garden: the herbs that could ease pain or cure disease; the ways that beings talk together in the terrible but holy encounters of eating and being eaten. We are like blind people now, and it will take us many years and much close attention to learn again how to see, how to accept the circle of being. And because we have destroyed so much of it, we must also learn to help reconstruct the Garden itself. We must learn to farm without destroying the soil. We must learn to deliberately rebuild ecosystems that can with help from nature evolve again into the exquisite har-

130

mony of a climax forest or a savannah grassland—natural communities such as this continent once knew, which supported humans then and could support us again if we give them the right kind of chance." ("Hallelujah!")

"But first we must mourn, and accept our Sin, and know it for what it was and is, and repent, and resolve to go and sin no more. And let us always keep in our hearts, O sisters and brothers, the dream of the Garden, and of how life went on there before the Fall, so that we have a standard, a measure for our actions now, a holy ground on which to stand. Amen."

The long days of summer were filled, for Lou, with nonstop work. Hoping to get clues to the physical mechanism driving her cell from its responses to different light frequencies, she had built rigs that would expose a cell first to the yellow light from sodium-vapor lamps, then to the almost invisible ultraviolet, then to infrared. She measured output characteristics at different intensities, and for both the "improved" cell and the standard cell—hoping to find some interesting anomaly that might suggest what was going on. She also prepared sections of the cell material and had it looked at with an electron microscope to see whether some kind of layering might be taking place within the silicon.

Sometimes, however, it was just too much, and if somebody proposed to make an expedition to her uncle Andy's place she would go along happily. Andrew Swift was a lawyer and lived in Orinda, an upper-middle-class suburb where the climate was much warmer than in Bolinas. They didn't get to Andy's as much any more, but Lou had many happy early memories of driving over with Jan in the summer to spend days lazing around the swimming pool. Sarah and Andy had two kids, a few years younger than Lou. In the summers they practically lived in the water. Sometimes Roger would come too, but he complained of the chlorine in the pool and spent most of his time reading or taking walks. The best times were in the warm, slow evenings. Andy would come home from his office in downtown San Francisco, and the grownups would have glasses of wine and sit around talking while the kids built a fire in the barbecue pit. In Orinda they could sit out late in the evenings, safe from the Bay chill. Lou remembered cuddling into her father's lap by the fire, with a long whittled

131

stick in her hand, toasting marshmallows to the exact even light brown that he liked. Sometimes she burned one. But Roger helped her understand the radiation pattern in the fire's embers and logs, and how to rotate the stick so no side of the marshmallow got too hot, and how to judge the softening of the inside by the marshmallow's tendency to sag. And when she did one just right, all creamy warm inside and toasty golden outside, Roger gave her extravagant praise. He praised her cousins too, when they managed a good one, but Lou noticed it was *her* marshmallows that mattered!

During those years, Andy had worked for a lot of good causes. He took civil liberties cases, he did labor law, he worked for public-interest organizations. He and Sarah had met, at college, through both being members of a lettuce-boycott group helping the Farm Workers Union. For a while they had gone on living in Berkeley. Sarah taught at an alternate school, doing dance and art with kids.

But after her children were born Sarah adopted a more traditional role. She stopped working, and once Andy was making a fair amount of money they moved to the suburbs. The house, though it had a sensational view of Mount Diablo, was isolated. It wasn't that her old friends didn't have a fine time when she invited them out for the day, but somehow it always required a special effort. Nobody just dropped by for a quick cup of coffee any more. So Sarah always welcomed visits from Jan. They talked art, swapped news of friends, argued about books and movies, and helped each other when their relations with their husbands were rocky.

By the time Lou was five or six, she had recognized that there were important differences between her aunt and her mother. Sarah would seldom make up her mind about anything important until she had consulted with Andy, whereas Jan was always very clear about what she wanted. Though Sarah still liked to dance, she didn't take it as seriously as Jan took her work. And Jan seemed to draw people around her easily—they'd drop in from all over the Bay Area, at odd hours, often bringing their strange friends with them, while Sarah tended to only have one friend around at a time.

Lou sensed these differences, along with the fact that, though two years younger, Andy made a lot more money than Roger. But the main thing for her was that the families spent time together often. The Orinda house was a warm, sunny part of her young world. Best of all was when, on a long lazy evening, after some crazy singing of rounds and maybe a last dip in the pool, and then wrapping up in a big towel to do a couple of final marshmallows, she would lie on the deck in the middle of the family group, looking up at the stars, and drift off to sleep amid the murmur of familiar voices.

The Ecotopia Institute, Raye Dutra's idea, came into existence in August. As the Survivalists steadily gained followers and influence, Raye realized they needed to give more systematic attention to a whole range of policy issues. They needed their own think tank, which could generate a series of authoritative position papers. If these were done well enough, they could help channel public debate toward the issues that mattered, and forcefully expose the weaknesses of the traditional parties' views. Raye even had a name for the series, echoing that of the Federalist Papers which had shaped debate on the formation of the American republic. "Let's call them the Survivalist Papers," she said.

Vera was enthusiastic about the idea. She knew the credibility of the Survivalists' general position would be put to severe tests before long. She wanted a range of action proposals available, and the back-up information and thinking to meet the onslaught of criticism which would surely meet the announcement of any such radical plans.

"Well, all right, you've got a new job," Vera said. "Build us your Institute."

Raye gulped. "But I've never run anything like that!"

Vera raised her hands and smiled. "And I've never run anything like the Survivalist Party, either."

"But Vera, I'm so—well, you know, I lack social graces, shall we say? I just focus on ideas, I miss the people side—"

"Raye, you can't get out of it. We *need* you because you can't let go of the ideas. The people will fit in, don't worry about that. Get the ideas right, the rest will follow. Look at it as a giant laboratory. Were your best professors all such hotshots at human relationships?" Raye laughed and shook her head. "But it worked, didn't it, in the best labs? Well, what we need here is testable ideas. So get yourself a crew of demon idea-testers. Remember Einstein—he'd forget to brush his teeth. Find us some people who forget to pee because they're too busy figuring something out, and they'll tell us what we need to know to run this country! You and Nick get on the phones. I want a list of 20 candidates by Wednesday night."

And thus the Institute was born. Raye brought in, wherever she could, people without ideological commitments to any fixed existing approach. She assigned them to study water, sewage recycling, energy problems, housing and population questions, medical systems, transportation. Many of the people she chose were young—assistant professors from the area's universities who had reputations for being "brilliant but erratic," junior staff members in public agencies—and many were women. Raye had noticed that in the past certain women had played an essential critical role. Jane Jacobs had been close enough to the architectural and planning profession that she knew what was going on, but as a woman she was kept out of real power centers and was thus forced to have an independent perspective. Her book *The Death and Life of Great American Cities* had changed the direction of the profession. Rachel Carson's *Silent Spring* had done the same for people's thinking about chemical pesticides.

What Raye was after, basically, were documents that focused the underlying issues and presented clear alternatives. The choices were seldom easy, but they had to be operative, feasible, practical. Vera once said to her, "Look, Raye, we're shipwreck survivors. Everybody else in politics is just drifting around in circles, thinking about how to keep their noses above water. You tell us which way to paddle and how far it is to land. If we lay out a sensible course, people will go along."

Raye, always the skeptical scientist, was not so sure. "What gives you such confidence?" she asked.

"I can't help myself," Vera replied with a shrug. "I have faith in people. They're ultimately reasonable, they can be persuaded by truth. If you don't believe that, even if you can never prove it, you should stay out of politics—go into business and try to make money out of people's foolishness! In politics we have to keep the faith. That's the only way it's worth doing."

Vera's clarity and determination always made Raye a little ashamed of her doubts, and calmed her. Vera, Raye knew, was not *afraid* of anything. To Vera the truth was bound to turn out hospitable, or at least neutral. To Raye it was always potentially treacherous, to be placated and approached with careful methodologies and precautions, as if it might bite. So there was something about Vera's placid confidence that moved Raye deeply. Raye did not think of herself as an emotional person. Yet often, after such a conversation with Vera, she felt tears just behind her eyes, and knew why she was here doing this difficult, demanding, threatening work instead of cranking out safe, easy little papers in a laboratory somewhere. Vera, after all, knew what mattered. She served the people, and her example was so strong that you saw you too cared, more than you had known you could.

As the century drew near its end, Washington, Oregon and California had experienced a continuing influx of population. From all over the Northeast and Midwest people streamed toward the Pacific—some drawn by the benign climate, some by the atmosphere of social innovation, some by the lure of jobs in the government-subsidized aerospace and electronics industries. So great was the growth of population that growth itself became a major industry: the provision of housing, shopping and transportation facilities alone created many jobs. For a long time it appeared the boom would last forever, or at least as long as anybody mobile remained in the decaying Eastern cities.

In time, however, this great national shift of population began to slow. The turn to a stagnant service economy made good jobs scarce all over the country, and people who thought of migrating could no longer count on easily finding work. Land and car transportation costs in the West had risen so steeply that the rush to exploit new areas for commuter tract housing had come to a stop, and the filling in of urban areas was a slower and more demanding and expensive process; even professional people with good job offers found they could not move to a Western city and maintain the living standard they had in Cleveland or St. Louis. It seemed the migration pattern might soon even reverse itself, with Westerners moving east to take advantage of lower living costs there.

The Survivalists had a clear perspective on these confusing developments. There were already too many people in the Ecotopian territory, they proclaimed. Sheer numbers exacerbated every social problem, and constituted a prime cause for pollution and destruction of the environment, the extermination of species, the mining and contamination of groundwater, the clear-cutting of forests, the overburdening of local services. Further cancerous growth would reduce the region to the same desperate straits the Northeast found itself in. Only by stopping in-migration could random growth be restrained,

135

permitting resources to be channeled to the re-creation of livable cities surrounded with a rich and productive countryside.

These ideas found favor with many people. As a practical matter, however, when California in the great depression of the thirties had turned back Okie migrants at the border, the practice was declared unconstitutional. American citizens, the courts held, could move anywhere they wanted. Some Westerners therefore resigned themselves to trying to receive a permanent tide of refugees. Within the Survivalist Party, however, some people (especially those who had begun to share the vision of an ultimately independent Ecotopia) began to draw a different conclusion: though a state border was not a bar to unlimited immigration, a national border certainly could be.

The secession idea also had the virtue of making the Ecotopian region seem more human-scale. America was a country of 230 million disparate people, stretching over a vast area. In recent decades it had often seemed barely governable, lurching from crisis to crisis. Relations between the central government and the people were inevitably tenuous, impersonal, bureaucratic and distorted if not monopolized by powerful business interests. Appealing to Washington, people often felt, was like shouting down a narrow tube three thousand miles long. But if Ecotopia was an independent country, the government would be much closer at hand. With Southern California's population excluded, the whole nation would only amount to some 15 million people. Officials would be known; they could be yelled at when necessary. It would feel good to have your destiny in the hands of people you could know.

As such ideas were reported in the national press, they had a curious double effect. Some Easterners who had been considering migrating to the West accelerated their plans, feeling they had better make their move while there was still time. These on the whole were adventuresome people sympathetic to Survivalist ideas. Also, as conservatives gutted regulatory and environmental protection programs in Washington, professionals in many fields decided that the only part of the country where their expertise would be appreciated was the Northwest. Thus set in a steady brain-drain of people experienced in agricultural research, forestry, consumer and environmental affairs, antitrust law, and many other fields.

Other Easterners, however, abandoned their moving plans because they feared the consequences of Survivalist separatism. And within the Ecotopian territory itself, some people who distrusted the trend of self-sufficiency as the forerunner of some kind of dangerous isolationism began to think of moving east.

Thus occurred a sifting out whereby both old and new citizens of the Ecotopian territory became more separatist in their thinking, and people out of sympathy with Survivalist ideas tended to leave. Slowly and almost imperceptibly, this process helped to shift the balance of political feeling in the area toward Survivalist positions.

In a small town in northern California an enterprising young man who had been making a living by doing garden work had a bright idea: a couple of goats might be better at cleaning up overgrown yards than he was, and they'd certainly be a lot less environmentally obnoxious than herbicides. He found two lovely Nubians and put them to work on an experimental half-acre plot. In two weeks they had stripped it clean and in the process distributed a lot of bean-sized odorless droppings that would enrich the soil.

The goats attracted attention, and soon the city manager heard of them. With reluctance he pointed out that an ancient ordinance prohibited the keeping of oxen, pigs, horses, sheep and goats within the city limits. But the young gardener did not give up. He went before the city council with photographs of his goats nibbling bravely at huge weeds. He praised their cleanliness, their agility, their general chemical-free lovableness, and emphasized that since they ate the weeds, no gasoline had to be burned hauling cuttings to the dump.

Agitated public discussion followed. Some citizens felt that the goats were an embarrassing throwback to the rural past. Others argued that they were an inspiring harbinger of the ecological future. Finally the city council, concluding that the goats did the job and gave no one cancer, amended the ordinance. The young gardener soon had a dozen goats chewing away at overgrown lots all over town. He got phone calls from public agencies with large grassy areas needing to be kept clear. He had to start keeping a waiting list. He also received a letter of commendation from the Survivalist Party, which he tacked on the wall of his goat shed—very high up, so that the goats couldn't pull it down and eat it. The Survivalists, who believed in small scale and teaching by example, wanted him to run classes showing people in other places how they too could use goats.

We have been following up on the idea of applying a bioeconomic methodology derived from net-energy analysis to a range of basic social processes. This enables us to focus on questions of "primary productivity": the amount of real products (food, timber, fibers, energy, metals, etc.) created, and their corresponding total real-world costs—not just those which appear on corporate balance-sheets, but also those paid by government, the public, etc.; also how these costs are borne by different sectors of society. This approach seems to offer the great virtue of transcending ordinary party-defined issues and moving toward operationally framed questions which an electorate, if reasonably well informed, could judge rationally. We treat the traditional party-government machinery as essentially a bargaining battleground in which social costs and benefits are moved from one sector of the system to another—a sort of hydraulic contraption which, in recent times, has operated as a zero-sum game. Thus, to over-simplify one major example, the armaments program has functioned in two major modes: to siphon resources from the population at large to certain high-technology corporations mainly located in western metropolitan areas, and to concentrate public subsidies among a diminishing number of dominant firms in the manufacturing sector. Since the output of this huge industry is almost entirely non-reproductive—that is, its products do not contribute to further production—its net drain on the economic system is a major factor in the long-term economic decline in productivity. Ceasing armaments manufacturing would thus probably be the single most positive real-world step a US government could contemplate. As I need hardly point out, most recent official thinking has moved in the diametrically opposite direction, with the predictable results: exacerbated inflationary pressure and further relative industrial decline. After some trial runs, we believe it is possible to describe pragmatically—and dramatically—the beneficial effects of a reversal of policy in this area.

For an example of whole-systems analysis nearer home, we have studied water policy. A few economists have developed comprehensive analyses on a few individual dam projects, but no systematic methodology for evaluating system operations has existed heretofore. (Of course the traditional Corps of Engineers cost/benefit ratios are critically deficient from a whole-system viewpoint, and also are based

138

on an unexamined enthusiasm for hydropower, wishful thinking about the economics of flood control, and a rosy view of the over-whelming social need for more motorboating.) Our general findings are that, since dam-building has been done more on the basis of polit-ical clout (pork-barrel construction contracts and cheap-water supplies) no rational assessment of the system as a whole, as it oper-ates in the national agricultural market, has ever been attempted. The bioeconomic pattern is this: dams are built at costs so high that result-ing irrigation water "could not" be sold at its true costs; hence it is heavily subsidized, normally by selling it at one-third or even one-tenth of its real-world costs. In general, simply buying the land pro-posed to be irrigated, and turning it into national parks, would have been cheaper than building the dams, even after deducting hydro in-come. The over-all effect of the dams has thus been to heavily sub-sidize farmers in irrigated districts, at thousands of dollars per acre, enabling them to out-compete farmers in rainy districts. The result is that, for instance, almost all the broccoli eaten in Massachusetts is grown in California and shipped east at heavy costs in oil for transpor-tation, although it is in reality considerably cheaper to grow broccoli in Massachusetts during much of the year. Thus dam policy has sub-stantially *diminished* the over-all efficiency of the national food-production system, causing a rise in the real total costs of food—though some of these costs are rendered "invisible" by being paid in taxes rather than at the supermarket.

We have also been working on the transportation system. Our figures so far can quantify fairly exactly the penalties imposed on the system as a whole by measures that subsidize high-energy-consumption modes such as trucks, autos and planes while penaliz-ing low-consumption modes such as trains, streetcars and bicycles. It seems likely that the over-all depressive effects of recent government policies in this area are almost as severe as those of military expendi-tures. Our analyses indicate that even a perfectly neutral policy here could generate savings easily sufficient to both offset the capital ex-penditures required (chiefly for new roadbeds and equipment) and to contribute substantially to over-all national productivity investment. This is altogether aside from lessening of the coming necessity for Mid-East military intervention and a highly beneficial impact on the petroleum balance of payments problem.

As these examples suggest, I believe we can readily put together a stunning package of policy-reversal documents, all pointing toward

139

rational steps that would conduce to bioeconomic survival. Comments please?

At the bottom of Raye's last page, Vera wrote in large letters:
GOOD—DO IT!

Dimmy was a zoologist by training, and worked part-time as a curator in a natural history museum. He kept the Swift household full of talk about many species of animals, but his particular love was grizzly bears—perhaps because he was a burly, bear-like person. Grizzlies were his totem animal. He had studied their habits, their life histories, their ill-fated encounters with humankind. He knew their anatomy, their mating habits, their former ranges. He had spent long summers in their remaining haunts in Idaho, Wyoming, Montana. Whenever anyone would listen, he would explain that grizzlies were fearsome beasts, lords of creation, standing unchallenged at the top of a number of food chains since they ate fish, fowl, animals, plants, even insects, depending on season and circumstance. In the distance they were splendid creatures, commanding awe from other, lesser species. At close range—where Dimmy had once or twice found himself, by mistake—the grizzly left little doubt about who was naturally boss. It was only the human invention of guns which gave us the capacity to intrude on grizzly territory.

This was, in Dimmy's view of things, a tragic imbalance. One evening when he and Roger were sitting around with their feet up on the wood stove, with Theo crawling first on one lap and then on the other, Dimmy began to wax particularly eloquent about it. "Now the Indians—they knew how to let Old Griz alone. You don't face off with an animal that's two hundred pounds heavier, quick as a damn rattlesnake, and faster on his feet than you are—especially when he's at least as mean. You give him *respect*. You look the other way. You move the other way, and slowly. You hang your head a little, maybe—if you had a tail, you'd put it between your legs."

Roger could never help kidding Dimmy about his passion for the great beasts. "How about saying 'Excuse me, Griz, just passin' through'? And maybe a little bow while you were at it?"

"Couldn't hurt," said Dimmy obliviously. "You don't want to offend a grizzly! He's easy to offend, too. Just walk a little bit toward where he doesn't want you to walk, or get too close to something he figures is his . . . and so, naturally, when the whites came, they couldn't *stand* it. Their egos were even bigger than his. And here was this bear, this *animal*, that wouldn't go away and hide. It would kill their cows, even their horses sometimes. If you cornered it, it would stand up and fight, and maybe take a man with it in a showdown, all clawed and chewed to death."

"Horrible," said Roger, egging him on.

"What do you mean, horrible? They had it coming. It was the grizzly's turf, and those dumb miner assholes started rampaging all over the landscape, shooting anything that moved—killing the deer, the mountain lions, the bears, the Indians. Who had all got along perfectly okay till then, you know!"

"Yeah, that must have been tough for Griz. And they finished him off in what—"

"In 1924," said Dimmy. "But that," he added in a conspiratorial tone, "may not be the last of that story."

"Meaning what?" asked Roger.

"I'm beginning to make plans, big plans. Can I swear you to secrecy?" Theo was messing around adding wood to the stove, but evidently Dimmy didn't worry about him hearing.

"Sure," said Roger, beginning to believe Dimmy had something serious on his mind.

"You remember I've been active in campaigns to get people to grow native plants in their gardens and in parks—to reestablish the original species that inhabited these parts before the Europeans brought in all their so-called ornamentals and all those grasses. And there are a lot of people trying to get the salmon back into the rivers—even up through the Delta where the poor devils have to swim through pollution so strong they can hardly tell where home base is."

"Yeah," said Roger. "I realize you've done a lot of that stuff. I really admire it, Dimmy."

"The point of it all is to get people to recognize and remember what a natural ecosystem looks like. Especially if we can get them when they're young, like Theo here. I don't want him to grow up to think nature is something you only see on TV! If we can just get through their heads the beauty and the complexity and the stability of nature, they'll know why we humans have to somehow fit into those marvelous natural webs without tearing them all up—and why, when

they've been rent asunder by the irresponsible profit-mongering assholes, it's up to us good responsible people to patch 'em up again."

"I'm with you so far. We owe it to the next generation to teach
them to live with decent respect for the natural order. Otherwise
there's no meaning to anything. But I don't see what all that has to do
with Griz."

A crafty grin spread over Dimmy's face. "Every ecosystem sup-
ports numerous food chains, right? Now by exterminating the grizzly
in this region, we have effectively removed the top anchor of these
chains. This is a fundamentally unstable and unnatural condition, and
an offense to anybody who understands what nature had wrought
before we got here to mess it up."

"So?"

"Well, remember when I was up around Yellowstone last summer?
I went out and hung around in grizzly territory. Got to know the
habits of a couple. And it occurred to me that three or four of 'em
might like to migrate—it's kinda crowded with tourists up there."

"But grizzlies don't migrate. They hibernate."

"They don't migrate unless somebody *helps* them. And that's my
plan. Capture them and bring them down and turn them loose in the
Sierras. They'd fend for themselves pretty quick. Did I ever explain to
you just how smart grizzlies are?"

"Yes, several times," said Roger. "They're related to pigs, the most
intelligent of domestic animals."

"Right, right. So no question they'd survive."

"If people let 'em."

"Yes, that's the problem. Of course they wouldn't be discovered
for a while. But sooner or later somebody would get close enough to
recognize one."

"And then there'll be a dandy bear hunt and poor Griz will be
extinct in California again."

"That's where you're not thinking far enough ahead, Roger. We
spring in first with our well-oiled propaganda machine. We give interviews, we give beautiful film to the TV stations. We explain nature's
way. We explain why God put grizzlies there, and that it was a sin for
humans to exterminate them. We give simple handy hints for campers
on what to do if they encounter a grizzly. We point out that grizzlies
are far less of a menace to humankind than automobiles."

"And they still end up stuffed on somebody's wall."

"Nope, I don't think so. You forget that grizzlies are an endangered species. It is against the law to harm even the tiniest hair on their heads, and illegal for anybody who isn't an Indian and a member of a bear clan to wear their claws or teeth upon their person. Listen, we could make Griz almost as popular as Flipper the dolphin. And if worse comes to worst, we could confess and take the heat off the grizzlies for a while."

"Is it a crime?"

"Probably, but I don't know the proper label. Transporting wild animals across state lines maybe, like the Mann Act? Stealing government property from Yellowstone? Causing a public nuisance, for sure." Dimmy chuckled. "I really *like* that—Griz as a public nuisance!"

"So you think you'd get away with it."

"Yeah, I do. The time is getting right. We could do it."

"What do you mean, 'we'?"

"Well, of course I want you in on it, Roger."

"Oh, no you don't! Listen, even German shepherds give me cold sweats. I don't like big sharp teeth."

"You won't have to worry about teeth."

"I see, you're going to walk up to a grizzly and offer him a train ticket?"

"No, we're going to use tranquillizer guns, just like the rangers do. I got very friendly with the rangers last summer. Sometimes they even let me carry their supplies."

"So you made off with the equipment."

"Yep. And I've built a sling that six people carry, and I've got a pickup truck lined up, with a welded re-bar cage covered over to look like a camper. Two-three trips and we'd have done it."

Roger looked at Dimmy with new appreciation. "You really mean it, don't you? When you planning to pull this off?"

"Next week," replied Dimmy.

Roger began to laugh, a bit hysterically. "All right, all right," he said. "Let's think about the other members of this gang of ours." Then he added, "I just can't wait till Fish & Wildlife hears about this!" and began laughing again.

Vera Allwen had known the D'Amato family for years. Angelo had been in her class in school, and he and Laura had lived most of their lives in Vera's neighborhood. After Angelo's death Vera hadn't seen much of Laura and had lost track of their son Ben and daughter Marissa. Marissa had been a self-confident, passionate girl. Ben had always seemed a little surly and truculent. Vera could never quite figure him out—he always seemed to have dark schemes afoot. So she was a little mystified when Ben dropped in at her office. "Come sit down," she said. "I'm working on my next 'sermon' and could use a break." But Ben had not come for a sociable visit. He and a group of friends, he said, had become convinced that the logic of the Survivalist program would sooner or later lead to the necessity of secession.

"And that," he said with a rather malicious grin, "has been tried before. The South lost."

"It won't come to that," said Vera. "Everybody remembers the Civil War."

"But if it ever comes close, you'd find yourself in the same position as the South—militarily weak, whatever the constitutional arguments."

Vera smiled. "I'm not really thinking about constitutional arguments, Ben. And I don't think you are either." She looked at him sharply. "What did you come here for, anyway?"

Ben glanced around nervously. "Do you think this place is safe from bugs?"

Vera shrugged. "I'm not really sure. We've had it swept—two days ago was the last time, I think. Maggie's the one who cares about things like that. I don't mind if anybody hears what *I* say."

"I wouldn't want *anybody* to know what I am about to say."

"I think you can proceed."

"No, too much risk," said Ben. "Why don't we go for a little walk? Just down toward the channel."

Vera disliked anything conspiratorial. But she also wondered what this intense young man was up to. And she could use the exercise. "All right," she said. "A quick walk."

Once they got onto the street Ben began talking, low and fast. "My friends and I believe you are headed for a confrontation with federal power. We know only one way you can survive that. We are working on something that could provide it."

"Come on, Ben, out with it."

"We believe we can build a couple of nuclear mines and plant them in New York and Washington, say."

"Nuclear *mines*?"

"Bombs. Small bombs—Hiroshima size. Concealable."

"That's an atrocious idea, Ben."

"Shall I tell you how? First, sources of weapons-grade uranium are—"

"No, I will not listen to that," said Vera. "It's out of the question. It goes against our most fundamental commitments."

Ben's eyes grew fierce, with some deep anger in them. "You're not being realistic! You'll end up losing everything."

Vera wondered at this intensity, and thought of trying to reach it, somehow—perhaps to try and detoxify it. But she gave up the idea and simply said, "If it comes to that, sometimes you have to accept losing, when the alternative is to win by doing something that really means you've lost."

"So you won't authorize us to go ahead? We're not asking for funds—we have sources of funds."

Vera frowned. "I hate to think of whom those sources might be tied to."

"No, you're wrong. It's clean money."

"Very hard to believe, obviously. In any case, the answer is no—absolutely no."

Ben's face twisted unhappily. "Too bad," he said. "You'll be sorry later, Vera, that's all I can say."

They walked on in silence until they came to the old ship channel. "You see this mess?" said Vera. "Someday it should be a waterfront park. We'll get rid of the old hulks and the rubble left from the warehouses. People will paddle around in clear water in their kayaks and canoes, and even take a dip if they feel like it. They'll be able to picnic on the grassy banks where trees will grow, and there'll be egrets and herons in the marshy places. You'll be able to get a water-taxi that will run you around the embarcadero to the piers and restaurants—"

"You may *try* to do all that, and just get it shot out from under you!" Ben turned back abruptly; Vera noticed that he had hardly looked at the precious little waterway that to her seemed so promising for the future.

"Ben," she said, "don't you realize the means must be appropriate to the ends? That otherwise the means you use distort and change the ends you meant to serve?"

"All I know," he replied, "is that you are going to be up against real enemies, and they are going to destroy you, and all your pretty dreams of egrets and parks, unless you can *fight* them."

"There are other ways to fight than bombs," said Vera softly. "And we'll just have to learn them. As Gandhi did." Ben said nothing more, and after a minute Vera changed the subject. "How's Marissa? And your mother?"

"Marissa's fine. Spending her time up in the woods, doing forest work. Seems to like it a lot—we don't see much of her since she got out of college."

"And Laura? I haven't seen her for six months. Saw her name on a membership list so I know she's with us, but she hasn't come round, and I wish she would. Will you pass on the message?"

"Sure. She's busy doing Planet People stuff—on pesticides mostly. Keeping a little too busy, but you know her."

"Yes, I do! Well, give her my love and tell her to come by soon. We need all our old friends." They had now reached the Survivalist office again and as they went in Vera added, "Now listen, forget that crazy idea of yours. Tell Maggie I said to give you something useful to do—she's over at that end, the red-haired one who never sits down."

But Ben did not go to find Maggie; he didn't need any new assignments to take up precious time. He headed back into the street, and Vera returned to her desk to work on her television talk—which she had called a sermon because she had been rereading Biblical parables for inspiration.

"Once upon a time there were a rich man and a poor man. The rich man had been told that it was necessary to take care of the earth, from which all our blessings flow. So he looked around for some land he could take care of. And he found a piece of untouched country land that was in danger of being turned into a suburban tract. He bought this lovely land, to preserve it in its original pristine state. He was very proud of what he had done. From time to time he would walk over his land—listening to the babbling brook, hearing the wind in the trees, enjoying the sunny meadows, and rejoicing that it had been in his power to do this truly good act.

"But the money that the rich man had paid for the land did not sit quietly in somebody's bank. It found its way to oil companies, who used it on strip-mining for coal and uranium, contributing to the country's burden of air pollution and destroying the landscape. It reached utility companies, who used it on nuclear reactors dangerous

146

to the nation's health and safety. It reached aerospace firms, which were building ever more dangerous missiles. Some of it went to chemical companies. Some of it even ended up in the commodities market, where people speculate on the hunger of millions of other people in countries ten thousand miles away. Wherever the rich man's former money flowed, it wreaked havoc and destruction.

"Now the poor man, meanwhile, had no money and no property. He rented a tiny house with a small yard, and he lived very simply. He didn't have enough money to buy a car; instead he rode buses and streetcars, which saved a great deal of energy. In order to save money on fertilizer he carefully composted all his kitchen wastes, and so his garden was lush and productive. His house was so small that it required little gas to heat, and he was also in the habit of collecting scrap wood that he found around the neighborhood to burn in his stove. He recycled old items—hinges, hardware, even nails. He bought recycled clothes in secondhand stores. He was very resourceful, and so he used up few resources.

"Now it came to pass that the rich man loved his piece of wilderness so much that he decided he should build a house there, on one small corner, so he could keep watch on his property. This house was four times the size of the poor man's house. It had a three-car garage. It consumed more energy in a week than the poor man's did in a whole year. It had required the cutting of ten times as many trees, the manufacture of six times as much cement, four times as much glass, five times as much roofing. The rich man was too busy making money to keep a garden, and he had his kitchen garbage and yard clippings hauled away to a dump. He had no time to recycle things and so whenever he felt he needed something he bought it new. His diet was full of expensive meats and exotic foods imported from abroad through great outlays of energy for shipping. Trips from the country house to the city used up immense extra amounts of gasoline and contributed to the supposed need for more highway construction.

"Now the moral of this story is that the rich man, even though he was trying to be good to the earth, actually did a great deal of damage to it. The poor man, who was too busy trying to survive to pay much attention to ecology, caused far less damage. And so we can see the new truth in a very old saying, 'Blessed are the poor'—for they cause minimal damage to our environment. Blessed especially are the thrifty and resourceful, for they shall have a margin of survival when the rich cannot find what they are used to in the stores. Blessed are the producers of their own necessities, in their gardens and garages and kitchens, for they can be poor in money but rich in delights. And so I say unto you, verily it is easier for a camel to pass through the eye of a needle than for a rich man to enter into a world of ecological sanity.

"This is Vera Allwen. Good night."

The Crow's Nest was a restaurant overlooking the Willamette River just north of Corvallis. Formerly a roadhouse, it had fallen on hard times when an interstate diverted the through traffic away from its door. Then it was bought and rehabilitated by new people. They built a terrace and deck overlooking the river, planted bushes, scraped off layers of dingy paint down to the raw wood, and began serving simple meals. They found some locally produced beers to go along with the variety of teas they offered. Gradually the place became the haunt for people in the vicinity who were interested in new ideas. Intense talk ran long into the night at the Nest. For many habitues it was more like somebody's house than a restaurant. People would bring their children and let them play on the back terrace, keeping an eye on them while they ate lunch or had a beer at the end of the day. If waitresses or waiters happened to be feeling like it, they would sit down next to your table while they took your order, and they'd ask whether you wanted things quickly or would rather take it easy. Some people who dropped in found this personal dealing hard to take; they didn't come back. The ones who liked it, however, liked it a lot, and despite its modest prices the place flourished. The crows from which it took its name still inhabited a row of tall trees on the opposite bank. The river still flowed past as always. From its headwaters in the southern mountains it ran past almost all the major population centers of Oregon—through all the rich, flat, wet agricultural lands of the state, until it finally joined the Columbia at Portland. Inscrutable in its sinuous flow, it equitably carried occasional lost logs, the debris of spring floods, a brown load of sediment from clear-cut uplands, and occasional fishermen in little boats. By night as by day it rustled faintly at the reeds and bushes along its banks—a powerful presence, yet always on its way somewhere else.

"The biggest difference between them and us," Vera Allwen often remarked, "is that we know the automobile is the enemy and they don't."

As the work of the Ecotopia Institute progressed, it became clearer that the economic future for America turned on the agonizing question of whether it would be willing and able to kick its addiction to cars. When Raye's researchers began to pile up the full indictment of cars, Vera was astounded at its seriousness. In the first half of the eighties, they told her, the net outflow of dollars to pay OPEC nations for oil amounted to the value of half the stocks and bonds listed on the New York Stock Exchange. Translated into real-world terms, this meant that in only five years the country had given away in order to maintain its car habit half of all the productive machinery, laboratories, land, buildings, transportation facilities, and food production resources accumulated by its corporations over the previous 200 years.

Ray confessed, "I didn't really think the term 'junkie' applied until I looked at these figures!"

"So the car," Vera said, has been a major cause of inflation?"

"Yes, though not the only one, of course. It's maybe worse that these payments have transferred so much *power* abroad. The capital markets are increasingly dominated by foreign money. Remember the old phrase, 'capital has no country.' If it can reliably and permanently raise its profit rates by bankrupting the United States, of course that's what it will do."

"Well then," mused Vera, "the car could be an identifiable enemy: the car is a foreign agent! — We aren't going to be able to attack the other factors frontally right away. We can't propose austerity all around. What 'reward' can we offer people if we start talking about a serious move against cars—like a really stiff gas tax?"

"It'll reduce interest rates and strengthen the dollar. It'll free domestic capital that could go into improvements in productivity, into jobs—including public transportation and rebuilding cities in less transportation-dependent patterns. There'd be really visible results in only a year or so."

"Anything else?"

"It'd also cut our chances of nuclear war over Saudi Arabia down to zero. Let those who live by the car die for the car."

Vera laughed. "All right. Let's work out a detailed plan. Year by year: key the tax to the import reductions achieved, so people can look ahead to it disappearing once we get to zero imports. Find ways to channel the surplus capital into new housing and new jobs."

"Tearing up battered highways?" Raye asked, smiling.

"Not yet. Reforestation first of all—very labor-intensive. Cleaning up the waterfronts, river banks, central cities. Adapting the interstates for fast intercity buses running on separated lanes—getting ready for the new trains when we get to that. Building energy facilities—*any* kind of renewable energy resources."

"But Vera, some of those things aren't really justifiable economically."

"Not at the moment, maybe. But we have to talk in longer-range terms, Raye. If we build them now, we'll have them in a couple of years when oil prices have gone up enough to *make* them economically justifiable. We have to make educated guesses on the discount rate. Besides, if we don't develop them, and right now, we have no credible long-term economic leverage on oil-supplying nations."

"Which leaves only military leverage."

"Exactly. Which in a panic situation might look attractive to some people in Washington."

There was a silence. Raye said, "What makes you think people in our region will go along with a real anti-car program when nobody in Washington is willing to risk it?"

Vera glanced up as Henry came into the room. "I'm not sure they will, Raye. It's just that we don't have much alternative, do we? We'll be asking them whether they want to survive economically. We'll put the choice in clear, inescapable terms. We'll propose to channel *all* the revenues into housing and jobs. Then, if people study the question and decide they'd rather go down with their cars—well, that's their right, isn't it? Nothing says a country has to survive forever. Countries get old and sick and incompetent and their minds wander. If people really want to drive off a cliff in a Cadillac rather than hike along the edge and enjoy the view, maybe that's truly their idea of what's best—who else is to decide, after all? We're here to make the choice *clear*. And to be geared up to act if the choice goes our way."

"So we propose a heavy gas tax, maybe a hundred percent, on a regional basis?"

"Yes. We'll say it's time to save ourselves, since the federal government is too paralyzed to do it. And if the rest of the country can't or won't act, they'll have to take the consequences."

Now Henry spoke up. "Bravo. But you're forgetting that a lot of

150

men identify psychologically with their cars. The car embodies phallic power. Men who need that *varoom* as a prop for weak sexual egos aren't going to give it up, no matter how much you tax it. And they'll react as if you're trying to castrate them."

"So what can we do about that?" asked Vera.

"We could try to help them feel better about their bodies, about their sexuality, so they can shake their car addiction without feeling emotionally destroyed. If their lives are more gratifying sexually, they won't need the car substitutes so much."

Raye looked provoked. "Henry, what the hell are you talking about—Survivalist whorehouses?"

"No. Maybe car-kicking clinics, where men learn to know and love their own bodies, and what they're capable of sexually. Learn to rely on them, so they don't need a car's power to feel all right. Help them learn about other sources of pleasure and reassurance—ones that don't require heavy expenditures of petrochemicals."

"Like sex?"

"Sex, and dancing, and soaking in hot tubs. Anything that promotes body-awareness will diminish car-dependency."

Vera had been thinking. "You mean Raye's tax is just the stick, and we have to make sure there are also carrots?"

Henry smiled benignly. "I am always in favor of carrots," he said.

One early fall day Lou and Jan went crabbing. They headed for a half-ruined pier on the Bay, taking bread and cheese and beer, and had a lazy time dropping their old star trap into the water. They'd chat a while, then haul it up, often with a crab inside. It gave you plenty of time to talk, and Lou brought up an idea that had recently come into her head—to have a celebration of her coming 18th birthday. It seemed much more important than highschool graduation, which was a matter of routine. At first she had thought of calling it a coming-out party, on the theory that rich young women and gays shouldn't have a monopoly on the term. But maybe it should be called an initiation (into adulthood) party? Finally she just called it "my party." Jan was very taken with the idea. It would be a great event. What with Lou's own friends, and Carol and Roger's, as well as Jan's, there'd be a hundred people easily! "And there'll be a ceremony," said Lou, "with some kind of dancing. There's got to be a part of it where I dance across this open space to where a group of young men are standing and watching—"

Jan said, "I guess if this was a so-called primitive society that would signify you were ready for marriage?"

Lou hesitated. "Well, I am sort of announcing I'm grown up. So I suppose that *does* mean I'm available for something serious.

Jan frowned and started pulling up the crab trap. "I hope you're not—"

"Oh, Mom, of course I'm not thinking about getting married right away, or having children, or any of that! But one of these days I might want to live with somebody."

"That would sound like a reasonable next step. When the maiden becomes an adult, she moves out of the father's house, not to mention the mother's."

"Now there's something about my name," said Lou. "You know there are cultures where you get a chance to pick a new name when you're initiated into adulthood."

"That might be a bit weird, but if you want to do it, do it."

"Trouble is, I really *like* 'Lou,' and I can't think of any name I'd prefer. Tell you what I *don't* like, though!"

"What's that, my dear?"

"I don't want you to call me Loulou any more, ever! From 18 on, I am just Lou, okay?" Then, seeing a hurt look in Jan's eyes, Lou moved over and hugged her. "It's nothing against you," she said. "It's just that little Loulou is metamorphosing into Big Lou! Or Ms. Louisa, in you insist," she added with a giggle.

When their bucket was finally full, they trudged home. "Here come the hunters and gatherers!" yelled Jan as they came into the warehouse. Her housemates Janine and Gary were there, and Janine's son Kevin, and Miriam, and Marcia who had lived there a while back; and so, to Lou's delight, was Jeffrey, whom she hadn't seen in months. They all gathered around, impressed, and looked at the crabs clawing each other. Then everybody helped prepare dipping sauce and salad and bread. When the cauldron of water began to boil, Lou and Jan took turns dropping crabs into it. But before they threw each crab in they picked it up, looked into its strange stalked eyes, and said something like, "Sister crab, we are about to eat you—to merge your life force with our own. We do so in full consciousness, knowing that we too will be eaten in our turn. Thank you."

Jan had felt silly when she first decided to make such little speeches

152

to live creatures she was about to eat. But the members of the household now readily shared what seemed to them all a solemn yet also festive rite. They watched the crabs steaming in the pot. Then followed an orgy of eating, everybody cracking claws with gleefully savage expressions, empty shells lying everywhere—a wonderful mess. Lou explained her celebration idea and it appealed to Marcia and Janine immensely. They began planning their costumes and tossed in ideas for the ceremony itself. They also offered help with the food and wine.

"I just wish I had thought of doing it myself, when I was 18," said Marcia. "All I can do now is start suggesting it to friends' daughters!"

Jeffrey asked if he was included in the plans. "Of course!" said Lou. "I want that line-up of young men to include everybody I've loved. Which means especially you. But you have to wear an elegant costume."

"What are you going to wear?" asked Jan.

"I don't know yet."

"I'd like you to have my silk dress, if you feel it's right for the situation."

"Oh, yes, it's beautiful! It'll be perfect, with all those swirly patterns, and it moves so gracefully when you dance—oh, thank you so much!" But then Lou's expression changed. "Does it mean I'm *becoming* you?"

"The dress? No, it's just that it'll be your dress now. I used it for a while, you can use it for a while. If you want to. You're always you, my Lou."

"I guess I have to do some serious thinking about it, don't I. There are a lot of things I have to think hard about. I'll add that to the list for my retreat."

"Retreat?"

"Yeah, I'm thinking I'll need to go away to the country for a few days before the ceremony. To clear my head, get really ready, you know?"

"I can see that," put in Jeffrey. "But why all alone?"

"I think that's an essential part of it," said Lou. "Pack in one day, stay a day, come out. Nothing fancy in the way of terrain, though—just up the coast."

"I don't want you breaking a leg or something," said Jan.

"Just flat country, I promise you," Lou replied. "And mostly just sitting and thinking, not hotdogging up any mountains or anything.

153

When I come back I'll have made up my mind about the dress."

SURVIVALIST PAPER NUMBER 6:
NEW TIMES, NEW TRAINS

Like persons, societies are sometimes seized by unconscious suicidal impulses which remain inexplicable to outsiders. Individuals may drive recklessly or drink or smoke too much; societies may become addicted to impressive but precarious technologies which actually contribute to friction and ultimate social breakdown. Sooner or later societies, like individuals, must seek to replace such destructive behavior patterns with constructive ones—or they will die.

An example is close at hand. In the fifties and sixties the United States indulged in persistently self-destructive behavior regarding its transportation system. Inheriting an extensive, efficient (and rapacious) railroad industry, the country proceeded to displace it by a truck-based freight industry and airplane- and automobile-based passenger-moving industries—all heavily subsidized from the public treasury.

Commonsense might have pointed out that railroads require only about a fourth of the fuel required, ton for ton and mile for mile, by trucks. However, energy was then too cheap to be a determining factor, and through a complex combination of political pressures the highway and air lobbies defeated the railroad lobby for government favor. In the decades following World War II, railroads had to maintain their tracks and stations at their own expense, while $525 billion of federal, state and local funds were spent on highways and streets, $23 billion on dredging and locks for barges, and $50 billion on air transportation facilities.

The resulting decay of rail transport seemed relatively painless at the time. The slow rise of one industry and the decline of another does not normally cause great anguish to the public—although, in this case, a small but vocal group protested the strangulation of passenger train service. However, without realizing it, the general public was in fact paying heavily for this particular change. The true total shipping costs of many goods were several times higher on the highway system than they would have been for shipping by rail; but the part of these costs met by government subsidies was paid indirectly and invisibly in taxes rather than in higher retail prices.

154

By the late seventies, when rising energy costs began to make it plain that the oil-dependent trucking system was a major contributor to the nation's energy problem, the railroads had deteriorated in many parts of the country almost to the disaster level. (The roadbed was so bad in places that trains had to move at a walker's pace.) Even determined efforts to rebuild the rail system would take many years—while the enormous drain put on the economy by the need to purchase foreign oil would continue.

Worse still, while double-track railway decently maintained could carry the traffic of a 20-lane superhighway, the once-proud interstates were proving so vulnerable to the pounding of trucks that further massive capital subsidies would be required to keep them in passable shape, since truck taxes came nowhere near the sums needed. (A single truck caused 10,000 times the wear on a highway that a passenger car did.)

Thus decisions made on the basis of short-term economic and political calculations in the energy-flush earlier years have returned in later times to haunt us, the children of their makers, with increased costs for every item of merchandise that moves in the American economy, and every plane trip.

What is to be done?

We must move immediately toward restoration of the financial and energy efficiency of rail transport as the foundation of our transportation system. The freight-moving capacity of railroads must be made more widely available—through piggyback trailer service, through railroad cooperatives serving areas that rail corporations have abandoned, through rate policies that distribute true costs to the goods and activities that incur those costs.

Despite the popularity of passenger trains, the passenger-moving capacities of our rail system, in the West as in most of the rest of the country, have been cut virtually to zero. We therefore propose to abandon the existing western rail network entirely to freight hauling, and to build an altogether new system of spacious, comfortable, ultra-high-speed passenger trains with magnetic suspension and linear motors. These new trains, based on Japanese designs but of American manufacture, will connect all major cities up and down the coast, and many secondary cities, either on the main line or through branch lines. The technology to build them is already in place within our region through the aerospace facilities of the Boeing Company in Seattle. Some of the guide rails required for this new system can be constructed between the lanes of interstate highways, taking advantage of the grading already done to provide relatively straight and level routes. Massive construction work, creating tens of thousands of jobs, will be required for additional tunnels, bridges, cuts and fills.

When completed, the system will move people, baggage and light freight such as mail from center city to center city in the same times as present air travel, and at greatly reduced costs in money and energy. Once this system is in place, with frequent service, air transportation with its huge energy consumption will be required only to points distant from the West Coast. Major airports will need no further costly expansion and many small airports can be closed. Intercity automobile and truck traffic, especially with appropriate taxes levied on petroleum fuels, will decline greatly, bringing us within striking distance of oil self-sufficiency.

By these policies we will build a sensible new transportation system from the ruins of the old. In time, the rest of the country will be forced to follow our example. But we cannot wait to follow their timetable. The Survivalist Party has therefore begun detailed engineering studies for the new system we need. We must get our part of the country moving again!

Survivalist proposals for reorienting policies on such matters as energy and transportation did not sit well with President Maynard and his administration. Ideologically committed as they were to continued reliance on automobiles and nuclear energy, they had no alternative but to dismiss Survivalist economic analyses of the disastrous consequences as arrogant and visionary. They were dimly aware that those analyses, since they were in fact based on hard new thinking, were having an impact among business people as well as in political circles. But it was inconceivable to them that such ideas be given serious governmental consideration; they called into question the basic assumptions of the administration.

At bottom, it came down to the question of growth. Always before it had been possible to quell domestic discontent with the promise that tomorrow there would be more. Now the Survivalists had gotten through to many people, at least on the West Coast, with the news that there would *not* be more. Indeed there might be less, as people had begun to see for themselves. Rising wages in inflated dollars no longer concealed the fact that the actual standard of living was declining. And so the Survivalist aim of establishing a stable-state economy, reliably and self-reliantly living within its own resources, not dependent upon oil sheiks or armaments sales or the endless export of wheat, had suddenly begun to have a dramatic appeal to people seeking some minimum degree of security in the world.

It was time for a counterattack. Interviews by high government officials were given to the press, hinting at the subversive nature of Survivalist ideas. Legislators known to be sympathetic to Survivalist positions were edged out of congressional committee posts, and party support was withdrawn from those who faced re-election campaigns. Bipartisan condemnations of Survivalist positions were issued. (These were not hard to arrange since both major parties had steadily moved toward the right for the whole preceding decade.) President Maynard himself put his waning popularity on the line: in a major speech, dealing mainly with the importance of maintaining American control over critical parts of Central and South America, he took time to attack "those who do not share the objectives of the American people, and of this government—to expand our production and regain the industrial leadership of the free world. The modern world is a tumultuous and competitive place. To seek for mere stability is a dangerous illusion. We must grow or we will perish. Growth may mean sacrifice for a time. But growth will only come through the sensible, tested, free-market principles of this administration, and not through the nostrums of visionaries."

Nonetheless, the administration had come to take the Survivalist "visionaries" seriously enough to direct the FBI to develop infiltration and provocation teams who could attempt to harass the Survivalist movement. It had sometimes worked with the civil rights movement and the anti-Vietnam War movement. Maybe it would work again. If you can't defeat people's ideas, you can always try to disrupt their organizations.

As the first European colonists landed on the coast of North America they faced a vast, forbidding sea of trees stretching from the Atlantic beaches all the way to the Great Plains. The settlers hacked at these trees in a frenzy. They chopped them down to make room for agricultural plantings; they sawed them up for lumber to build houses and piers and even roads. They burned them to stay warm. But they also

157

cleared the land simply because trees constituted the hateful wilderness, which they felt it was their God-given mission to subdue. Only in the Northwest, whose immense stands of virgin timber were isolated from Eastern markets, did sections of the original forest survive; and after the second World War these too fell rapidly to the chainsaws of the logging companies.

The original forest floors were rich reservoirs of nutrients, accumulated by the leaf and twig droppings and the rotted trunks of hundreds of generations of trees. The forest floor was tunnelled by worms and insect larvae, penetrated by roots, inhabited by microorganisms busily decomposing materials that would soon be recomposed into the next cycle of growth. The thick tree and undergrowth cover gentled the impact of even the heaviest storms, so that rainwater percolated into the earth instead of running off, and the creeks ran steadily and clear year round.

Once the trees were chopped down, the immense fertility they had created could be exploited. Farms spread throughout the areas that had enough rainfall to support crops, with only small woodlots as reminders of what had been. Year after year, in all the vast farmland stretching from Boston to Colorado, farmers extracted from the earth the richness that the trees (or, farther west, grasses) had built up. Driven by market forces controlled by speculators in the cities, they abandoned the ancient peasant wisdom of crop rotation and mixed farming; they became corn farmers or wheat farmers, dependent on the fluctuations of international markets. They no longer planted ground-holding legumes to replenish the soil's nitrogen, but turned to chemical fertilizers. Seventy percent of available agricultural land was devoted to the production of grain for meat animals. Professional agricultural experts began to speak of "factory farms."

Once the soil was denuded of its tree cover, erosion had set in. Where there was heavy rainfall, as in the South, poverty-stricken tenant farmers were driven to such desperate practices that gully erosion sometimes consumed half a farm's acreage. In the dry Plains area, grasslands plowed up for wheat simply blew away in dry years, leaving the desolation of the Dust Bowl.

Gradually, most farmers had learned to plow with the contours of the land, to plant windbreak trees, to sow soil-holding crops. Nonetheless, even in years of benign climate and with the best possible farming methods, topsoil losses through wind and water erosion greatly exceeded soil build-up through organic processes. From each row in each

158

field, in all the thousands of fields making up the watersheds of the nation, rivulets of rain carried soil particles to the ditches and the creeks and the rivers, which became brown with the soil suspended in them. The land lost the absorbency it had had when forested, so run-off became rapid and great floods were common. In dry seasons, wind scoured the fields, blowing loose soil into the gullies. By the seventies, for each bushel of corn grown in Iowa, six bushels of soil eroded away; in eastern Washington, 20 pounds of topsoil were lost for every pound of wheat produced. Even in well-tended farm country such as Wisconsin, about eight tons of topsoil were being lost from each acre each year, and only about four tons regenerated. The national average net loss was almost nine tons per acre. Three million acres of cropland per year were being lost to highways, factories, subdivisions, but the equivalent of another three million was blowing and washing away.

The declining yields which would otherwise have resulted from these inexorable processes were averted only by heavier doses of chemical fertilizers at constantly increasing expense. Rebuilding the soil, if feasible at all, would require decades of devoted effort. And the process would not begin so long as the existing agricultural technology remained dominant.

In the great farm belts of America, vast tracts of land were worked by machines which consumed large quantities of petroleum fuel. Further expenditures of costly energy were made in food processing, packaging and distribution. Indeed, for every calorie of food energy consumed, more than one calorie of fossil fuel energy was being expended in producing and delivering it. The overall energy budget of American agriculture had thus begun to show a net loss. Paradoxically, the situation would have been improved if human beings or their livestock could eat oil directly—and in fact during the sixties, when oil was very cheap, researchers had tried to develop bacteria that ate oil and could then be made into porridge or cattle feed.

However, most people preferred to believe that the natural abundance of the American soil was eternal. After all, corporate advertising told them that the ingenuity of American agribusiness could control nature and extract unimagined productivity from the land. The underlying energy consumption of the system remained invisible, except in steadily rising prices for foodstuffs. Few Americans would have relished the idea that their food supply was in reality critically dependent on oil wells in feudal countries half a world away, prey to sudden revolution and disruption. The point at which energy outlays would no

159

longer be able to make up for declining soil fertility came ever nearer.
But the prospect of food shortages in America seemed as remote as the
prospect of gas shortages had seemed a decade earlier.

Despite denunciations from Washington, the Survivalist Party went on growing rapidly, operating out of a network of rented storefront offices in the cities, and out of members' garages and back bedrooms in smaller places. Conventional political wisdom said that third parties never got anywhere in America; their ideas were always co-opted by one of the two major parties before their strength became too threatening. Yet in this situation the existing parties were remaining obstinately committed to business as usual. They could contemplate minor compromises; they could not envision real change. And so they left the Survivalists a *de facto* monopoly on new ideas.

As the number of people committed to the Survivalist cause grew, the Party could afford more and more detailed attention to the actions of existing government bodies. By early October they had adopted, on Maggie Glennon's suggestion, the old British custom of "shadow governments," whereby Survivalist counterparts followed all the chief officials of the state and city governments on a day-by-day basis, criticizing their doings and proposing alternatives. There were Survivalist sympathizers working at various levels in virtually every public office on the West Coast, so a steady stream of leaks and inside information poured out to the Survivalist shadow staffs.

By this time there was some sentiment among party members for emphasizing their increasing strength and respectability by renting an imposing headquarters facility, either in the financial district of San Francisco or somewhere near the civic center and federal building. Vera Allwen didn't much like this. "It might seem like a sign we were moving in among 'them'," she said. "Better they have to come to *us*, on our own turf!" Besides, Henry Engelsdorf argued, operating out of a conventional office structure would mean fitting the party's people into a physical arrangement designed for authoritarian corporate operations. It would mean giving up much of the directness, the creativity spontaneity, which were fostered by their informal facilities. The Party must always practice what it preaches, he urged.

Maggie and Nick began looking for some kind of warehouse to replace their present rented storefronts. When they found one, they held meetings there to brainstorm its possibilities and lay out the basic necessities. Vera and the other founders sat in on these meetings but said little; the idea was not to do something that would please them, but something that would work for everybody. And so, in productive confusion, the Survivalists made the gradual move to their new quarters. First they insulated the whole structure and added a solar-heat greenhouse all along the south wall, with a couple of slow, quiet fans to push warmed air back toward the north side of the building. The greenhouse had massive concrete planting boxes to store and re-radiate heat. In them people grew tomatoes, peas, beans, zucchini, cucumbers; many Survivalists were either vegetarians or followed diets in which dishes tended toward a Chinese pattern—meat and fish were used sparingly. A kitchen was soon added, using methane from a sewage digester rig for cooking-gas. Solar water heating panels were installed on the roof, along with solar roof tanks to provide further interior heating.

To reflect Survivalist ideas about democratic organization, the central southern part of the warehouse became "the commons"—an area for socializing, eating together, holding big group meetings, and working on projects that required a lot of space. An openable skylight was put in overhead, with plenty of hanging plants. Circling around this central area were offices of various sizes, all easily reached. There were no corridors or executive suites. Furniture was home-made or comfortably worn. Several stoves, often fed by wood salvaged from debris boxes and scrap piles, were scattered here and there amid a profusion of carpets and rugs. There were no fluourescent lights, no air conditioning, no private washrooms. After some discussion it was decided not even to have one person regularly working as a receptionist; people would take turns being responsible for dealing with visitors and answering phones. And a large, gracefully hand-carved wooden sign was made by one of Henry's friends to hang above the main door. It read:

THE GREEN HOUSE

Bert had been diligent. By fall he had mobilized enough people to build solar cells that Lou's bluff to Gleason was now more than half justified. The cells were in actual use powering small radios, stereos and other light appliances. Bert had also helped Lou write an article

161

that explained in technical detail how to put such cells together. A San Francisco magazine that Bert had lined up was itching to publish it.

But Lou hung back, even though she knew it made Roger anxious and Bert angry. "There are still too many unknowns!" she lamented. "We don't know the basic mechanism, but beyond that we don't know how the output will hold up over time. We don't know the optimum scale of the things. It would just be *weak* to publish it now. Give me a little more time!"

Bert took to coming out to Bolinas with Lou every day after school, and she put him to work constructing new cells, doping, setting up experimental rigs. Bert had a systematic mind, and he worked out a schedule to enable them to develop output-over-time curves for a variety of cells, comparisons of various sizes and configurations, fail-ure-rate tables. He worked on circuit connection problems and im-proved some of the processes of manufacture in small-scale facilities. He added the resulting information to Lou's basic article.

And still Lou stubbornly refused to publish it. "It's *my* cell!" she said. "So it's *my* risk."

"There are tens of millions of other people who will suffer if you lose this gamble," replied Bert, his voice unsteady with anger. "They'll pay for your pride! I say you're being selfish and irresponsi-ble and childish. And greedy—for fame. What do you think you're really doing, trying to win the Nobel Prize or trying to help human-ity?"

Lou stamped her foot and glared at him. "You make me sound so horrible!" she said. "But I want to do both—I want it *all*! If only I could crack the thing. Oh, Bert, why can't I get it?"

"Look, Lou," said Bert, "how about setting a fixed time limit? That will make me feel easier, and your family will relax a little, and we can begin thinking ahead to a real public announcement—you know, a television spectacular! We'll invent our own Ecotopia Medal for you."

Lou sniffed. "I don't want your medal," she said determinedly. "I want time." Bert stared at her.

Finally she said, "All right. We'll set a date. I get six more weeks. Okay?"

"A month."

"No, I want six weeks."

"All right, six weeks. Now let's take a break. There's a Survivalist

162

Party meeting tonight. Vera Allwen's going to be there, I hear. We can tell her about the deadline. Then you can't get out of it!"

Though she resisted the idea initially, thinking she should spend the evening working on her cells, Lou finally agreed to come. She expected the meeting to be either a dry political gathering or a rather rowdy affair like meetings of the Bolinas town council. But she had been intrigued to hear that Vera Allwen would attend a meeting of only 15 or 20 people. "Everything Survivalist groups do is *personal*," Bert explained. "They're more like little tribes than just political groups. So they have to stay small."

When they got to the meeting place, a little late, Lou and Bert found that people had taken off their shoes and were engaged in what appeared to be yoga exercises. They joined in. Bert didn't need to point out Vera, who was leading the exercises along with a man of perhaps 35; she was a friendly looking person who, Lou noticed, immediately commanded your attention, though in the exercises she didn't say a lot. The group went through a series of deceptive stretches. Nothing much seemed to be happening, but as Lou angled a leg in a certain way she would realize where the connections were, and how other parts of the body responded. "Keep breathing!" Vera reminded them, since the tensions of the exercises tended to make them concentrate and cut down their breathing. "Keep that front leg strong! Don't go over too far, just till it feels like you'll have to bend. Remember to keep feet firm on the floor . . . "

The people were serious, Lou noticed; they really put energy into the movements. Then the leaders had them do a series of cooling-down exercises, inventorying the sensations in feet, ankles, pelvis, back, shoulders, neck. Most people did these lying on the carpet; Lou saw they looked at home in their bodies—calm, soft-eyed. They breathed evenly and deeply, and paradoxically seemed both relaxed and full of energy.

A quiet descended on the room and people retrieved their shoes, put sweaters or other outer garments back on, and settled themselves in chairs or on the floor. "Most political groups," Vera began, speaking in a direct, conversational way, "address themselves to your head—and perhaps also to your stomach, that is, to your narrow self-interest. We Survivalists are trying to do something basically different. We think the head is important, of course, but it is only part of your whole body. *All* parts of the body are essential to your health and life. So we think it's essential, when we come together for a political meeting, to begin by renewing our consciousness of our whole bodies, and particularly of our breathing. Our breath is a very emotional thing. By observing it we can learn to breathe more deeply, more fully, more openly." (Here Vera pulled her shoulders back, to open up her own chest cavity in illustration, and Lou, like everybody in the room, found herself imitating the movement.) "We can develop our breath in ways that we cannot develop our hearts or our digestion. And you can get an idea of what Survivalists are really up to when we say that we're trying to deal *politically* with the person you are when you've done some exercises and are being conscious of your breathing."

Vera paused and looked patiently around the room, meeting the eyes of all present. "We don't particularly want you to get excited and go out marching—though we do like it when people become conscious of their muscle tone! We're not even necessarily trying to persuade you to write letters, or knock on doors, or phone your representatives. We want you to see that it's possible to *change your lives*. That's what these Survivalist meetings are all about. They are supposed to be part of our lives—not something separate that we go to, and then go home and forget about. This *is* your life, right here, right now.

"We have the chance to learn things here, about each other and from each other. We can join our strengths together to do things that we really care about. We can be crazy and have fun—if we *don't* have any fun, we shouldn't be here!"

She paused and looked around the group, her eyes sparkling in an inviting way. "What's on your mind?"

Lou had imagined a political meeting would always involve lots of maneuvering for position and parliamentary rules and votes—a kind of game that only certain aggressive and verbal people were good at playing. But this was all personal and direct. It didn't feel preplanned. People began to volunteer some of their feelings about how they were living. Vera's reassuring presence evidently made them feel it was all right to bring out very emotional concerns. They talked about fears—of losing jobs, of pollution, of cancer, of contaminated or adulterated food. They told stories of impersonal and misdirected and ruinously expensive medical services. They talked about loneliness—the breakdown of traditional families, the difficulty of constructing new groupings of people to live with, their confusions over new sexual roles. Lou found herself, along with the others, expressing painful anxieties about living in a society where people were

164

impersonally controlled—by governments, corporations, faceless economic forces—and felt they had no defense for their own private space. They talked about hopes for their children—and here several people broke down and wept, in despair at the bleakness they saw ahead.

Lou had half expected that Vera Allwen would tell them that the Survivalists would fix everything, ask for their votes, and then go home. But Vera and the other party leader doggedly pursued the issues people raised—exploring all their emotional components, their cultural components, their political components. They sometimes focused the group's attention on special issues: what this person might do about her housing problem, diet improvements that might help that person, things that another person might do to be less exploited on his job. When things got too painful they led more exercises to refresh spirits and bodies. Teas and fruit that people had brought were shared. It was not until later that questions of practical political action came up, and when they did they flowed naturally out of the preceding events of the evening. A number of members of the group, it turned out, had been working to divert county money to develop separated bike paths through downtowns and parallel to main roads; an election was in the offing, and various plans were put into action. Survivalist candidates were also on the ballot, and campaign work was going on. A plan was afoot to establish a neighborhood food buying club. Somebody needed volunteers to help erect a greenhouse on the coming weekend.

As the meeting ended, Bert asked Vera if she could speak with them for a few minutes. It had been some months since Bert had first approached the Survivalists about Lou's cell, but Vera responded with enthusiasm and greeted Lou warmly. She looked at her curiously. "So now you're about ready to publish the story?" Lou was taken aback. How had Vera guessed?

"Well, in six weeks," she said. "I'm still hoping to figure out the mechanism."

"Yes, I can see that," said Vera. "It would be beautiful to present it all in one package." She hesitated. "But Bert told me there are risks involved." Vera looked at Lou more sharply, and Lou felt herself blushing. "Well," added Vera with a smile, "I suppose if you didn't have a lot of pride you wouldn't have discovered it in the first place."

Lou looked down in silence; for once she was unable to think of anything to say.

"If you wanted, we could provide you with some protection," said

165

Vera. "But Bert said you were taking sensible precautions. And I don't believe in doing something for people when they're already doing it for themselves."

"That's very nice of you to offer," said Lou. "I think we're okay. Nothing weird has happened yet, anyhow."

"I hope you get it, Lou," said Vera. "We want to make a big thing of it, as Bert has surely told you. It's a beautiful and generous plan, to make it public. In any case, we'll be ready when you are."

Then Vera headed back to San Francisco. As Lou and Bert left the meeting room, Lou actually felt herself looking forward to the next meeting. "Are there a *lot* of Survivalist meetings like this?" she asked.

Bert laughed. "Yes, rather a lot," he said. "Thousands by now, probably. In neighborhoods all over the region."

"And they meet every two weeks?"

"Some meet every week."

"And then they go out and *do* these things—actually help each other?"

"Yes indeed."

"So they might, for instance, be helping each other build photovoltaic cells?"

Bert laughed again. "Now you know how I found people to build cells and put them to work! That's why I wanted you to come. Or at least one of the reasons." He nudged her affectionately, and gestured at the sleeping bag he had brought along on the back of his motorbike. "It's full moon," he said. "Great night to go up on the mountain."

"And howl?" said Lou.

"And bark."

"And nip?"

"And play."

"Okay."

Independent family farming had not been completely overrun by corporate farms, even in California, and in the seventies a few determined farmers had begun to carry out experiments in novel ways of farming. Economically pinched by high mortgage and financing costs, they found that labor-intensive practices like cultivation to control weeds began to look good compared to ever more expensive herbicides. Going against the standard advice of university experts, government advisors, and the sales people of the chemical fertilizer companies, they cut down on the application of pesticides to their fields. Instead of routinely spraying everything, they waited for signs of infestation and then applied modest quantities of pesticide only to the areas actually infested. Their neighbors predicted dire outbreaks of insect damage. But when the experimenting farmers actually experienced only a modest increase in damage, more than offset by massive savings in money, these neighbors took grudging notice and began to experiment a little themselves.

Other farmers were appalled at the sharply rising costs of fertilizer (whose nitrogen was produced by processes requiring high energy input). They tried recycling animal manure back onto their fields—something that for many years had been considered uneconomical by agricultural cost accountants. The discredited practice proved profitable again, and monocropping of corn or wheat began to look less attractive compared to mixed farming, using crop rotation, with some cows or even horses or mules around. Official doctrines, however, were slow to change; most of the advice given to farmers discouraged them from innovation and pushed them toward reliance on larger, more expensive and more breakdown-prone technologies. A few of them, nonetheless, emboldened by their own successful experiments and not intimidated by "experts" who said they were exceptions, began to think of farms that could be almost entirely selfcontained, recycling all wastes back onto the land and utilizing nitrogen-fixing legume crops to replace much of their commercial-fertilizer needs.

One such farmer was Ralph Burns, about 50, a wiry, windblown, thoughtful person who had inherited 640 good acres in the fertile Willamette Valley of Oregon. On one balmy, drowsy evening Ralph had been studying his farm accounts and preparing to pay his bill from the oil and gas distributing co-op. As was his custom on such melancholy occasions, he poured himself a glass of whiskey before he got out his check ledger. He sipped, he sighed, he looked at the bill. Then he flipped back to the bills for preceding periods and noted the implacable increases.

Ralph was a resourceful man who tried to use his head in independent ways. He did not want to pay that fuel bill. He stared at the glass in his hand. He sipped again, feeling the warmth of the whiskey as it slid down toward his stomach.

At this point, Ralph recalled later, something clicked: whiskey-warmth—fuel. He had read in some magazine about the Brazilians turning sugar-cane into alcohol and mixing it with gasoline, one part in ten. It was supposed to eliminate engine-knock on lower octane gas, in fact, and thus could substitute for leaded gas. If the Brazilians were doing it, there might be something in it. And if you could ferment sugar-cane you could probably do it with corn too. Or spoiled fruit or grain. And as far as fermenting went, well, he had that old leaky water tank out by the barn, could weld on some patches. . . .

A few days later, Ralph went in to town for the morning and at the post office he ran into Hank Latham. Latham had moved out to Oregon from the South almost 20 years before and started a hardware store. He carried quality merchandise and stood behind it. And he was an ingenious cuss who could usually help you improvise a solution to your problem.

"Say Hank," said Ralph, "I was going to come over and ask you about something. Got a minute?"

"Sure. What you up to?"

"You know anything about gasohol?"

"A little. Ten percent alcohol. You don't need a new tune-up."

"That's it. I'm going over to the University one of these days and see what they have on it. The fermentation part sounds easy enough. But I don't know anything much about distilling except that the feds don't like it much."

"Well, actually I hear these days you can get a permit without much trouble. It isn't like the old days in Tennessee! —Of course I admit I owe the revenuers a lot. If it wasn't for them, I would never have gone into the hardware business. I figured somebody else could *use* the copper tubing and get busted, and I'd just be the one who *sold* it to them!"

Ralph began to think he had found the right man. "You mean you—"

"Yeah, buddy, I did it all right. Now what exactly did you want to know?"

"What's it take? Could I do it out on the farm? How much work would it be? Is it legal?"

Latham laughed again. "Jesus, you sound serious."

"Yeah. I was just paying my gas bill the other night, and you know, Hank, it *is* serious, sure it is."

Latham said, "Well, you best know what you're getting into, then.

168

Sure you can do it. Any idiot moonshiner can do it, you can do it. It isn't even that much work, depending on the quantity."

"I was thinking of like a thousand gallons."

Latham whistled. "I can see it now. Headlines about 'Local Farmer Arrested by Marshals.' Claims he never tasted a drop. When asked why he had a thousand gallons of high-test alcohol in his barn, he said he was innocent!"

"Well, goddamn it, I *would* be innocent. I'd be glad to put something in it to make you retch if you drank it. I just want something to put in my tractors and truck."

"Sure," said Latham, abandoning his kidding. "We all do. So what do you need from me, besides some copper tubing?"

"Can you teach me how to set it up and run it?"

Latham thought for a moment. "I'll tell you, Ralph. If you get five or six men together who want to do it, and you make it okay with the law, sure enough I'll set up a little postgraduate moonshine school for you. I'll help build the first still, it'd be a kick."

Ralph stuck out his hand. "Henry, you just made yourself a deal."

The Crow's Nest collective wanted to put its electric and telephone lines underground, and Vickie the cashier-accountant was assigned to get it done. She checked with the utility companies about their requirements, got her plans approved by the county, and called an excavation company in Corvallis. There was, she calculated, about 60 feet of trenching to be done. A man named George called back with an estimate, but it seemed high to Vickie and she talked to her friends about it. One of them said, "Hell, that ground is river loam, why don't you just hire somebody to dig it by hand?"

Vickie got the Laborers Union on the phone, and a couple of telephone numbers. A few days later two hulking characters came over in the early evening to take a look at the job. They studied it, went back to their car to drink a beer and think it over, and gave Vickie an estimate that was well below the company's. She called George back next day and needled him a little. She said she'd found a way to get the job done cheaper, and why were their rates so high?

"Honey," began George, "I—

"My name isn't Honey," broke in Vickie, "it's Vickie. Anyway, I'm just trying to understand how you work on these things. We'll probably have some other jobs coming along."

"Great, great! Okay, remember we have to drive the back-hoe out there, and it eats a lot of expensive gas—so we have a mileage charge first of all. And both ways, don't forget."

"Yes, I can *see* that, George. I don't want to keep the damn thing."

"Uh, right. Well, then there's gas used in the job itself, plus the labor charge—that's a skilled operator rate. Half-day minimum, of course. And we have to put a charge on the machine itself—you know, amortize its cost over its working lifetime. Then we have a little overhead for the shop and the office here. So it mounts up. We're not trying to take you. —How much you going to pay these other guys?"

"Well, they're 20 percent under you, George."

"Oh. I was going to say, you know, we could shave our estimate a little. But not *that* low. What are they gonna do, scratch at it with a spoon?"

"No, just old-fashioned pick and shovel. Powered by sandwiches and beer instead of gas. I guess that makes the difference. And they can dig a narrower trench too."

"Son of a bitch. That's the first time I've heard of *that* in a while. Have to think about that. Let me know how it turns out, will you?"

"Sure, Honey."

"My name isn't Honey, it's George. Listen, if I come out and make sure those guys dig a straight trench, will you buy me a beer?"

As a scientist, Raye Dutra was accustomed to a sharp distinction between the real world and the things that people said or wrote or thought about it. As she and her colleagues plowed through the labyrinths of the nation's tax policies, they became increasingly appalled at the disjunctures between reality and these mental constructs—which, unfortunately, often had disastrous effects on reality. But, unlike many economists, Raye did not succumb to the soothing belief that money simply had a life of its own.

"My God, listen to this!" she said one day, bursting in on Vera. "Here's a capital-gains regulation for you! Hog investors can treat income from the sale of breeding stock as capital gains—which means you only have to pay tax on 40 percent of it. Know what that does?"

Vera shook her head.

"It means that if you are raising hogs your most profitable move is to sell your sows after only one litter, to maximize your tax-savings turnovers."

"So what? Somebody eats the sows anyhow."

"But later litters produce more and larger piglets, with less sow feed needed to produce each one. In other words, the regulation leads to less total meat per pound of feed, as well as per dollar. And then it siphons away tax dollars besides."

"How did the hog industry get that one through?"

"I can guess. But it isn't just the hog industry. It's an absolutely general pattern. The tax system is set up to *create* financial efficiency and productive inefficiency. Economic rationality becomes biological insanity."

"You sound almost like one of those corporate anti-tax people!"

"Not quite. When you push those folks, they turn out to be against tax regulations that help *other* people—especially poorer people—but they love things like this that will help *them*. If we manage to simplify the tax system so that pigs is just pigs and income is just income, they'll be screaming. Like stuck pigs."

"What other schemes are you cooking up, Raye?"

"We're nearly finished with the report on how tax policies have been favoring the use of virgin materials. We've figured out how to encourage the recycling of paper, metals, glass by turning those policies around. And we're proposing to revamp government purchasing and licensing and building-code regulations to favor recycled materials too. We've even got something for gardeners."

Vera looked particularly pleased at this last item, and Raye went on, "Yes, actually household recycling generally. You remember those statistics about the impressive weight of the domestic or home economy? Some aspects of it totally dwarf industrial activity. So any little things we can accomplish there will have enormous effects. For a start we want to issue tax credit chits through recycling centers for newspapers, cans and bottles. And households that use composting facilities and cut their garbage volume could claim a yearly tax deduction."

"The opposition will yell about tax cheaters. Phantom compost bins."

"Sure, but the amount from each household is small enough that a certain amount of cheating would easily be offset by the overall in-

171

creases in recycling income. Actually there will be so much money to be made that cities will probably begin to franchise the collection systems."

Vera sighed. "You're getting pretty clever at this business of harnessing greed to accomplish ecological good, aren't you? Well, be sure to leave us some scope for idealism, Raye. Maybe even a little sacrifice. People know that the most important things can't ultimately be measured by money."

Bob Glenn was a vice president of the Raussen Chemical Corporation. He was a large man, and with prosperity he had put on weight; his neck had grown bull-like; his ears sank into the flab behind his jowls. He had not risen to his present eminence by being nice to people, and subordinates felt their stomachs clutch if they noticed his attention had fallen on them.

One morning he was discussing with Terry, a young man on his engineering staff, a report Terry had prepared on a leaking Raussen dump in the central valley. Chemical wastes from pesticide and herbicide manufacturing, along with what the newspapers liked to call "a witches' brew" of other carcinogenic compounds, had been stored in drums which were then buried under a thin earth cover. This process had gone on from 1953 to 1976 at this site, and the older drums, some years earlier, had begun to corrode through—releasing chemicals into the underlying earth. Seepage was first detected when odd-colored liquids began to appear in nearby creeks during the wet season, and the company had set up a small monitoring program. Few people, luckily, lived in the immediate area, which was mostly farmland. But one farmer's drinking-water well, almost a half mile from the dump, had recently become contaminated; state health inspectors had closed it down. Upon further checks it was discovered that chemicals had migrated through the water table to irrigation wells in several directions from the dump. A small public outcry had been generated by local conservation groups and some television coverage had ensued when the farmer's wife delivered a malformed baby a few months later. But, as Raussen's public relations genius Morton Jensen had pointed out, malformed babies were born everywhere all the time, and nobody could establish any legally warranted cause and effect in this case.

172

"Actually," said Bob Glenn, "let's get Mort in on this for a few minutes. You sent him your report?"

"Yes, he's read it."

"Fine, fine." Glenn pushed buttons authoritatively, and directed a secretary to round up the PR man. "All right," he said when the three of them were assembled. "What the hell can we do about this thing?" He looked at Terry's report and frowned. "I don't much like this stuff about 'time bombs we must defuse'."

"Well, Bob," said Terry, squirming slightly, "I'm not married to that language. But it could get much worse out there if we don't make a serious containment effort." He looked at Jensen, who looked back without encouragement. "That stuff is getting into the aquifer in bigger and bigger quantities. Some of it's oozing toward the town well. At the present rate, it'll take a couple more years. But you can't really predict these things."

Glenn looked at Jensen. "Could we handle that, Mort?"

"You mean the state closing down the whole town's water? Christ, Bob! That's about ten thousand people screaming about cancer, deformed babies, Raussen poisoning them—you'd have women miscarrying in the streets just out of hysteria. Dozens of law suits. Those damn Survivalists would pick up on it and beat us with it in the media too."

"Yeah, but we've got to look at the bottom line. To do a containment job on that mess out there isn't going to be chickenfeed. We're talking about a half mill, maybe more."

"Actually," put in Terry, "it all needs to be moved—put onto a new sealed bottom. We can't just do a drainage ditch job."

Glenn's thick neck settled lower on his shoulders. "You're telling me to spend a half million dollars on the chance we might give some peckerwood's wife a miscarriage? That's not the kind of poker game I play in."

There was a brief and ominous silence, and then Mort asked, "Uh, look, Terry, is there anybody else up there generating wastes of the same general kind?"

Terry replied, "Not really. There's a small plastics plant, but—"

"Well, couldn't we say the stuff comes from *their* dump?"

Terry had a startled look. "You mean—?"

The two older men had pained expressions. Mort put his fingertips together and said, "Terry, things can be more complex than we imagine. Pollutants percolate around underground. Who knows where

173

they come from? We're asking you whether it could be *proved* that the stuff heading for the town well comes from our dump."

"Yes, it could. All they have to do is drill two holes about 20 feet deep."

"That's too bad," Glenn said. "Really too bad." He fell silent for a few moments. "All right," he said finally. "We'll sell the site. Purty it up a little, maybe even give it to the town for a park—they could use one, God knows! That'll give us some legal insulation, anyway, if it comes to that."

Terry said, "But Bob, selling the site won't stop that leaching. *Somebody*'s going to have to clean it up!"

Glenn looked at the engineer with the pity of one who deals in superior realities. "Yeah, I suppose they will. But I don't intend to have it be us." He nodded dismissal to the two subordinates, and Mort, from well-honed bureaucratic instinct, made it through the door first. As Terry approached the safety of the exit, Glenn stopped him. "Terry—one more thing. Next time you give me a report with something in it about a bomb, I'm going to stuff it right up your ass."

After Lou had discovered that the cell process was a two-step one, the conceptual problem had seemed much more straightforward. She had now managed to identify more than a dozen compounds produced when the cell ran "backwards." Then, starting with the ones that involved elements commonest in seawater, she added these one by one to new cells, and checked to see if output rose. She tried sodium compounds, magnesium, sulfur, chlorine, potassium, even bromine. Arsenic and phosphorus were already present in standard doping compounds and didn't produce the results she was getting. She even thought briefly of porphyrins—organic substances that had electrical properties and might exist in seawater. Seawater also contained manganese, zinc, rubidium, indium, barium—all in sufficient concentrations that the atomic ratios with the silicon would not be unreasonable. And some of their compounds were interesting, with little-known properties—not to mention their possible interactions with the silicon.

Rubidium looked promising because it had been used in primitive photoelectric cells and seawater contained 0.12 parts per million. Something might happen to it in contact with the arsenic or phos-

174

phorus. This lead, however, was soon proved unfruitful. Lou turned to other ideas. The process seemed to be sensitive to the total number of molecules available of *something*. When Lou had tried a cell conformation that passed more seawater over the cell surface, the output went up slightly. But that didn't mean every silicon atom was getting one of whatever it was. There was still the outside possibility that a relatively rare element was the key to the puzzle. Cesium? She focused, however, on iodine and barium, both highly concentrated in seawater and also capable of forming several intriguing compounds.

It was maddening to see the thing work and not to be able to tell why. For a while Dimmy was writing up some research reports so he was around a lot and he helped when he could. Bert developed a cascade pattern for experiments that cut down the number of new cells they had to prepare. But it was slow, tedious work. And Lou's promised six weeks had now shrunk to three.

It was morning rush hour in Sacramento. In the sixties and seventies the city had developed a suburban periphery occupying untold thousands of acres of prime farmland, but it still possessed a compact central residential ring made up of large old houses and modest-sized apartment buildings fronting on tree-lined streets. From these each morning streamed bureaucrats and legislators and aides and clerical workers, heading for the capitol area in buses, cars and a vastly increased fleet of bicycles. Sacramento is situated on a flood plain and is dead level—ideal bicycle territory. So numerous had the bicycles become (mostly reliable three-speeds with ample baskets for carrying briefcases or grocery bags) that they now sometimes outnumbered cars and traveled three abreast, taking up a street lane and moving at only slightly less than auto speed.

A group of five cyclists was approaching an intersection when a big car accelerated around them and made an unbraked right turn across in front of them. The brakes on the lead bicycles screeched as their riders made crash stops to avoid broadsiding the car. Then, furious, all five cyclists pedalled after the car, which they caught at a red light a block away.

One of them leaned his bike against the car's radiator grille. Another banged on the driver's window, while the others surrounded the car. "You trying to *kill* somebody?"

"Why no, I just, I—uh—" The driver looked around at the outraged cyclists.

"You know what we *should* do, don't you? You endangered five lives. You made a reckless and illegal turn from the wrong lane at a dangerous speed. You oughta have your goddamn license taken away! Do you think you *own* the streets just because you're sitting in that road hog? Do you think we don't pay the same taxes you do?"

The driver already had two moving violations on his record; this one could indeed cost him his precious right to drive. If they called a cop, there were plenty of witnesses. He looked worried. "I'm sorry, I know I shouldn't have done it, I—"

"You know what we'd really like to do to that fancy car of yours? We could kick out some tail lights, and put some cracks in that expensive windshield. We could put a knife through a couple of tires. Scratch up that nice shiny paint job. Think *that* would teach you a lesson?"

"Look, I promise to be more careful. I really didn't mean—"

"Yeah, that's what they all say, when there's a body under the wheels—some poor cyclist who was just trying to save *you* gas, you fucking *driver!*"

At this point a passing patrol car happened to notice the obstruction of the intersection. Soon Sacramento had another bicyclist, and another big car for sale.

Ralph Burns went to Corvallis to find out more on gasohol. He was nervous about going into University offices unprepared, so he spent a few hours in the library. He poked through the periodicals index and turned up a couple of magazine articles, but most of them were in obscure publications that the library didn't have. He got their addresses from a directory volume, however, so he could write away to them.

Ralph had dressed up in his town clothes and actually looked just like everybody else, but he felt a little out of place all the same. The campus was full of young people looking fresh and shiny and naive. He was glad he was carrying his manila folder because it made him look as if he belonged there, somehow. But he felt irritation, too. Why should a university be an enclave of leisurely, clean, healthy, well-to-do kids where a person like him felt out of place? His own children had gone here and he didn't begrudge the taxes he contributed to maintain it. But he instinctively disliked its isolation. Today, he knew, as he went from office to laboratory to library, he would have to insist—quietly but stubbornly—on his right to have the university serve him as well as the corporations that provided its research grants and the federal government that set its research priorities. He figured he'd start in the Ag Engineering building. If they didn't know anything about gasohol, he'd try Biology. In some cubbyhole or other he'd find somebody who could at least tell him how to go about looking for what he needed to know.

After Ralph had amassed what information existed on small-scale fermentation and distillation, he and his friends called on Hank Latham. Working in Ralph's barn and using piping and pumps and parts mostly scrounged from here and there, they assembled a fermentation rig. It was an improvised-looking contraption, but it was easy to fill and empty; it could be warmed by either a small fire, an alcohol flame, or propane. Then they hung up the government letter of exemption and began to put together the still. It too could use a variety of heat sources and was designed to be operable at different times of the year, sometimes using air cooling and sometimes water for its condensation cycle. It stood in Ralph's barn like a small misplaced section of an oil refinery, a maze of ungainly pipes and tanks and coils.

The inauguration of the still had to await the fermenting of some moldy grain and half-rotten apples that the farmers collected. The daytime temperatures were still high enough that this process took about a week with no added heat applied to the fermenting mixture. Ralph went out and stirred it occasionally and checked the surface to make sure gas bubbles were still rising satisfactorily. Finally he was able to phone Latham and tell him it looked ready for filtering and distillation.

The entire group of farmers assembled that evening, excited. They were all supremely practical men who had survived in a period when independent farmers were being subjected to murderous pressures from economic forces, government policies, and the competition of massive agribusiness corporations. They had seen many of their brothers sell out and leave the land. They were tired of having to play by other people's rules, and they saw gasohol as a means of recapturing a little of their lost independence. They gathered around the still, helping Latham to make a few last adjustments before the fire was lit.

177

It took a while for the still to reach operating temperature, and there was a good bit of joking at Latham's expense. He remained unruffled, however, and busied himself cleaning and re-cleaning a small glass, into which he placed a wad of cotton wool. Finally a few drops and then a thin stream of clear liquid began to flow from the condenser outlet. Latham captured some in his glass. He passed it under his own nose, then around the group. Nobody quite dared to taste it. "It looks like alcohol, it smells like alcohol, and I'm sure it would taste like alcohol," said Latham. "But what we want to know is, does it *burn* like alcohol?" With this he lighted a match and tossed it onto the damp cotton wool.

A small blue flame flared up. The group cheered, and Ralph Burns noted with satisfaction that the stream of alcohol continued to run steadily into the storage tank. He went into the house and brought out his bottle of whiskey. The men passed it around, watching fascinated as the still dribbled its precious output. Finally they began to break up. Ralph leaned against his barn. "Listen, everybody," he said, "let's not tell Exxon, okay?" There was a last burst of laughter in the Oregon night.

In the ensuing months word of what Ralph and his friends were doing spread by gossip in feed stores and at co-op fuel outlets. Ralph was a meticulous book-keeper and he could demonstrate that he was producing fuel considerably below market prices, and could do so even if he had to pay for the material he fermented. Of course, as he pointed out, his system had been constructed largely from surplus items; if you had to buy the equipment and borrow the money for it, the figures would not look so good. This, however, did not mean much to resourceful small farmers. Individually and in groups, they set about building their own systems.

The process did not require refined, precarious high technology, or the expensive engineering talent that such technology springs from, or an elaborate division of labor to manage. Fermentation is a natural process that has been utilized by untutored human beings for several thousand years; distillation is a technique that any highschool student can carry out. The necessary equipment could be improvised cheaply anywhere. There was no particular economy of scale pushing toward construction of enormous gasohol plants, and there were strong reasons for the farmers to wish to retain close control over this independent source of fuel in an era when gas supplies were in danger of periodic interruption.

In time Ralph learned that sophisticated economists had studied the process. Basing their figures on costs reported by large companies that bought fermentation ingredients on the open market and produced high-purity ethanol for vodka or for laboratory use, they had concluded that gasohol was uneconomic. Only in footnotes did they acknowledge that for farmers with "waste" biomass material available for fermentation and for fuel, the situation might be rather different; wastes, or produce that could not be sold in the fluctuating markets except below production cost, did not figure in their equations.

But Ralph Burns, sipping his whiskey and doing his accounts, knew that he had reduced his outlays for fuel by about five percent, while producing enough fermentation yeast by-product to cut his cattle feed outlays a couple of percent too. He was still paying rising prices for the nine-tenths of each gallon that was gasoline. But he was also preparing to rebuild several farm machine engines so they could burn pure alcohol, as racing cars did. During World War II, he remembered, the Germans had used alcohol for their tanks. And damn it, this was a war too.

The Survivalists, recognizing that traditional American politics tended to work from the top down, expended a great deal of effort in encouraging popular participation in their new movement. They had worked out a federation network structure that fed people's ideas, needs and perspectives upward to the party's central committee. Like mushroom spores so light they can float through the air for miles, Survivalist ideas had penetrated every town and city and neighborhood in the Northwest. Now Survivalist organizers helped them take root and grow. In some places party chapters were set up to cover a whole small town. In larger communities there were a number of neighborhood organizations. Sometimes people who had started working together for other purposes gradually developed a political identity and began to call themselves Survivalists. In other cases new groups formed, brought together by the usual techniques of meetings, pamphlets, posters, leaflets. But always, as Vera Allwen said in one her broadcasts, the emphasis was on the direct and personal.

"You may have a hopeless feeling about politics—as many Americans do. The idea of a new party may not exactly fill you with en-

179

thusiasm if you think it means just more speeches, more compromises, more meetings. You may not really enjoy talking or even thinking about politics.

"Well, we who have formed the Survivalist Party have many of the same feelings, and that's why we are a different kind of party. We don't ask you to 'support' us with votes and then forget about us for four years. We ask you to *join* us. That doesn't mean signing a form, as it does with the Democratic and Republican parties. It means linking up with people and actually doing things together, things that make sense to you—whether that's to form a neighborhood childcare service or to try and pass legislation to protect our food and water supplies from chemical contamination. It means talking frankly about what matters to you, and what can be done about it. We want you to realize that, in the end, power over this society is in our hands, and we can exercise it if we want to. What's more, we can start doing it tomorrow morning.

"Now that's a large statement, obviously, and I owe it to you to spell it out. Here is how we Survivalists think about it. It's easy to feel that all the important decisions and actions are taken by people in high places—those are the things that get written about in the newspapers and reported on television. Big plans, strong statements, conflict and controversy—all that.

"But have you noticed too that for all this noisy drama, things tend to remain pretty much the same? Well, there is a reason. A country is like a huge, heavy wheel that's spinning, and it's made up of the habits and expectations of all of us. No single politician, no corporation no matter how powerful, no single bank has much power to alter the rotation of that wheel. Its resistance can be overcome only if very large numbers of us change our ways of doing things.

"If *that* happens, we see the rise and fall of whole institutions and industries. If we decide to buy smaller, more fuel-efficient cars, which our auto industry can't or won't produce, that industry declines drastically. Huge corporations go bankrupt. If the food industry can't or won't produce foods free of additives, preservatives, flavorings, colorings and other questionable ingredients, then a new natural foods industry springs up to displace it. And if we come to recognize overwhelming needs for pure air and water, for the conservation of our few remaining wilderness areas, for the rehabilitation of our cities, and our politicians do not move toward providing these things—we throw them out and find politicians who will.

180

"Now what's important about these huge, slow changes is that we *all* participate in them every day, whether we think about it or not. And basically all the Survivalist Party invites you to do is to become conscious of this process and participate in it with your friends in a systematic way. Your actions will add themselves to the actions of millions of other people, so it doesn't even make that much difference what you choose to concentrate on. As the proverb truly says, 'Every little bit helps.' You don't have to feel guilty if you're not saving the world all by yourself. You can just do your small fair share, and added to all the other shares it *will* change the world. It isn't necessary for everyone to do the same thing. What is necessary is for everyone to do *something*.

"Let me give you some practical examples from daily life. You may be concerned, for example, with crime. Well, the single most effective thing you can do, which also happens to be an enrichment of your daily life, is to organize a neighborhood association so that people on your street get to know each other. Then they can learn to trust and help each other and keep an eye on strangers or suspicious characters. Your neighborhood association could be a Survivalist Party chapter—we can give you some advice and help in getting started—but you can also just do it yourselves.

"Or say you are concerned about food. As a region we need to shift away from our unhealthy level of meat and fat intake, which is particularly energy-consumptive, and redevelop our vegetable-growing areas close to cities—both for greater freshness and so we're not so vulnerable to oil shortages. But in your own private life, even if you live in a heavily built-up city area, you can do your part by finding some place to grow zucchini and tomatoes and beans. You might form a community garden with neighbors and friends. You can study non-chemical methods of fertilization and control of insects. Here again, you will have a lot of fun by learning to do things in better ways—but you will also produce a lot of inexpensive, fresh, tasty pure food. You'll get to know people while doing it, and you'll decrease your dependence on the commercial food industry, which is more interested in its profits than it is in your health.

"Every day offers us many small choices that are more important than we think. We can drive to work—or take the bus or walk. We can eat foods with less sugar and fat—saving money and improving our health. If you love trees, you can help people in your neighborhood to choose and plant them—they're amazingly cheap and make a

181

lasting contribution to your community, in shade or fruit or nuts or beauty. If you work in an office or factory or a warehouse, don't just accept its ways of doing things as fixed—get together with people and analyze what's being done wrong. Then work out how, in the better world that we have to create for ourselves—because nobody else is going to do it for us—you would run it better.

"There is good work for us all to do, no matter where or how we live. So do what you can, what feels appropriate in your life situation. Do what brings you the deepest satisfaction. Join us or work alongside us; we all need each other. We *can* take charge of our lives, little by little. We *are* this country. We love it and must make it run to benefit our health, our security, our happiness, our freedom. We live here. Let's begin to live right."

Lou came to her mother's place one afternoon in an uncertain mood. "Here I am," she said, "planning my adulthood ceremony, and I don't really know how I'm going to live afterwards."

"You look upset, my dear Lou."

"Well, it just hit me today. I've been assuming that I'd go on living out at Roger's, I guess. But I'd still be playing a child's role there. So maybe I ought to move out. But I don't know where to go!"

Jan knew that her daughter, who was ordinarily so self-confident and self-propelled, also had crises of confidence, just as she herself did. She had half been waiting for this one. She controlled her natural impulse to invite Lou to come live with her—better, she thought, for Lou to bring up that possibility herself if she wanted to.

"I also realized that I don't really remember how you started living the way you do. I was only about eight, wasn't I?"

"Yes, just past eight. Shall I tell you the story, all in one piece?"

"Oh, please do, Mom. I need clues!"

"Let's make a pot of tea and get comfortable. I don't want to over-simplify it." They assembled cups and mint tea and then settled down in some old soft chairs. Jan was a large, physical woman; she had Lou's curly hair. When she folded her legs under her, it seemed to give her the power to spring, like a cat. "I have to begin with the beginning, which was why I didn't want to live out at Bolinas any more. You understand that well enough, I think—how I had gotten fed up with monogamous marriage and was trying to concentrate

182

more of my energy on creative work. Roger and I didn't want to try some kind of non-monogamous arrangement. Neither of us thought we could stand it if we were still living together. So—" Jan paused and sighed and then continued. "So we decided to try living apart. It was a shock; your change of abode won't be nearly so bad! And we were both worried about the effect it would have on you, of course. So we wanted to make sure both of us had full, solid supportive environments to bring you to. That wasn't much of a problem for Roger. He started seeing Carol pretty soon after I left."

"That must have been hard for you."

"No, actually it was a relief. Till he met her he always really wanted to get back together. We did keep on sleeping together occasionally, but I started sleeping with other people too, and he couldn't stand that. And he couldn't stand it that he couldn't stand it, either, because he knew it was my right. He fought his own possessiveness as well as he could." Jan shrugged. "By that point, a lot of men were already being more possessive than their women—the roles had switched. Anyway, from the moment I decided to move out I knew two things: I didn't want to live alone, and I didn't want to move in with some other man. I had to invent a new alternative.

"It was my work that kept leading me along. I wanted to have a space where I could live and work, both. That meant a big space, and something other than a conventional house—which I couldn't afford anyway because I only wanted to put in part time at a money job. So then I heard about this warehouse for rent, and it sounded good. Of course I had models—I knew artists in other places around the Bay who had taken over run-down places or commercial space that wasn't being used. And so what happened was that once I got hold of the place I realized I couldn't really make the rent. I had put all my share of the money that Roger and I divided up into building the partitions to make my bedroom and bathroom, putting in the kiln and the ventilation system, and so on. Then I was stuck.

"So I looked around for help. About that time Marcia was breaking up with her first husband and she needed a place to live."

"You turned to Marcia first?"

"There's a whole other side to Marcia. You know her as just a suburbanite, always giving cocktail parties. She does do that, especially now that she's married to Marty. But at that time she read a lot and was always trying to figure life out. Very dramatic—we had good talks. Anyway, she really needed help. So she moved in. And that was a big help to me. I mean at 55 she wasn't about to live in a filthy artist's studio, and she had the money to buy carpets for the living areas and that super stove, and of course to enclose her own bedroom and bathroom—that whole northeast corner of the place. And she brought a big group of new men around. Some of them were married, sixty-ish. Some of them were younger than I was. There was a lot of intrigue—it was like living in one of the novels Marcia was always reading. I used to have to console the men she dumped. And she had terrible judgment—she always dumped the really promising ones who had brains and something to say. Some of the most interesting men I have as friends now, I owe to Marcia."

"That's certainly news to me! —But then she moved out?"

"No, not for about two years. And in the meantime we added to the crew. Janine came next. Janine and Kevin. At least Janine wasn't coming out of a marriage. She was just an independent artist—doing those huge tapestries and making out pretty well with them—even selling them to banks for their lobbies! She had found herself at 35 and never married and decided to have Kevin by herself. After he was born she had tried living by herself with him, but it was driving her crazy: enormous problems with child care while she worked, babysitting at night so she could get out, the usual story. You liked Kevin a lot and were really good to him. That mattered a great deal in Janine's coming here—since you were around most weekends, it gave Kevin some live-in child company. And I could understand Janine's problems since I had most of them myself. We made a good team, subbing for each other. And I learned Lesson One about joint living arrangements: you have to approve of each other's ways of relating to children or you're going to have a lot of serious trouble.

"Janine took over the southeast corner and built her room, and Kevin's loft space over that. So that left the fourth corner unbuilt. We put in the skylights about that time, and the water tank along the roof—incidentally, it's about time to close the flap, don't you think?"

Lou got up and went over to the pulley arrangement that opened and closed the insulating shutter flap. During the day the sun warmed a huge pan of water, 30 feet long, built into the roof and covered with black plastic sheeting. By the time the sun had lost its force, as it had by now in the late afternoon, the water in the pan was too hot to touch. Closing the flap at this time ensured that the water's heat did not radiate off into space during the night but instead slowly diffused downward into the building. Jan was very proud of this arrangement;

184

it was not original with her but it had been easy to build because of the heavy beam structure of the warehouse roof. It provided soft, even warmth for the main living areas; the stove was only needed for rainy periods and sometimes in the mornings.

"By this time," Jan resumed, "we had begun to realize that we had stumbled into a good thing in a lot of other ways too. We were spending about half of what people who lived in conventional ways spent per capita on gas and electricity and food. We shared expensive stuff like stereos and cars. Sometimes we even wore each other's clothes. And we had better lives—we all felt our social lives had greatly improved since we stopped trying to maintain separate, isolated existences. Of course we had quarrels, and sometimes they were painful. But so did 'normal' families. We felt we had more lively friends, more vital social relationships, more contacts with the outside world, more freedom to manage our time sensibly, more energetic and productive lives—and more exciting sex lives—than women we knew who had typical marriages. It began to look pretty permanent—Marcia and Janine and Kevin and you part-time and I. Marcia would get into some hot affair and talk about leaving, but she was still around. So we began looking for another person. At the beginning we expected it would be another woman. But then Gary heard about it and came to ask if he could join us."

"That must have been a big issue."

"It really was. We didn't know what to do. We all really *liked* Gary, too. That almost made it worse—we didn't know what would happen if one of us got involved with him. In a house that can hold ten or twelve people, having paired couples can be fine, but at that point we were all jealously guarding our independence. In fact I used to make it a point to have three concurrent lovers, so none of them would get the idea he could take over. —I don't know if you realized that."

"I just remember seeing a lot of men around!"

"But you probably didn't recognize there was a sort of system to it."

"No. I do remember once, though, you were having a fight with Paul and you kept saying 'But Paul, it isn't *your day*'!"

"Well, when I was living like that I felt the need for some kind of schedule. Paul wanted to be able to drop in any time. He fell in love with me and began to get crazy ideas—he couldn't face the fact that I was not in love the same way with him. I loved him in certain ways, but that wasn't enough. He couldn't even stand that Marcia and I were so close. He'd come over and we'd be talking, and he'd manage to break up the conversation. If he saw us giving each other a hug, he'd accuse me of being lesbian. In fact that's how I finally got rid of him—I told him I was entering a bisexual phase."

"You never told me about that."

"Well, about that time I did have a serious affair with a woman. She lived in San Francisco—you don't know her. A very beautiful, very elegant person. We had wonderful times. But I've never found it possible to put myself forward as a bisexual person. Even if we really all *are* capable of bisexual behavior, most people can't handle the idea. You can have bisexual flings or bisexual friendships that involve occasional sex, but mostly you still have to choose between presenting yourself as straight or gay. There isn't any in-between social world. Yet."

"So it isn't just sexual preference—who you like to make love with?"

"That's very important, of course, but even more it's who you associate with, who you identify with—and that begins to define who you meet, who you sleep with."

"So you decided to stay in the straight world."

"Yes. I put my sexual feelings for women into my art, I guess. And I like men too well to give them up. Though I can understand my women friends who just think men aren't worth all the damn trouble! Well, back to Gary. By that time, we had realized that what we were doing was constructing a sort of family for ourselves. Marcia would probably be leaving, but then people leave every kind of family—and she'd still be a friend. The rest of us were settling down for the long haul. We didn't want to make mistakes. So we talked about Gary, and with Gary, for a month. He was a writer, not a visual artist, and we liked that, for variety. It turned out that Gary wanted to keep his sexual life out of the house and didn't have sexual designs on any of us. In fact he was more certain on that point than we were. Janine even made a wee play for him but he didn't respond. Finally we all felt settled and it seemed natural that he would move in. So that took the fourth corner and filled us up."

"But Marcia did leave. When was that?"

"Not for almost a year. She met Marty and started spending a lot of time in the city. Then Marty would go away on a business trip and she'd come back home. Or they'd fight—Marcia has always had a sharp tongue—and she'd tell him she could never live with him, that

186

living here was essential to her independence. Which was true, of course. Marty wanted her to be his hostess."

"But why did she decide to do it, then?"

"I'm still not quite sure. She does love Marty, for one thing, and he's quite a touching man under all that business bullshit. And Marcia likes to have things altogether her own way, so when he offered to buy her a house and let her run it just the way she wanted to run it, it must have seemed worth it to her. And besides, she is a very *good* hostess. She doesn't just make sure everybody has drinks—she gets things to happen at those parties.

"So she announced she was leaving. It was really awful—she was our first loss. It was like the break-up of a marriage. We all cried a lot, tried to argue with her—all that. You and Kevin didn't like it much either. She promised to live as near by as she could, and come have lunch once a week. And she does, you know, but it's not the same. I miss her." Jan looked sad, and Lou was touched.

"It must have been hard to find someone to take her place," Lou said thoughtfully.

"Very hard," Jan replied. "For one thing, we had enjoyed having some age spread. I was about 31, Janine was 36 or 37, Gary was maybe 25. We wanted either somebody older, maybe Marcia's age, or somebody around 20. So when Miriam turned up, we were really pleased—she was probably almost 60, and clearly a very wise and warm person. She wanted to establish her practice in the building, and that made some problems—we had to add that room on the corner and the little waiting room and terrace outside it. And do a little soundproofing, since she works best in a really quiet environment."

"I can remember helping build that room. She used to give us all massages afterwards. I especially remember her hands, how cool and strong they were. And how she closed her eyes when she worked on you. I used to imagine she saw into my body with her hands."

"Well, that's what *I* think she does, too! She became a sort of grandmother figure in the household. And so we settled down into the pattern you're familiar with from the last four or five years."

"And it'll go on like this?"

Jan laughed. "Unless it changes! —You mean, do I want something else? No, I don't. This suits me better than anything else I can think of. I don't want to be married again—I'm too attached to my own ways for that. I don't want to live alone: it's lonely and scary and

187

not safe. I want other people to look after, who will also look after me when I need it. I want to be able to work, and this system lets me do that. It gives me a kind of family. We plan to live together indefinitely. And if it doesn't last forever, well, these days, what does? We've already lasted longer than the average marriage, you know!"

Lou looked at her mother. "You're such an optimistic person! You just go ahead and *do* things, don't you?"

Jan lifted her eyebrows. "I've never felt there was much alternative," she said. "I'd rather go ahead and do something, and think about it afterward, than sit around thinking about it to the point where I don't do *any*thing. —It gets me in a certain amount of trouble, of course."

"I guess I'm like you in that, huh? —I'm glad you're my mother! I couldn't imagine a better mother to have." Lou's hand reached out for Jan's and they sat there together, not needing to say anything more.

Nick Ballard was in Sacramento talking to legislators and labor lobbyists about ways of extending the Survivalists' successful foray into that most intractable of American problems, housing. In a government cafeteria he ran into Bill King, head of the local developers association. Last Nick had heard, Bill was running sprawled-out tracts through the nearby foothills, having earlier paved over some thousands of acres of prime valley farm land. The two men knew each other from previous encounters. Bill recognized that Nick was a skillful political operator—smart and shrewd and practical despite a lot of hare-brained ideas. Nick couldn't help being impressed by Bill's phony western style: broad-shouldered and sun-tanned, he affected a cowboy hat and boots, though the only things he rode were his gold-colored Toronado and his office calculator. As Nick knew well, Bill's corrals were the corridors of the county offices and his watering hole was the public treasury.

"Hello, you old horsethief. You look thinner—we must be doing something right."

"Nicky, tell me, what have you people got against us, anyway?"

"Why, not much of anything, Bill. Except that you've covered half the landscape of California with your stucco boxes. Everything so far apart you can't get anywhere without a car. About fifty billion dollars worth of trash on the landscape, which we're going to have to clean up someday. That's all."

"Well, I plead guilty. We used to call it Progress."

"I know you did. But that era is over. You guys have got to learn some new tricks. Build near the jobs. Build dense."

"Well, shit, Nicky, what makes you think we can't do that? People wanted sprawl, we gave 'em sprawl. People start to want dense, we'll give 'em dense. We don't give a damn what they want, we just want to make some *money* out of it! We think it's great if their wants change—gives us something new to do. Might even be more profitable. The only thing we cannot tolerate is *wantlessness*."

"Yeah, I know. And you won't have to confront that for a while yet."

"Listen, we can live with these ideas of yours. Just give us the chance. Shared-wall construction? Hell, yes, gives a higher profit rate! Less hot asphalt for streets and parking? Sure, lower land costs per unit. Passive solar heating? You bet your sweet ass. We'll even throw in some trees. But no more 'Walnut Acres'—it'll be 'Walnut Courts' from now on!"

"Bill, you're a prince. But you know what? Sooner or later we *are* going to get you. Ever hear of employee ownership?"

"Sure. Puttin' the monkeys in charge of the zoo."

"Giving power to the people who do the work. One of these days you're going to wake up and find that you're just an employee, with only one vote, just like every carpenter in the outfit."

"I'll move back to Ohio first. Where free enterprise is rewarded."

"That's fine. But if you hang around these parts, you'll have to work for a living like everybody else."

"Americans will never stand for that."

"Well, then you just get up and run for the board of directors in your company and see if you can persuade the boys to give you a free ride."

Most Bolinas houses had watchdogs, and some hours after midnight on a foggy night Roger was awakened by persistent barking. Rousing himself, he decided it was coming from the houses to the east. "Might just be the dogs after a raccoon," he said to himself hopefully. But the barking did not die down. Roger got out of bed.

He debated whether to turn on a light. On the one hand, if intruders were about a light might discourage them; on the other hand, they'd probably just come back some other night. Maybe it was best to get it over with now? He woke Carol. Then he went into Lou's room and shook her awake. "I'm afraid we have visitors," he said.

"Shit," Lou replied, groggily. "All right, I'm getting dressed."

"Everything secure?" asked Roger. "No papers lying around in the lab or on the roof or under the bed?" Lou fished around under the bed, just to be sure.

"Nope," she said. They all put on clothes and shoes and began peering out various windows. Lou saw a shadowy figure slip past the end of the garage. At least they weren't coming in with helicopters and playing Wagner on loudspeakers—this was a sneak attack! Just the sort of thing, in fact, that Roger in his paranoid way had fantasized about. Carol got a glimpse of a dark figure half hidden against a cypress tree. "Should we try the PA system?" she whispered to Roger. "You know, 'You have been seen, the police are on the way to arrest you for trespassing—'"

"No," said Roger. "Besides, they've cut the phone line—it's dead."

A chill went down Lou's back. They sounded like professionals; the situation could get serious. She and Roger had never agreed on whether a raiding party, if one came, would probably be armed or not. If they were caught as burglars, being armed meant obligatory jail sentences. It might not seem worth it. Then again, the types likely to be hired for such a task might not regard jail sentences as all that fearsome. But a cat-burglar approach seemed the most probable, so that what what the Swifts had mostly prepared for. They continued to watch and listen. The garage had only one door, clearly visible from a nearby house window. It had a burglar alarm on it, and a warning plaque next to the lock. Roger saw a figure approach the door, illuminate the plaque with a tiny flashlight, and hesitate. Soon another person joined him, and they seemed to confer in whispers. This was good, Roger thought; they would try the roof first. Were there others? Maybe a lookout somewhere, but these two seemed to be the only ones actually near the house. At any rate, it was time for action. No use letting them wreck anything on the roof! They were standing by the ladder now, ready to go up—perhaps made uneasy by the intermittent continuing barks from next door.

Roger went into Lou's bedroom and climbed into a sort of cockpit

190

just under the roof. There he took a loaded shotgun from an improvised rack. Stationing himself carefully, he looked down at Lou and waved. Lou pushed three times on a button attached to a wire that came up through the floor. This was the community alarm signal, wired underground to adjacent houses. Then they heard the creaking of feet on the rooftop decking, and a red light went on, activated by Mike's rooftop alarm system. Lou threw a wall switch. Instantly powerful flood lights illuminated the roof and the whole area surrounding the house. At the same moment Roger pushed up the trapdoor over his head and covered the two men with his shotgun. Blinded by the light, they froze. Then one of them bolted for the ladder. As he disappeared over the edge of the roof, Roger fired one barrel over his head. Then he covered the other man. "Move and you're dead!" he growled. The first man, going hurriedly down Lou's ladder, came to a rung that was suddenly missing (because Lou had given a yank to a small wire attached to it) and hurtled off balance toward the ground. On the way down, however, his leg passed into a cable loop hidden under the remaining ladder rungs, and Lou pulled on this cable, as he fell, with all her might. Now he was hanging upside down by the heel from the roof edge, flailing about and cursing.

At this point other shadows approached the house from all directions—neighbors with assorted and excited dogs and carrying an impressive arsenal of firearms. No other intruders were discovered in the neighborhood. The two whom Roger and Lou had captured were duly hauled off to the county jail. The neighbors took the precaution of searching them thoroughly before the sheriff's men came; they had no identification, no papers, no guns or other weapons—only a collection of small housebreaking tools. However, an unknown car was found parked downtown, and an ingenious Bolinesian promptly broke into it. Under the seat was a notebook with sketches of the Swift house, indicating the layout of Lou's lab and the rooftop cell array. The notebook also contained telephone numbers. One of them turned out to be the office of a Mr. Barber at Omni Oil; another was an FBI office.

These facts were conveyed not only to the district attorney but also to the press, which loved the story: "DID OIL COMPANY BURGLARIZE LAB OF HIGHSCHOOL SCIENCE WHIZ KID?" "FBI IMPLICATED IN BOLINAS CAPER." Both the oil company and the FBI issued firm denials of any connection to the case. It would certainly be some time until the links between the burglars and whoever had employed them could be

191

worked out. Meanwhile, Lou and Roger felt that at least for a while they were relatively safe from further attempts. All the same, they never kept any research documents around the house.

Whitey Whitehead drove up to Portland looking for some action. He had heard about these big fountains in the downtown parks—lots of girls hung around there, just waiting to be picked up. So he washed his big old Dodge and headed for town.

When he hit the outskirts he got off the interstate and took the road along the river. There was a lot of building going on there—condominiums and shops and offices—and a new waterfront park where warehouses and old factory buildings had once been. There seemed to be an awful lot of bicycles around—and not ridden just by kids, either; he saw a couple of really old people cycling too. They pedalled along the highway inside a row of little round white markers. Must be one of them bike paths, thought Whitey. Chickenshit bike riders, taking up good road space!

He drove on downtown. But when he neared the first group of large buildings he came to an intersection blocked off by some kind of barricade. There was a sign there, but Whitey didn't bother to read it. He cut hard left and roared up the hill, figuring to make a right at the next corner. But it was blocked off too, except for a single lane marked BUSES AND TAXIS ONLY. Damn, thought Whitey, this must be that mall crap I heard about. He went another block and stopped: that street was blocked too. A pedestrian crossed next to the Dodge, and Whitey leaned out. "Hey, buddy, what's going on—I want to get on downtown, and everything's blocked!"

The walker was young and lanky; he strolled over, smiling faintly. Whitey didn't like the smart-ass look on his face. "You're on the edge of the car-free zone," the man said. "No private cars allowed downtown anymore. Free buses, though."

"For Christ's sake!" Whitey looked over at the narrow bus lane. "They ticket you, huh, if you just drive in?"

"They sure do. Fifty bucks. Best to park at the lot up there at the corner and take the bus. They come every couple minutes. Or just walk—it's only six or eight blocks."

"*Walk?*" said Whitey. "What the hell are cars for, buddy?"

The man shrugged. "Not much in downtown Portland, that's for sure," and began to walk away.

192

"Hey," said Whitey, "you know where those fountains are?"

The man turned back. Now he seemed friendlier. "Why, yes," he said, "you're practically there! Two blocks down and on your right." Seeing Whitey hesitate, he added, "It's really worth the walk."

Whitey's jaw set. "We'll see," he said, and jammed his foot on the gas. He went up the hill to the parking garage, stopped in front of it, and studied the fees posted outside. "I'll be goddamned," he said. He turned around abruptly and headed back toward the interstate. He had noticed a roadhouse bar on the way in. He could park *there* for nothing, have a few drinks, decide what to do next. "Car-free zone, my ass," he muttered to himself.

In the early eighties, stimulated by federal grants, aircraft and electrical equipment corporations had begun developing large-scale wind machines for the generation of electricity. Their installations, however, like many other engineering projects attempting to deploy space-age technology for relatively mundane purposes, were plagued by exotic troubles. The huge scale of the machines required sophisticated and costly structural design, but the results still did not always meet the severe and fluctuating challenges of wind and storm. Giant blades developed metal fatigue and disintegrated, scattering fragments at high velocity. Support towers developed oscillatory vibration patterns that shook them from their foundations. Large blades moving at high speeds reflected broadcast television signals, causing loud distress in nearby communities, and sometimes they even produced an unnerving low-pitched noise. When breakdowns occurred, they were often catastrophic, taking a long time and heavy investment to repair.

These drawbacks did not cause the corporate engineers to rethink the scale of their efforts, however. They considered that the only realistic market for electric power lay in the utility companies, and those companies were interested in big machines. So were the bureaucrats in the federal research establishment, who wanted to serve the utilities. Mostly corporation people themselves, or used to dealing with corporation people and their university counterparts, they preferred operating in large institutional settings. When such people contemplated utilizing wind or solar energy, they thought not of widespread resources that ordinary people and their communities could use, but of devices to be constructed at central points, subject to cor-

193

porate control and capable of extracting massive profits. Unless such profits were certain, they considered new technology "premature."

Small entrepreneurs and inventors thus got little attention and few grants, especially after the national government abandoned its flirtation with solar and wind energy alternatives. But they studied the failures of the big machines closely. One small company in California, calling itself MiniWind, had been started by a trio of engineers who had become disgusted with working in big corporate engineering departments where their designs were always being downgraded by the sales and finance people. They had decided that an entirely different approach was likely to prove more satisfactory and more reliable. They therefore devised not one giant windmill which might be unreliable though elegant, but instead a windmill "farm" system, composed of elements that were simple, sturdy and forgiving. To minimize construction costs, they utilized components already available. Heavy-duty generators came from the truck industry; gearboxes and hubs and wiring and bearings were off-the-shelf parts too, mostly from the automotive industry. Only the blades and housings had to be specially fabricated.

To make assembly and repair easy, they went for modest size: each MiniWind machine would have a blade diameter of only about 20 feet, but there would be many of them, scattered over a whole hillside. Mounted on a piece of standard oilwell-casing pipe, supported by guy wires, the operating works could slide down to ground level for easy maintenance work. The soil need not be disturbed by massive foundations. Experimental installations that MiniWind constructed proved astonishingly reliable.

A number of small Western communities had succeeded, through ordinances that made contractors orient buildings for solar input, shade windows to avoid the need for airconditioning, and install other conserving measures, in reducing their per capita energy consumption—and thus the capital drain out of the community into the utility company's coffers. Encouraged by drops of 40 per cent in natural gas consumption and 25 per cent in electricity use, they now began studying the possibility of acquiring their own power distributing systems from the utilities (as a number of Western cities had done many years before, saving their citizens very large sums over the years). One of these towns, Rio Vista on the banks of the Sacramento River, decided to install a MiniWind generating facility. Several thousand wind machines would be built on nearby hills where, espe-

194

cially in summer, the winds blew strongly and steadily. (In fact they blew strongest on summer afternoons, precisely when airconditioning electrical demand peaked.)

The utilities fought the municipal take-over, but the citizens persisted. Construction of nuclear plants had required between five and ten years. The wind farm took little more than a year. Repairs proved cheap and rapid. Moreover, while individual machines broke down from time to time, the temporary absence of a few of them was insignificant in the output of the whole system. Thus virtually all its capacity was available all the time, while the breakdown of a large machine, like the refueling of a nuclear plant, created a serious and lengthy disruption to the power network of which it was a part. As it happened, this feature also proved some safeguard against sabotage. Shortly after the wind farm opened, several windmills were damaged at night and a destructive short-circuit was deliberately caused in the transformer yard. Rio Vistans suspected the power company might be behind the damage, but in any case repairs took only a few days.

More reassuring still, the Rio Vista wind farm's lifetime would be indefinite. Like a biological organism, it would be constantly repaired piecemeal as weaknesses surfaced. It would never get to the point where, like a nuclear plant after 20 or 30 years, it would have to be expensively decommissioned, abandoned, and buried under a mountain of concrete. Rio Vista people often went out to picnic on the grassy hillsides near their windmill farm and to fish in the river as it flowed past. Cattle grazed on the slopes. Little gravel roads used by the maintenance crews led out from the control building and maintenance shop, winding here and there among the irregularly scattered wind machines. Glorious feats of engineering might be in spectacular disarray elsewhere, but these humble machines turned quietly, their blades glinting in the sun, sometimes spinning leisurely, sometimes racing in a gust—producing power without belching sulfurous smoke or particulates, without fouling the river, without creating radioactivity, and without disturbing the heat balance of earth and atmosphere.

Marissa's brother Ben had always tried to boss her around. Perhaps that had helped give her a tough kind of independence, she sometimes thought: she had had to fight for it! But she still resented Ben's tendency to check up on her friendships or her relationships with men. As she sometimes accused him, it was as if after their father's death Ben had decided to appoint himself patriarch. He even took to spending evenings in the Italian restaurants of North Beach with Angelo's brothers, whom he had never had much use for earlier. But he would still drop around to see Laura and Marissa in the old family house.

One day when Marissa had come back to the city for a week with her mother, Ben came by for a visit. It proved rather hurried. Ben seemed distracted, and he had brought along a friend whom he introduced vaguely as Steve. Marissa took an instant dislike to Steve. He was obviously very smart, but he was also very self-centered. The conversation always somehow seemed to come around to how he understood everything better than anybody else. And he and Ben got into a competitive mood, talking about hang-gliding and the beauty of "big risks." After a bit of this Laura went to take a nap. Marissa excused herself and went out to the garden for a while to pick some lettuce. When she came back she heard the two men discussing something about centrifuges, but they stopped suddenly when she reappeared. Soon Steve had to go run an errand, and Marissa turned on Ben.

"You've been awfully secretive lately," she said. "What are you up to, anyway? Who is this self-appointed genius Steve? And what's this about centrifuges?"

Ben practically snarled at her. "What did you hear about centrifuges?"

"Just something about concentration processes. Using several centrifuges would make something go faster. What are you trying to concentrate?"

"Marissa," said Ben, "this is serious business. I want you to swear that you'll never mention to *any*body that you heard anything like that!"

Part of Marissa resented this request and wanted to argue. Part of her agreed that she had overheard something by accident and that it was only fair to keep quiet about it. Part of her was dying of curiosity about Ben's secret. And part of her was taken aback by the intensity of Ben's demand.

"You want me just to shut up without knowing why it's so goddamned important?"

"That's right. I can't possibly explain to you how important it is, or how dangerous it would be to all of us if you evened *mentioned* it!"

196

"Ben, are you into something criminal?"

"No, I assure you it's not criminal. It's not drugs. But it's something very big. Now will you swear?"

Ben was a large, rather awkward man. Sometimes, when they were children, he had used his superior strength against his sister. She was not afraid of him now, but she had learned to know when he was near the capacity for violence, and this, surprisingly, was one of those times.

"All right," she said. "I swear. But someday, I want to know what it was all about."

Ben smiled, a crooked sort of grin. "You'll know, all right," he said.

Traditional politicians were not in the habit of visiting sewage treatment plants, but because Vera Allwen understood such plants to be key elements in a future biologically stable food production system, she made it a practice to drop in on new ones. On such expeditions she took along a couple of people from the Ecotopia Institute and any journalists she could corral. Thus when a new and innovative plant in a suburb of San Francisco announced it was having a two-year anniversary celebration, Vera made it a point to attend. By now her public appearances were sufficiently newsworthy that a TV crew appeared at the party too.

People wandered around the facility, marvelling at the luxuriant growth of the hyacinth plants that extracted pollutant substances from the sewage stream, enjoying the steamy and not too odoriferous atmosphere under the solar-pillow plastic roof. They read the signs that explained the system to visitors. Once the only pretty part of a sewage plant had been the giant flares of methane gas. But the big fluttery yellow flames had been extinguished: now the methane was captured and used to run office heating equipment and giant dryers that turned sewage sludge into crumbly brown fertilizer powder. Working for the sewage district was still not exactly a glamor job, but it had become intensely interesting to certain young people, and Vera was thus happy to tour the facility, talking with the staff members. Nowadays a lot of them had degrees in ecological management rather than just sewer engineering. They realized that sewage was not a "waste" problem, but rather a resource to be used. They did computerized studies of inflow and effluent chemistry. They were alert to the hazards of chemicals and toxic metal wastes that industries liked to dump into sewer systems. They had come of age in the water-shortage era and instinctively knew you couldn't solve problems by washing them away somewhere. When Vera was asked to make a few remarks to the crowd, she praised this new generation for recognizing that "Dilution is no longer the solution to pollution." Once upon a time, Vera pointed out, nobody had really thought seriously about sewage—you just gave it primary treatment and washed it away downstream. People who said that valuable organic material was being wasted were laughed at as harmless lunatics. Then gradually the health problems and the sludge disposal problems mounted to the point where a few of the more imaginative engineers began to realize that the existing system couldn't really work much longer. But the solutions they proposed tended to be elaborate, partial, and hugely expensive, and sometimes they did not work. Gradually, over a period of several years, new ideas found supporters. The price crunch on chemically produced fertilizers became worse. Experiments were made with sludge drying and with innovative treatment methods. The prohibition of dumping toxic wastes into the sewers was investigated on a practical basis. Lawsuits and countersuits and legislation followed. In the end people interested in new and better ways usually prevail, and later nobody can quite remember why anybody ever wanted to do it differently. This was the normal way of change in our society, Vera said. And what was important to remember, in the stage where you're still being laughed at, is that if your cause is just, it will win in the end.

This particular plant, Vera learned, had been much sought after as a neighbor by a golf course adjacent to the community, since sewage plant effluent was now recognized as a prime source of irrigation water. Instead of desperately seeking remote dumping sites to dispose of sludge and effluent, the community had thus been able to bargain competitively on contracts and pipeline routes. In the end, the plant had been located on abandoned land that had once been used by wartime factories. It was bulldozed back to its natural contours and with spray irrigation had become a fantastically productive pasture—making the surprised community a considerable exporter of milk.

In her ceremonial speech, the manager of the plant noted that its hyacinth pond system, once thought "experimental," had now been duplicated at dozens of sites along the West Coast. She gave impressive figures of the tons of cattle fodder derived from the chopped-up hyacinth plants. "Our fertilizer," she boasted, "is the most toxic-free in the entire four-county area." It had long been certified for use on vegetable gardens as well as lawns and fruit trees. About 40 percent of the region's sewage output was now being recycled back onto the land as fertilizer—to produce more food, to produce more sewage, to produce more sludge, and so on, indefinitely, in what the biologists at the Ecotopia Institute called, with the satisfaction of those who have seen the good and the beautiful, a "stable-state system."

As Vera pointed out in her interview with the TV crew, if these practices could be expanded to cover the entire agricultural and sewage system of the region, they would ensure that Ecotopian food production could continue on a bountiful basis for thousands of years, as it had in Europe and China "Ultimately," she reflected, "all societies are agricultural, despite the high technology they may develop. If we don't take care of this fundamental aspect of our region's biological health, we will not survive here for long. That's why the Survivalist Party puts so much emphasis on these neglected matters. Like a person, a society is what it eats. And if we recycle well, we'll eat well!"

Nils Anderson came from a solid Minnesota farm family; he loved the rich earth of the Midwest. He discovered early in life that he also had a good head for chemistry. After college he found a job with Farmchem, a large manufacturer of fertilizers, pesticides and herbicides. He was happy enough when the company asked him to relocate in the West. He married and had a child, but his relationship with his wife was difficult. Sometimes he would think of leaving the family. But then a business trip would take him out of town for a while and when he came back his wife looked very good to him again. In time, partly because he had found he enjoyed traveling and partly because it got him back closer to the land, he moved into the applications end of the business, working with farm advisors in the counties. These were men who supposedly educated farmers on what possibilities were open to them for combatting pests and increasing productivity. In practice, they sold products for the chemical companies. But at this period nobody was questioning the massive application of chemicals to American farm land (and to farm workers and neighbors) and Nils felt he was doing good work in the cause of feeding the country.

Even later, when alarms had been raised about the consequences of a chemicalized agriculture, Nils felt few doubts that what was going on was essential, even if perhaps not ideal. He felt he had had a well-spent life, and when he realized at 55 that he had been with Farmchem so long that he was eligible for favorable terms on early retirement, he seized the opportunity. He looked forward to doing a little teaching on the side, expanding his garden, maybe doing a few experiments he hadn't had the chance to carry out while he was working.

However, as soon as Nils retired, the relationship with his wife began to deteriorate. He no longer had the escape valve of his business trips. The annoyances he stored up against her took their toll, and they no longer had their passionate reunions to look forward to. In less than a year the marriage broke up; Nils found himself alone and with very little money.

Realizing he could not afford suburban living expenses, he sold everything and moved north to Mendocino County. He found a small, dilapidated cabin back in the hills which he could rent for virtually nothing in return for doing some fix-up work on it. He settled in, planted a garden, started raising a few chickens. As time went on, he found that the local people he enjoyed talking to were city refugees like himself. But most of them were young—hip men who wore denim and beads and headbands, and women who wore no bras or make-up—and it took him a year or so to understand that the differences between their ways and his were not insuperable.

The most difficult part of the process was his introduction to marijuana. Nils had always assumed that marijuana was a terribly dangerous narcotic. He had seen alcohol ruin the lives of some sales people he knew at Farmchem, and he had heard grim stories about teen-agers' destructive dependence on pot. But finally a friend did persuade him to try a few puffs. Nils had been afraid that, "under the influence," he might become deranged and violent. When he discovered that, quite to the contrary, the dope softened and quietened and loosened him, and that he had been in the grip of ignorant fantasies about it, his world view was shaken. It suddenly occurred to him that he might have been wrong about a whole series of things. He began to talk openly to people about drugs and sex. He let his beard grow and discovered it gave him some mysterious new appeal to women. And

200

he listened more carefully now to the people who talked about little plots of marijuana hidden out in the forests.

He had not realized that marijuana, a tropical plant, could thrive in Mendocino. But a few miles back from the coast the summer weather was blazing hot and the growing days quite satisfactorily long. By Nils's standards the soil wasn't much good, really. But if you found or created a little clearing, barely big enough to be visible from the air, you could grow marijuana as a cash crop and maintain a modest lifestyle on very little work.

There was, of course, a serious risk. Growing and selling dope remained a felony, though possession of small quantities was now a trivial misdemeanor. But the growers Nils talked to were used to the risks, even from the paramilitary invasion mounted each year by the state—which remained complacent about the damage caused by the middle-class drugs, alcohol and nicotine. Even the state didn't possess resources to cover the huge county with any realistic kind of surveillance. The planter of a confiscated plot probably had another one or two hidden away somewhere and wouldn't starve. Mafia narcotics dealers had never intruded into the Mendocino scene; it was too diffuse and decentralized. And among the few remaining loggers and other timber industry people a certain sympathy had grown up for the marijuana farmers. After all, as the lumber industry declined, they were bringing lots of new money into the county. Marijuana was rumored to be the county's second biggest industry now. That seemed to explain why, even though lumbering jobs were in decline as the old timber was finally all cut, the county's economy as a whole remained relatively stable, or even grew a bit. So a timber cruiser who happened to notice a little marijuana growing somewhere on a lumber company's land might keep quiet about it.

In this atmosphere of live and let live, Nils began thinking of growing some marijuana himself. He tried a few plants indoors as a starter. He read some of the surprisingly sophisticated books available about marijuana culture. He talked genetics with some of the growers. Marijuana, he discovered, was a very *interesting* species scientifically. His plants thrived, but he began to see some ways in which a more methodical approach could probably increase both yield and potency.

In the fall of 1987 Nils received a visit from his son John, now 23. John had done some college, dropped out, worked a little, drifted around, then gone back for a while to live with his mother, but that hadn't worked out. He couldn't seem to find anything he really wanted to do. When John arrived, he had expected severe chastising from a stern father who would chide him for not making anything of himself, or at least not going on to an advanced degree. Instead, he found a relaxed man who wanted to talk about living a just life, and contributing happiness to human beings, and the challenges of growing better dope! John couldn't believe it. He mostly stayed stoned for three days.

One morning Nils brought him coffee and said there was an important matter he wanted to discuss. "I've been thinking of starting a business, and I'm going to need a reliable partner. It just occurred to me last night that you might be the one. It would certainly give you something to do with yourself for a couple of years."

"What you up to?" asked John. The sun through the window hit his feet and warmed him; he sipped his coffee.

"Dope growing," replied Nils, and smiled at the expression on John's face. "Well, don't look so surprised. After all, I'm basically a farm person."

"Yeah," said John, "it's just that—"

"Can't get used to the idea of your father as a criminal, hm?"

"Oh, come on, Dad. It's just a big change. I mean it's as if you decided pesticides cause cancer."

"Well, as a matter of fact they do. I've had to admit that to myself."

"But you always used to have all these arguments about how nobody had ever proved—"

"Well, I've had more time to think, up here, and do more reading. I was wrong. *We* were wrong—the industry, the company."

John examined his father as if he had never met him before. "That must not have been easy to admit."

"No," said Nils, "it was not easy at all."

John sat quietly for a few moments, thinking how strange it was that a son might never really know his father until some stroke of fate changed his fortunes and brought a revelation like this: his father the dope farmer!

"What I've been thinking of," said Nils, "is a large greenhouse, against the hill where there's all-day sun. I'm going to need help building it, and running it—I've worked out a whole series of experiments. And we'll need to set up warning systems on the roads and other approaches. There'll be quite a lot to it."

John's eyes brightened. "Well, I happen to have taken some electrical engineering, you know."

202

"Yeah, that'll be fun for you. But there's a lot of dumb heavy work too. We're going to dig a cave back into the hill, and everything will grow on a sliding platform. The sheriff shows up, we slide it all back under the hill and bring out our tomato vines and green peas."

"That's pretty clever, but is it worth all the work?"

"I've got some botanical refinements in mind that will make it worth it. You can't do controlled experiments back in the woods."

"The world's best dope, huh?"

"Safest, Johnny. It doesn't do anybody any good to put smoke into their lungs. So I want to develop marijuana strains that give off the least tars and other junk. And ones you can make into a sort of tea."

"Paying for your earlier sins?"

"Something like that. You know the term they have up here, 'righteous'? It'll be righteous work."

By this time the penetration of Survivalist ideas into the Ecotopian territory was such that Raye Dutra's proposal for a heavy gasoline tax had been enacted by the state legislatures. In the absence of federal action, the states had reluctantly decided they themselves had to defend their weakening economies against the hemorrhage of oil dollars. There was a certain amount of public grumbling against the resulting higher prices at the gas pumps, but no concerted resistance, and gas consumption did indeed drop substantially. Some months after this success, with the economy already showing some faint signs of improvement, the Survivalists were emboldened to introduce a new measure which would tax cars themselves and assign the resulting revenue to improve bus, streetcar, taxi and train services.

At this, the automotive industry realized that it was under full-scale assault. It mounted expensive publicity campaigns all along the coast, aimed at preserving the holy right of "automobility." More important, a suit was filed in federal district court by an auto dealer named Madera, charging that the new law was an unconstitutional interference with interstate commerce: automobiles made in Detroit were being penalized in the Northwest. If the people of the Northwest wished redress against the alleged damages they were suffering from automobiles, Madera's lawyers argued, their only remedy was to appeal to Congress. The Western states were forbidden to apply unilateral regional measures that would discriminate against a particular commodity; the federal government had pre-empted the regulation of interstate trade.

The Madera case was quickly recognized as being potentially explosive in the same way as the Dred Scott case had been in the bitter conflict over slavery just before the Civil War. That case had made it clear that the Southerner-dominated Supreme Court was adamantly pro-slavery. The result was the formation of the Republican Party, largely as the vehicle for the anti-slavery movement. Now it was the Survivalist Party whose actions against the automobile (a "peculiar institution" at least as important in the nation's life as slavery had been) were posing agonizing constitutional issues.

As debated by lawyers, these issues might seem abstract—matters of arcane precedent and constitutional interpretation. But just as in the case of slavery, the issues became bitterly personal for ordinary people. Some argued that anti-car measures infringed on their personal freedom, which they equated with the untrammeled right to drive wherever and whenever and whatever they pleased. On the other side it was argued that the domination of the society by the automobile, through its impoverishment of the economy, its carcinogenic air pollution, its accident death toll, infringed on basic human rights to health and welfare. The possession and use of cars had thus become a central moral and political issue. It divided families, exacerbated class struggle, and further polarized the political machinery between the growing Survivalist power and the waning strength of the two old parties. Amid this growing ferment, the Madera case went on appeal to the Supreme Court of the land.

With the success of the Rio Vista installation, the MiniWind company began to have more orders than they could fill. By now about 50 people were working in the shop; this was a dramatic increase, since they had started out in a garage. The founding partners discussed the prospects with the rest of the staff. Should they go to the banks for expansion capital to build a bigger plant? How could they arrange things so that the company provided a good life for all of them?

Such questions had begun to seem quite natural among people who worked in the small, local-oriented firms that had been arising in the Bay Area. Often these firms were employee-owned, or at least managed by more democratic and open means than a traditional business.

From its beginnings in cultural industries like publishing or service industries like food stores and restaurants, this trend had spread into specialized science-based research and manufacturing companies. This new kind of company did computer program development and genetic engineering. They made camping equipment, woodstoves, furniture, garden implements and other fine tools, greenhouse kits. They produced exotic teas and herbal remedies and soaps and lotions. They brewed strong, tasty beer, and made wine—and taught their customers to make both on their own. They ventured into the production and distribution of locally grown organic foods. They were ignored by the ineffectual government bureaus that supposedly helped small businesses, and they soon discovered that government funds theoretically intended to foster innovation were in fact only available to large corporations whose record of innovation was poor and getting worse. So they were generally lean and efficient; they knew their markets intimately and learned to prosper in economic niches too limited to be of interest to a multinational conglomerate.

MiniWind's staff, after lengthy debates on the experience of firms they knew about, moved toward a full employee-ownership-and-control system. The employee association bought out the founders so that all the employees became stockholders. They elected a board of directors to make basic policy decisions and hire a management staff to carry these policies out. Like many other small businesses in the area, MiniWind began to keep open books so that employees, customers, and anybody else interested could know what they were doing with the money they took in. (An early basic decision was to accept somewhat lower personal incomes in exchange for shorter and more flexible hours of work.)

Once the people who made up MiniWind fully realized that they were in control of their own work situation, a great burst of creative ideas occurred. The company hired a chef to cook delectable and nutritious lunches—and found this helped people develop more solidarity and pay more concerted daily attention to the firm's collective problems. They built a shower room for people who liked to bicycle to work or go running on their noon breaks. They set up a child-care facility next door so parents and children could see each other during the day; that way children also knew what their parents did for a living, and it fostered more family feeling around the organization. Like other employee-controlled companies, MiniWind evaluated every aspect of the work situation for its health impacts; since government agencies protecting against toxic substances on the job had been gutted in the early eighties, workers knew they had to look out for themselves.

MiniWind also made many experiments in work arrangements. Through a program of job rotation they built up a staff deep in varied experience and capabilities—and less subject to boredom, stagnation and absenteeism. A small apartment where a couple of people actually lived was created over part of the office, thus providing guard service nights and weekends. In these and many other ways, MiniWind and its companion firms broke down the traditional division between work life and private life. They recognized that the quality of life they provided for themselves on the job was just as much a "product" of the company as its wind machines were.

And their wind machines were the best in the business: high-output but simple, reliable, repairable. Nonetheless, the company kept a low profile. It got little media attention and attracted no conglomerate buy-out offers. Flexible, fast in response, capable of mobilizing the best energies of its employee-owners, it could survive crises that would crack a rigid, bureaucratized corporation into disruption and collapse.

But such large corporations still dominated the American economy. Their capital resources enabled them to buy, sell and control smaller companies with ease. From the inside, their operations had an impressive look of economic rationality—they resulted in high profits and retained fickle investors. Seen from the outside, however, they were very costly to society; they generated huge damages in pollution, unemployment, death, welfare costs, and the decay of cities when they abandoned plants. These costs had for a long time been considered as "normal" burdens to be borne by the public, passively. But many people had begun to doubt the justice of this arrangement.

Moreover, some people began to notice that the giant corporations were often not as efficient as their partisans proclaimed. They were powerful in buying and selling companies that somebody else had built up, but their own productivity was hardly increasing at all. They had become bureaucratic, like the government upon which they suckled. They took six months to change the box design on a detergent, two years to redesign trivial features of a car. In head-on competition with German or Japanese firms, they proved backward and unenterprising. Their search for the quick buck was coming to a dead end.

Finally the time arrived when Lou would go on her "retreat." She loaded her pack methodically, as she had done many times before, with the necessities to take care of herself in the wilds for three days. She patched her jacket; she washed out and filled her canteen; she started up her little camp-stove to make sure it was in working order. She rolled her sleeping bag and foam pad into tight rolls and strapped them to the pack. Then, curious as always, she stepped onto the bathroom scales to check the pack's weight. "Only 29 pounds," she noted to Roger with satisfaction. "That's living pretty light on the land, right?"

"Okay, kid. Got your ground cloth? Got matches?"

"Roger! What do you think I am?"

"Oh, all right, excuse me! I *know* you've got it all. I think this whole event is throwing me a little, actually. Part of me must want you to stay about 12 forever, Lou. Even though most of me is proud you're so grown up."

Lou was glad her father didn't mind confessing such things. "Well, I've got plenty of mixed feelings myself! In fact I think that's probably why I got the idea of the ritual—to work through all that stuff and settle it."

"I know it's made all of us face some things. We have to recognize your new status in the generations. You'll be an adult, capable of having your own kids. You'll be a producer, not just a dependent. —What an awful word!"

"Yeah. Lots of big issues to think about." Lou put on her jacket. "I better get down to catch the bus. Gonna go up the coast a ways, then head inland. See you Sunday afternoon. I want to make my grand entrance just as the sun sets."

Lou had half expected she might be followed on her trip; from time to time strange people had appeared in the neighborhood following the burglary attempt. She kept watch out the bus rear window. But no cars seemed to be paying any attention to the bus. When she got out, at a remote crossroads bus stop, the only other person to get out was an old man, who started walking back along the highway. Then a car passed, perhaps slowing down slightly, but its occupants seemed to pay no attention to her. Lou relaxed and set out uphill at a brisk pace. It was a sunny fall day and the pines along the road sighed in an occasional breeze. How wonderful it was to be young and strong and alone! It was an essential part of her plan that for these three days nobody would know exactly where she was. She was on her own.

207

There was something exhilarating and also frightening about that. But she felt ready to take care of herself.

Her map showed a creek branching off from the road half a mile further on. At this time of year, before the rains had begun, it might not have much water in it; since the county had been lumbered off the summer flow of the creeks had dropped badly. But Lou liked to sleep near the sound of running water, so it was worth a look. When she got to the old trusswork bridge over the creek, there was still a little water flowing. A path led off along the creek, graced with a battered "No Trespassing" sign hanging on a steel cable. Lou hopped over the cable and set out upstream.

As always happened when she spent time outdoors, she began to realize that her senses were picking up far more interesting information than they did in town, or even in Bolinas. She welcomed this condition of receptiveness, imagining she could feel little lines of contact and appreciation coming to her from the grasses, the trees, the creek, the little birds. She was entering their world and would become one of them, one of the earth's creatures. It made her happy in a way she seldom experienced among people, who by contrast seemed so bent on *controlling* things.

The road was now far behind and she was climbing through forest with occasional patches of meadow. Her map showed an old Indian rancheria somewhere up near the crest of the adjacent ridge; maybe she could hike over next day and see if anybody still lived there. Finally, following an obscure fisherman's trail along the creek, she came out onto flatter higher ground. Here the creek went over a tiny falls near some spongy grass she could camp on—so soft she really wouldn't need her foam pad. She checked around for poison oak and found a tree nearby with a horizontal branch she could hang her food supply from—to frustrate raccoons or other camp thieves. This, Lou decided, was the place. She slipped out of her pack. Then she set up her sleeping area, her cooking area, and dug a small hole for a latrine. She got out her notebook and, leaning back against the big tree, began to jot down some of her thoughts. Other creatures observed her and gradually became used to her quiet presence. A groundsquirrel sentinel on the rocks watched her nervously for a while, then decided she posed no danger. A bluejay, naturally inquisitive, grew bold enough to hop near and examine her pack. Though Lou did not notice a faint glint of light on binoculars, from a hill half a mile away, she was also being watched by the deadliest species of all, her own.

However, she cooked her supper without incident. As the light faded she lay in her cozy sleeping bag looking up at the stars, so heartbreakingly beautiful in their intricacy. You never realized except on camping trips how extraordinarily *many* stars there were! And she knew that the visible stars were only an insignificant fraction of those in the universe. An old fantasy of hers came to mind again: that our solar system was only a single atom in this great flood of stars, and that together all the billions of trillions of star-atoms made up the blood stream of some immense creature. To that creature—who, she always imagined, with a giggle, was rather like Smokey the Bear—the bloodstream would appear a continuous liquid, just as rocks which are in reality mostly space, dotted with tiny specks of matter, seem solid to us. In our boundless self-importance the earth seems huge and indeed the center of the universe; and we have even conceived a universe without bounds (or a past, beyond some speculative Big Bang). This, Lou thought, must seem pretty funny to Smokey, who knows exactly where his skin boundary is, realizes that everything must come from somewhere, and must have been born like any bear.

It was chilly and damp when Lou awoke. She stuck her head out of the sleeping bag and debated whether to crawl out or wait a little longer. She decided to snuggle down again; after all, she was here to think, not to *do* anything. She dozed until the sun came up enough to warm her face a little. After that she pulled her clothes back on and crawled awkwardly from the bag. Then she started the little stove and made her breakfast.

The rest of the day she spent thinking and writing. The ritual she was planning involved a speech by her; she wanted it to be brief and powerful, like a song. Taking little walks from time to time, she worked most of the day. On one of her walks, following the creek further upstream, she came upon an old campsite. Perhaps it was made by people from the rancheria? After so much immersion in nature, it was startling to come upon the works of humans here in the middle of the forest. But Lou was always curious and she poked around, finding boards nailed to trees for shelves, and spikes in trees to hang things on, and a proper fire circle made of big stones. There was even an arrangement of notched branches over the fire to hang cooking pots from—an old settlers' or Indians' technique. Anyway, whoever camped here must have liked it and stayed a while. The idea pleased her.

But it was time to get back, she thought. As she neared her own camp she had what she first took to be an olfactory hallucination—she thought she smelled stew cooking. There was a slight breeze from the northwest and she faced into it, her nose at attention like a dog's. The smell seemed to be coming from a distant hill. "It *is* stew!" she said to herself. "Somebody must be camped over there." The smell made her hungry and she began to rummage in her pack for the makings of her own evening meal.

With a shock that seemed to run from her hands up her arms and down her back, she realized that her notebook was gone.

She looked around her camp, thinking some animal might have gotten into the pack and, perhaps liking the binding glue, dragged the notebook away. But the pack had been firmly strapped shut, and there were no signs of animal activity. She tried to remember exactly how she had left the pack earlier, and whether it had been moved. But everything seemed just as it had been. Some human had stolen the notebook.

Suddenly the forest around the camp seemed sinister. Who would want her notebook, her innocent notebook—unless somebody thought it was her *research* notebook? And what else might they be up to?

Lou's heart began to race. Adrenalin pumped through her system; her biological mechanism prepared for flight. But she held off panic long enough to throw her stove and clothes into the pack and strap the sleeping bag lumpily onto the frame. Then she crept off into the woods, making as little noise as possible. Once in hiding, she studied her map, laid a course taking her away from the source of the stew smell, and set off downhill as briskly as she dared. After she came to the road, she listened carefully for cars and hid in the brush whenever one approached.

Finally she reached the coast, near a little crossroads grocery. She phoned home, her voice shaking even after her exertion. By now it was almost dark, and the storekeeper was closing. Roger ordered her not to stay there alone, and Lou persuaded the storekeeper to take her down the road to the next town, where he lived. There was a coffeeshop there that she could wait in, till Roger came to get her.

"You kids," said the storekeeper, "got no more sense 'n a grasshopper, out on the highways by yourselves." He looked Lou over. "From what I hear, half the guys who pick up girl hitch-hikers aren't even goin' anywhere. You're lucky to have a father who cares about you enough to come up and get you, but he sure has some work to do talkin' a little sense into your head!"

"Well, I'm not hitch-hiking," Lou pointed out. "I came up on the bus. And I didn't get scared by a rapist, but by a thief." She sighed. "It's all too complicated to explain. But I'm sure glad you were here."

When Roger finally came, she had reconstructed a good part of her speech on some scraps of paper she found in the coffeeshop. "What was in the notebook?" Roger wanted to know.

"Poems, notes about the ceremony."

"Any research notes?"

"No, none of that at all."

Roger laughed. "Think of it—some poor assholes go to all that trouble, sneaking around up there in the woods, snatch your notebook, haul it home, and find out it's all about a rite of passage!" But then he realized that Lou, now that she felt safe again at last, was on the verge of tears. "My poor baby," he said, "let's go get some sleep." And so Roger led his daughter, who seemed so near to being a woman and yet so young and fragile, outside to the pickup truck and took her back to Bolinas.

Howard Penderton, president of Raussen Chemical Corporation, was not only a major figure in the California business world, but also a pillar of the San Francisco cultural community. He sat on the boards of the Opera and of drama companies; he and his wife donated large sums to educational institutions; they served on official cultural commissions. This Sunday afternoon they were presiding over a gathering at their Peninsula estate.

Surrounded by neatly fenced paddocks and acres of lawns, the Penderton mansion was approached by a long tree-lined drive; along it, this afternoon, dozens of large automobiles and limousines were parked, looking like a row of silver and black beetles against the well-irrigated green fields. The house itself, which boasted 34 rooms, plus a servants' wing, was done in fake-Tudor style. It was set among carefully planted patio areas of different sizes. The Pendertons' guests circulated from one to another, sampling canapes from tables shaded by awnings put up for the occasion, while waiters kept their champagne glasses comfortably full. The women wore light, flowing dresses and their jewelry flashed in the sun. A few well-mannered teen-agers and children—Penderton offspring and cousins and friends—mingled with the crowd or drifted off to the swimming pool. This tranquil event was scheduled to last all afternoon. An excellent

211

string quartet played demurely under a wisteria trellis, its sounds mingling agreeably with the soft buzz of conversation.

Mrs. Penderton, expert at her duties after a lifetime of such gatherings, discreetly supervised the serving staff and insured that guests had somebody to talk to—not difficult today, since most of them were either old friends or had business dealings with Raussen or enterprises connected with Raussen. Mr. Penderton moved about among the guests, inquiring affably about their family news, chatting about their business ventures. Knowing that Penderton had excellent contacts with the administration in Washington, some guests sought his advice about securing preferential treatment from one agency or another. Others asked his opinion on the new threat from the Survivalist Party, expressing their fears that the dying bureaucratic dragon in Washington might be replaced by a new and far more dangerous threat here at home: demagogues who proposed not just to control the manufacture of dangerous chemical compounds, but actually to prohibit it! To these alarmists Penderton replied that the chemical industry had never before had any real trouble fighting off regulation or turning it to advantage, and it had never been so influential in Washington as now; he saw no cause for worry, and asked if they wanted a little more champagne.

This elegantly relaxed scene was suddenly disturbed by the insistent clap-clap-slap sound of a helicopter. The guests watched with curiosity as a small agricultural spray copter swooped across the ample Penderton fields. Like a giant dragonfly, it gracefully banked against a row of distant eucalyptus trees and seemed ready to go on about its mysterious business. But then it turned and came toward the mansion. When it was a hundred yards away its spray boom began to emit a spreading cloud of white vapor. Before the guests could grasp what was happening, the copter had roared over the gardens and house and was gone, but its vapor cloud settled softly, stinging faces and burning eyes.

Uncertain what the acrid stuff might be, the guests panicked. Some scurried indoors and began frantically closing windows. Some simply ran about this way and that, looking for the people they had come with. Others headed for the line of limousines in the estate drive. Mr. Penderton, who had sudden suspicions what the spray was, crisscrossed the gardens, yelling at people, "Don't panic!" But the helicopter approached again, and the panic redoubled. Some people jumped into the pool fully clothed, and had to be rescued by the teen-agers.

Everybody was shouting suggestions at everybody else, but nobody paid any attention. Several guests reached their cars only to find that their chauffeurs were off somewhere, probably trying to "rescue" them, and had the only keys. Other drivers could not locate their own keys in the confusion. Still others, in their haste to escape, hooked bumpers with adjacent cars. And others simply headed out on foot over the fields, climbing fences and ripping clothing as they went.

Inside the mansion, a few determined souls had located small rooms with tight-fitting windows and had locked themselves inside, putting towels or bedspreads along the bottom of the doors; if there was pounding on the doors from outside, they gave no response. By this time Mrs. Penderton had telephoned the police and, for good measure, the fire department rescue squad. Her gardens were full of overturned furniture, spilled food, and hysterical guests. Amid this chaos she could hear the helicopter in the distance, turning and approaching on another run. Resigning herself, she went off to look for Mr. Penderton in the gardens. This time, however, the copter emitted no more spray—only a shower of tiny leaflets fluttered slowly to the ground. In fear or astonishment, the remaining guests saw them land in the pool, in half-empty champagne glasses, on damp clothing— thousands of them.

Mr. Penderton, it turned out, had gone to the pool but had been unable to find his bathing trunks—somebody had appropriated them. By now almost certain what the spray was, he had taken the precaution of stripping to his undershorts and jumping into the pool to clean himself off. Now he trudged across the lawns, bedraggled, holding one of the leaflets in his fingers. "Look at this!" he said, holding it out to his wife. She took it and read:

THIS SPRAY CONTAINS 2,4,5-T,
A WIDELY USED DEFOLIANT
MANUFACTURED BY RAUSSEN.

"2,4,5-T is perfectly safe." —Raussen
"Ye shall reap as ye sow." —God

Mr. Penderton looked around wildly for something to shake his executive fist at, but the helicopter had disappeared. Here and there, his friends were picking up the leaflets, looking at them, and tossing them quickly away as if they were contaminated—which they were.

Lou's initiation ceremony was held at a favorite family picnic spot high up on the slopes of nearby Mt. Tamalpais: a natural bowl with a flat bottom facing a grove of old oak trees where a circle of campfire rocks gave a focus to the scene. It was a brilliant, warm October day. Roger had the food and wine organized by mid-afternoon, and the guests began arriving and settling down to chatting and drinking and turning on and nibbling. Roger had asked some Caribbean friends to help him do a lamb roast and so a carcass was turning slowly on a borrowed spit frame with a low, hot fire under it; the drippings smelled marvelous.

The Bolinas contingent of neighbors and friends was there in force. Jan and her friends made up another large group. The ceremony had become an occasion for a gathering of clans—an expression of solidarity among old friends who had often helped each other before and stood ready to do so again. Ellen had promised Lou to arrange the music, so she and the other band members had rented a tiny generator to power their instruments and had hidden it in the ravine behind the oaks, where its muffled putt-putt couldn't be heard. Theo and dozens of other small children ran about, staring at the roasting lamb and taking turns at the handle, or climbing the grassy hills that made up the little bowl and rolling down like logs. People wore their best party finery, including many extravagant home-made garments: cloaks, capes, ornamented vests, spectacularly gaudy shirts and jackets and skirts. There were dramatic hats and elegant boots. Some outfits, of both men and women, were tight and revealing; others were loose, flowing and dramatic. There was the sense of a magical event in the air, and people wanted to live up to it. As the sun sank toward the ocean their expectancy rose, and they watched curiously as preparations went forward. Lou was nowhere to be seen; as Jan explained, "She's planning her grand entrance." The band, set up at one side of the fire circle, played a couple of soft, slow numbers with a melodic line dipping and swooping effortlessly like a gull in the wind. Then they paused, and in the silence people saw that the edge of the

214

sun had touched the horizon. Just at that moment the band began a slow rumbling crescendo that rose and shook and grew and then, with a crash of drums and an earsplitting whine from the guitar, stopped. Opposite them, where the hill met the sky, Lou appeared, silhouetted against the darkening blue, wearing her mother's silk dress, which moved slightly in the breeze. She paused there an instant, surveying the gathered crowd like a young goddess about to join her subjects on earth, and everybody applauded. Just as the sun sank below the horizon, she skipped down the slope to the fire.

Then, as if she were stepping out of character on a stage, Lou stood stock-still and smiled. "Hello!" she said, in a vibrant and almost husky voice. "I'm so glad and grateful you're all here!" She looked down half shyly, but was also obviously enjoying herself. "I want you to look back with me over the story of my life. So far, that is. Of course some of you remember things I can't remember. Jan and Roger have told me what it was like when I was born—both me and the doctor getting there late, about three o'clock in the morning, under Aries. I want to particularly thank my parents for bringing me into being on this wonderful planet.

"I know I was a kind of impulsive kid, and not easy to deal with—and I realize it isn't always easy now, either! But they always encouraged me, and so has Carol, even when the kind of encouragement I needed most was to be let alone to do my studies or my experiments. I can remember Roger taking me out on the beaches and just letting me figure things out—in fact one time he let me find out the hard way that crawling on the rocks when the tide's coming in can get you knocked around by waves. He saved me, and warmed me up in his big coat, and never said anything. But as a teacher I'm sure he noticed I never took chances about *that* again!

"And I can remember Jan teaching me by her example—and also by a certain amount of yelling—that when people are doing something that's really important to them, like painting, you'd better stay out of their way for a while. Jan showed me that having work you care about is really important, especially for women. And Carol, by the way she brought up Mike, taught me a lot too about mothering, and now that I'm declaring myself an adult, I've been thinking about all those things.

"I don't imagine I'll be having any kids for a long time—too many adventures I want to try first! But sometimes I look at my body and think how wonderfully adapted it is to all these survival tasks. When it was really little, it knew how to curl up in Jan's uterus. Then it knew just how to worm its way through the birth canal, and how to start breathing, and crying for milk and attention. And then how to crawl, and walk, and talk. And these fingers got so clever they could draw and tie knots and write equations and build experimental equipment. And my muscles got strong and supple enough to run and swim. And I found out how to have orgasms—what a lovely surprise! And my breasts grew, getting ready to produce milk in their turn. So it all felt like a comfortable cycle, just moving slowly from one phase to the next."

Lou smiled at the crowd assembled in a ring around her. Many people had arms or hands entwined. They were smiling back at her, softly and proudly: she was one of them.

"But at 18, it feels like the cycle takes a bit of a jump. It's really scary, I'm ready to admit that. I'll be done with school, and as soon as I get this cell research done—which has been going very well, as most of you know—I'm going to try living on my own for the first time. Probably right around here somewhere, with friends. I'll want you all to come and visit. I love you all. Thank you for being part of my life!"

She blew kisses toward the group, and the band began playing again. They had written some strange material for this part of the event: almost free-form music, with unorthodox tonal transitions, little interspersed rhythmic interludes, a sense of dance rhythms searching for a way to express themselves yet somehow held back. Against this musical background, Lou was carried around the fire on chairs-of-hands made by Roger and Carol and Jan and Mike; then she was encircled by these members of her biological family, and then Dimmy and other friends began inserting themselves into the basic circle, weaving around Lou in a serpentine line, sometimes singing or humming along with the band's wordless sounds.

Inside this dancing circle, Roger and Jan separated themselves and stood with Lou between them. They faced away from the fire, toward the circle of darkening hills. Opposite them a line of young men arranged themselves—David, who left the band for a few minutes, Jeffrey, Bert, and four or five others Lou knew from Bolinas or from school. Then Roger and Jan in turn hugged Lou and whirled her around, then finally turned her loose and stood behind her, arms at their sides. Now the music changed character, taking on a strong, driving dance beat. Lou went over and grasped Bert's hand, and as if this were a signal the circling crowd broke up into leaps and prances

216

and swung along to the band's impulsion. Bert was gangly and a terrible dancer, but even his gawkiness now seemed beautiful. Then Lou moved on to dance with the others in turn, feeling strangely light on her feet, as if she truly had some goddess-like presence which it felt wonderful to lend to them all.

The music and the dancing went on for almost an hour and then, finally, the lamb was pronounced roasted and the tired dancers descended on the food. They cut and tore off chunks of the lamb and ate with greasy fingers. They consumed great quantities of home-baked bread, and nourishing soups, and salads loaded with morsels of cheese and shrimp and avocado and fruit. They drank gallons upon gallons of wine. And Lou moved among them, seeming about an inch taller than most of them remembered her, conscious of her new dignity. She particularly enjoyed a subtle, almost subliminal sensation that Jan and Carol were treating her differently: as if she were now one of the adults of the tribe.

"Anderson & Son" read the carved wooden sign over Nils Anderson's doorway. He and John had prospered at their marijuana growing and research, but they continued living modestly in the little cabin. Nils gave himself the luxury of a decent car, however—an unobtrusive grey Oldsmobile—so that he could make more frequent trips to visit friends near San Francisco. He was also becoming active in an anti-pesticide campaign being mounted by Planet People, an ecological group based in San Francisco with chapters in several other cities and alliances with the Farm Workers Union and other unions whose members were especially exposed to chemical hazards. As his commitment to PP deepened, Nils found it difficult to continue visiting the old friends he had kept from his working days. He didn't want to start a lot of arguments; on the other hand, he couldn't just keep quiet about his new convictions either.

One day a PP member he hadn't yet met telephoned; it was Laura D'Amato. She asked if he would testify for the group at a coming Sacramento legislative hearing. He agreed to come to her house in San Francisco and talk about it.

They sat in Laura's pleasant, airy living room and drank a glass of wine. The PP, it turned out, needed expertise on the exposure of farm families to pesticides sprayed near their dwellings, and this was a subject Nils was well acquainted with. "But Laura," he objected, "if I get up there—you know who's going to be testifying on the other side, don't you? My old colleagues."

Laura looked at him quietly. "I wouldn't have asked you," she said, "without thinking about all that. But I also know that sooner or later you *will* have to choose."

"And you think you know which side I'll choose."

"Yes! All I'm really doing is asking you to choose now rather than later. Now happens to be an unusually good opportunity, that's all. It would be very dramatic, having you testify for us."

Nils hated public controversy and politicians' practiced voices and the distortions of the newspapers and television. He still felt loyalty to some of the people he had worked with at Farmchem. They had been good folks in their way, he knew, trying to do a useful job. It was just that they didn't know certain things that later became clear. But now the companies knew, all right—and still they went on, until determined people like Laura managed to mobilize enough public opinion, wangle enough legislative support, to stop them. Nils was well aware of the odds they struggled against, from his experiences on the other side. He knew the industry slush funds, the political inside tracks, the media contacts. There were all these executives in their dark suits, scuttling about the state making connections, smooth and smiling and confident, just as he had been once. And then on the other side were Laura and her friends, bright-faced and naive, but full of determination and capable of bringing political imagination and energy to bear that the companies and their hired ad agencies could somehow rarely match.

"I'll lose a lot of friends through this, you know," Nils said to her.

"You'll make a lot of new ones through it, too," Laura said. She took his arm and led him out into the garden hidden behind the house where a small group of people were sitting around a table in the sun. "This is Nils Anderson. I'd like you to meet Vera Allwen—I think you know her role in the Survivalist Party? This is my daughter Marissa—she works in forestry. And this is Dennis Tureau, our regular pesticide watcher on the legislative front."

"Well, Nils," asked Vera, "has Laura talked you into it yet?" The group laughed; they often had cause to marvel at Vera's persuasive powers and they knew she would join in if necessary.

"Yes, she has," said Nils. Suddenly there were smiles everywhere. Standing rather awkwardly at Laura's side, he was surrounded by people stepping up to give him enthusiastic hugs. He had to admit that it felt a lot better than the hand-pumping at a Farmchem sales meeting, or even sitting around drinking with old friends. But still his heart jumped a beat as he sat down to join the group, and the saying "Out with the old, in with the new" went running through his head. Why did life keep making you choose?

◆⧈◆

Roger came back from a supposedly leisurely stroll to the post office in a rage. "Clowns, assholes, miserable goddamn creeps!" were his first words as he came in, slamming the heavy carved door so that the house shook.

"Uh-oh!" said Dimmy, who was standing at the stove. "What hath the heathen wrought now?"

The gossip downtown, it seemed, was that the county had discovered that several of the good citizens of Bolinas had asked the power company to disconnect their dwellings. They had solar heat and wood stoves, they cooked with propane, they had solar water heaters, they ran their stereos and small refrigerators off of Lou's cells or wind generators. They used kerosene lamps. These self-reliant practices, it appeared, were in conflict with a county regulation that a habitable house must have electric power, indeed a specified number of outlets per room. The county had issued orders to the householders to get themselves reconnected or else face condemnation of their dwellings.

The householders, of course, had torn up the notices with many flourishes, to the applause of the Bolinesians hanging around the post office. Now the matter would go before the town council. "Well, if you're so into all this," Carol said to Roger, "maybe you ought to get yourself elected to the council. Now that we've joined the Survivalists, we really ought to get more active. And I hear Jerry isn't going to stay on."

"Really? Why not?"

"He's adding a room to his house, I think."

"Well," mused Roger, "then maybe I should try for it. This kind of crap has got to be stopped!"

So it was that Roger Swift became a Survivalist candidate, soon joined the group of town fathers and mothers, and began to be instructed in the ungentle relationships between large government organs and small ones.

◆⧈◆

The period after Nils was recruited to the Survivalist cause by Laura was a whirlwind of new activity for him. He took to spending a great deal of time in the Bay Area, mostly at Laura's house. It was an informal center of Survivalist activities, always full of devoted people making plans, organizing campaigns, and rushing around excitedly. Their enthusiasm was contagious and Nils got involved in more of their activities than he had planned. But his son, after all, could manage the pot farm without much help at this point.

Gradually the relationship between Nils and Laura deepened into a sexual one—to Marissa's delight, since her mother had not really had any important involvement after her father's death six years before. Nils, despite his rather formal Scandinavian manners, proved to have a definite romantic streak. He had even begun to think that, although Laura was accustomed to protesting her independence, marriage might not be out of the question.

And then one fine, crisp, lovely San Francisco day, Laura came back to the house and announced that her doctor had diagnosed her as having lung cancer. Inoperable, it was fatal in 90 percent of cases. She had perhaps a year to live. For some months it would not make much difference in her life. Later, she would become weaker, especially if she underwent treatments that might give her a greater than 10 percent chance. It all seemed crushingly unfair; she had never even smoked.

A slow, deadly rage began to build up in Laura. All the terrible statistics she had read now suddenly came crashing down upon her in urgent personal reality: she was going to die, senselessly and pointlessly, and at a time when her life had never seemed so hopeful, so productive. She stamped her feet, and screamed in anguish, for she had never been one to take adversity quietly; when Nils counseled calm, she only raged the louder. Then, through some subterranean process—she could never later remember just how—her rage turned to defiance: she would fight back!

She clenched her fists and chuckled at Nils in a way that made his blood chill. "No, by God," she said, "I will *not* go quietly. These murderers will hear from me!" She paced the room as if her bottled-up energy were looking for an escape route. Then she stopped and looked at Nils. "Since I have to go, I think I'll take a chemical plant with me! I'm free to do that now—after all, what can they do, put me in jail?" She laughed, but an air of determination had come over her.

Nils asked mildly, "How are you going to do that?"

"Form an organization made up of people like me—the Cancer Commandos! Doomed cancer victims who can *afford* to act." She went over to Nils and looked at him with an intentness he had never seen in her before. "This may sound a little odd, but I feel freer now than I have ever felt in my life. You know I'm basically a pacifist. But frankly if there was some person I could kill and be sure it would do the world some important good, I would do it without a qualm. Uncanny, isn't it?"

Nils was appalled. And yet there was a strange beauty in Laura's readiness to take desperate measures. Was she doing now only what everybody should have had the courage to do?

"How can I help?" he asked.

"You know how chemical plants are laid out. You can show me where a bomb would do the most lasting damage to the plant but not spread poisons all over the place. It has to be done very carefully— the exact opposite of the neutron bomb, because we want to damage only property, not people!"

"You're really serious, aren't you?"

Laura looked at him with cold eyes. "I have never been so serious about anything in my life. I'm going to *get* them, Nils! Where it hurts."

They went on to talk about the requirements for explosives, about how to find other cancer victims who would be willing to participate, about plans to handle reporters and media people so as to maximize the political impact of the bombing: the goal, after all, was not mere revenge but a symbolic action that could help halt the manufacture of carcinogenic chemicals—to bring home that this was indeed a matter of life and death.

Now that she had a new enterprise to be concerned with, Laura's depression about the diagnosis lifted somewhat. She stopped talking about her illness, even when asked about it by Marissa or Ben; she didn't want them involved in the aftermath of her act, so she simply told them she was going to live out her remaining days doing good things through Planet People. They couldn't decide if she was concealing her real feelings, or had somehow repressed them; but they noticed she stayed busier than ever, and they knew from long experience that this was how she dealt with pain, whether psychological or physical. She had never had much use for doctors. She would go in her own way.

Laura's diagnosis alarmed Nils into thinking of a full-scale check-up himself; it had been many years since he had bothered with one. He finally got around to it a month later. By one of those coincidences that go against all probability, Nils was told that he too had cancer—of the colon. It could be operated on, but probably not successfully. There would be other operations, also probably not successful. He too would perhaps survive for a year.

When he came home and told Laura she cried, and cuddled him, just as he had tried to comfort her. She knew the fear behind his soft, kind eyes. They would share, now, the terror and the rage. She looked at him and gave him the only gift in her waning power: "Welcome, my dearest, dearest Nils, to the Cancer Commandos! We will make a great avenging team, you and I."

They were both energetic, effective persons with a wealth of organizational experience. They were working against time. They soon found the few comrades they needed, and laid their plans.

FEDS ORDER START-UP
OF CLOSED NUKE

Washington, Nov. 12 (WPI). Department of Energy officials today announced that the Humboldt Bay nuclear plant at Eureka, California, which had been taken out of operation in 1976, was to be reopened. It had been closed because of the discovery of earthquake faults a short distance from the plant, leading to fears that a nuclear disaster could occur if the plant was damaged by earth movement. DOE declared that the national energy emergency demanded reopening of the plant, even if some small danger existed. "Everything in life involves some risk," said Department spokesperson Michelle Danton. "Additional safety precautions will be taken to preserve the plant's integrity even in a strong earthquake."

Under questioning, Danton stated that the plant's earthquake resistance might be extended to as high as 7.5 on the Richter scale. The last major quake in the area, in 1980, had registered only 7.1, she pointed out, and had caused only "minor" damage to the inoperative plant. However, earthquakes of greater intensity have been relatively common on the California coast.

Asked about evacuation plans for the downwind population in the event of a quake that severely damaged the Humboldt plant, Danton revealed that the Department has not yet developed such a program. "We are counting on state officials to work out those details," she said.

The Raussen public relations office issued a press release following the spraying of the Penderton estate. It condemned the "terrorist assault" and offered a reward for information leading to the helicopter pilot's arrest and conviction. It was a sorry day for our society, the statement continued, when extremists take advantage of the exposed position of executives like Mr. Penderton to publicize their own minority views. Of course, the release pointed out, Raussen laboratories had conclusively established that 2,4,5-T was harmless to human beings; nonetheless, the spraying had inflicted mental anguish on many innocent people.

Betty Castillo, an ambitious television reporter, happened to see the Raussen story. Betty came from a family of Mexican agricultural workers, and she knew from personal experience that pesticides and herbicides were not good for you—one of her uncles had nearly died after a pesticide accident. The small UHF station Betty worked for was desperately trying to improve its audience ratings. She had a hunch that something big could be made of this thing. So Betty began digging around and soon discovered that in fact Howard Penderton had arranged immediate medical attention for all of his guests. With her suspicions about Raussen's real views on the safety of 2,4,5-T thus confirmed, Betty got assigned to pursue the story in a serious way. She took a camera crew to the Penderton mansion and filmed the remnants of its once lovely gardens—whose plants had been almost completely killed by the spray. This scene of devastation, shown as the attractive reporter walked through it in a protective white space-suit, was particularly effective on TV. At the end of the tour Betty announced that in her next program she would present an exclusive interview with the helicopter pilot.

Through family contacts in the agricultural community, Betty had succeeded where the police had failed, and the pilot agreed to be filmed if he could wear a disguise—a gas mask. A series of promotional teasers and newspaper ads made the story a hot one, and the little station's viewer ratings leaped upward.

When the main story finally aired, the pilot stated under Betty's questioning that he was a member of a group called "Ecotopians for Corporate Personal Responsibility."

"What's that?" asked Betty. "As I understand it, a corporation is precisely a device to *avoid* personal responsibility. 2,4,5-T is not manufactured by Mr. Penderton, who is a nice man and loves music, but by the Raussen Corporation."

"That's exactly our point," replied the pilot. "You can't put a corporation in jail. In fact it's almost impossible to put individual corporation officials in jail, no matter what you can prove they did. So we decided that direct action is the only answer. Somehow, people must be made to bear responsibility for what they do. We dramatized for Mr. Penderton the actual consequences of his actions. Now he knows he's responsible for stopping them."

"What makes you think your gambit will work?"

"Well, first of all it makes millions of people remember what's really going on—that people like Penderton are poisoning us! And second, it offers a kind of deal."

"What deal?" asked Betty.

"You know this 2,4,5-T is all over the place—on farms and in forests and parks and in water supplies and in people's bodies. But we have ways to make sure it gets to Mr. Penderton and all his rich friends too, just like everybody else."

"So what's the deal?"

"Simple—if he stops spraying us, we'll stop spraying him."

NUKE START-UP SPARKS MASSIVE PROTESTS

Eureka, Calif., Nov. 15. Plans to reopen the nuclear power generating plant on Humboldt Bay were met today by massive public demonstrations. The plant is situated on a narrow spit of land, and about 10,000 demonstrators completely blocked access to the area for several hours. However, the crowds were well organized and no violence occurred. Police said the protest was the largest ever held in Humboldt County.

While the mood of the demonstrations was non-violent, anger ran deep in the crowd. As one participant told a reporter, "If the federal government forcibly subjects its citizens to the danger of a nuclear plant disaster, it makes you wonder just what we need that federal government for!" Demonstrators carried many placards, but the most common bore the Survivalist Party slogan popularized throughout Washington, Oregon and Northern California: "Nuclear-Free Northwest Now!" The protest was organized partly by the local Survivalist organization and partly by a coalition of anti-nuclear groups from the region.

Several county supervisors participated in the protests, commenting angrily that the federal government was not listening to the voice of the people—who had voted by a two-thirds majority to keep the plant closed.

Power company officials declined official comment on the situation. Privately, however, the company was said to be worried about damage and liability questions if a Three Mile Island situation should occur here. Federal disaster back-up and private insurance would cover only a fraction of the damage from a major nuclear accident. Moreover, the costs of bringing the plant up to safety standards would make its output very high priced—a questionable business risk in a period when electrical generating reserves considerably exceed consumption. Some utility observers believe the company is chiefly concerned with getting a federal bail-out for the expensive process of decommissioning the plant, which would be the first such final closure in nuclear history.

By this time the Survivalist campaign to cut back on cars had had considerable effect. Corporations had been persuaded to offer employees a choice between free parking spaces and raises equivalent to the "rent" on the land area freed for other uses if they turned to bicycles or carpools, and individual commuting had dropped 25 percent as a result. Bus and streetcar services were markedly improved. New taxis were on the streets: compact, rather square and high looking but very energy-efficient, they were also designed for easy passenger entry and exit, minimal parking-space requirements, and quick bag storage; already they were replacing a great number of private vehicles, and few commuters now ventured to drive downtown. Experiments were being made in downtown areas with the free-bicycle plan pioneered in Amsterdam many decades before: white city-owned bikes were provided, unlocked, in dense areas for easy availability to all. Inner city parking lots, often now partly empty, were being turned into small parks or used for new buildings devoted partly to commercial and office purposes and partly to apartments. Indeed, among large sectors of the population car ownership was becoming something of a social stigma, just as smoking had earlier. People felt they had to make apologies if they bought a new car; regional car sales, which had been dropping since the early eighties, were now at less than half earlier levels. On the roads old rusted-out cars held together by wire sported bumper stickers that read: "Don't Laugh—This Car Will Be My Last!"

It was in this context that, as Vera Allwen and her strategists had foreseen, the Supreme Court decision in the Madera case went against the states: their special tax on cars was declared unconstitutional by a 7 to 2 vote. In Eastern newspapers and in auto industry headquarters in Detroit there was rejoicing: a formidable threat to the country's major industry had been decisively beaten.

But the reaction in the Ecotopian territory, as Vera had also foreseen, was widespread rage: the will of the people, duly expressed through their democratically elected state governments, was being thwarted by brutal national power. Mass meetings suddenly erupted, with placards reading "SMASH MADERA, THE SUICIDE MANDATE!" and a wave of vandalism swept the streets. Car tires were slashed; graffiti reading "KILLER KAR" and various obsenities were spray-painted on cars; impromptu barricades were thrown up at major intersections, causing city-wide traffic jams. Vera Allwen made a public appeal for the destructiveness to stop. "We can only counter this unjust Supreme Court decision by *political* means," she said. "I understand your anger. I share it. But we must turn it into constructive channels. History is full of examples of people overturning unjust rulings. We will find a way to nullify this judicial error.

"And we have already made great headway in our regional program to lessen our dependence on cars. We have already begun to enjoy the benefits of our reduced oil outlays, in the form of a stronger economy. We enjoy cleaner air, safer streets. If the Supreme Court has failed to recognize the crucial importance of such achievements, it had made a grave mistake, whose consequences will be severe. We will persist. If the rest of the country is happy with the Madera decision, let them suffocate in their own fumes! We must find a new way. And we will."

Few people had any clear idea of what alternatives Vera might

226

have in mind. But the Madera ruling, for millions who ordinarily did not think of themselves as particularly radical, dashed their last hopes for sanity in Washington. And within the Survivalist Party Vera found that the decision had caused a massive and sharp turn toward outright secessionist sentiment.

STATE QUESTIONS HUMBOLDT NUCLEAR DECISION

Sacramento, Nov. 13. Governor Timothy Clark held an emergency meeting with key members of the state Energy Board this morning. The group, it was learned, discussed yesterday's surprise order from the federal Department of Energy directing that the Humboldt Bay nuclear generating plant be reopened.

The Governor later issued a brief, carefully worded statement that the federal order conflicted with state safety requirements. However, he did not mention any action the state might take.

Capitol observers noted that the federal order also flouts a Humboldt County referendum vote of a decade ago, which strongly opposed reopening of the plant. Moreover, in recent months the Survivalist Party has made great inroads throughout the region with its "Nuclear-Free Northwest" slogan, and local officials have reportedly warned Clark of trouble if the federal order is carried out.

Clark's relations with the federal administration have been increasingly shaky this year, and some political analysts here suspect that Washington is not averse to tossing him this political hot potato. However, the analysts add, Washington may have little understanding of local political pressures, which might force the governor to try to counter or at least delay the federal plan.

From the onset of the Industrial Revolution, it had been an article of faith that there were always economies in greater scale: if a factory could be doubled in size, it could turn out more than twice as many goods and return more than twice the profits. This belief led to ever-increasing size in corporate enterprises, and it was applied, by powerful analogy, to every aspect of life. The bigger a power-generating station,

the better. The bigger a steamship, the better. The bigger a city, the better.

This tendency, however, came to stand in fundamental opposition to another principle, which might be called the irreducibility of error. Careful design of human–machine "interfaces" such as control panels could reduce human errors, especially if operators were carefully trained and frequently tested. But, surprising though it might seem in the abstract, errors could never be eliminated entirely. It was never entirely possible to foresee all possible breakdowns. Moreover, the human mind was more complexly flexible than any computer; evolution had equipped it to deal with rapidly changing situations that required instinctive judgment and the balancing of uncertain risks, but the very qualities of broad adaptability that gave it survival potential also made it more erratic than simpler organisms. And no machine remained reliable forever. The strongest metals in the end developed fatigue; insulation broke down; even computers aged and developed electronic failures or mysterious bugs in their complex programs.

The establishment of extremely dangerous large technologies, such as those of nuclear warfare or nuclear plants or those involving the production of immensely toxic chemicals like dioxin, thus brought the possibility of large-scale disasters to human populations into juxtaposition with the unavoidability of error. Clever military designers inserted fail-safe devices into command and control systems, and they surrounded bomb trigger mechanisms with multiple layers of protective devices. Their industrial counterparts interposed computer links between human operators and reactor cores, wrote ever more complex programs, provided more warning bells, left fewer human over-ride possibilities.

Nonetheless, both human and machine error persists. A pilot of 20 years' experience, landing with ample ground control contact on a clear day, puts an airliner down in the middle of San Francisco Bay. Operators of a nuclear plant forget that certain valves have been left open, a partial core meltdown occurs, a hundred thousand people must be evacuated. A bomber inexplicably drops a hydrogen bomb by accident; five of the bomb's six safety devices fail, and only the sixth prevents the destruction of much of North Carolina.

Under such circumstances, the art of risk assessment becomes metaphysical. Professional insurance statisticians opt out of these games, knowing that the risks are not amenable to normal actuarial analysis. Nonetheless, sophisticated calculations are made by eminent scientific committees, and then revised and re-revised. They provide estimates of the likelihood of irreparably catastrophic events—making a major American city uninhabitable, for instance, or mistakenly believing a Russian missile attack was in progress and responding by devastating the entire Northern Hemisphere.

The risks in such calculations always turn out to be impressively small, indeed minute—smaller by far than the risk the ordinary citizen takes in crossing town by car. However, ordinary citizens do not possess the statistical refinement needed to evaluate a risk expressed as .00001% And so the normal political process, which depends upon the judgment of ordinary citizens fitfully informed by the news media and by a few conscientious scientists, cannot come to terms with such risks.

It is only when a major disaster occurs, as in the explosion that scattered dioxin over the town of Seveso in Italy, or a near-disaster such as the Three Mile Island nuclear accident in Pennsylvania, that the political process re-exerts control over technology. Then the trend toward ever greater scale may be checked or even reversed; people demand security against super-catastrophic risks even at the cost of more frequent smaller risks.

In the United States as elsewhere in the world, people began to discover that nuclear installations suffered far more "minor" accidents than had been publicly revealed. Moreover, as existing nuclear plants aged, many experts placed the risk of further Three-Mile-Island type accidents at near certainty over a range of ten years or so. The chances of worse accidents—seriously contaminating a few miles around a plant, with large but perhaps acceptable damage to property and some lives lost through radiation exposure—still seemed bearable to some. But the risks of a meltdown accident, which would render several counties uninhabitable, perhaps for generations, and which directly or indirectly caused tens of thousands of deaths, might be statistically very small and yet be politically and morally insupportable.

In the end, thus, commonsense reasserted itself over arcane statistics. People decided that they would rather expose themselves to a 1% chance of a solar boiler blowing up and killing three people than run the .00001% chance of a nuclear meltdown. But in the country as a whole, which was significantly dependent on nuclear plants, the resulting political pressure was contained through a regulatory system that, while supposedly enforcing more stringent safety requirements, actually ignored several potentially fatal defects in operating reactors. Only in the West, where the Survivalist Party proposed to do away with nu-

229

clear altogether, did popular unease find direct political expression.

As months passed after the spraying "accident," which the Forest Service continued to deny had ever happened, most of Mary McBride's symptoms disappeared and she and Jamie decided it was safe to start a pregnancy. When she was two months along, however, she developed new and more alarming symptoms, and the diagnosis was leukemia. By this time leukemia in adults was no longer rare, and while no certain causal links had yet been established, it was widely believed by researchers that radiation and chemical exposure were responsible. Mary and Jamie, at least, had few doubts that her exposure to the herbicide had caused her illness.

"We'll sue the bastards," said Jamie. "I'm going to ask the anti-spraying people for the name of their lawyer."

"Oh, Jamie," said Mary, "I don't know if it's worth it. We'll lose—and all that money! We really need it for the place. For the baby, if—"

Jamie saw, with despair, that already Mary's delicate fair complexion was becoming routinely pale and grey. She had always been a quiet person, but now she seemed to have lost all her vigor.

"Mary, we just can't let them get away with it, that's all! Somebody has got to fight them on this stuff. It's for you, for the baby. All the babies!"

Mary dreaded the idea of a court fight. She knew their medical insurance would cover only a fraction of the coming medical bills. And all Jamie's arguments could not shake her foreboding that they would lose the case. Nonetheless, she allowed Jamie to persuade her, and she found she enjoyed contact with the dedicated anti-spraying groups that had sprung up through the region.

With their aid the McBrides duly filed suit against the Forest Service, against the Fir-Aid Company which operated spray copters in the area, and against a certain unknown John Doe, pilot of the copter that sprayed their land. But Mary went on losing weight, and her red cell count steadily dropped. When she was in her fifth month, she had a miscarriage.

The legal proceedings dragged on; Mary's condition worsened. She had to visit the hospital frequently for painful bone-marrow tests. The defense challenged the validity of the lab analyses the McBrides had obtained after the spraying. The expert medical testimony was contradictory and confusing. The pilot turned out to be named William Whitehead; he testified that he had followed the prescribed flight plan, well east of the McBrides' land. The jury, drawn as it was from a lumbering community, hesitated to accept the idea that a standard forestry practice, said to be essential to the health of the industry, could be condemned in a court of law. The McBrides lost their suit, and in order to pay legal fees as well as Mary's medical bills, they sold their land and house and moved to an apartment in town.

A month after the trial ended, Mary died. Jamie got the new owners of his land, Jane and Mack, to let him build a teepee nearby and live there for a while. He worked for them a little, and he also worked at his old job repairing trucks. Mack had no gun, so Jamie asked to keep his rifle on the spikes above the front door.

SURVIVALIST PAPER NUMBER 12:
THE REVENGE OF THE SNAIL DARTER

A resilient and resourceful people who are serious about surviving in the part of the world they occupy must learn to assess traditional political practices in new ways. In the thirties and forties, for example, dams were built throughout the United States for flood control and power generation. At the time, most of these dams were sensible propositions economically—relatively cheap to build, and posing few safety hazards.

As the sixties and seventies passed, however, reasonable sites for new dams became scarcer and scarcer. Prospective costs grew, and prospective benefits—even by generous calculations—shrank. Nonetheless, dam building had long been popular with voters who felt it must somehow contribute to Progress. And it was profitable to influential construction-industry corporations who worked in a mutual support relationship with the government's Corps of Engineers. Thus many dams continued to be planned, authorized, financed, and built.

One ambitious and instructive dam project was in Tennessee on a small river that had escaped damming earlier, the Tellico. While this dam was under construction, ecologists discovered that a minnow-sized fish, the snail darter, would have its sole remaining river habitat destroyed when the valley was turned into a stagnant lake—and thus the fish would be made extinct.

Congress had not much earlier passed the Endangered Species Act, which recognized that animal and plant species, even those of no obvious usefulness to human beings, constituted precious and irreplaceable parts of the earth's web of life, toward which we were obliged to act with due respect. Under this act, suits were filed by environmental defense groups to halt completion of the Tellico Dam. For a time these suits were surprisingly successful. Work on the dam ceased, amid widespread consternation on the part of politicians and business people, who considered that any needs on the part of humans must outweigh any needs on the part of fish, however endangered they might be. Moreover, as it happened the snail darter was not a particularly beautiful or impressive fish. It was not even edible by humans, though it had its proper place in several food chains. So a great many jokes were made at the snail darter's supposed expense.

However, the delay caused by the little fish gave time for careful new cost-benefit studies to be made of the dam project as a whole. These studies, as has often proved to be the case with other dams as well, revealed that the dam was turning out to be inordinately more expensive than originally foreseen. Moreover, the figures that had been used to prove that the dam would richly repay its investment by the provision of electric power, flood control, and recreation facilities, turned out to be vastly exaggerated. In fact the dam would flood rich valley bottom-land, and it would also pre-empt other land useful for timber growing. The electricity it produced would be more expensive than new power from thermal power plants, not to mention power "produced" by conservation investment—increasing the efficiency of existing energy use—which was by then widely known to be the cheapest method for improving the energy-supply situation. The dam might provide additional water surface for motorboats and waterskiers in an area already full of recreational lakes, but the public subsidy for their amusement would run to many dollars per hour. Fish caught in the reservoir, if all their costs had been openly acknowledged, would have cost more than the choicest caviar.

In any case, what the region really needed, like the country as a whole, was not more electric power but substitutes for petroleum—for example, gasohol made from crops that could have been grown on the land to be submerged by the filling of the dam.

The Tellico Dam, in short, was discovered to be a certifiable disaster from a hardheaded economic point of view as well as an instance of irretrievable eco-crime against a fellow species. It also constituted an irresponsible waste of ever more precious agricultural resources.

However, there it stood, almost finished. Studies showed that, even so, the most rational policy would *still* be to abandon it, preserve the valley's productivity, and devote the remaining funds to alternate sources of energy production. This, however, the nation and its leaders were not wise enough or courageous enough to do. Angered and frightened by gasoline shortages, the populace felt that any new energy source must be good—despite the existence even at that time of a glut of electric power-generating capacity. Congress moved, herd-like, toward the destruction of the Endangered Species Act itself if the dam could not be exempted from its provisions. The president caved in and signed the year's energy appropriation bill into which the dam's completion had been incorporated. Twelve hours later the bulldozers resumed work.

Proponents of "Progress" were delighted by this demonstration of their political clout and considered the case successfully closed. As it turned out, however, the snail darter gets the last laugh. It is impossible to foresee whether this tiny fish, like many plants that provide the basis for new medicines, might have turned out some day to be of direct utility to humans. But it is certain that with its extermination a little more of the inherent variety and beauty of the earth had been destroyed. More directly, the Tellico Dam continued to exact a heavy and inexorable price from the people. It did provide some excess reserve electric power. But its flood control benefits were negligible and in any case were far outweighed by the permanent submerging of valuable lands. The fundamental effect of the dam's financing and operation was to put a steady long-term drain on the Tennessee Valley's economy, and on the nation's. The seemingly proud achievement of the dam was in reality a symbol of stupidity, impoverishment, and decline.

When it was completed, however, no newspaper editorial writers chose to take notice of that unpalatable fact. Blind to the future as well as to the lessons of the past, they left it to us to draw wise conclusions from this sorry tale. We of the Survivalist Party do not wish to suffer, in our part of the world, the revenge of the lowly snail darter as it is being visited upon the unhappy people of Tennessee. So when we contemplate and assess projects for the damming and diversion of our remaining wild rivers, we must not be carried away by false symbolism. We must know the facts and be guided by them. Let the snail darter remind us that nature does not forgive fools nor does she spare them the penalties of their folly.

After her ceremony Lou immediately went back to work. She had the pleasant new feeling that, as a certified grown-up, she was now free to come and go in her father's house. But there was no question of moving out until the six weeks was up, anyway. She got Bert to come and camp out in the Bolinas house, and they often worked almost around the clock.

It turned out to be an obscure compound of selenium which was responsible for the Swift Effect. As Bert put it wryly, "I might have known, because Luckman's Law predicts that whatever solution you try last will be the one that works!"

As Lou first realized what was going on, she rushed into the house to tell Roger, who was writing some letters. When he looked up he exclaimed, "Lou, what is it? You look as if you were just caught at the cookie jar!"

"I've got it, I think I've finally got it!" She stuck a sheet of paper under his nose and began to explain, whispering breathlessly and drawing little diagrams and chemical formulas. "And," she concluded triumphantly, "I also know how to verify it!" Then she explained a critical experiment that would reveal whether or not her hypothetical mechanism was in fact operating in the experimental cells. It would be conclusive, she thought. At last!

Now she and Bert stopped sleeping at all. Carol and Roger organized extra-tight security on a 24-hour basis. Lou and Bert constructed a new piece of test equipment designed to prove definitively how the process worked, in a way that would be easy for other laboratories to repeat. They redrafted parts of Lou's article. They prepared new drawings. They showed the results to Roger, who made a few suggestions. Then Bert carried the manuscript off to San Francisco; it would appear in a week. "Public disclosure" could not be more complete!

Lou fell into bed and slept for 14 hours straight. When she got up she and Bert began revising the terse scientific paper they had prepared for *Science* magazine—if it was published there, it became a part of the official record of science, and who knows, might indeed make Lou a contender for a Nobel Prize. With glee they boiled the paper down to the absolute minimum number of words. "Let's show 'em Ecotopian elegance!" Lou gloated as she made a final count. "It's 402 words."

"Well," said Bert, "we can get rid of a couple more somewhere—get it down to a round 400."

And so the article went off, with duplicate copies for protection purposes flying in various other directions. The *Science* editors, wary of "amateur scientists," delayed publication until another laboratory could repeat Lou's crucial experiment. But then the piece appeared as the lead report in its issue, titled simply "A New Mechanism for Photovoltaic Cells."

When the San Francisco magazine article appeared, journalists began phoning again and Lou decided it was time to deal with them, explaining that the public disclosure meant the invention was now in the public domain and that in fact she was planning with the Survivalist Party a program to help people build their own rooftop cells. The resulting stories, as she had feared, ranged from the sensational ("GIRL SCIENTIST GIVES UP MILLIONS") to the skeptical ("YOUNG INVENTOR HOPES TO LIBERATE HOMES FROM POWER LINES"). She kept the clippings in a pile in one corner of her lab. And she sent a copy of the *Science* article to Professor Gleason.

As Roger had expected, the announcement of Lou's process created panic in the utilities corporations. There were anguished discussions in the executive suites as captains of the industry explored possible ways to counter or delay the cell's probable impact. Some officials hoped that technological problems of hooking cell arrays into house circuits that remained connected to the electrical grid might be exploited. Others argued that building codes could be invoked to prevent people from disconnecting from the grid entirely—but of course nobody could force people to actually consume electricity, so a basic connection charge would have to be devised to make up for the lost revenue—a move that even a docile state public utility commission might hesitate to rubber-stamp. No question about it: if the Swift cell was widely used, electrical grid demand would fall substantially. The major remaining consumers of electrical power would be manufacturing and processing industries, which had fought bitterly to maintain preferential low rates and would now undoubtedly redouble their efforts at co-generation—the use of waste heat to generate electricity on their own premises.

The utility executives could hardly help wondering what they had done wrong. Had the government deliberately suckered them into nuclear to make nuclear weapons seem more acceptable? Had they, like Detroit with its devotion to gas-guzzlers, simply been unable to see what was coming because it was too transparently obvious to be believable? And would they now be able, like so many corporations before them, to obtain government bail-out funds until they could reorient their operations to meet the new realities? If not, utilities like Great Northwestern, already on the verge of bankruptcy, perceived that in the Survivalist Party program for an entirely renewable-resource energy system their doom was sealed.

The only hope for the utilities lay in the possibility that since the Swift Effect had been put in the public domain, nobody might seriously attempt to make cells based on it. This, after all, had been the pattern with penicillin: for 20 years after its discovery, the drug companies had not felt the possible profits were worthwhile, so they didn't bother with it until World War II forced them into it. The Survivalist crazies on the Pacific Coast might put their plans for do-it-yourself cells into limited effect there. But for the rest of the country, unless the Japanese jumped into the cell market, or the damned government decided to sabotage them again, the utilities might squeak through for a few more years.

Sometimes Jamie McBride got so moody that his friends worried about him. After Mary's death he had worked a lot in the shop, paying off some of his debts and keeping busy. But he could be light-hearted and charming too, and women who had coveted him while he was with Mary seized the chance and dropped around to his teepee. He refused to get serious with any of them, however, and when they tried to probe into his feelings in their gentle country way he would say things like, "Well, since Mary's trouble I just can't get into anything where I feel responsible." So they mostly loved him and left him, in their fashions. But one particular woman, Lucy, was persistent and after a while Jamie took to letting her stay overnight in the teepee. Mary had been small and lithe; Lucy was lush and pillowy—

as different from Mary (she suspected) as Jamie could find. Still, they had terrific times in bed, especially after a little of the old home-grown got Jamie firmly into the here and now.

In the early morning hours of November 20th, they were lolling about on the mattress in the teepee, giggly and still a little sleepy after a particularly cozy night. Jamie had offered to get up and make some coffee. Lucy had said she'd do it in a little while. Then, tussling over who was to do it, they found themselves feeling sexy again. It was later, as they were dozing, that Jamie was wakened by a helicopter, whose clap-clap-clap filtered through the cloth of the teepee. He sat up suddenly with a strange look in his eyes. "Honey," he said, "I can't let them get you!"

"Jamie, what are you talking about?" said Lucy, rolling over.

"It's coming back!" Jamie yelled, and ran out of the teepee nude. Lucy crept over to the teepee door. The copter was coming on slowly, trailing its toxic cloud. Jamie stared at it, then ran into the house. In a moment he reappeared followed by Jane and Mack, with his rifle in his hand, fumbling with the ammunition box. "Wait, Jamie!" Lucy cried. But he had run toward the edge of the forest, paying no atten-tion. The helicopter, she realized, was much nearer; it seemed to be heading almost directly for them. Then there was a sharp crack, and after that the helicopter noise faded away.

Jamie rushed into the teepee, pale and sweating, and grabbed his clothes. "We've got to get out, *fast!* Those spray bastards have done it again!"

Throwing on clothes haphazardly, they all four ran down the lane, just ahead of the spray cloud. As they ran, they heard a faint explo-sion off to the northeast. "Christ, Jamie, you must have got him!" said Mack. Jamie stopped. "Got to get rid of that gun," he said. He ran back toward the teepee, into the herbicide fog. In a few moments he caught up and they reached their old truck. Jumping into it, they headed toward town. On the way they stopped along the river, filed off the rifle's serial number, and buried it under heavy rocks in the river bed. Then they went to Lucy's place, cleaned up thoroughly, and coordinated their stories. Jamie went to the shop and picked up with an engine rebuilding job he had been in the middle of. The other men joshed him about being late. "Well, you know, I spent the night with Lucy," he said. They smiled appreciatively.

The next day, after an extensive search, a rescue party reached the wreckage of the copter. The pilot, William Whitehead, was dead. The sheriff's office stated that a rifle bullet hole had been found in the control panel of the burned-out craft, indicating it had been fired upon by persons unknown, resulting in engine malfunction and thus the crash.

Many people in the district secretly or openly felt that the death of the pilot was in some obscure way justified. Whitehead, after all, had probably sprayed the McBride homestead earlier, no matter what the jury said. There were 30 or 40 families living along that ridge, and any member of any of them might have felt murderous if a copter pilot strayed near their land. There were now plenty of people in the county, the sheriff knew, who were capable of going out into the forest and just waiting, on a day scheduled for spraying, in hopes of getting a good shot. He knew Jamie McBride's story, of course, and sent a man around to interrogate him. Jamie replied evenly to the questioning. "No," he said, "we didn't hear any copter. We got up and got organized and headed for town pretty early. Jane and Mack had shopping to do and I had to get to work. Fact it was real quiet that morning. I just wish it was always so quiet."

"Yeah," said the sheriff's man, "I guess I know how you feel, Jamie."

GUERRILLA CONFLICT FLARES
IN BRAZILIAN NORTHEAST

Brasilia, Nov. 21 (WPI). Government sources revealed here today that the Brazilian armed forces have committed another 75,000 troops to the struggle against the FLB rebels. Airborne units make up a large proportion of the new forces. Government officials said these units had been specially trained by American advisors in helicopter assault strategy developed for search-and-destroy missions in the Vietnam War.

A major new headquarters for the ongoing anti-guerrilla struggle is being established near Campo Formosa in the poverty-stricken "sertao" areas. However, government troops have also been combatting rebel forces, said to be armed with Soviet weaponry, in the fringe Amazon jungles further north.

Cuban sources have denied that the rebel forces in Brazil have been receiving Cuban aid. The size of the Brazilian reinforcements, however, has led some observers to speculate that the government

238

suspects Cuban troops may be present in the area.

In other developments in Brazil, a large oil installation near the town of Petrolina was blown up yesterday by guerrilla saboteurs. Authorities insisted that the loss of oil from this source was not significant in the total national supply picture. Guerrilla leaders, however, declared that further attacks would be made, claiming that no physical facility in the area could ever be made secure against them.

The Brazilian government has asked the United States to provide 200 new attack helicopters of the Destructor type, also known as the HS-14. They are equipped with night-seeing infra-red equipment especially adapted to guerrilla warfare, and are armored against small-arms and rocket fire of the types most encountered in Vietnam. The Pentagon has announced that top priority will be given to the Brazilian order because of the "increasing gravity" of the Brazilian situation.

All her life Laura had hated hospitals, hated their bureaucratic atmosphere, their chemical smells, their air of depression, and their increasingly intimidating scale. She had even managed to give birth to Ben and Marissa at home, though it had been hard to find obstetricians willing to do home deliveries, and with Marissa she'd been assisted by a midwife. Her early relationships with doctors had often been edgy, but finally, in her late twenties, she had found one she could get along with. Pete, as she called him, practiced general medicine out of an old shingled house converted into offices which he shared with an obstetrician, a pediatrician and an internist. At a time when it was not yet fashionable, Laura had insisted that the central responsibility for her health, mental and physical, was her own. She had studied nutrition and first aid; she had amassed a stock of herbal remedies for various family ailments; she had tried bioenergetics and other unconventional therapies. Little by little, in areas of more traditional medicine, she had also trained Pete to treat her as a person entitled to and capable of decision-making about treatment options. She asked to be told the factors involved, to be given the opportunity to follow up by her own reading if she felt the need, and to decide what was to be done or not done. Sometimes she accepted Pete's advice; sometimes she went against it. She would take the consequences of her own decisions, just as she did in other aspects of her life.

Pete's office was in her neighborhood, and she could walk to it. But now she had to go to a central hospital for tests, which never gave good news, though at least the news was not always significantly worse. And she had to consider the choices about therapy: whether to concentrate on strengthening her system's defenses to help it ward off the cancer or to experiment with radiation and chemotherapy techniques—none of them notably effective against lung cancer, and with probable side effects of nausea, loss of her hair, and loss of her appetites for food or sexual pleasure. She inclined toward conserving her strength, foregoing the hopeless treatments, trying to mobilize her body's own remarkable energies. "I don't intend to let all my attention turn inward against me," she said to Pete. "I'm going to focus all that anger *outward*. Much healthier!"

"Mmm," said Pete. "How are you going to manage that?"

"Leave it to me," said Laura. "I've thought of some ways."

"Well, you've always been an easy patient in not pushing for treatment. I could hardly get you to take aspirin! But you know, if you want us to try these things, you're entitled. Half of all our medical expenditures are spent in the last 180 days of patients' lives. And you haven't come near using up your other half yet."

Laura contemplated the workings of the medical establishment with some irony. She had always complained bitterly of its gross neglect of public health, nutrition, and medical prevention that could have made the entirety of people's lives much healthier. Only 15 percent of the country's medical outlays went to keep people well; a vast amount went on caring for trivial colds and other minor complaints that people should know how to treat for themselves, and half went for "crisis medicine" in those last dying days. Sprawling new hospitals incurred heavy expenses for administration, construction, paperwork, litigation, spectacular machinery. But what was really needed was a network of small neighborhood hospitals or clinics which would practice preventive medicine and deal with people as human beings, not just as numbers in the anonymous "patient flow."

Meanwhile, it was some slight consolation to know that when doctors went on strike and a community was denied their services, the death rate actually *declined*. Nobody knew why. Perhaps there were fewer deaths from profitable but unnecessary surgery. Perhaps, left to their own devices, people somehow decided to take better care of themselves. Perhaps, by remaining outside hospitals, they caught fewer contagious diseases. Laura was always glad to know there were such mysteries in the world. It helped keep her awake, she sometimes said.

Lou's aunt Sarah had invited Roger and Carol and the kids over to Orinda to spend Sunday. It was a crisp winter day so they all took a walk up the hill to an overlook where there was a lovely view down toward the reservoir lake to the north. After they got back they sat down to lunch, and Andy held up his wine glass.

"Ahem! Now I'd like to make an important family announcement. Attention, please!" He looked around as silence fell. "I wanted you to be the first to know that Uncle Andrew has taken a new job. A very *good* new job."

Roger clinked his glass against Andy's. "Congratulations," he said. "That's terrific. What *is* it?"

"I'm going to ConCo. They have this huge—"

"*ConCo?*" said Roger. His face, Lou saw, had gone very pale. "You mean ConCo?" Roger's hand shook; he had to put down his glass.

"Yes, the engineering company. Their contract department is—"

Roger glared at his brother. "Andrew, what the fuck have you done? What are you doing, going to work for them?"

Andy shrugged defensively. "Oh, come on, Roger. They do very interesting projects. Very big things, that matter. That last. I can't accept that good guys versus bad guys stuff you Survivalist people are peddling. It's too complicated for that."

"They made you an offer you couldn't refuse. That jackass Bentley, I'll bet. When you creamed him in that discrimination suit he figured they'd better get you on their side!"

"Sure, Bentley wanted me. So what? Look, Roger, I'm just getting tired of beating my brains out for nothing, that's all."

"You call this nothing?" said Roger, waving around at the house and pool and view. Everybody else had stopped eating.

"ConCo is the big time. It'll give me some real scope, a real base to work from."

"Yeah, a real base all right. A pack of militarist sons of bitches with their noses up tight to the ass of every Corps of Engineers bureaucrat, and every Arab sheik, and every power-company executive, and every Defense Department guy they can get within licking range of!"

241

"It's business, Roger, that's all. Sooner or later we've got to face it. That's how things are done in this society."

"Things like nuclear plants, maybe? Andrew, you are going to have *blood* on your hands!"

Lou thought her uncle looked a little pale too, at this. Roger, on the other hand, had now regained his color and in fact turned quite red in the face. His voice, normally low and calm, was harsh and sarcastic. She had seen Roger angry often enough—he would bark or yell, but his anger never lasted very long and he was never mean. This was different. She knew Roger loved his younger brother and never criticized him, at least when anybody else was around. This argument was therefore doubly terrible.

"You're being unrealistic, Roger. Nuclear is safer than *coal*, for Christ's sake, which is the real alternative: less immediate deaths, less pollution, in fact less *radiation*, even. But the main thing is, we need it. And if somebody's going to build plants, they ought to be built as well as possible. That's what ConCo happens to be good at."

"But not good enough. *Nobody* is good enough to shave those odds! Sooner or later we'll have a meltdown, we'll have a containment blow, we'll lose a city. You know that!" Roger pointed his finger at his brother. "Andy, they're the enemy, remember? They trample over everybody and everything. They're so big they can't help doing harm, even if they tried to do good—which they don't! They're centralizers, authoritarians, promoters, profiteers, exploiters. They'll build whatever anybody will pay for, without any qualms about its effects on people or the environment or the future."

"Well," said Andy with a smug expression that Lou did not remember seeing before, "decisions about things like that are made in the political arena. I've paid my dues in that arena several times over. Now I'm willing to let others argue about those issues. And when they're decided I'll come in and do the contracts and deal with the regulations and get the job done."

"Spoken like a true sell-out technocrat—just itching to do your job and forget about the consequences!"

Andy looked at his brother. "If you're trying to hurt me," he said slowly, "you're succeeding. But it won't change my mind. I'm moving over to ConCo next week. Even if you feel betrayed. Even if I lose your respect."

Roger sat back in his chair. "You'll never lose my love, Andy. But yes, you are losing my respect. And my trust. You're going over to the

242

wrong side, Andy. You may regret it, but then again you may not. As far as I'm concerned, it'll be worse if you don't. It would be awful to see you make your million and get fat and complacent and begin to hang aroung with people like Bentley, until you forget what you're really doing."

"I know what I'm doing."

"Well, if you do you're selling your soul. You're becoming an expensive hired gun. You might even get to be the best in the business. Fine, enjoy it, but don't get to thinking that justice is on your side. History *isn't* going to absolve ConCo, you know. Or you."

They ate a few more bites without anybody saying much. Roger swallowed several glasses of wine too quickly, and invented an excuse to go home. Usually he threw his arm around Andy's shoulder as they left. This time they did not touch, and after he said goodbye and had settled into the car Roger sighed heavily, and then again. "Shit!" he said, as Carol put the car in gear. "Shit, shit, shit."

As the membership of the Survivalist Party increasingly abandoned hopes of rational government in Washington, Vera Allwen felt as if she were coming to live in the shadow country of Ecotopia, rather than in "the old country," as her associates had now begun to call the United States. Nonetheless, she was startled when a visitor to the Green House announced that he was a representative of the Quebec government and wished to discuss establishing an official diplomatic mission.

"But we aren't a country. You can't maintain diplomatic relations except with countries, surely?"

"We are not particularly concerned with official labels," said the emissary. "Our desire is simply to establish a close relationship. We feel a certain kinship with you, after all, since you are striving to defend yourself against the rest of your country, just as we have been against the rest of ours."

"I can understand that. We might have ideas to share."

"We might be able to *help* each other."

"That seems unlikely—you're three thousand miles away."

The Quebecois smiled. "But we are only a few hundred miles from New York. If another oil crisis comes, New York will be needing our hydro power to keep all those air conditioners running."

A few days later a small building across the street from the Green House was sandblasted down to its original brick. It had once been a corner cafe for warehouse workers, featuring chili dogs, beer, and juke-box music. Now the flag of Quebec, bearing four crisp white fleurs-de-lys, flew over its front door.

The episode started some new ideas circulating among Vera and her colleagues. Soon an Ecotopia Institute research team began studying other incipient "international relations" for Ecotopia. In certain critical minerals, as well as in oil, the United States was heavily dependent upon two of the world's most reactionary governments, South Africa and Saudi Arabia. Sooner or later they would fall, probably in the flames of civil war. The sooner Ecotopia could extricate its economy from such dangerous dependency, the better. The team was instructed to come up with practical alternatives—substitutes, recycling, other sources. Ecotopia needed new, less sinister friends.

. "All right, class," Midge Murray began, "you know where we're going on today's field trip?"

"Omni Oil!" came the chorus from her eighth-graders.

"And what are we going to be looking for?"

"Technological processes!" said Nathan, the class's best scientific head.

"Chain of command!" said Carlotta, who always wanted to know how people related to each other. "And how it compares with the co-op we visited last week."

"Propaganda!" said Natalie. "I want to see if they try to tell us how great Omni is."

"Division of labor," said Nathan, realizing that nobody else thought technology could be talked about all by itself.

"Anything else?" asked Midge.

"Well, uh, products," said Kenny. "You know, what they're making out there."

"And raw materials," added Sue.

"And energy!" said Natalie.

"What about energy?" asked Midge.

"Where they get it, how much they use, how much comes out."

"Good. I see you'll have plenty of questions to ask. Now before we

244

get on the bus, remember that the people working in this plant are no better than you and no worse than you. It'll probably seem like a pretty strange place at first, but you might find yourself working in a plant like it some day. We want to find out what's going on. Then when we get back here we'll analyze and discuss it. Our two aides, Laura and Nils, will be along with us. Nils knows a lot about chemical plants because he used to work for a chemical company. So they'll help us sort it all out later. Any questions?"

The class of 24, lively and buzzing as usual, trooped off the bus a half hour later at Omni Plant 37. This morning Laura seemed pale and preoccupied, and her heavy handbag seemed to weigh her down; sometimes Nils took a turn carrying it for her. The class was met by one of the company's smooth public relations people and, in a straggly clump which Midge Murray herded like a good sheep dog, they moved through the plant—a complex of buildings, pipes, cracking towers, tanks, pumps, runways. Only a few employees were to be seen; like a refinery, the plant was highly automated. The work of monitoring and controlling its operations was performed in a sealed, windowless control room in an office tower—carefully air-conditioned and thus the only part of the plant where chemical odors did not penetrate. Repair and cleaning crews moved about occasionally, the latter in space-age protection suits. Armed guards periodically patrolled the area.

Finally the tour guide led the class to the exit, passing through the plant's office building. "So there you are, boys and girls," he concluded. "The story of how Omni makes the chemicals that contribute to the food you eat and to the healthy economy of our great state. Hope you enjoyed the tour!" The students began filing out the door, but Laura went up to the guide.

"There is a bomb in Unit 12," she said quietly.

To the guide Laura looked like a harmless, rather wan old woman. "That's very kind of you to tell us," he said condescendingly. "Now what did you see out there that looked like a bomb?"

"No," said Laura, "it *is* a bomb. I put it there. You had better evacuate the plant instantly. And tell people not to touch the bomb—it'll go off if it's touched. It's in a large brown fabric bag."

The guide was perplexed. "Ma'am," he said, "are you joking? Bomb threats are no laughing matter—"

"It's not a joke," said Laura. "It's a real bomb, and it will go off in six more minutes." Seeing she was having no effect, she finally raised

245

her voice. "Get your people out of there, *now!*" Then she added with a half smile, "I'll just wait here till you get around to having me arrested. We also have a public statement to make," she added, indicating Nils, who had come to stand beside her.

"My God," said the guide, "I think you mean it!" He rushed to a telephone. The children, meanwhile, had reached their bus. Then Midge realized that Laura and Nils were not with them. Having noticed how pale Laura looked, Midge worried that she might have tripped or even fainted, and she ran back to look for her. Just as she reached the office door, the wail of a siren hit her. Moments later people began pouring out of the building, and she had to push her way through them to get back to the office area. There next to Nils Laura stood, hands in her coat pockets, watching the excitement with a strange air of calm. "Laura, come on!" said Midge. "It must be some kind of fire drill or something. Let's get going!"

"No," said Laura. "We're staying for a while, Midge. You take the kids and go on. We'll see you later. I'll be okay. You know I love excitement!" Seeing Midge was doubtful, she added a white lie. "Nils and I are going to have a good argument with that Mr. Sissonen, maybe go to lunch. We'll take the bus back and see you this afternoon."

As the remaining Omni employees streamed from the offices, the control rooms, the shops, and headed for their evacuation stations, the automatic machinery continued its operations untended, having for the most part little need of human supervision. Ten minutes after she had primed it and placed it behind a control panel, Laura's bomb went off. Because she and Nils had taken pains to arrange the blast so that no finished herbicides were within range, the explosion created no poisonous cloud to drift over nearby residential areas. But the bomb did destroy the entire control system for Unit 12 and a great deal of expensive nearby equipment. Unit 12 would produce no more dioxin-contaminated herbicides for at least a year.

Laura and Nils had prearranged that several Cancer Commando comrades would be waiting in a van outside the plant. One of them had stood at a nearby pay phone to contact the media as soon as the plant evacuation siren sounded, so a TV crew arrived only a few minutes after the police did. Presented with a prepared statement by the group of thin, haggard people in the van, the news team realized they had a very hot story indeed, and they managed to get a few moments of footage showing Laura and Nils being led away by the police. Then, to their astonishment, several people from the van identified themselves as accomplices in the bombing who would shortly turn themselves in too, but who would be glad to be interviewed beforehand.

The TV crew knew the network guidelines against letting themselves be "used" by radical groups. But here? A huge chemical installation lies smoking in ruins; a sweet old woman had just been dragged away by the cops, saying she and her gaunt man friend did it. And now these other sick-looking people say they're in on it too, and they're all condemned cancer victims and just wanted to take a poison-plant with them before they go—nobody could suppress this story! So the camera operator got out his camera again and ran two reels of questions and answers. Then the Cancer Commandos phoned the police who duly came back and, shaking their heads as the camera whirred, took them away.

"CANCER COMMANDOS" STRIKE OMNI PLANT

San Francisco, Nov. 23 (WPI). Damage estimated at $1,500,000 was caused to an Omni Oil chemical plant east of Richmond yesterday. A bomb was set off in the plant by a group calling itself "The Cancer Commandos," claiming to be made up of persons condemned to die from chemical-induced cancer. Leaders who gave themselves up to arresting officers immediately after the blast were Laura D'Amato, 54, of San Francisco, and Nils Anderson, 59, a Mendocino County resident. Three others associated with the group were also arrested outside the plant, where they were handing out leaflets after the explosion.

The Contra Costa sheriff's office, which has jurisdiction over the plant area, expressed skepticism at the group's claim to be terminally ill cancer patients. "Complete medical tests will be made immediately on all the arrested persons," a spokesman announced. Asked if special hospital facilities might be required while the arrestees are held for trial, the spokesman had no comment. "In any case, the medical status of these people will have no effect on how we handle the case," he said. "A serious crime against property has been committed. It will

Text of Cancer Commando Communique:—

WE BLEW THE OMNI PLANT FOR YOU!

Fellow citizens, you know you are being poisoned. You know that American cancer rates, already intolerably high, are rising again. And you know that one of the major causes is the irresponsible proliferation of herbicide and pesticide chemicals in the environment and in food and water. Last year more than three billion pounds of pesticide were produced in this country, as compared with 100,000 pounds in 1940. Yet the proportion of our crops consumed by insect pests remains just about the same.

In other words, all this dispersion of poisons is not "saving our food supply," as the chemical corporation death-merchants argue. It is just making them money.

We say it has to stop. We say it is just as much a crime to pour cancer- and mutation-causing chemicals into the environment as it is to go out on the streets and stick people up with guns. We don't want cancer to go on claiming one out of every four Americans, and more in the future. And since our government refuses to protect us, we must protect ourselves!

Most people don't see much that they can do. But we are a group of people diagnosed as terminally ill from cancer. We are going to die soon, and we wanted to do something for humanity before we go. We can ACT, without fear of the consequences. So we have decided to make an example of the dangerous Omni plant—the producer of immense quantities of deadly chemical poisons. We have shown Omni that they, and the other chemical merchants, cannot continue on their criminal path with impunity any longer. In the interests of this generation, and of all the generations yet unborn, the Cancer Commandos say, "Stop! Enough!"

Please join with us. Let the government know we will not take it any more! Outlaw cancer-causing chemicals in our food, water, air! And if the government will not act, help those in your midst who will strike at the criminals directly. A determined people can be a free people. Dare to struggle, dare to win, dare to survive! —THE CANCER COMMANDOS

248

be prosecuted with vigor. It was just great good luck that nobody was killed."

The Cancer Commando group has issued a communique claiming responsibility for the bombing and giving its reasons for the action (see box for text).

Omni officials expressed outrage at the bombing. "This is a vindictive vigilante act," said Thomas Littrell, president of Omni. "Even though this group evidently knew enough about the plant to avoid spreading harmful substances in the vicinity, their bombing was still reckless and dangerous to public health. Moreover, the bombing strikes at the freedom of American business to conduct manufacturing operations that conform to local, state and federal law. If these people do indeed have cancer, I am sorry to hear it. But there is no way they can establish in a court of law that our plant was responsible for that. We will cooperate fully with the district attorney in making sure that they receive the severest sentences possible."

Sometimes Lou had to get away from Bert and the preparations for disseminating information about her cell. When she heard that Sharp & Natural was doing a concert in a little town called Point Reyes Station, on Tomales Bay, she went up to have some fun. The session was terrific, she thought, and she felt very proud of the band. Afterwards, David took her to an old farm house in a nearby valley where he now lived part of the time. As a change from the intensity of his own music, David put on some Hawaiian records and they had a couple of tokes and made love. The music was soft, sinuous, gentle, playful. Lou found herself floating happily along with it almost as if she were in some soft, swelling warm ocean, and she had a series of long, sweet orgasms that made her feel as if the boundaries between herself and David and the universe had melted. It was all pure motion, pure energy, and her body moved without her having to think in the slightest about what it was doing. "I've got it! I've got it!" she cried, with an angelic, beaming smile.

"What have you got?" asked David, pulling himself back so he could really see her, though their bodies continued moving, ever so gently, in a kind of polyphonic theme and response. "Something about your cell?"

Lou began to giggle helplessly. "No, no! Something much nicer. It's—uh—"

She had drifted off for a moment. David kissed her on the ear.

"It's—well, I just realized that music is *frozen sex*." A happy grin spread over her face.

"Frozen? What are you talking about?"

"Well, see, now I understand why it *gets* to you so. It's because it takes all those sexual energy patterns, which usually just vanish totally as soon as they've happened, and it *preserves* them—so you can experience it again. You can record it, or write it down, or play it again. You save it from the passing of time."

Lou looked at him with her large grey eyes, now wide and serious. "So now I also understand why I've always been fascinated by your being a musician, you see?"

"No—tell more."

"Well, when I watch you playing, it's almost the same thing as making love with you. The music is audible fucking-feelings. They're not just inside anymore—you and the band have this wonderful gift of getting them out into the public eye. —I mean ear."

Now David laughed. "I get you. There's *some* music like that, anyway. Though I also have to tell you that sex can also be frozen music."

TOP SECRET
TO: STATION CHIEFS

An instance of low-level penetration of the Agency by adherents of the Survivalist Party/Ecotopian movement has been uncovered in the Seattle area. Infiltration into government bodies, corporations, and the armed forces is suspected and may have been in progress for at least a year. Intelligence agencies have certainly been targeted for such activities.

All stations are ordered to review the security of their key personnel within the next ten days. This is a national order; Survivalist sympathizer groups exist in all parts of the country. Precautions against access to sensitive documents should be strengthened, especially regarding personnel taken aboard in the past three years. Since many of the leaders of the SP are female, this security review should not neglect women staff members, no matter how innocuous their personalities or professional roles may appear to be.

After the public disorders caused by the Madera decision, Vera Allwen's television speeches became more urgent. "My friends, we must consider the possibility that the federal government has become quite irrational in its decisions about fundamental energy problems. What else can we think of a government that refuses to move seriously against the automobile oil costs which are draining the economy dry? A government that puts its research and development money almost entirely into nuclear power when we already have sufficient electrical generating capacity for reasonable uses? A government that tries to force the reopening of a nuclear plant situated on an active, dangerous earthquake fault? A government that refuses to help the poor people in cold areas to insulate their houses and thus cut oil imports? A government that strikes down, through its Supreme Court, our attempts to save ourselves from such disastrous policies?

"Who is crazy here—we who are attempting to take care of ourselves, or the national government which seems bent on economic and social suicide?

"The answer, I suspect, lies in the fact that in the past decade we who live here on the Northern Pacific coast have become a new and different people. We have learned to think differently—more realistically and over a longer time frame—than the people in Washington, who can think ahead only four years at the most.

"We did not seek this. Our history has given it to us. Through a million different experiences in the lives of millions of us, we have come to hold different values from those prevalent in the rest of the country. We conserve and preserve; they waste and spend. We treasure our natural resources; they despoil them.

"Our part of the continent is relatively uncontaminated. Its forests and seashores and mountains provide a timeless uplift for our spirits when we go camping or hiking. Thus we have learned more rapidly than people elsewhere to respect the lives of our fellow species—the mammals our nearest kin, the trees whose lumber shelters us, the tiniest fish, the very grasses that give soft cover to our hillsides. And so, as fellow travelers on the planet, in this region we have enacted many environmental protections. We have expanded our parks, and fought for the preservation of our coastline public spaces. We have recovered rich farmland from suburban sprawl. We are defending the relative purity of our air and water.

"Here on the Pacific shores, we are also a healthier people. We live outdoor lives and are accustomed to getting around on our own two

251

feet. We have learned again to enjoy walking—whether on solitary forest trails or on our lively streets that we have been making safe again for pedestrians, by night and by day. We have understood, earlier and more clearly than people elsewhere, the need to curb the imperial power of the car—which not only threatens to destroy our economy, but also disrupts our neighborhoods, pollutes our air, and involves us in the danger of a nuclear war over oil. We have refused to let our cars be held hostage by the oil countries. Instead, we have developed minibuses and streetcars and trains and new kinds of efficient taxis—alternatives which make it easier to live well without cars. And we are working to reorganize our cities so people need to move around less in their daily lives.

"We have been doing all these sane things right here, in our lucky little green strip along the Pacific. We have been tending to our business here, despite interference from outside, while the national government was daydreaming and flexing its military muscles to intimidate people all over the world. I ask you, my friends, what can we do when we are confronted with this kind of madness? It sucks away our tax money and pours it down the armaments drain. It risks our lives in conflicts we did not choose. Its actions oppress the poor, the old, the weak, and shower favors on the already rich and powerful. Is there not some point at which we must say that we cannot participate any longer in this? When we will decide that we must have a society toward which we can feel loyalty?

"A free people must have a government that embodies the ideals of that people. We are a people who want to feel at home here on the earth, serene in the knowledge that we are living in harmony with the other beings on the planet. If the federal government is hostile to these values, we must find our own ways to survive together, taking our proper places in the great circle of being, joining our hands and our hearts. A suicidal national government, a government that seems bent on devouring its people rather than nurturing them, forfeits our allegiance. We did not choose this situation. But we must recognize realities. My friends, dear friends—we are on our own."

Frank Werdon was a friend of Jamie McBride's who had ten acres on the other side of the valley. He worked in Myrtle Grove at the hardware store, and he and Jamie sometimes went to listen to music together at the Hot Spot. Frank possessed a 1960 Ford sedan which he had kept running by pure blind determination and some help from Jamie. They regarded it, by this time, as a challenge: if the damned thing had run this long, there was no way they were going to let it die! Most parts were still available, luckily, though once or twice Jamie had to machine something specially. Of course it ate gas, but what old car didn't?

Finally, however, the gas costs and frequency of repairs got to Frank. He was pouring money into the wreck, but for what—just a kind of a dare, really. Still, how could he afford a new car, even a new used car? He talked about it with Jamie one night, over some beers. "Well," said Jamie at one point, "maybe it's back to the horse!" He swallowed a gulp of beer, and Frank laughed.

But then Jamie looked at him again. "Frank, you've got all that *grass* out there."

"Let's just stick to beer tonight, Jamie."

"No, I mean green grass that horses eat. You've got three acres of great pasture."

"I still don't get it."

"Horses *eat* grass. You have grass. You could get a horse."

"But I don't know anything about horses! —I gave 'em apples when I was a kid."

"It can't be that hard. This country used to have more horses than it had people."

"I thought horses were for rich people in the suburbs and to bet on at the races."

"Well, used to be that everything that moved was drawn by horses. Or mules. Plows, streetcars, carts, stagecoaches—you know all about that."

"Yeah, I've seen it in the movies, anyway."

"Hell, they can't be much harder to raise than a goat, and you've had goats out there."

"That's true." The idea began to grow on Frank. "Grass power, huh? I could fix up that little barn for a stable. But I don't much like the idea of riding around on a smelly wet saddle in the rain."

"You'll just have to find a buggy. Or build one. Motorbike wheels. Nice two-wheel job with a sort of cabin on it, made out of that stuff they do convertible tops with."

"Hey, I like that! But what about at night? I don't want some driver to turn me and my horse into stew."

253

"You carry a battery, like the old Amish farmers in Pennsylvania do, for a headlight and some tail lights. Plug it into a charger in the stable."

"Okay, but how about speed? I'm ten miles out, don't forget."

"Aw, no problem. A good horse'll do 20 miles an hour easy. Besides, you got to remember you're getting really cheap transportation—sun-powered. Think of all the hours you used to work to support that heap. If you added in those hours as part of your travel time, you were only doing about five miles an hour anyway."

"Whutt?"

"Well, you can't just figure on the time when you're *in* the car. You've got to add in the time you spend to *get* into it. Working to pay the depreciation, the maintenance, the gas and oil, the insurance, the license, all that."

"But it still goes at least 70, with a tailwind."

"Sure it does. But that's only one piece of the puzzle. While you're working to support the car, that's *part* of the travel process too. Can't just leave it out."

Frank got it, suddenly, and smiled broadly. "Jamie, I see what you mean! It's not just the here-to-there, it's how much time it takes you to get set to go!"

"Right. So if a horse and cart cost a quarter as much to run as that car, you are suddenly going to have either a lot of free time or a lot of extra money, and you'll get to town practically as fast anyhow, considering the shape that road is in."

Jamie fished a pencil out of his pocket and the two men began drawing, on paper napkins, sketches for a light, two-wheeled horse-drawn buggy with a snug passenger compartment and a sort of trunk underneath the seat for luggage.

In the labyrinthine piping of the Puget 1 reactor, the hairline crack that had shown up on the X-rays had gradually lengthened. Under the relentless pressure of the coolant water that it carried, the pipe finally ruptured. Water began to flood the great spherical containment su__ __e that housed the reactor, and pressure in the primary coolant circuit dropped precipitously. In theory, automatic control devices were supposed to sense such events and react by closing huge valves to prevent further water loss while opening others that would direct emergency core-cooling water into the reactor vessel. Generation of heat and power would also be slowed by the insertion of neutron-absorbing control rods into the fissioning uranium core.

However, maintenance and inspection work in an operating reactor is difficult and costly at best, and to minimize interruption of output from the expensive plant, Great Northwestern had attempted to carry out such work while the plant was running—a common practice among the owners of nuclear reactors—and safety checks afterward were often omitted. In this case, maintenance work on a subsidiary water system had necessitated temporary closing of a large valve that normally provided water for emergency core-cooling, and technicians had neglected to reopen the valve after they finished work. When the accident began, therefore, the emergency cooling system was ineffective. However, because the position indicator for the valve was inoperative, possibly because it had been disabled during the maintenance work, this fact was not grasped by the operators in the control room until many minutes had passed. By this time the sudden rise in temperature within the reactor core had already caused some deformation of the fuel assembly. Possibly for this reason—though later investigations also pointed to the possibility of electronic failure in certain relay equipment—the control rods did not drop smoothly into the core. Thus temperatures in the reactor rose even more rapidly and unevenly. Finally additional emergency cooling systems went into action, but by this point a mass of fuel rods had crumpled into the bottom of the reactor vessel where the water could not cool them effectively—the dread situation known as a meltdown. This intensely hot and radioactive mass of uranium began to melt its way through the bottom of the reactor vessel and the reinforced concrete floor beneath. In addition, intensely radioactive gases under high pressure filled the containment sphere, mingled with hydrogen produced by the reaction of the rod cladding with water.

Since this situation was what all the elaborate safety equipment of the plant had been designed to prevent, the operators had a natural reluctance to believe it was actually happening. In the confusion of the emergency they did not always believe the control-board indicators, and for some crucial minutes they continued to alter programs and reset controls in the belief that the "scram," or shut-down process, was probably working—even though some instruments indicated otherwise. Meanwhile, the molten mass of uranium continued to work its way downward.

When the fuel had nearly burned its way through the concrete foundation, a spark from a pump motor ignited the hydrogen bubble in the reactor vessel above it. The resulting explosion not only demolished the vessel and spread highly radioactive material throughout the containment sphere, but it also drove the molten fuel mass downward, giving it the last push to break through the remaining concrete.

When the hot fuel came in contact with the water-laden earth beneath, great quantities of steam were suddenly generated. With an unearthly shriek that deepened into a roar, its explosive force pushed out a channel through the soil and rock under the reactor foundation. The radioactive contents of the containment sphere, along with radioactive debris, earth and water vapor, were blown out through this excavated tunnel into the surrounding atmosphere. The explosion was heard for some miles, and a cloud of radioactive steam and small particles rose several thousand feet into the air.

Because the steam escape fissure happened to run underneath the nearby generating buildings, these now listed into the crevass formed when the channel collapsed. Multimillion-dollar generators, their polished blades of stainless steel whirling helplessly, tumbled into the wound of the earth amid the debris of buildings, huge transformers, control room computers. The mass of molten fuel settled into a cavern of its own construction, apparently dispersed by some lucky formation of rock strata enough that it no longer burned its way downward; as water seeped into the hole, it was transformed into a giant tower of steam which rose toward the stratosphere like the plume of a volcano.

Plant officials in an office building that survived the explosion phoned the governor's office. A state of emergency was immediately declared, and an attempt was begun to evacuate all persons downwind from the plant, while hastily deployed monitors tried to keep track of the main path of the radioactive fallout. However, the state had no serious evacuation plan, and total confusion ensued. Lines of communication were jumbled; local authorities found they could get no coherent advice from state or federal offices. In some places evacuation sirens sounded but citizens had no idea of what they meant and ignored them. Rumors spread both true and false information. People leaped into automobiles, clambered onto buses, and literally ran. In the panic and confusion, cars stalled at crossings and on bridges; desperate drivers rammed them, hoping to push them out of the way, but only added to the pile-ups. Emergency instructions broadcast after an hour or so over the civil-defense network advised people to remain indoors with closed windows to await instructions. However, these messages were heard only by a fraction of the population, and many of these people did not trust the government's motives or accuracy; they set out anyway.

Perhaps because the fall-out from the Mount St. Helens volcano eruptions had tended to drift northeastward, most evacuees tried to head west. But the highways were soon hopelessly clogged, even their shoulders littered with abandoned vehicles. On foot and by bicycle, like refugees in a war, the victims of Puget 1 did their best to head around the southern shores of Puget Sound toward the clean air coming in off the Pacific.

The next day federal nuclear authorities from Washington arrived on the scene, but their pronouncements were contradictory and not reassuring. An area populated by almost two hundred thousand people had suffered fall-out sufficient to make it uninhabitable for the foreseeable future. The state prepared emergency shelters west of Olympia, which itself was partially evacuated, and vast tent cities were hastily constructed. Recriminations flew between the officials of Great Northwestern and local and state officials. Estimates of long-term damages ranged up to nearly 50 billion dollars, and Northwestern lawyers secretly began preparations for salvaging as many assets as possible through bankruptcy proceedings.

The state Survivalist Party announced plans to impeach the pro-nuke governor. The signatures required for a special recall election were amassed in three days.

One morning Jake, the owner of the hardware store in Myrtle Grove, was sweeping his sidewalk when Frank Werdon clattered up in his new cart, drawn by a handsome brown mare. Frank was not yet a good driver, but he maneuvered into a parking space, tied the reins to the parking meter, and solemnly put in a coin. The horse snuffled, just as horses do after they're tied up in the movies. Jake laughed himself silly. "My God, Frank, I knew that car was driving you crazy, but I never thought it would come to this!"

"Well, I'll tell you something, this little mare is turning out to be a whole lot more fun than any internal combustion engine I ever knew.

Aren't you, Gertie?" He patted the horse on the nose, and she looked at him with her huge round eyes. Then she delicately lifted her tail and dropped about five pounds of horse manure on the city pavement.

"Frank, you just lost your dime. Now take that critter around back and put her in the corner under the tree. And come back with a shovel. And you also just bought yourself a garbage can, wholesale."

"Sure, Jake. And I'll give you wholesale rates for compost horseshit, too."

And thus it was that among the mopeds and bicycles that increasingly provided transportation in the Ecotopian territory, the citizens of Myrtle Grove saw a half-dozen horsedrawn buggies appear; in a few months, only tourists bothered to gawk at them.

WASHINGTON GOVERNOR RECALLED; NUCLEAR PLANTS BANNED IN STATE

Olympia, Dec. 15 (WPI). Washington state's special recall election yesterday unseated Democratic Governor Talcott Dennison by a margin of 68% to 32%, an unprecedented landslide in state politics. Dennison had been a strong proponent of nuclear power and military installations. The campaign to recall him from office was initiated by the Survivalist Party immediately after the accident and evacuation at the Puget 1 nuclear plant near Seattle.

Dennison, 57, had been given grudging support by many Republicans in the recall contest, and his defeat is seen as a stunning rebuff to both major parties. The governorship will now be held by Margaret Engstrom, 32, one of the original leaders of the Survivalists in the state. She and her little-known new party ran on the program of making the state "nuclear-free now."

Engstrom announced last night, after Dennison conceded defeat, that the Survivalists had built a strong statewide organization during the recall fight, and would contest all seats in the next election. She also said that state inspectors would be sent today into the remaining nuclear plants operating in Washington, at Aberdeen and Hanford, to verify that state safety requirements are being met. "If there's any danger of another Puget disaster, you can rest assured we will close the installation down immediately," she declared. This statement indicates that Engstrom will not wait until the deadline established by the referendum to take actions ending nuclear operations in the state.

When asked about her attitude toward the federal nuclear installations at Hanford and the problem of huge volumes of nuclear wastes stored there, Engstrom said that Survivalist scientists were readying recommendations in the matter. Hanford has been a bone of contention between state and federal authorities since an initiative in 1980 banned deposit of nuclear wastes in the state. "We are particularly concerned," the new governor added, "that at Hanford the territory of this state is being used for work on breeder reactors. Breeders produce large quantities of plutonium and will greatly contribute to health dangers and world political instability."

Some observers foresee a confrontation between Engstrom and federal officials on the Hanford issue. The huge Trident submarine base on Puget Sound is also a sore point with Engstrom's militants, but it is believed she favors dealing with the perhaps more manageable Hanford issues first.

Observers noted that one faction of the Survivalist Party favors ceding the eastern section of the state around Hanford to the federal government if nuclear research and storage there cannot be stopped. Other Survivalists, however, point out that radioactive leakage from the Hanford storage facilities is likely to become more severe as the holding tanks rust away. (Coyotes and jackrabbits in the area have already been discovered to be radioactive.) They feel that retaining some state control over such leakage, through regulations prohibiting pollutant discharge into rivers, may be the state's sole chance of preventing substantial radioactivity from entering the Columbia River.

Officials of the federal Nuclear Regulatory Commission expressed dismay at the election results while conceding that the scope of the Puget 1 disaster could hardly help having major political repercussions. A strongly anti-nuclear bill is pending in the Illinois legislature, and sweeping anti-nuclear initiatives have been filed in Oregon and California. (These three states have a total of nine operating reactors among them and several more in construction.) Bills or initiatives have also been proposed in several states which so far have no reactors. The Illinois bill is expected to produce especially bitter conflict, since that state is heavily dependent on nuclear plants, many of which are sited near the city of Chicago. However, observers generally concede that the three Pacific Coast states will be nuclear-free within a year.

The Survivalist victory in Washington state startled the national political establishment into action. President Maynard himself issued a sharp statement. While deploring the recent unfortunate nuclear accident which, he recognized, had caused immense damage and great distress to the people of the state, he nonetheless condemned the voters for rushing headlong into the arms of the Survivalist Party. That party, he declared, was an unprincipled and opportunist organization. Moreover, in recent months it had been flirting with treason in its continued criticism of the Supreme Court's Madera decision. The federal government was the arena in which great decisions were properly made, whether they concerned accepting the necessary risks of nuclear power or the essential contributions made by the automobile to our national life. The states should not meddle in them, he declared. These were difficult times for the whole country; it was irresponsible for the Survivalists to try to secure favored status for the Northwest at the expense of other Americans. Where was their sense of patriotism, he asked, where their dedication to the great American dream of a continent united from sea to shining sea? ("Yukk!" exclaimed Lou Swift, reading a newspaper account of the President's remarks.)

But Maynard did not confine himself to moral condemnation; he also issued a veiled threat. "This nation," he solemnly proclaimed, "has already confronted in a great civil war the question of whether states, in pursuing what they take to be the protection of their citizens' rights, can abrogate federal power. The majesty of the Union arose from the firm establishment through bloody sacrifice of the principle of federal sovereignty over this land—all of it. The states have an important and honorable role to play in our system of government. Let them play it, keeping in mind always that it is a subordinate role. Let them also remember that if any of the states overstep their limits, the united country will turn against them and remind them of their proper place in the commonwealth.

"Our problems may be serious, and they call for serious remedies. But solutions must be found, as my administration has been finding them, within the normal procedures of American government. We do not need a new party which arrogantly tells us it can solve our environmental problems, our economic problems, our health problems, by new and untried nostrums. These are hard times. We must pull together, within the wisdom of the two-party system that has given us stable government in this country."

The President's statement reinforced beliefs in the rest of the country that something was going haywire on the West Coast. In Washington state, however, where the death toll from Puget 1 was rising, it was met with incredulity and anger. Margaret Engstrom was able to point to Maynard's remarks as the latest example of gross federal insensitivity. Elsewhere in the Ecotopian territory, the speech was greeted with derision by Survivalists and with fervent appreciation by anti-Survivalists; instead of defusing Survivalist activity, it merely polarized the citizenry further.

As Lou had worked toward isolating the mechanism that made her cell work, she had also made improvements in the basic design of its component parts. These refinements simplified its construction and maximized the output she was able to achieve. She calculated that a cell area of 150 square feet on a south-facing roof could produce a peak output (on a sunny day) of more than 2000 watts. Although suburban houses in places where air conditioning was common were still being wired for an electric consumption ten times greater than that, Lou knew her 2000 watts was enough for basic needs—refrigerator, lighting, stereo or television, and occasional use of heavy-current items like irons and toasters. Her cell could also charge storage batteries providing for evening use. On cloudy days the output was much lower, but still enough for the essentials.

Roger pointed out that she was being modest in calculating on the basis of 150 square feet. "After all," he said, "we have 1500 square feet of roof on this place. If the cell is going to be easy to make, people will just add more, won't they? Then they can have their hairdryers and their air conditioners."

"I suppose some would," agreed Lou. "But let's set a reasonable example, huh?"

At first Lou had been worried that Bert Luckman's ideas about inaugurating wide usage of her cell might be utterly unworkable. Gradually, though, she had had to admit he was ingenious. He saw how commercially available plug connectors that were weatherproof could enable individual cell units to be removed and replaced or repaired as needed. Working with the MiniWind designers who had put together microprocessor control circuits for windmill units, he found ways to use inexpensive solid-state components to maximize the effectiveness of the charging systems.

But more than that, Bert had a consistent vision of how people could use Lou's invention: turning somebody's garage into a shared neighborhood cell-building center, cooperating to install the rooftop units and wire them into the houses' circuits. "It should be like the old-time barn-raisings!" he told her enthusiastically. "Everybody gets together, the work goes faster, you have fun doing it, and when it's done everybody knows how it was done, so they will know how to fix it. It gives you *resilience*! *Flexibility*! Many hands make light work!"

"All right, all right," Lou would say. "I believe you. Now how are we going to teach people to tap into the house wires without electrocuting themselves?"

Bert was tireless. Now that she had cracked the basic process, Lou felt a bit bored with the whole thing. She would walk downtown and borrow a boat and row out into the lagoon to watch the egrets feeding, or take long walks along the beach. But Bert drew diagrams, he wrote manuals and tried them out on friends, then revised them. He set up experimental workshops to see what messes people got into, then figured out how to forestall them, and revised the teaching procedures. He drafted background articles for newspapers and magazines. And, with a few friends, he and Lou prepared for the big television broadcast that would inaugurate the Survivalist program to disseminate Swift cells into every community in the Ecotopian territory. The broadcast, they knew, would be watched by a lot of people—utility rates were skyrocketing again. It was hard to think of anything more welcome than a way to disconnect yourself from the power company wires.

Negotiations between the Bolinas town council and the county had dragged on for weeks. As often happens in times of crisis, procedural issues soon eclipsed the original dispute over electrical disconnections. The county found ways to put pressure on the town, the town found ways to evade or neutralize county power. After protracted talks, however, the situation finally stabilized beyond further discussion. The county was going to come in and bulldoze any houses that remained nonconforming after ten days.

The dispute had welded the Bolinesians together into a solid community in which personal feuds and disagreements were forgotten.

With a sense of unanimous fury, the town council appointed a drafting committee which would prepare a declaration of secession from the county. As somebody said, "By God, we'll give 'em *real* disconnection!" If San Francisco could be both a city and a county, why couldn't Bolinas? Roger was made a member of the drafting committee, whose members secluded themselves in a backyard cottage for ten hours nonstop. That evening they took to the council meeting a document they titled, without mincing words,

THE BOLINAS DECLARATION OF INDEPENDENCE

"We are American people. But we are human beings before we are Americans, and we would still be human beings if we ceased being American citizens. Governments are created to serve people, not the other way around. And so, when institutions have become bureaucratized and rigid, when the laws and applications of the laws no longer protect the people but have instead become a burden and a danger to them, then the people have the right, and indeed the duty, to take the management of their health, their welfare, and their happiness back into their own hands.

"At such times old institutions become null and void. The people no longer pay attention to them. They do not pay taxes; they do not obey officials and the regulations they issue; they deny the power of the police, which must come from the consent of the people or it is mere armed tyranny.

"In recent months we have seen the development of an intolerable situation in many parts of the territories which have become known as Ecotopia. Citizens despairing at the ineffectuality of government measures to protect them against the abuses and dangers of the chemical and nuclear industries have been forced to take direct action in self-defense. The citizens' just demands for healthy conditions of life, such as contaminant-free food and water supplies, air to breathe which does not contain dangerous levels of pollutants, freedom from the threat of nuclear plant accidents, and a reduction of the influx of carcinogenic substances into the biosphere, have been ignored or even derided—in government documents which call upon us to sacrifice human life upon the altar of profit. The attempts of our state governments to protect their citizens against the economic and health dangers of the automobile have been overturned by federal court order. Arrogant county bureaucracies and criminals employed by corporations have obstructed citizen attempts to achieve independent,

263

renewable-source energy systems. In a time when experimentation and novelty are essential to our very survival, citizens have been forced into lock-step with outmoded standards.

"Our petitions for redress of these grievances have been met with silence or outright refusal. Now, therefore, we the elected officials of the Town of Bolinas proclaim that a state of civil emergency exists. The people must take the power over their destiny back into their own hands and form new institutions to defend their welfare.

"From this date forward the Town of Bolinas is hereby declared an independent territory in which the laws of the county of Marin, the state of California, and the United States of America no longer have legal force whenever they run counter to duly instituted ordinances of the Bolinas Town Council. A Bolinas Militia responsible only to the Town Council will be constituted immediately to provide for the maintenance of order and for the defense of the Town if need should arise. A Bolinas Court will be established, with a judge to be elected immediately from the citizenry. A new tax structure, controlled by the town, will be implemented, and citizens should immediately, wherever possible, cease paying sales taxes to the state, real estate taxes to the county, and income taxes to the state or federal governments.

"We take these steps with heavy hearts, for all citizens have a stake in the continuity of institutions, to which we develop a natural and healthy attachment. But our highest loyalty must be to ourselves and to our survival, and to the survival of our children and our children's children. At some point we must say to the state: This far and no farther! We draw that line today at the boundaries of our town. And we say to the world that we will defend ourselves and our future with our strength, our determination, and our honor."

Having adopted this document, the Bolinesians felt they should plan a celebration. Some among them, including Dimmy, had long been arguing that the big commercialized holidays ought to be replaced, or at least transformed into something both more serious and more fun. The ancient solar festivals that fell on the solstices and equinoxes (the shortest and longest days of the year, and the midway points when day and night were equally long) had degenerated into what we know as Christmas and the Fourth of July for the solstices, and Easter and Thanksgiving for the equinoxes. But they had lost all the original sacredness holidays had as literal matters of climatic life and death, markers of the earth's slow movement through the seasons as it ponderously swung in its course around the sun. People who were devoted to a decent life on the earth and honored the gift of life that the sun gave us should take all that seriously again, Dimmy argued. And so he proposed that since they had just passed the winter solstice this would be an excellent time to begin a new cycle of festivals. He suggested feasting and music and staying up all night dancing in the streets, Mardi Gras style. He proposed a couple of days moratorium on monogamy so that people who hankered after sexual variety could have some, but without endangering their long-term commitments. For just a few days, he said, let gratification be undelayed! It would be a time to rejoice, a time to share hopes, a time to drop the usual routines of life and meet people freely and openly, come what may—a time for surprises, for changes of pace, a time for reflection on where the earth and all its inhabitants, human and nonhuman, were headed as they spun around the sun.

After only a few weeks in jail, while the lawyers were still busy with their preparations, Laura's Cancer Commando comrade Haskell grew very weak. He had been the one who was stationed at the telephone to alert the media. Soon he was removed from his cell and taken to the hospital where, in three days time, he died. The fact, noted by the media, caused an outpouring of sentiment for the survivors. They received great stacks of mail, more favorable than before; they received presents of candy, and flowers, and mufflers, and slippers, and little hand-written letters and poems from children. For Laura especially, these were hard to take; they made her cry, and crying hurt. After a while she stopped reading them and saved her energy for the trial.

More weeks passed, and Stacy who had handled out the leaflets also died. Her family was an old one and prominent in San Francisco; Stacy, despite being a bit of a black sheep, had been loved by many friends of the family. A modest funeral was planned for the Cathedral, and a small notice appeared in the paper. But when the day came, more than five thousand people attempted to attend, and loudspeakers had to be hastily set up so the overflow crowd on the plaza outside could hear the service.

The priest, normally a cautious man, spoke poetically of Stacy (who

265

had no children) dying in hopes that the children of others might live. Seeing the tearful response of the crowd, he extended his remarks beyond his notes and stressed the need for the faithful to manifest Christian devotion through active concern for the environment in which our bodies, the vessels for our immortal souls, must after all survive while here on earth. The Church, he ventured, must follow the Lord's example and be a good shepherd; it must not lead its flocks to pasture upon contaminated grass, nor to walk in the valley of chemical death. The next day the priest was severely reprimanded by his bishop. But when he remembered that unexpected sea of dismayed faces, he felt unrepentant. The Church, too, he muttered to himself, was going to have to learn some new lessons. He'd have to look into what these Survivalist people were saying.

TOP SECRET

TO: THE PRESIDENT

COPIES TO ALL STATION CHIEFS

An underground group, probably affiliated with the "Ecotopian" movement, whose overt arm is the Survivalist Party, may have obtained supplies of weapons-grade uranium sufficient to build several nuclear devices. Agents believe the group's purpose is political blackmail of the federal government in order to facilitate secession of the Ecotopia region—Washington, Oregon, and California as far south as the Tehachapi range. See previous memoranda No. A3564 and No. A3992.

Continuing surveillance of shortages of nuclear material in processing plants leaves several hundred pounds of fissionable material unaccounted for. Discrepancies in reactor fuel inventories at nuclear plants are also sizable enough that groups with access to centrifuge equipment might have concentrated such materials to explosive grade in quantities large enough for the construction of two or three bombs. (Note: Materials mentioned in memorandum No. 3564 as shipped to Seattle area were later identified as destined for sanctioned reactor project in South Korea.)

Physics advisors state that if an underground unit has constructed devices to plant in Eastern cities, detection with current ultrasensitive radiation monitors should be possible. However, vast wilderness areas still intact in the West complicate detection efforts; abandoned underground mine sites might be involved, making even low-level radiation-scanning sweeps ineffectual. Main recommendation is permanent installation of USRD equipment at all truck check points on east-west highways. Highways lacking such check points should have detectors mounted on overpasses where appropriate pursuit measures could be rapidly instituted.

All stations in Ecotopian area are advised to alert agents to any reports of unusual radiation-connected events. We are also tracing recent sales by metals-supply companies to locate purchasers of substantial amounts of lead, which a clandestine bomb operation would require for shielding.

It is impossible to establish a recommendation for level of emergency at this time. The technology of constructing a nuclear explosive device is demanding, but is within the capacity of a sophisticated machine shop. Health hazards to operators would be severe, but it is believed that underground militants might be sufficiently motivated to sacrifice themselves to the building of such devices.

"You're not suggesting a 'diminished-capacity' defense, I hope!" said Laura to her defense attorney, Ruth Lehrmann. "We won't stand for that, you know. If anybody's going to look crazy in this case, we want to make sure it's the chemical companies."

"But Laura, there's a good chance we can get you off!" said Ruth in exasperation. "Look at the precedents. Dan White walks into San Francisco City Hall, shoots the mayor, walks down the hall, shoots a leading supervisor, and gets off because he was demented from eating junkfood! You and Nils are in danger of actually *dying*. Naturally you'd be distraught. It's a far stronger case. Besides, you didn't actually kill anybody."

Laura sighed. "Ruth, my dear, I know you're a lawyer and you have to think in legal terms. But please remember that we don't really need to get off. We're dying. We're perfectly content to be found guilty in the legal sense. Besides, there are times in history when people have to be willing to accept that society, or at least the law, will condemn them for doing what's right. With Nils and me—well, I'm not sure we'd have been willing to face that if we weren't sick, but—"

267

"But Laura, I can't let you just fatalistically accept that you're bound to die. People have remissions. Cancers do go away, even lung cancers. Suppose they convict you, and then you have a remission, and you spend ten years in prison? I can't have that on my conscience!"

Laura eyed her young friend. "You had better either strengthen your conscience or find us a new lawyer," she said flatly. "What we need you for is to make sure we get to say in open court everything we have to say. We want the case on the public record in the most powerful possible way. That's the only kind of maneuvering we will tolerate. Can you handle it that way, and forget this strategizing to get us off?"

"Laura, it isn't so simple. If you just plead guilty, they sentence you and it's over. Twenty minutes. Page 23 in the papers."

"Well, then, we'll plead not guilty."

"Not guilty by reason of what? You're not willing to say momentary insanity, or diminshed capacity, or external compulsion. The judge is going to require relevance in the testimony—including yours."

"There must be other alternatives. Not guilty because we were protecting our children."

"You'd have to prove clear and present danger. It may be present, but it isn't yet very clear, at least to the courts. You'd have to prove imminent harm to somebody."

"How about us? Haven't we in fact suffered harm? Isn't it self-defense?"

Ruth brightened. "Self-defense? My God, maybe that *is* the way to do it! You're not dead yet—" She stopped, in red-faced embarrassment.

"Go on," said Laura mildly. "I think I see what you mean."

"Well, you're not dead yet but you're in obviously mortal danger, and the continuation of the plant's operation would have probably increased the danger. We can make an indirect statistical case on all that, anyway. And it'll have the advantage of bearing on everybody in the airshed, not just you—sort of a class-action aspect. You acted out of moral duty, a social and personal responsibility. You're the sentries stationed outside the camp! Of course you have to defend yourselves, or the whole camp will be killed—"

"Ah, Ruthie, I can see you're happier now."

"You know, with the right jury, there's even a tiny chance we might win?"

There was fire in Ruth's eyes now. She hated to lose, even honorably against overwhelming odds. This approach gave her a fighting chance; she knew she could be eloquent with juries. Already her mind was racing ahead to the argumentation she would use. Laura sat quietly facing her, her patient eyes studying her ardent young defender, contemplating this last astonishing episode in her life. She was tired, but not too tired to see it through. She folded her hands, as if to conserve her waning strength, and ran through her mind an ancient comforting quotation:

> *If it be now, 'tis not to come;*
> *if it be not to come, it will be now;*
> *if it be not now, yet it will come;*
> *the readiness is all.*

In the wake of all the publicity about the Swift cell, the Department of Energy finally decided to give Lou a medal. She hesitated about going to Washington to receive it, and Bert thought it would be a total waste of time. But Lou had never been east of the Sierra, and when a corporation in Baltimore offered to pay her for a day of consultation, she accepted; she could go to Washington to get the medal on the same trip. "You realize the basic invention is in the public domain?" she had insisted when the Baltimore people phoned. They were still interested—the market on the West Coast might be pre-empted by people doing it themselves, but elsewhere there might be profits to be made, if mass production could turn out the cells cheaply enough. Lou didn't mind. Cheap was *good*. She envisioned healthy competition between many companies in many countries, bringing the price down to ludicrous levels so that even the poorest of people could afford their own installation.

She flew to Baltimore. Riding in from the airport, she was astounded at the rows of tiny, cramped, broken-down houses, the abandoned cars, the junk and filth everywhere. The city looked as if it were covered with a 200-year accumulation of old chewing gum and spit. She had never seen anything to match it in the worst slums of Oakland. When she arrived at her hotel, the first thing that caught her attention was three armed policemen who stood guard in the lobby. Her room had elaborate instructions about double-locking posted on

269

the door. She went down to the desk and inquired about a restaurant that was supposed to specialize in unique Maryland crab-cakes, and the desk man advised her to take a cab, though the place was only four blocks away. She went out, nonetheless, for a brief walk in a nearby redeveloped area and noticed several middle-class business types wearing holsters on their hips. It seemed a city under siege. At nightfall, she guessed, everybody went home and hid by their television sets until morning. It was nothing like San Francisco, where she was accustomed to wandering around in North Beach or Noe Valley, feeling fairly safe because of the number of people on the streets. Looking out from her 23rd-story hotel window, Lou felt suddenly that her trip was pointless. She had been filled with fantasies of her cell lighting up the world. But nothing was going to light up this place, it appeared—not for a long time.

Nonetheless, the next morning she went to the company's plant. The firm had originally been in the transformer business and then had branched out into other electrical equipment, including some electronics. Now it was looking for direct consumer items. Lou was taken through the labs. She talked to the staff of the research department, essentially giving the talk she was preparing for the Survivalist broadcast. They asked questions that seemed to indicate that they suspected Lou was holding something essential back. "You mean that's all there is to it?" an engineer finally asked.

"Yeah," Lou replied. "The only way that you could get an edge would be to develop a continuous extrusion process. But you couldn't price it very high, or the do-it-yourselfers would kill you." She smiled. The company officials, however, were not at all happy. They began to murmur among themselves about profit margins and Japanese competition. In mid-afternoon they politely took Lou to the train station, where she was to catch the Metroliner to Washington. "We'll let you know if we get serious about it," the company people said.

The Metroliner was almost an hour late. Lou wandered around the station. Then she sat down on a bench and started talking with a well-dressed man of about 35 who said his name was Norman Borden. He worked in the Department of Interior—something to do with the leasing of coal and oil-shale lands. Lou told him about her coming award.

"Well, then, I know who you are! Of course I've heard about that work of yours. It sounds very clever. The only problem seems to be

that nobody can figure out how to make enough money out of it."
Norman smiled slightly. "It's an invention without a constituency."

"A constituency?"

"They can't figure out what to do with it in the boondocks."

"Well, we certainly know what to do with it on the West Coast, but that is the impression I got in Baltimore," replied Lou. "They'll let the Japanese do it."

"You don't care about that?" asked Norman.

"No. My idea is that the cells should be cheap, that's all. And if they aren't cheap enough, people can always make their own. I think that's neat."

"Tough young person, aren't you?" Norman appraised her. "Look, I like your spirit. Why don't you come out to the house for dinner with my wife and me? I'll give Paulette a ring at her office. We can take you down to your hotel later."

Lou accepted happily. Paulette also worked in the government; she was tall and blonde and stylish. The three of them sat at a small, intimate round table, and the dinner was delicious; it was served, to Lou's surprise, by a maid. Lou had some wine with dinner. She wasn't used to it, and got rather blurry. Norman and Paulette were telling about life in Washington—the intrigues, the parties, the gossip, the suppressed scandals. Lou giggled. Her cheeks felt unusually rosy.

Then she sensed a hand on her thigh—Paulette's hand. It was cool and gentle, and it moved slowly and softly, almost stealthily. This was a situation Lou had never faced before. Norman was smiling across the table at them. Did he know what was happening under the elegant table setting?

The answer was evidently yes, because in a moment *his* hand arrived on Lou's other thigh. Paulette stared into Lou's eyes. "Honey," she said, "you are just unbelievably beautiful!"

Lou was filled with contradictory feelings. This was evidently one of those adventures she had been thinking of in her initiation ceremony speech. And she had had some vaguely sexual feelings about Norman when they first started talking on the train platform in Baltimore. On the other hand, she said to herself—and then giggled again: which hand was the "other" hand?

"That laugh is absolutely delicious!" said Paulette. "Come here, come on!" She got Lou to her feet and, with Norman helping to guide her, led the unsteady Lou through the living room and toward what Lou thought must be a bedroom.

271

Lou stopped and planted her feet sturdily. There was, she noticed, a slightly feverish look in Paulette's eyes. Norman was watching them benignly, but she didn't altogether like his look either. "I'm really not up to anything like this," Lou said. "A threesome is just, well—"

Norman said, "Who's talking about threesomes, necessarily? Paulette likes you a lot. I can watch television while you two go enjoy yourselves! —Later, who knows?"

Lou thought about her mother's affair with a woman. She knew a lot of women who had made love to other women, and some who had become committed to lesbian lives. She had often thought that someday, somewhere, she might have gay experiences of her own. But with these people she barely knew, who seemed to have some secret program going? No, it didn't feel right.

"I want to go to the hotel," she said. A look of desperate sadness crept over Paulette's face. Lou, moved, gave her a hug, which Paulette returned with passionate kisses. But then Lou pushed her away. "The country needs me early in the morning," she joked, trying to ease the tension.

Norman drove Lou downtown. He seemed apologetic and as he dropped her off he said, "I'm sorry we were too much for you." He looked at her, perched warily at the door edge of the car's seat. "Maybe we're both just too tempted by beauty."

Then Lou understood. "You were wanting my so-called beauty, but not wanting *me*." She shrugged. "It turned me off, that's all."

On the way to the Department of Energy next morning, Lou asked the taxi driver to stop for a moment at the monument to Thomas Jefferson—most democratic-minded of all the U.S. presidents. She stared at the statue and wondered what that strange man's mind was really like. He was a slave-owner, of course, like many of the founders. Yet he had a wonderful faith that human institutions could be molded to aid freedom, not to suppress it. And he understood that land, and human beings' relations to the land, were the ultimate foundations of everything. It must have been stupendously exciting, to be one of the founders of a new country! Jefferson's expression, Lou thought, was confident yet a little melancholy. And she noticed that his marble figure was softening at the edges—it was being eaten away by acid rain.

She got back in the taxi and after a short ride was dropped off at the Department of Energy building. She found her way through a labyrinth of corridors to the Secretary's office and announced herself.

The Secretary himself was away, inaugurating a synfuels plant in Wyoming which, Lou knew, would permanently exhaust the underground water supply of an entire river basin, turning its grazing lands into desert. But a small ceremony was planned for a sort of lecture hall, presided over by a deputy assistant secretary. Several press photographers and reporters were on hand, looking bored. There was a dull speech, supposedly on behalf of the Secretary and the President, and the country at large, about how important the Swift Effect could be to the country's energy future, and how Lou Swift symbolized the creative spark of America's youth. The Department would be working with America's corporate leaders to exploit this new resource.

There was no mention of the fact that ordinary people could construct their own Swift cells, and no mention of the dismay that the cell had caused in the utility industry. Lou listened with growing irritation. Whoever wrote the speech either didn't know what was going on or else was trying to conceal it.

She got more and more angry. When the time came for her to accept the award (it was actually a small, rather tacky-looking plaque) she had decided to speak her mind. "Thank you for the award," she began. "But I believe I must be ungrateful and say some things that somehow did not get said." There was a stirring of life among the press representatives—could something actually be going to *happen*? "First of all, this invention, which will sooner or later benefit almost every human being on earth, was treated as a terrible threat by the utilities and the oil industry. They see ecological progress as a danger to their *profits*. As you may know, a court trial is shortly scheduled to determine whether Omni Oil, possibly using F.B.I. operatives, was responsible for a criminal burglary attempt on my laboratory. Second, since Swift Effect cells can be produced on a do-it-yourself basis and cannot be monopolized by any corporation, we are not exactly seeing a rush to put them into production. I wonder why? Is this the penicillin story all over again? And third, on the West Coast, in the region we nowadays like to call Ecotopia, we *are* doing something to put them into production—a regionwide Survivalist Party program of neighborhood workshops will shortly be announced, and within a year we expect most dwellings to be equipped with Swift cells. We will then have a permanent electricity *surplus*. As far as the rest of the country goes—" Lou stopped and shrugged. "Well, you can either get your own programs going, or just slide on down the drain. Good luck."

She stepped from the dais amid a group of frozen-faced bureaucrats. Reporters crowded around to ask questions. Now they had a story: feisty girl genius snubs award ceremony, condemns industry skulduggery and inaction, predicts West Coast energy independence. One reporter asked, "Miss Swift, considering you have achieved this great breakthrough and gotten this national award, why are your criticisms so harsh?"

Lou was taken aback. "I'm not trying to be harsh," she said. "But I get impatient when the truth is not being told. Now it's up to you."

Lou found the westbound flight much longer than her eastbound one. She dozed and occasionally looked out. The plane moved over the industrial belt of Ohio and Indiana, over the great flat Midwest and the rolling high plains. What was going on down there, Lou wondered, in this strange contradictory country? Was there hope for those people? Would they realize in time, as the Ecotopians had, that they too had to defend themselves? Finally the plane reached the Rockies, then headed over the barren high desert of Utah and Nevada. To Lou's Ecotopian eyes this region looked forlorn, treeless, uninhabitable, like the moon. Then finally she saw the sharp uplift of the Sierra. Here the dead tan moonscape gave way first to craggy snowcovered peaks and then to the dark greens of the Sierra forests. Ahead lay the foothills with their oaks and grasslands, the verdant central valley, the cool coastal redwood belt.

Now, as the plane descended, Lou began to peer down eagerly. The sun was lowering, sending graceful shadows scross the grassy slopes of the Diablo range, emerald green from the winter rains. Here and there she saw a farmhouse with its solar collectors gleaming on the roof, its pond and windmill tower, and cattle grazing on the hills. Suddenly Lou realized how relieved she was to be back.

The trial of Laura and Nils was as spectacular as they had hoped. Ruth got them on the stand early, and over prosecution objections the judge ruled that evidence bearing on their state of mind at the time of the alleged crime was relevant, as the jury would be obliged to assess their motivation. Laura spoke from a wheelchair, which Marissa pushed up near the witness box. Two networks were covering Laura's testimony.

"We have committed a crime," she began, "and we have never denied it. You have heard the details of how we Cancer Commandos constructed the bomb, carried it into the chemical plant, and caused it to explode—taking careful precautions that no persons would be harmed. We committed this crime in order to prevent the continued commission of much *worse* crimes by the company, and I want to explain how Nils and I felt about those crimes."

"Objection!" called the chief prosecutor.

"Overruled, same grounds," said the judge, nodding to Laura to proceed.

"Being condemned to die from cancer gives you a special clarity of mind," Laura went on. "Since you have nothing to lose, you have a certain incredible freedom of action. You can think in terms of justice—and not just the justice of the law, for the verdict of the law too often touches only the fringes of human actions, the little edges to which legalities apply. If you are condemned to die, as we are, you can think in terms of moral justice—of what lies behind and above the law, and which we attempt to approximate by means of the law.

"Nils and I knew that the fate we faced, death from cancer, was also being visited upon millions of our fellow Americans. We knew that this year about 800,000 of these millions will die, while many others suffer. We knew that of all the people killed by cancer, a substantial percentage of deaths are due to environmental factors—contamination of our food, our water, our air. And we knew that many other damages—malformed babies, miscarriages, kidney dysfunction, and a host of other maladies—also stemmed from the chemicalization of our environment. We are even endangering the very genetic material upon which the future biological health and survival of the human species depends.

"And certain herbicides are among the worst offenders against us and against our environmental health. So to protest in the most direct and effective way, we Cancer Commandos chose a chemical plant manufacturing 2,4,5-T. It is difficult to calculate the exact damage done by that one facility in its 22 years of existence, but a low, conservative estimate (on which you will hear expert testimony later) is that its operations caused or will cause several hundred deaths, several hundred deformed or abnormal babies, and a vast array of medical problems of varying severity affecting tens of thousands.

"Our political and legal mechanisms have not put a stop to such slaughter, such death and destruction. So we who are victims decided we must fight back. We stopped that plant before it could kill more. And we know that others elsewhere will carry on the struggle until

275

the poisoning ceases and we are free to live in health and happiness.

"You must understand too that we would do it again if we had the chance. Some of our comrades have already died. We are weak in body, we will die soon. But we will know that we accomplished something in our dying. And we say to all those millions of people whose fates are even now being prepared in the laboratories and chemical plants: Do not go gladly! This is a matter of self-defense. It is us or them. And we are many, and they are few!"

Cheering broke out in the courtroom. The judge, banging his gavel for order, noticed that many eyes in the jury box were wet. The chief prosecutor himself looked rather rattled and thought it best to pass over this chance for cross-examination. The cameras followed Laura as Marissa wheeled her back to her place next to Ruth.

"How did I do?" Laura whispered. Then she noticed that Ruth's eyes too were filled with tears.

PENTAGON DENIES AMERICAN
TROOPS FIGHTING IN BRAZIL

Washington, Jan. 9 (WPI). The Pentagon today issued a formal denial that American ground troops are engaged in combat with the rebel forces now operating from an expanded guerrilla base in northeastern Brazil. In recent weeks rumors have circulated in Washington that secret troop movements from stateside bases have been carried out through flights of giant C-7 planes, and European papers have published accounts based on alleged eyewitness reports of landings and deployments in Brazil.

Defense Department spokesmen released a statement which acknowledged that American aid to the Brazilian army has increased in recent weeks. However, the air supply flights involved only the delivery of equipment and munitions believed to be essential to the Brazilian military. False and inflammatory reports, the DoD statement said, endangered our efforts to preserve peace in the Hemisphere.

The statement admitted that American advisors have been present in Brazil for some months, training Brazilian pilots and crews in use of the new Destructor attack helicopters. These aircraft are heavily armed, complex, and utilize sophisticated electronic equipment; they require expertly trained crews, the report explained. Some Americans have also been necessary to act as ground crews and for repairs of the craft.

Pentagon officials declined to comment when asked for an estimate of the total number of Americans now serving in the Brazil conflict.

Sometimes, in her television talks, Vera spoke meditatively, as if she were taking the viewers, her people, into her confidence as she thought about the crises that deepened on every hand.

"My friends, we are approaching a time of revolutionary change. We all sense it—some kind of momentous event is about to come upon us, but we don't yet know what it is. That can be exciting or it can be frightening, or both at once. How can we prepare for it?

"Perhaps it will help if we remember, first of all, that basic change is always really a slow process. For a society to change, its millions of people must change, and that happens so slowly, as the decades and generations pass, that we cannot perceive it directly, and have to measure it by statistics and records. And the political arrangements of any people are therefore conservative by nature: they exist to serve economic and social and personal interests which change very slowly.

"Yet we also know that crises do arise when things seem to move very swiftly, and we must be prepared to act properly to meet them.

"Crises come, I think, at times in history when extensive changes have happened in a society but have not yet found expression on a political level. People have new beliefs, which have not yet found expression under the old arrangements. People have new desires, which the old arrangements forbid fulfillment. People have new fears, which the old arrangements cannot assuage. In time, a mighty pressure builds up against these old arrangements.

"Social crises are created in much the same way as earthquakes. Huge stresses accumulate over many years through the gradual movements of two great sections of the earth's crust. They strain to slide alongside each other, but are jammed tight, and for a long time nothing happens. Then finally there is a rupture, and the stresses are released—in rapid and cataclysmic realignments.

"We are nearing a social earthquake now. Our political system has failed to respond to fundamental changes in the life of our people. And though the normal pace of political life is placid, with most seeming crises turning out to be less critical than they looked, now I think

277

we are entering a period of truly revolutionary events. Things will move with blinding speed and significant political realignments will take place.

"In such a period we may be tempted to think that our political actions are 'causing' change. Of course political acts may facilitate some new developments and inhibit others; they *are* important. It is not a mere detail when a sweeping new law is passed, or one government is replaced by another. But such changes are always the expression of a complex web of interconnected pressures which flow from the daily life of a society.

"Americans, especially, like to imagine that it is individuals, such as individual politicians, who are in charge of things. But in fact, we political figures only express the forces of our time, even when we speak most bravely. It is easy for me now to demand that new government regulations must be used to protect us against contaminated water and air and food, for the job of convincing us all that that is necessary has been done by thousands of knowledgeable people who have worked in that area for decades. It is easy for me to speak against the vast power of the oil and automobile corporations, not because I know more than what you know, but because we have *all* learned, in the past few years, of the toll the automobile takes on our economy, our cities, our lives. And I can speak of a vision of a new Ecotopian way of life not because I am terribly clever and made it all up, but because this is a vision that millions of us have contributed to and shared among ourselves.

"We can have confidence, then, even when events seem chaotic, that this is just the brief earthquake period. Our society is attending to long overdue business. There will be a lot of shaking, and some termite-eaten houses will go down. But when the realignment has been accomplished and the shaking has stopped, life will again seem placid and normal, and we will wonder how we could ever have lived in the old wasteful and destructive ways.

"So the paradox of these times, my friends, is that our new Ecotopian world already exists, just under the official surface. The people who are still in power try to pretend that things are the way they were 20 or 30 years ago. But the stresses are so great that they are being shaken away, and with each shock wave on the political level we see more of the new reality revealed. And that new reality looks to me like a world we can live in, with safety and shared delight."

278

As if she had concentrated all her remaining strength for her appearance at the trial, Laura collapsed immediately afterward and was put into the prison hospital. The verdict was a foregone conclusion; in the eyes of the law as it stood, she and Nils were guilty. The actual sentence was a matter of indifference. Laura knew that, although her carefully placed bomb had damaged only property and not harmed any persons, she would be condemned to a longer sentence than if she had, through negligence, actually killed somebody with a car. That was only manslaughter; she had willfully destroyed private property. But what really counted, she said, was that in the aftermath of the trial huge public demonstrations for the banning of the manufacture of all dioxin-containing substances had been held. The Cancer Commandos had lost this battle, but might yet win their war.

Laura and Marissa discussed these ironies occasionally; it felt good to joke a little. It preserved a healthy sense of the comedy of history. But Laura's strength waned steadily. At first, when the trial was over, she had a secret hope that some mysterious reward process would be activated that would cause the cancer to leave her. But it grew worse, and she grew weaker. Finally when she and Nils barely had strength to get out of bed, Marissa and the lawyers prevailed on the judge to let them spend their last days at home.

To Marissa, it was as if her beloved mother were literally fading away. Sometimes she revived, with her old liveliness, but those times grew rarer.

Nils was anxious to spend a couple of days in Mendocino with John, making arrangements so his own death would not cause legal problems and assuring himself that John was doing all right with the farm. He set out one day with a friend he had persuaded to drive him, leaving behind a supply of his best grass. Laura hated goodbyes; mustering her strength, she told him that she was sure she'd still be around to welcome him back.

Ben came by later in the morning. Laura seemed very weak to him, compared to a few days before, and so, against all conspiratorial good judgment, he told her about the bomb project. Laura was horrified, though she had to confess she was impressed with his caper, which completely outclassed hers. She also felt it was wrong for Ben and his group to go against Vera Allwen's clearly expressed views. Ben listened to his mother's criticisms a little sullenly and without comment. He and his friends had gone through these arguments many times, in anguish and confusion, but always had decided they must push on.

Finally Ben said, "But Mother, aren't you the woman who blows up chemical plants?"

Laura laughed. "Like mother, like son? Maybe. But we took pains not to endanger people. Whereas I assume you're putting these 'devices' of yours in the middle of cities?"

"I can't tell you where they are."

Laura looked at her son closely. "But would you really ever set them off?"

"Of course I hope they'll never be used. We take the same position as the Pentagon, basically. The devices are there simply to give Vera and the political people the most possible room for maneuvering."

"But Ben, you've seen those pictures from Hiroshima and Nagasaki. Could you *do* that?"

Ben looked away. "I could tell you things like 'That depends' or 'Only as a last resort'—but that's just a way of saying yes without really facing it. We've faced it! And Vera will have to face it too. She isn't quite ready yet. But soon the situation will force her hand. Then she'll be glad our devices are there."

Laura knew her history. Revolutionary situations always throw up a few individuals at the extremes who are willing to undertake actions that most people, however dedicated to their cause, cannot or will not consider. Such groups have killed kings, destroyed the property of colonial tea-merchants, and set bombs in the desks of Palestinian administrators. Initially they were regarded as criminals; later, they were redefined as heroes of their new countries. Still, it saddened Laura that such a role should be played by her son.

"I wish it hadn't been you who had to do this," she said. "Some day, I suppose everyone may agree you took the right course. But I myself don't see how you can do it." She shuddered a little, and looked out over the city, as if seeing it devastated.

It was not news to Ben that Laura did not quite approve of him. He took her small, thin hand in his large, rough one. "We all work for the cause in our own ways, Mother," he said. And then he added, with an awkward, haunted smile. "I didn't really expect you to understand it."

They said goodbye, with Ben promising to come back next day. Soon Marissa returned, cheerful and full of news from friends she had run into on the streets, where mass meetings seemed to be springing up like mushrooms. People were telling Bolinas jokes—about how the Bolinesians had formed their own coast guard, whose purpose was to *help* smugglers; about how they were going to sign a mutual defense treaty with Monaco, Lichtenstein, and Vatican City. There seemed to be a great surge of popular feeling in defense of the heroic, embattled Bolinesians, who had dared to tell constituted authority to go screw itself.

Laura listened to this news with apparent good humor, but her pain had returned and it seemed to Marissa that she could no longer concentrate on anything; it was as if her attention was far away. She had lost any appetite for several days now, and Marissa could only get her to swallow a little juice and a few crumbs of bread. She could no longer sit up by herself, and even breathing seemed to be hard work. But Marissa knew her mother liked small changes, and she decided it would be nice to move her over to a big soft couch that faced the huge windows to the west. There they could lie back comfortably, smoke a little of Nils's grass, and listen to some Indian music.

It had been raining, but the clouds were breaking at last, and they were more puffy than they had been earlier in the storm. The wind, gusty now, made a tree in the garden wave in a slow, erratic rhythm counterpointing the intricacy of the music. And once, when the sun behind a particularly dark cloud gave it a rim of bright pearly light, Laura sighed and smiled at Marissa, and squeezed her hand.

"How beautiful it all is!" she said. Then she closed her eyes, and put her head on her daughter's strong shoulder, and in a little while she was dead.

ANGRY PRESIDENT DENIES
BRAZIL TROOP ACTION

Washington, Jan. 13 (WPI). In his first press conference in almost three months, President Maynard firmly denied persistent rumors of massive secret American troop involvement in the war in Brazil. Appearing surprised and somewhat confused at persistent questioning about European press reports of American forces being involved in heavy fighting, Mr. Maynard at one point lost his temper. "There are liars everywhere, sir," he replied to one questioner, "so it would be surprising if there were none in the European press. Do *you* believe everything you read? Or for that matter, everything you write?"

Regaining his composure after this outburst, which was not characteristic of his generally calm demeanor in press conferences, Mr. Maynard repeated that the Brazilian government has assured him that only technical aid and military supplies are needed from the United States in order to bring the war to a successful conclusion.

The President conceded that American pilots have occasionally flown helicopters in combat situations, as trainers in anti-guerrilla methods. He declined to comment further on the role of advisors to Brazilian ground forces.

Pressed as to whether American ground troops might be deployed in Brazil in large numbers if the government's position deteriorates, Mr. Maynard replied that he could only conceive of such a possibility if vital U.S. interests were threatened. When asked whether he thought the steady expansion of guerrilla-controlled territory suggested the pattern seen earlier in Cuba and Vietnam, he smiled and remarked, "Not at all—we've learned a lot since then."

The President's statements were received with relief by most observers. Sen. Arnold Tucker (D., N.Y.) who has previously criticized the level of American involvement with the Brazilian regime, said that he was "pleased, indeed delighted, at the President's assurances of restraint." However, a group calling itself the Council for Peace in Brazil held its own press conference to present photographs and other evidence of a troop build-up involving the presence of American combat divisions in Brazil. Some of this evidence consisted of the stories published in European newspapers, which President Maynard had branded as lies.

The crisis came at Bolinas because the citizens had decided their Festival of Independence should include the traditional fireworks. They had experimented with Dimmy's holiday ideas from Friday night onward, and there had been a great round of partying. Lou's brother Mike and a couple of other people had made an expedition to San Francisco's Chinatown where they tracked down a supply of out-of-season skyrockets and roman candles to be set off Sunday evening.

The afternoon turned out to be unseasonably warm and almost windless. Virtually the whole population of the town, many of them rather hung over, gathered on the beach downtown. Lou wandered about happily, talking to people she hadn't seen for months because of her cell work, she took off her shoes and ran around barefoot on the sand. From about five o'clock on, the small children began asking when the fireworks would start. But people had brought food along, and wine and beer, and they were having fun talking over the growing regional crisis as well as their own exasperating negotiations with the county. They speculated about whether the little guard post they had established on the approach road would deter the bulldozers when they came. Moods ranged wildly from the fatalistic to the defiant. There was talk of lying down in front of the machines, and other talk of shooting at the operators. When it came right down to it, nobody knew what was going to happen. Finally it was dark enough for the fireworks. The roman candles spewed their colored fire. Rockets zoomed unpredictably upward, some fizzling into a mass of gunpowder smoke, others spraying into the night sky a vast globe of glowing rays of light.

Whether it was because some of the rockets exploded over homes on the Stinson Beach spit across the inlet and alarmed the owners, or simply because the celebration had attracted police attention, shortly after the fireworks began a county sheriff's car approached the checkpoint on the Bolinas road.

A little uncertainly, Dimmy (who was taking a turn at guard duty at the time) held up his hand to the approaching car. "Entry permit?" he asked.

The sheriff's deputy got out of his car. "What's your name?" he asked.

"What's yours?" said Dimmy. But then, not wishing to cause trouble, he added, "You guys know we don't want you in here, so what's up?"

The officer noticed that Dimmy had a .38 revolver in a holster on his hip, and a green jacket like a National Park ranger's with a green patch reading "Bolinas Militia."

"Fireworks," the officer said. "No permit from the county." Dimmy said nothing. "In my duty as a peace officer I'm obliged to check out these fireworks. Interfering with my duty is a criminal offense."

"It might be, on your side of that line there. But on our side of the line, letting you in would be dereliction of *my* duty." Then Dimmy added, "Look, why make trouble? Those fireworks'll be over any time now. A little party, you know? It isn't hurting anybody. Why don't you just radio in that everything's under control. No hassle."

283

The deputy considered. Then he got into his cruiser, backed off a few yards, and talked to headquarters. Dimmy couldn't hear what was being said, but from the way the deputy looked around as he talked, Dimmy suspected he was planning something. Then he got out again.

"Listen, we're giving you one more chance. Raise that damned bar or you're gonna be sorry."

Dimmy stood with his hand on his revolver handle. "No way," he said. "We've seceded, brother. Just leave us alone."

"We'll see about this secession shit," said the officer. He drove off in a hurry.

Dimmy picked up a walkie-talkie in the guard booth. "We've had a little visit from the sheriff," he said. "Just one guy. But he checked with headquarters and I have a feeling they're coming back."

About 45 minutes later, a heavy four-wheel drive pickup and two county cruisers assembled at the highway and headed in on the Bolinas road. They stopped 50 feet back from the guard box, their headlights pointed at the little structure, and hailed Dimmy on their loudspeaker. "This is assistant sheriff Dawson speaking. We are here on county business to investigate a complaint. Please raise that bar across the road."

Dimmy stepped out. "Sorry," he said. "We've had no complaint. And this is no longer part of the county."

"Put your hands up!" said the loudspeaker. "You're under arrest!"

Dimmy ducked behind the guard box and from there scooted into the underbrush nearby. After a moment the pickup, which had a heavy pushbar mounted on the front, revved up speed and crashed through the wooden bar, followed by the two cruisers. From the cover of the trees, Dimmy could see that there were three helmeted men in each vehicle, shotguns at the ready.

They roared ahead about a hundred yards, but then the lead driver braked to a sudden stop: a heavy log lay across the road. Just as he stopped, there was a rifle shot, followed by another. Two tires on the pickup sagged to the ground. The officers got out, cautiously now, whispering; it was dead silent except for a faint sighing of wind in the trees, and there was no moon. Heavy brush lay to their right, trees and hedges and the lagoon to their left. Not a happy situation—in fact, a goddamned ambush! There was a click, as of something being done to a weapon's safety catch, off in the bushes somewhere. The officers whirled in that direction, guns at the ready, but could see nothing.

Dawson considered. There might be two snipers hidden out there, or a dozen. Some of these Bolinas people were harmless hippies, but others were Vietnam vets, and some of them had lived in the country and hunted and knew guns. It was best not to take chances. They'd see about it in the daylight. If it got to be a real show of strength thing, they could use the helicopter.

He gave orders, in a whisper. The men abandoned the pickup, piled into the two cars, and slowly backed up beyond the guard box. Then they turned around and drove away.

By early in the new year the relationships between the Ecotopian shadow government and the state governments in the Ecotopian territory had become very complex and delicate. After the Puget 1 disaster and recall election, Washington state had a *de facto* Survivalist government. Margaret Engstrom and her followers, however, knew that they could not exist long in isolation, and that the drama between the regional Survivalists and the federal government had only begun. They marked time, awaiting developments to the south. In Oregon, the state government had been a national leader in environmental matters for years, and there were many Survivalists in government departments on all levels. No confrontational issues had yet tested the relative loyalties of either the state apparatus or the citizenry at large. It was known to everyone, however, that the Survivalist Party was laying plans to contest all posts in the next election, and its support was solid and widespread; political observers predicted wholesale defections from both Democratic and Republican ranks.

It was in California, where the conflict over the Madera decision had been especially sharp, that the situation was most tense and problematic. Governor Clark's political base lay chiefly in the southern part of the state. He regarded the Survivalists as an insult to his federalist instincts and to his presidential ambitions, but he realized that their ideas were now deeply entrenched throughout the northern areas. He was not greatly worried by the direct electoral threat this constituted—he was confident that his solid southern backing could win him re-election. But the widening split between north and south on water and other questions seemed increasingly forbidding, and with this Bolinas nonsense the prospect of actual civil disorder had begun to arise. Attempted secession from a county could be put down and laughed off. But the idea of secession from the nation was, he had

285

been forced to admit, no longer merely a lunatic-fringe notion; and the idea of splitting the state had also developed a dangerous appeal in the north. If Bolinas actually defied the county's authority, he would call in the National Guard as a show of force; that should stabilize the situation. But it was a calculated risk. Bolinas could blow up into a shooting confrontation. And there were angry people in the streets in all the major cities.

The Guard's readiness for domestic policing was debatable. During uprisings in Detroit following the assassination of black leader Martin Luther King, badly trained Guard units fought serious battles—generating many casualties—which turned out to be between different Guard forces unaware of each other's identities. Moreover, Guard units were drawn from nearby communities; they might not have the stomach to get tough with their fellow citizens. And if a show of federal armed force thus became necessary, it would mobilize all the "home rule" sentiments that the Survivalists had been cultivating so skillfully.

They had even come forward with an ingenious plan to reorganize the Guard into forces known as the Home Guard. It was particularly clever in its provisions for meeting the Guard's perennial problem of retaining enlisted personnel for more than brief periods. But it also contained a crucial omission—of provisions whereby the Guard, under certain circumstances, could be put under federal command and control. The Home Guard would be a regional army.

The Survivalist plan was too sensible in its details to be dismissed. Yet to discuss its crucial feature meant debating the political role of federal armed force in controlling the people. Either way, Governor Clark knew, lay trouble. In his worst fantasies, he envisaged a pitched battle in the sand dunes near Fort Ord between demoralized elements of the regular Sixth Army stationed there and diehard militant guerrillas who had taken over the Guard—with the guerrillas winning. Maybe, he thought, when everything was added up, splitting the state wasn't the worst idea in the world. If he were merely governor of Southern California, maybe he would be a happier man.

As if to oblige him, Survivalist sleuths announced they had unearthed a secret agreement Clark had made with certain Southern California interests at the time of his election campaign. The deal, as usual in California politics, involved water and land. The land was south of Los Angeles along the coast, and largely in the possession of

286

a few big corporations. The water was in the few still undammed Northern rivers. If the two could be joined—over the dead bodies of the environmental movement and about four fifths of the voters of Northern California—immense amounts of money would be generated. Clark, the Survivalists had discovered, had been promised some of it.

Clark's predecessor had pushed through the essential authorization of the Peripheral Canal, a giant concrete ditch capable of carrying almost the entire flow of the Sacramento River—the output of the whole watershed of the northern valley. But, at least in public, he had defended the sanctity of the remaining free rivers, whose salmon-rich waters still ran undammed to the Pacific. Clark, however, believed that the southern part of the state would soon run short of Colorado river imports. Pressures to save dying Mono Lake from total draining by the Los Angeles water system were mounting, and decreased imports from that area might not be made up for by conservation measures such as more efficient irrigation. But Southern California demand for growth and the profits of growth was not going to go away. The Northern rivers would have to be sacrificed. Clark, far more dependent on Southern votes than his predecessor, had felt the risk worth taking. The Northerners could scream all they wanted about him turning Sacramento into "L.A. North." A successful politician did what the voters wanted, didn't he?

The headlines, however, proved unnerving. "GOVERNOR'S HAND SEEN IN WATER SWINDLE," said the normally conservative San Francisco *Chronicle*. "DEAL TO PLUNDER NORTHERN RIVERS INVOLVED CLARK," said the even more conservative *Examiner*. Most unsettling of all, a position paper was simultaneously released by the Survivalist Party, concluding that dividing the state in half was the only sure way to preserve Northern water against further Southern depredations. The newspapers and even television commentators had brought this idea into the public eye. In the long run, the Survivalists maintained, each river basin on the coast should be a self-sufficient entity, living within the resources present in its own watershed on a sustainable basis, neither "mining" its own stores of underground water nor importing water from other areas—which meant constantly increasing costs for pumping. But, as a stopgap and transition program, the Survivalists had proposed a ten-year "water compact" under which the new state of Northern California would sell fixed and gradually decreasing amounts of water to the state of Southern California—at real costs. This obviously sensible notion meant that water pricing policies in Southern California would also be exposed to public scrutiny. The "surplus" pricing system by which residential users (and national tax-payers) unknowingly subsidized agricultural land-owning interests would be jeopardized.

The jaws of the political trap closed around Clark's feet. His Southern backers were adamant that this was a struggle to the death and that the Northern rivers deal must be defended. But throughout the North, in small towns and large cities, masses of people organized by the Survivalists marched in protests bearing signs that read "Save Our Water! Split the State!" At an all-day rally called by the Survivalist Party in San Francico's Golden Gate Park, an amazing 150,000 people turned up. And along the hundreds of miles of canal which snaked its way from the Delta southward, and around the giant pumps that consumed more energy than a major city in lifting water over the Tehachapis, state police guards were posted against the possibility of sabotage. The uneasy compromise that had kept California one state despite the divergent interests of North and South had finally broken down.

The morning after the shooting incident at the Bolinas checkpoint, the sheriff himself came out with four carloads of officers. The smashed bar over the road at the guard box had been replaced with an unpainted board. The flat-tired pickup had been pushed back onto county territory. Roger was now on duty and he waved down the sheriff's car. The others stayed in their cruisers, but the sheriff got out and identified himself. Roger in turn said that he was a member of the Town Council and a signer of the Declaration of Independence. The two men eyed one another.

"What happened last night was a criminal obstruction of the duty of my men," the sheriff began.

"The duty of your department stops at that line," replied Roger. "Bolinas is no longer part of your county."

"Your saying it doesn't make it so," said the sheriff. "I don't care what you signed, we're still the law out here. And we're going to go on in."

In Roger's mind the old Marx Brothers riposte, "This means war!" struggled to get out, but he kept a straight face. "In the name of the people of Bolinas and their democratic decision, I deny you permission to enter," he said.

"They we'll go in without it," said the sheriff. "Crank up that bar."

Roger looked at him grimly. "You'll have heavy casualties," he said. "Is it really worth it?"

The sheriff looked back. "Casualties? You wouldn't be crazy enough to—"

"What do you think we have a militia for, sheriff? Just take a look. Those big trees, those rocks, that brush. You wouldn't get downtown with a man alive."

The sheriff looked around. If these people were desperate or crazy enough to actually take up arms at all, they could have the whole road lined with snipers. And it was the only road in. He had to hand it to them, they'd taken advantage of their situation. In guerrilla war the natives always had the advantage.

"You know you can't get away with this," he said. "You may be able to hold *us* off, but we can have the National Guard in here this afternoon and it'll be all over."

"Well," said Roger stubbornly, "it isn't their territory either. We'll deal with that if the time comes."

After the Madera decision, the administration in Washington relaxed in the belief that Survivalist ideas had been satisfactorily discredited (with the regrettable exception of the state of Washington); the president and his aides turned their attention once more fully upon foreign policy. They had in fact secretly sent more than a hundred thousand ground troops to Brazil and had plans to send more if necessary. They had also committed themselves to related military spending that further accelerated the chronic inflation.

Like many administrations before it, the Maynard White House found the drama of foreign adventures far more appealing than domestic issues, where it seemed paralyzed by the very interest groups that had brought it to power in the first place. The inflationary drain of dollars to pay for oil continued unabated. Except in armaments production, the manufacturing sector of the economy continued to weaken, creating a new wave of unemployment in Eastern cities, many of which tottered toward bankruptcy along with several major corporations.

A wave of environmental depredation begun by the dismantling of protective agencies in the early eighties continued, spreading illness and death, especially among the working population whose medical protection had now been largely eroded by uncontrollable rises in medical costs. A vast program of prison expansion had put more people behind bars than in any other country in the world. Nonetheless, violence on the streets had reached epidemic proportions. Crime and sabotage seemed the only means available for people to express their resentment of a government which lacked either the ability or the desire to manage a stagnant economy with even a modest degree of economic justice. Public opinion polls gave the Maynard administration the lowest ratings that had ever been recorded—ratings that were especially abysmal along the West Coast.

The presidency had become increasingly media-dependent and unstable, and now, after almost three years in office, President Maynard's political future looked bleak. Moreover, his angry outburst at the press conference on Brazil had been followed, according to stories circulating around the White House and on Capitol Hill, by increasingly frequent and bizarre accusations directed against cabinet members and aides. By mid-January rumors had it that the president was seriously depressed and receiving psychiatric treatment. The business of the executive branch, it appeared, was being transacted mostly by the president's chief of staff, who happened to be a general. But even he, it was widely felt, was showing signs of erratic behavior.

Washington observers began to speculate darkly that the country was no longer governable by the old rules. Some wondered if, as in ancient Rome, the constitution of the republic might be overthrown by a Caesar who would promise—and enforce—a reign of military order. To many in the Survivalist Party, such prospects effectively destroyed any remaining hopes that the national political and economic situation might be redeemable. Ecotopia would have to look out for itself.

Every morning just before dawn the fishing fleet puts out from Fisherman's Wharf in San Francisco. Graceful little shrimp boats, ungainly steel trawlers, topheavy power yachts, they pass under the long span of the Golden Gate Bridge and head to sea. On this particular morning the radio gossip among the skippers tended to favor an area near the Farallon Islands, and most of the boats set course in that direction. One small craft, however, continued north along the coast. It was rigged for salmon fishing, but nobody unlimbered the drag lines; instead, the skipper headed on toward Bolinas. The trip would take a couple of hours.

Vera Allwen sat on the afterdeck with Maggie Glennon, drinking tea from a thermos and enjoying the slow swell of the ocean; occasionally a little sun got through the overcast. They were en route to Bolinas to meet with the Town Council, and since word had come that the land approaches might soon be the scene of more "incidents," they were going by sea.

Maggie felt the Bolinas declaration of independence was a dramatic symbolic move that should be endorsed and defended by the Survivalist Party as a model and inspiration, a rallying point for northerners in the struggle to split the state. But Vera hesitated. "What if it backfires?" she asked. "The county is sure to come in and take them over. Losing on this could dampen the whole state campaign. And then on the other side, well, secession is one of those explosive ideas—once it's out of the box you can't tell how far it will go. This might have to be *it*. Are we ready for it?"

Among party strategists, *it* was code for some critical happening, some crystallizing, polarizing event that would lead a majority of people in the Northwest to see that removing themselves from the federal union was their only way to survive. Some thought such critical events could be created. Others, Vera among them, felt that they simply occurred, unpredictably, and could never be engineered; all the party could do was to try to recognize them and act on them. The Bolinas secession offered itself as a candidate event. But was this *it*?

"So far the papers and wire services are playing it for laughs," said Maggie. "That gives us a little time. But pretty soon it won't be funny any more. Somebody will get hurt."

"It'll escalate."

"Yeah. There could be a massacre. And the question will be, are these just a bunch of uppity hippies who got what they deserved, or are they the martyrs of the new Ecotopian life style that everybody is adopting? Well, I say they're our people and they deserve help!"

"But can we carry the case in the regional media?" mused Vera. "Some of them look a little weird, but of course most Bolinesians are really pretty standard citizens. Roger Swift's a well-known teacher with a lot of impressive contacts—and a brilliant scientist daughter.

They've got architects, writers, planners, all plenty articulate. But how will people read this story? Does it have a positive ending?"

"Well," said Maggie, "the county oppresses poor little Bolinas. There may be real trouble, and the governor brings in the Guard. For what? To keep the Bolinesians hooked up to the electric wires—just when we have Lou Swift about to tell ten million people how they can *un*hook! What the Bolinas people want is to save energy and live free lives and not bother anybody—and get government off their backs so they can do it. That is a program a lot of folks are extremely enthusiastic about. We shouldn't underestimate it, like we did the turnout at the Park. We are approaching critical mass!"

Vera was silent for a few minutes, watching the bow wave spread out to the sides of the little boat. They began edging through the narrow safe channel toward the entrance to the Bolinas lagoon and harbor. A handmade flag flew at the end of a small dock. On it a dark oak tree stood out against a light background, while its roots symmetrically showed light against a dark background. The effect was rather like that of a ying and yang symbol. "Some people like to be with the winners," said Vera. "Some like underdogs. Best of all is to be an underdog and still win! Well, let's talk to them."

At the Green House the sense of excitement and crisis had become almost normal, and great hopes alternated with dread and despair. Continual demonstrations and protest meetings indicated that a great many people were fed up with the deteriorating national situation and eager to go it alone. Things were clearly building toward some kind of climax. Despite a lack of recent public attacks from the Maynard administration, Washington had finally begun to react to the depth and breadth of secessionist sentiment in the Ecotopian territory. Reports from Nevada told of a major military build-up taking place around Johnson Air Force Base near Reno. An entire airborne division, equipped with hundreds upon hundreds of heavy attack helicopters, had assembled there and was busy flying practice missions into the surrounding desert. A division of infantry from Texas had also been brought in, with large numbers of fast personnel carriers capable of reaching San Francisco in a few hours. No inside intelligence of any real use had yet been received in the Green House, but no one doubted the troops were there for one purpose: to seize control of key points in the Ecotopian region and destroy the separatist movement.

Better information was available through Survivalists who had joined the National Guard. Commanders had received orders to prepare for widespread civil disorders. They were advised to purge their officer ranks of anyone suspected of Survivalist sympathies, but nothing much seemed to have happened as a result. Security at weapons and vehicle storage facilities had been tightened a little. However, since Guard members were basically civilians, they shared the widespread public discouragement and dismay at federal policies, and many of their families included staunch Survivalists. The chief concern of most Guard members, in fact, was not the domestic crisis at all, but the growing possibility that the conflict in Brazil might expand, or that the tense Mid-East situation might lead to war—in which case they might be mobilized into the regular army and sent to the jungles or deserts to die.

The Ecotopia Institute had quickly had to develop a military intelligence section—much to Raye Dutra's dismay. To her analysts studying Pentagon actions, the army seemed to be spreading its troops surprisingly thin. Actual tactical forces had dwindled in recent years because funds had been increasingly allocated to high-technology, high-cost weapons systems. And most of the men trained for combat assignments—including the occupation of a potentially rebellious region like Ecotopia—were already committed elsewhere. American forces in Europe remained massive, on guard against what was still considered a threat of Soviet invasion. No one yet knew just how substantial were the forces committed in Brazil, though reports continued to trickle out indicating they were very large. Clearly, withdrawal and defeat there would be as embarrassing as in Vietnam—and considerably more dangerous, since it would seriously threaten American dominance of the Western Hemisphere. The airborne division that had materialized in the Nevada desert was normally stationed in North Carolina, poised for deployment eastward across the Atlantic or south across the Caribbean. Could it be that it was the only strike-force unit available that was considered politically reliable enough for the task of subduing Ecotopia? It seemed possible, especially since Survivalists had devoted a great deal of energy to political organizing around (and where possible within) the army bases on the Pacific coast.

The great puzzle about the airborne division's appearance in

Nevada actually stemmed from the Mid-East situation. Survivalist contacts in Washington had been reporting persistent war rumors for several weeks. The CIA evidently expected some kind of offensive by Shi'ite Moslem rebels in Saudi Arabia, and the Saudi regime was so brittle that immediate American intervention might be the only way to maintain access to the essential oil fields—from which a vast proportion of Western oil imports came, not to mention much of Japan's. In such a crisis, with Russian tanks a couple of days' ride away through a collapsing Iran, American forces stationed nearby in Egypt and Somalia would surely be insufficient. So what were those divisions really doing up there in the Nevada desert—preparing to crush Ecotopia, or perhaps tempting the Soviets into a nuclear ambush? Jittery, Raye and her collaborators kept tabs on the situation as best they could and awaited the return of Vera and Maggie from Bolinas.

At this juncture, the Survivalist Party in Eugene decide to stage some kind of symbolic event that would polarize Oregon public opinion and put that state firmly in the secessionist camp. Thus it was that they revived the plans they had made the previous summer for a Great Ecotopian River Float—a flotilla of boats that would drift down the Willamette all the way to Portland. It would dramatize the river as the aboriginal link among Oregon's major cities. It would focus attention on the plan to create a park the whole length of the river. Since it would pass through areas where more than 80 percent of the state's population lived, if managed right it would converge a wave of Survivalist sympathizers upon Portland and, in passing, upon the nearby state capital, Salem. It would also be a great deal of fun.

As it happened, David Vandermeer was in Corvallis playing a couple of nights at the Crow's Nest with Sharp & Natural. He phoned Lou and asked if she'd like to come up; she got the bus the next day. They joined people who were busily scouring around for boats—rubber rafts if possible, but old rowboats and canoes also joined the flotilla. A large communal raft of truck inner tubes was lashed together with bamboo poles; on it little improvised tents were made in case of rain. There were ice chests, camp stoves, water containers—the mighty Willamette being much cleaner than it once was but still not fit to drink. With everything more or less ready, and the rag-tag

294

squadron tied up along the river bank near the Crow's Nest landing, they awaited the arrival of the Eugene fleet. Local newspapers had been alerted, and the departure from Eugene had been covered with sympathetic humor: ECOTOPIAN EXPEDITIONARY FORCE HEADS FOR PORT-LAND. A rousing declaration had been read, inviting Oregonians all through the green center of the state to rally to the cause—either get a boat and join the Float itself, or gather along the river to support the fleet as it drifted past.

Lou and David sat on the Crow's Nest dock to wait. They drank some peppermint tea and had a sandwich; then they took a nap. At last, about three o'clock, the Ecotopian flotilla appeared around the upstream bend. "They're coming!" Lou yelled, and people began streaming out to get ready to push off. The Eugene contingent made fast to willows along the bank and scrambled out to talk with their Corvallis counterparts. Some had discovered they were lacking essential provisions and went across the road to a market. Newspaper reporters and TV crews were on hand, and a bulletin was issued to them—reporting firsthand on the state of the river banks between Eugene and Corvallis, pointing out locations where the river park might include picnicking and camping spots, and describing the message being carried to the legislature and the governor from the people all along the meandering Willamette.

By the time everybody was ready to set out, a crowd lined the bank for several hundred yards, cheering as each boat was untied and released into the current. Lou celebrated the departure by falling spectacularly overboard for a newspaper photographer. But the water, she found, was icy, and she scrambled back into the boat, giving the photographer the finger when he asked for a wet T-shirt shot. Once in the current, the little rubber raft Lou and David were in tended to rotate slowly. So if they just sat still they got to see in all directions. Lou changed into dry clothes and soon she was warm again.

People were very excited at first; a few restless souls paddled off on side expeditions in canoes or kayaks. But gradually most of them relaxed, settled down into their makeshift craft, and chatted quietly. There were no rapids in the Willamette, only a dam near Portland that they would have to portage around. It was going to be a lazy trip. But they did have things to do besides get stoned, take quick dips in the river, and make camp on gravelly beaches at night. People with cameras documented the river's banks from the water side, taking photographs to be used in articles and slide-shows. Others with experience in landscape planning took notes on the location of the banks, natural land formations rather like levees that would make good boundaries for the park, and deep places that would be best for swimming and diving. When the fleet passed under a bridge scouts were sent to find a telephone from which they could notify people downstream to get ready for their passing.

The event did catch the public imagination, and at places where roads gave easy access to the river thousands of people sometimes gathered to watch the fleet pass. By now it numbered several hundred boats; only one had actually sunk and its passengers had continued the trip on the big raft. The vagaries of the river's currents stretched the fleet out into a long, straggling line, and like a big patriotic parade it took 20 minutes or more to pass any given point. Hand-made banners streamed from some of the bigger craft, and from a mast on the big raft: "Ecotopia Now!" "To Survive—Secede!" As these passed under bridges the watchers cheered, and some of them rushed down to the water's edge, asking to be picked up. Other people waited with their boats at crossings and landings, joining the flotilla when it reached them.

After Corvallis came Albany, where the Willamette is joined by the Calapooya. Then onward they sailed to Independence, and only a few miles further lay Salem. At Salem the entire fleet tied up to the banks, except for a few canoes and kayaks that could navigate the old canal which conveniently ran to within a few feet of the gold-domed capitol building. A Salem city delegation had met the fleet; joining Survivalist leaders who were part of the expedition, they boarded the little craft and were paddled briskly to the steps of the capitol, while about a thousand members of the expedition and local Survivalists trotted alongside the canal.

The governor was not in town, but one of his chief aides appeared on the steps, at first looking apprehensive, to talk with the crowd. Several prominent legislators known to have Survivalist sympathies also came out. They were presented with a petition asking that Oregon formally align itself with the Survivalist-controlled state of Washington and with the forces working to form a new state of Northern California in a Northwest federation dedicated to ecological sanity and survival. They promised to present the document as a resolution before the legislature. Then the fleet members trooped back to their boats, and prepared for their descent on Portland.

296

GOVERNOR ORDERS GUARD
TO QUELL BOLINAS RISING

Sacramento, Jan. 30. Governor Clark has ordered National Guard units to assist the Marin County sheriff's department in restoring order to the little coastal town of Bolinas, just north of San Francisco. Last night, according to county officials, Bolinas inhabitants at an improvised "checkpoint" refused entry to sheriffs trying to investigate an illegal fireworks display. Shots were reportedly fired, puncturing tires on a sheriff's department pickup truck. This morning, further threats of violence occurred, the governor's office said.

"This will *not* be a shot heard round the world," said the governor, referring to the Bolinas Town Council's recent attempt to declare independence from the county, and indeed the state and nation. Aides added that the governor was outraged at the incident and did not share the humorous view of it taken in some newspapers.

Bolinas, with a reputation as a largely self-contained and self-reliant community, is considered a hotbed of Survivalist Party followers and the Bolinas "Declaration of Independence" draws heavily on Survivalist ideas. As of this morning, however, the Survivalist headquarters in San Francisco has issued no official statement on the Bolinas situation. Party spokeswoman Maggie Glennon said in a telephone interview, "We know that many people all over the region, not just in Bolinas, are becoming desperate about governmental unwillingness to try to construct a more livable world. Solar technology is about to make it possible for almost anybody to unhook from utility lines, and the county is going to look pretty silly standing in the way, with or without the National Guard's help. No wonder people come to a point where they decide they have to take things into their own hands. After all, that's a good old-fashioned American tradition." However, she stressed that an official statement was in preparation and would be issued tomorrow.

News of the governor sending the Guard to Bolinas and of the continuing widespread demonstrations reached Lou in Salem. She phoned the house in Bolinas and asked Roger what was going on. "Nobody really knows," he said. "Our little declaration seems to have driven a lot of people completely crazy. It would be funny if it wasn't so damned dangerous. The whole society just seems to be teetering on the brink. The polls run about 50/50 on the state-splitting bill—people in Sacramento think it'll go through in a couple of days. But that may be the last straw for the feds, so the troops may come in. A lot of folks are talking like this was 1776—you know, the whites of their eyes and all that! But we had a big pow-wow with Vera Allwen and Maggie Glennon here yesterday, and it looks as if the Survivalist Party will come out for us. Vera thinks you're terrific, by the way. Anyhow, you've sure got your pick of crises—are you going to continue to Portland or come back here?"

"I think I'll come back. As Bolinas goes, so goes Ecotopia."

"That's probably about right. Anyway we've given the world a new human right—the freedom to disconnect!"

Lou got on the bus for Bolinas, but David went on with the River Float toward Portland, home not only of a majority of Oregon's population, but of most of its media. Though the River Float people were unarmed, a few newspaper commentators had criticized the event as an attempt to intimidate the state government. A farmer near Newberg had fired on the boats as they passed; nobody had been hurt, but the incident had been built up in the press. In response, Survivalist groups had stepped up their appeals for support, and in Oregon City and Oswego large crowds gathered to cheer the flotilla's passage.

The Portland media had been alerted that something interesting was going to happen when the fleet came ashore at the new park along the river to the south. So photographers, video crews, and reporters were on hand in force when the first boats hit the beach and were pulled up onto the shore. Over the next half hour the makeshift fleet landed most of its people. Local publicity for the event had been received with instant enthusiasm and tens of thousands of welcomers and curiosity-seekers had gathered on the grassy areas of the park. Finally the big raft tied up and the mayor of Eugene, a well-known state Survivalist figure, stepped out of it with a green flag bearing the increasingly familiar Ecotopian tree insignia. He marched up the bank onto the grass and stuck the flag's staff into the ground.

At that moment a couple of trumpet players David had recruited blew a fanfare. "Now hear ye, hear ye!" cried the Eugene mayor. "With the powers invested in me by the Executive Committee of the Survivalist Party of Oregon, I do hereby take possession of this territory in the name of—Ecotopia!" The crowd laughed and cheered, and the trumpeters blew again. The TV cameras zoomed in; interviewers, tongue in cheek, began to ask questions.

"Are you *really* authorized by the Survivalist Party?"

"Just as much as Cortez was authorized by Queen Isabella, or Sir Francis Drake by Queen Elizabeth."

"How are you going to take possession of Portland if you have no arms?"

"By force of example."

"Why do you think the Survivalist vision deserves to be dominant in Oregon politics?"

"What other vision is there?"

And finally, "Don't you fear that aligning Oregon with Washington and Northern California could risk secession and civil war?"

"Yes, it could. But to gain great objectives—and survival in the face of national suicide seems to us a very great objective indeed—risks must be taken."

At this point a big flatbed truck appeared carrying Sharp & Natural's instruments. David and Ellen and the rest climbed up, somebody plugged the system into a nearby pavilion outlet, and they began to play. For about an hour their music pulsed across the river as the huge crowd danced on the grass and knots of people gathered to lay plans for political activities in the next couple of days. Then there were murmurs from one edge of the crowd. A car had drawn up, and out of it stepped the mayor of Portland and several members of the city council. They got up on the truck to use the microphones; the band stopped playing. Now the crowd became alert, curious; what was happening? The Portland mayor stepped forward to speak. He was a widely respected figure, responsible for many solid, sensible environmentally sound innovations in city government. Though not a member of the Survivalist Party, he had worked smoothly with it on many occasions. It was often said that he would be the next governor. Now he took the microphone and looked out over the expectant crowd. David saw him take a deep breath, and suspected something big was coming.

"Fellow Ecotopians!" The crowd, taken by surprise, roared its delight. People pushed toward the truck so happily that it shook. Then the mayor read a proclamation which, he said, would be proposed to the city council that evening and which was virtually sure of adoption: a declaration of support for the Survivalist program in Oregon and its neighbor states, and a call for immediate emergency consultations among leaders of the legislatures of the three states with a view toward forming a consensus on what was to be done to face the worsening crisis. The crowd listened solemnly to this and did not immediately applaud when he was done. But when the mayor of Eugene crawled up beside him, put the little green flag into his hand, and gave him a fraternal hug, there was a great roaring cheer from the crowd. It appeared that Oregon could be counted on.

The National Guard unit that was ordered to Bolinas had done stalwart work in saving people from from floods but it was not a terribly effective military organization. Most of its members had joined for the money—they were working people and that weekend day's extra pay just enabled their families to get by. A few were on police forces, including some of the officers; they didn't mind the prospect of having to keep civilians in line, but even they were cynical about the outfit.

Thus, although a top-priority mobilization order had been issued, it took longer than the sheriff had predicted for the Guard to appear. It was not until the morning following his parley with Roger at the guard post that a line of big olive-drab trucks rumbled over the hills. In order to minimize the likelihood of some raw recruit driving a personnel truck off the cliff into the sea, they came the long route via Muir Woods. The troops bivouacked in a pasture near the highway. Then one party of several hundred men, with bayonets fixed on their rifles, marched toward the sea, skirting the Bolinas town boundaries on the north; another party approached the guard post. Both parties soon encountered posted signs and leaflets scattered about, and officers and men alike picked these up and read them.

BROTHERS!

You are approaching the boundaries of the independent Town of Bolinas. We the citizens of Bolinas have seceded from the county, state, and country. We ask only to be left alone. We are taking care of our own needs—we have our own courts, our own militia to preserve order, and our own democratically elected government.

> The sheriff of Marin County has tried to exert the county's authority over a territory whose citizens have seceded from that county. The Guard is being asked to assist in this illegal and oppressive action.
>
> We do not believe you wish to participate in a war against your fellow citizens. But if you cross the town boundaries, you will have committed an act of violence which will be met with violence; we are sworn to defend ourselves by any means necessary.
>
> Stop now, and discuss the situation with your fellow Guardsmen, before it is too late! You are safe as long as you remain outside the posted boundary lines. —BOLINAS TOWN COUNCIL

Little knots of Guardsmen collected near the boundary markers, talking. The officers hesitated. Their superiors had told them they were being sent in to control rioting hippies. Now it looked more complicated. The commanding officer had instructed them to fan out and sweep in toward the downtown area, arresting anybody who resisted. Tear gas was to be used to disperse gatherings. If hostile fire was encountered, it could be returned, the orders said. Some of the men had welcomed this. Others had been suspicious, and they were now looking particularly upset by the leaflets.

Still, orders were orders. "Okay, men, move on out!" yelled one lieutenant. But his men continued milling around, rifles slung over their shoulders. A few of them urged their fellows toward the boundary; they would move off a few feet in that direction, but when the others failed to follow, they would come back for further talk.

The lieutenant sensed trouble. "I said move out! That's an order!" He himself headed toward a nearby fencepost with a Council notice tacked to it. But his men did not follow. He pulled his automatic from his holster. "Are you guys going to move or not?" he growled.

But the men stood sullenly, holding the Bolinas leaflets in their hands. "Uh, lieutenant, may I ask a question, sir?" one of them said. "What is it?" the lieutenant snapped.

"Well, sir, we're worried by these leaflets. It doesn't sound like a riot, sir."

At this point the noise of a helicopter was heard. The Guardsmen and their uneasy officers looked up, hoping that the craft contained a higher officer who might clarify the situation for them. But it was a little civilian copter; taped to its side was a handmade sign reading PRESS. It fluttered gracefully along the boundary line for a moment, then headed back toward downtown Bolinas.

"Shit," said the lieutenant. "All right, men. Let me talk to the commander. Stay where you are."

When the rumor of the Guard's approach ran through Bolinas, most people stayed indoors; it was said there might be shooting, or at least tear-gas. Dimmy hadn't been seen for 24 hours and the Swifts had been looking after Theo. Roger went off on some mysterious official errand, telling everybody else to stay put. But Lou was not about to stay home and miss all the excitement. She sneaked out the back door so that Carol and Mike didn't hear her, got her bicycle, and headed downtown. There were few people about, but she ran into Jerry, a neighbor, who said that the Guard seemed to have abandoned its plan to take over the town. Instead they had set up two bivouacs, one on the mesa near the trans-Pacific radio transmission towers and one near the town's checkpoint on the road. Both were well back from the town's boundaries.

"Do you think it's safe to go take a look?" asked Lou. "I really don't know," Jerry replied. "You never can tell, in these things. There can be a lot of confusion—somebody gets scared and starts firing. It's been quiet for a while now, but if you do go out there, move slowly and keep in plain sight, and don't carry anything that might look like a weapon."

Lou bicycled on northward. A car that she recognized as belonging to another neighbor was parked near the boundary fence; there were a couple of people in it with a walkie-talkie. Lou leaned her bicycle on the car. She strolled slowly toward the fence. Three Guardsmen were lolling about near a big khaki tent, drinking coffee out of styrofoam cups. Lou leaned on a fence post and called, "Hey, you guys!" The Guardsmen ambled over, delighted that this attractive young woman wanted to talk to them.

"I wanted to say thanks for not messing up our town," said Lou. "And if there's anything we can do for you out here, let us know. It gets kind of cold at night, you might need firewood or something."

The men were embarrassed. Something about Lou's innocent looks kept them from making the obvious come-on reply. Besides, these people were still supposed to be the Enemy. According to new orders

302

that had just come down, the Guard's mission now was to confine the "civil disturbances" within the boundaries of the town and prevent confrontations between townspeople and outsiders.

"Well, listen," said one of the men, "you could tell us what's going on! What's your name, by the way?"

"I'm Lou."

"I'm Henry, and this is Slim, and that's Fred."

"Pleased to meet you. Well, nothing's going on. I mean, we're going on living, that's all. Just the way we were before all this fuss. We just want to be left alone."

The men saw their lieutenant glowering at them from beside the mess tent. "We better get away from the fence," said Jake.

"Take care," said Lou. "Here, catch this!" Smiling, she tossed a big yellow daisy toward them and then turned back toward her bicycle.

"Christ," said Henry, "am I ever glad I read that leaflet. Just look at those legs."

. The two-way format the Survivalists had pioneered had become immensely popular, both for local and regional coverage, and Vera's weekly TV broadcasts were now major regional political events watched by millions of people. In her quietly reassuring way, Vera seemed the only sane voice in the growing chaos, and many sought the opportunity to talk with her over the cable facilities. Tonight she began by explaining that the Survivalist Party had decided to support the Town of Bolinas in its move toward independence and energy self-sufficiency.

"Sometimes," she said, "a tiny community can see things that a larger, more complex community takes longer to learn. We believe that Bolinas is telling us all something: that local communities, in a spirit of self-reliance and cooperation, can move faster to solve energy and ecological and health problems than the often constipated machinery of county, state, or national government. Bolinas has a lot to offer us. One of its young people, Lou Swift, has developed a do-it-yourself photovoltaic solar cell which will be described next week on these broadcasts. Her invention will enable you too to unhook from utility company lines if you wish. Government authorities must recognize that people in the Ecotopian region are pushing ahead with many such innovations. And so the Survivalist Party has interceded with the county and state, and obtained a promise that the Guard forces on the borders of Bolinas will remain merely as a peacekeeping force."

After a few people called in to question Vera about this solution to the possibility of violence, she proceeded to drop her other bombshell of the evening: the as yet unconfirmed probability that Governor Clark would resign because of the water scandal. He would be replaced by the lieutenant governor, a northerner who had sworn to split the state before he would let the Clark water deal go through. In fact he would immediately go before the legislature to put the weight of the governor's office behind the bill providing for the orderly and constitutional division of the state. This made the bill now almost certain of passage, and Vera urged the people of the region to indicate their support for it in every way possible.

She also announced that, as a result of the River Float, the state legislature of Oregon had passed a resolution aligning the state with Survivalist-led Washington and with the Survivalist forces in California. Now if Northern California could take control of its own destiny, Vera said, there would be a solid tier of Ecotopian states that could stand firmly together against the madness in the federal government. "Let us support the separation bill with all our strength," she concluded. "We do not stand alone. And in just a little while, we will have our own place in the sun."

Vera and her colleagues were well aware of the treacherous territory that would be entered with this move. A legal division of the state would require the consent of Congress. Eastern states would not welcome the advent of two new West Coast senators, and other states with regional problems might not wish to encourage the process of state mitosis.

As the Survivalist Party went into high gear around the new governor's separation bill, a feeling of jubilation began to mix with the dread of military intervention. People had a sense that their common dream of a region organized with some kind of ecological sanity was coming tantalizingly within reach. If only they could control the territory, this tiny strip of earth, they knew they could create a new society there. Its technology would have a human face, it would be socially, economically and ecologically accountable, it would need make no apologies to the future. "We knew we had to choose," they could say. "We chose to start doing it right."

Shortly before dawn on a chilly winter morning, radio-controlled model airplanes with 8-foot wingspans took off from locations near all major military bases in the Ecotopian territory. They rose to several hundred feet altitude and then headed out over the bases. When they reached the barracks areas, their miniature bomb bays opened. Then packets of tiny leaflets tumbled out, one every few seconds. As they drifted toward the ground, the wind dispersed them. The planes then executed wide turns and came back toward their launching points, releasing more leaflets.

Troops asleep, as well as the few on guard duty, heard only what they took to be the sound of a small chain-saw. In the dawn's early light, however, soldiers moving about the bases saw small pieces of paper on the ground carrying the legend, PUT THIS IN YOUR POCKET, READ LATER. Some soldiers ignored them or treated them as litter. A good many, however, whether out of curiosity or thinking they might have something to do with dope deals or other excitements, did put the leaflets in their pockets. Later, behind mystery novels or comic books or in the privacy of latrines, they took them out and read the Survivalist Party's appeal for sympathy and support in case civil disorders broke out on the West Coast.

The new governor withdrew the Guard from Bolinas, to widespread relief, and the focus of political events in California moved to the measure providing for the division of the state. Public and legislative debate was, as expected, both bitter and prolonged. During this period Carol phoned Sarah in Orinda, hoping to arrange a visit. After all this tension and sense of crisis, she felt it would be nice to have a lazy family day together. But she got Andy on the phone instead. And he was sarcastic: "How's my brother the politician?"

"Fine," said Carol. "He's a little sick of meetings by now. But it's tremendously exciting, of course—so many new things happening! We've all gotten very caught up in it."

"Well, watch your step, Carol. Those people are toying with treason, you know. The government isn't going to put up with it forever."

Carol felt the threat in Andy's voice. "What do you mean?"

"I've heard talk about just locking the whole bunch up," he replied. "You remember the detention camps they built for the

Japanese in World War II? Well, they're still there, you know."

"But that would be unconstitutional!"

"Yeah, it would, wouldn't it? It was then, too."

Carol had been hoping she wouldn't have to ask for an invitation. But Andy didn't volunteer, so she plunged on. "Look, Andy, it's been a long time since we've all gotten together. I was wondering if we could come over this weekend. Take some walks and hang around."

Andy hesitated. "It *has* been a while. But Carol, I really don't know if it would be comfortable. I don't see Roger giving any ground, and I don't enjoy getting kicked in the teeth all the time. Every time we talk it's a real row."

"But Andy, we can't let political disagreements break up our family!"

"It's not just a political disagreement." Andy sighed. "Roger and I aren't seeing a lot of things the same way. I'll let you have it straight, Carol, and I'd tell him the same thing: I think he and those Survivalist people are being destructive and dangerous and nihilistic. I've earned pretty good credentials as a liberal. I know the difference between constructive reform and tearing everything apart. These mobs of people in the streets, and this Bolinas secession nonsense—what can they possibly accomplish?"

"So you don't want us in the house?"

"Don't be hurt, Carol. I just don't think it would be good, right now when things are so hot."

"Afraid it might compromise you at ConCo, to entertain your Ecotopian brother?"

"Come on, that's not fair. I love him, Carol, but I don't know how to handle this. We're on different sides now. It tears me up. I'm sure it's just as hard on Roger."

"And what about brotherly love?"

"That's what I'm trying to figure out. I know Roger has a right to his views, but so do I. He keeps insinuating that I'm a hypocrite, that I'm just selling out and must be feeling rotten inside from secret guilt. Well, I'm not! And until he sees that, and respects *my* right to *my* views, I don't know how to talk to him any more. I'm sorry, but I just don't know how."

"I wish your father was still alive, to mediate between you."

"So do I. Though he probably couldn't do much either, when things

306

have gotten to this point. Besides, he never hesitated to take sides, you know."

Carol had never met Lou's grandfather, though plenty of stories about him still circulated among the family. "Oh?" she said.

Andy's voice fell as he said, "Yeah, he'd probably take sides."

"And which side would he be on, Andy?"

"Yours, I'm afraid. He was always a sucker for underdogs."

TO: THE PRESIDENT

B-LEVEL ALERT

The Directorate now believes that nuclear devices constructed by a clandestine "Ecotopian" group have been hidden in Washington and New York City. Emergency measures are in progress to locate the devices. Electronic surveillance, clandestine searches of suspect locations, and other measures are being used.

However, technical advice based on CIA portable nuclear device experience indicates that detection may be impossible short of house-to-house search, which would require declaration of martial law and other extreme civil measures. It is believed that political blackmail regarding West Coast separatist movement is objective of emplacing suspected devices. We cannot estimate the time frame within which decision may be required for emergency measures; no communications have yet been received from the suspected group. At present, however, B-level precautions should be ordered in view of possibility of accidental detonation. We also recommend reconsideration of the hold put on assassination of key Survivalist leaders.

Unsophisticated weapons design of the type within capacity of an underground group is expected to produce relatively small but extremely "dirty" bombs. Casualty expectations under worst-case assumptions: approximately one million deaths and incapacitations from blast, fallout and radiation; extensive and protracted uninhabitability of areas within two miles of ground zero and downwind.

You've heard about it, now you can do it—
BUILD YOUR OWN SOLAR-ELECTRIC CELL!

Learn how you can unhook from the utility wires—how you and your neighbors can build cells that will generate electricity on your own rooftops!

Tomorrow night on Channel 33 at 8 p.m. the Survivalist Party presents its long-awaited special program on do-it-yourself photovoltaic cells. Learn how from Lou Swift, the 18-year-old inventor who beat the corporate laboratories.

Vera Allwen, leader of the Survivalist Party, will give a major address on the startling recent political developments in the West, and she will make a dramatic announcement of new policies to deal with the crisis. Tell your friends to be sure to tune in!

"Hello, Roger, this is Andy."

"Andy, how are you? I'm glad you called!"

"It's been a long time, brother. I felt awful when Carol called last week. I haven't been able to figure out what was happening between us. It feels terrible to be on opposite sides in all this—in this war, or whatever it is."

"It sure does." Roger was about to add something about Andy always being a stubborn son of a bitch, but he suppressed it, sensing that Andy had something important on his mind.

"Roger, I've got to tell you something. I don't know if you realize how serious the situation is. There are troops massed in Nevada."

"Sure, we know that."

"Roger, you remember the Civil War, don't you? This is going to be one bloody mess!"

"I'm not sure about that. I like to think the federal government still has some sense. At this point they probably don't want us much more than we want them. And they've got one war going in Brazil, why should they need another one? But Andy, what are you getting at?"

"Sarah and I are clearing out. I've had enough of it out here. I've got an offer in Chicago."

"They *love* nuclear in Chicago."

"Let's not get into an argument—I'm just calling to tell you what we're doing."

"Okay. When are you leaving?"

"We've put the house on the market already. Of course the damn real estate market is horribly depressed, but we can still get enough out of the place to buy something pretty elegant in Chicago, I think. I'm going in ten days, and Sarah will come as soon as the house is sold."

"What happens if you can't sell the house? I don't want to scare you, but most people have other things than real estate on their minds right now."

"Well, that's what I wanted to ask you, Roger. If worse comes to worst, do you want it?"

"You mean to live in? No, I've got my roots in over here in Bolinas."

"Yeah, I figured. Well, would you be willing to look after it for us?"

"Sure, Andy. I could rent it out for you. But what's your hurry?"

Andy's voice took on a dark tone. "It's all collapsing, Roger. This is the end. I don't want to get caught in the wreckage. Even ConCo is going to go down. Nobody's going to build anything here for a long time."

Roger wondered if he should argue. He and his Survivalist comrades were engaged daily in exhilaratingly ambitious and complex plans for constructing a whole new society: new technologies, new social institutions, new human relationships, new philosophies. All his rich brother could think about was building dams and nuclear plants for cost-plus profits—and clearing out if it was no longer possible. Well, thought Roger, some would leave but others would take their places; in the last weeks there had been a perceptible flow of people from the East, coming to lend their experience and energy and knowledge and hope to the Ecotopian dream. Old families broke apart yet new ones always formed. With a pang, Roger remembered the days when they all sat together in the warm evenings on Andy's patio, watching the stars come out and eating the kids' marshmallows.

"Well," said Roger, "I guess I can understand how you see it, even

309

though I think you're wrong. I'll remember the good times we've had. When this thing is all over, you can come back for a nice long visit. You may not recognize the place."

"If you live through it, Roger, I will. But you crazy fools don't know what you're up against. We're—they're going to blow you away."

"In that case I guess we'll see each other across the barricades. In a manner of speaking. Incidentally, who are you going to work for in Chicago?"

"Towne and Hatton."

Towne and Hatton—the giant military contractor out of Houston, Texas, now moving into the Midwest. A corporation experienced in building airfields, military port installations—all the facilities an occupying army might need, whether in Saudi Arabia or the Pacific Northwest. Roger spoke bitterly: "Those bastards make ConCo look like peacemongers! And I can guess what they're cooking up for us. Look, Andy, make sure you stay in Chicago. If they send you out here, I wouldn't be able to guarantee your safety. If it does turn into war, it'll be guerrilla war. There'll be saboteurs and sharpshooters and mines and things that blow up in your hands, and Survivalist agents everywhere. You hear me? There'll be no mercy then, even for brothers. Don't help make it happen, for God's sake!"

"Roger, it's *you* who are on the wrong side. You're in an illegal and subversive and treasonous movement."

"It's our only way to survive. That's all we've ever asked."

"Well, goodbye. I love you."

"I love you too. Goodbye."

"Bye."

Survivalist sympathizers in the little desert towns around Johnson Air Force Base noticed, the evening of February 12th, that the servicemen who customarily dropped by the local bars and brothels were not in evidence tonight. They phoned friends who lived out toward the base and learned that unusually intense loading activity was taking place around the helicopter pads. By prearranged coded signals, they notified San Francisco that the long-feared attack was probably about to begin. Watchers with binoculars in the hills near the base stood by

310

to provide immediate warning of the actual departure of the strike force.

Toward dawn the sleepy watchers were brought full awake by the distant roar of hundreds of engines. There was barely any light from the glowing sky to the east, but through the clear desert air vehicles could be seen scurrying around the take-off areas. The message went to San Francisco: the end was near, head for the hills! But back came the voice of Vera Allwen herself, calm as always. "No," she said, "we're not running. Let them come if they must. But give us a count, will you?"

Then, rising heavily from their pads, the fleet of helicopters took off. In the distance their heavy bodies made them resemble great lumbering beetles, but they rose in orderly military rows, each craft following its neighbor into the air and then off toward the south. After about a mile, they began slow turns—toward the east.

The watchers looked at each other in amazement and fingered their radio mikes. Were the copters going to head over Echo Summit, perhaps? No, as their formations became more definite they were clearly heading eastward—away from San Francisco, back toward their base in North Carolina. More ranks of aircraft rose from the ground and joined the advance squadrons—all heading east. Mechanically, the stunned watchers counted them as best they could—up past four hundred. They communicated the unbelievable news to San Francisco, where it was greeted with skepticism, and they talked with friends who lived to the east, along the flight's apparent route, who could confirm its continuation. In an hour, it was certain the fleet was in fact heading east because it had flown over Ely, darkening the sky there in its passage.

The Survivalists, as the news spread, speculated jubilantly on what could have happened to alter Washington's intentions. Vera sighed with relief; whatever the explanation turned out to be, it had been a very close call! It was not until mid-day that phone calls to contacts in Washington began to piece together the story. Ecotopia, it appeared, had been saved by the American obsession with oil.

311

MID-EAST WAR THREAT:
SAUDI REGIME TOTTERS AS
REFINERIES BLASTED

Russian Tanks in Iran?

Riyadh, Feb. 13 (WPI). Raging fires set by fanatic Shi'ite Moslem guerrillas swept through large areas in the refinery district along the Saudi Arabian coast after a series of massive explosions early this morning. Preliminary reports from the Saudi police indicate that they have arrested a number of saboteurs who claim allegiance to the messianic anti-American Muslim denomination whose followers overthrew the Shah of Iran in 1978.

American advisors, who have been airlifted into the troubled areas in sizable numbers in recent weeks, are aiding Saudi forces in combatting the rebels.

Unruly demonstrations by Shi'ite devotees were also reportedly taking place at several other points in Saudi Arabia. Armed exchanges were reported in Mecca, whose mosque was seized briefly by Shi'ite rebels in 1979. American observers here have noted that the Saudi royal family appears badly shaken by the events, and frequent jet departures from Riyadh airport have led to speculation that some members of the extensive family may be evacuating the country.

Officials of American and European oil companies operating here report that loading of crude oil from storage depots into tankers has been almost entirely disrupted .

Meanwhile, reports from Teheran indicate that Communist-oriented forces in the northern sectors of the civil war that has now spread over much of Iran have used Soviet-made tanks in combat with government troops. The Soviet government has issued repeated assurances that no Russian troops are involved in the fighting, but it has made no clear statement about the number of tanks that may be in Iran or about the conditions on which they have been supplied. The American concern is that the increasing Iranian disorders may provide cover under which a sizable force of Soviet armor could be accumulated within easy striking distance of both the Iranian and Saudi oil fields.

American embassy sources here revealed that American troops and naval forces in Egypt and Somalia had been on ready alert status for several weeks. These forces, whose precise dimensions are un-

312

known, are believed to include armored units capable of rapid deployment into the oil-producing areas around the Persian Gulf. They are reported to be equipped with nuclear artillery.

Word has been received in Riyadh of military mobilization in neighboring Iraq. The Iraqui government is strongly expansionist and may be inclined toward new military moves. It is still smarting from the humiliations of its inconclusive war with Iran and the Israeli destruction of its nuclear facilities. If a political vacuum should develop in Saudi territory, the Iraquis may attempt to take advantage of the situation. Their army has been vastly improved since the Iran war and has been given substantial new equipment by the Russians.

An additional military complication in the volatile Mid-East situation is that Pakistan, which has pursued an active nuclear development program and has recently attempted to establish itself as the military leader of the Muslim states, has declared that it will not tolerate an American military take-over of the Gulf area. Pakistan may possess some nuclear weapons, but the ability of its air force to deliver them in the face of concentrated American air power is doubtful.

In official circles here in the Saudi capital, the situation is regarded as extremely grave. Saudis remind themselves that President Maynard has repeatedly reaffirmed that America will defend its presence on the Arabian peninsula with all necessary force. Nontheless, the turmoil in the ancient kingdom could easily escalate toward nuclear confrontation.

Before she went to the studio for the big broadcast, Lou sat down to talk with Roger. They had had little time for quiet contact lately, and she missed it.

"Well, Dad, is it going to come off?"

"Your broadcast? Of course it is."

"No, I mean the splitting of the state. And all this talk about actual secession."

"I think we have a very good chance, now that those troops have been pulled back from Nevada. What more could we ask?"

Actually, Lou thought, Roger had never looked better. These last weeks of excitement had given people a sense of new energy, new possibilities. They didn't stand on ceremony or approach situations cautiously. There was no time for that—you just plunged in and took the consequences. It felt terrific, as if you were truly living at last. People felt caught up in a great wave of collective spirit, and Lou had noticed that nobody seemed to be getting colds or other minor illnesses. Even the crime rate had reportedly dropped.

"But suppose we lose," Lou persisted. "Other troops could come. You've got an awful lot at stake, haven't you?"

"My life, possibly," said Roger. "But you're thinking about the personal stake, the feelings? Yes, I've got everything at stake, Lou. More than I've ever had on anything before. Except you."

The two looked at each other. When she was younger, Lou had sometimes felt oppressed at being the apple of Roger's eye, as he would put it. She wondered if it was fair to Mike; she wondered if she had earned it. Now she was prepared just to accept it, as an emotional fact. He was her father, and he loved her and was proud of her. He loved her just for being, as she loved him. And now she *had* done something to deserve praise and admiration, not only from Roger but from lots of people. In some curious way, she realized that she felt the equal of her father. They were friends now, comrades.

"You know, Lou, whatever happens, people are going to talk about all this for a long time."

"They'll mess it up, too," said Lou. "The historians will think that the reporters really knew what was happening."

"And people invent and change things to make better stories. It'll all get mythologized. Who knows, maybe Vera Allwen on a white horse talking to God? Secession happening because women refused to make love unless the men went along with it? They'll believe those rumors that we had nuclear bombs. Conspiracy stories are always more fun than real politics."

"Secret laboratory on isolated promontory. A dark and stormy night—"

"You got it," said Roger, laughing. "But of course that part's perfectly true."

Lou was laughing too, and added, "For that matter, it *was* a conspiracy. We conspired to beat the corporations."

They grinned at each other and said as with a single voice, "And we did!"

The broadcasting studio, Lou found with relief, was a rather cluttered and make-shift place, full of old sets, mysterious equipment, people messing about with lights and cameras; it reminded her of a science lab. Still, she was nervous, and Vera tried to calm her down.

"You know, Lou, it'll just be us standing around talking."

"Yeah, but with a couple of million people watching! What if I get tongue-tied?"

"You won't. And remember you aren't talking to those people in one enormous crowd. You're really just talking to four or five in their living room. That's the personal reality of it. Or you can just talk to me."

"I wish you hadn't made such a big deal out of it, anyway."

"It happens to *be* a big deal. As you knew perfectly well when you went to work on it back in high school! And you're such a beautiful example of what we need more of. Look, Lou, suppose out there today you're talking to just a couple of young people who are capable of the same dedication as you are, who are as smart as you are—think what they might do in the next few years! Talk to *them*."

"Well, Bert has convinced me to emphasize the do-it-yourself side, the organizing side. There's so much going on out there among people, I want to connect the cell up to all that—that fervor."

"Sure, hit that too. But—look, Lou, I've been doing politics on television for a long time now. You know what people are really going to respond to? It's that sparkle in your eye, that happy little chuckle you have when you're talking about science. You look playful and strong and full of energy. That's contagious. The main message people will get is through the kind of being you are. They'll remember the cell because of you. And you just happen to be a visibly wonderful person."

Lou gulped. "Well," she said hesitantly, "I hope you're right!" She stopped pacing around and sat down on the edge of a set. "I haven't even asked," she said, "what the rest of the program is going to be. What is this big announcement I've been hearing about?"

Vera smiled. "Oh, I'll probably tell one of my stories. And then I'm going to propose a plan for secession from the United States of America."

The broadcast opened with Vera Allwen poking around at Lou's sample cell and chatting with Lou and the friends who had come to help in the demonstration. Then she addressed herself to the viewing audience.

"Friends, today you're participating in a remarkable historic event.

There are several extraordinary things about it. One is that with this broadcast we're inaugurating a standard two-way format for television in the whole Ecotopian region. We can talk to you—but you can also talk to us. Some of you on cable already have this capability and the necessary equipment. All of you can get it if you want it. We have great hopes for this system and will talk more about it soon.

"The second extraordinary thing today is that this young scientist, Lou Swift, is going to show you her invention, a do-it-yourself solar electric cell. She developed it in her last couple of years of high school. It will make it possible for you and your neighbors to build your own cell arrays for your own roofs. Which means you can achieve independence from the electrical utility grid at modest cost. Which will end our dangerous reliance on nuclear plants, and even cut down considerably on our need for oil-burning generating plants. Lou's achievement is especially remarkable because she brought it off when battalions of expensive scientists working for large corporations could not. Perhaps that was just luck, but perhaps it was because Lou was trying to develop a method that could be used by ordinary people and not something that had to be manufactured and sold by corporations. At any rate, she did it, and it works, and we're immensely proud of her, as a Survivalist and an Ecotopian!"

Lou shyly returned Vera's warm hug and stepped up to the cell display. "Hello," she said. "These are my friends, Bert and Carmen. First we want to explain just what a solar photovoltaic cell does." With the aid of some diagrams, Lou showed a schematic cell absorbing energy from solar input and transforming it into electrical current.

"What I've actually discovered is a special way of building these cells, using a process that involves salts from seawater. As you'll see, the materials needed are easy to get and we'll never run out of them. We can't actually build a whole cell for you here today because it would take too long, so we have a short film that shows us building a frame and melting the silicon in a kiln, just like a potter's kiln. Now here you see us 'doping' the silicon—that means we are adding to it very small quantities of other materials which enter the silicon molecular structure and help it to emit electrons.

"Here's an animated diagram of what happens when you add seawater and pass a little direct current through the cell. You see that now the electron transfers are greatly facilitated, and that's why this cell works so much better than earlier cell designs did.

"Now to capture the current off the cell when the sun shines on it,

316

you have to pick up the electrons from some kind of grid. So we bond onto it, through another brief pass in the kiln, this network of wires. And then the current comes out here. Each cell is hooked up to an array of other cells; it takes about a hundred of them, this size, to provide enough power for the ordinary electrical needs of a small house.

"Now as you know, the Survivalist Party has introduced legislation so that if you generate extra power during the day, it goes into the power company wires, and you get credit so you can draw on power company electricity later when you need it. But you can also totally unhook from the wires. For that, you'll also need an inverter and storage batteries and electrical control equipment. Carmen has produced this free booklet you can send in for. It explains the whole process—making the cells, hooking them up, mounting them on your roof, how often you need to clean them, and all that."

Carmen then ran through the high points of the booklet, and after that Bert stepped forward with his charts and graphs. He explained the output characteristics of the cells, their durability, and how they hooked up with various arrangements of batteries and inverters to provide enough power for different constellations of appliances. He also explained the neighborhood workshop program that the Survivalist Party was setting up. "In a year," he said, "almost everybody who wants to can have their house equipped with Lou's cells."

Lou came back on camera. "It's quite an easy thing to do, really, and thousands of people have begun doing it already. Our booklet explains everything you need, step by step. Get a copy at your neighborhood Survivalist Party center. If you work in teams and help each other, as Bert said, it goes quickly and you avoid mistakes. And we'll be having more programs about it, every week from now on, and you can call in and talk with us about any problems you might be having."

She smiled happily. "So there you have it," she said. "The power is in your hands."

After Lou finished, Vera spoke. She sat in a comfortable armchair, with Lou, Bert and Carmen seated nearby and the cell equipment in the background. The scene was informal and equalitarian, without lecterns or banners or other panoply of office; yet Vera's seriousness made the occasion seem personally urgent.

"My friends," she began, "we meet tonight at a crossroads in our

317

history. One fork in the road leads in the direction Lou Swift and her friends have just shown us. It will take us toward a society of self-reliance and independence and freedom. Surely that is the road we want to travel on. But there is another fork in the road, and our national government seems determined to follow that route, even though its destination is pollution, destruction, and the imminent threat of nuclear war.

"How did we get to this fateful junction? Let me first summarize our own actions. We on the West Coast have not only been arguing with our national government about what should be done, but we have actually gone ahead to *do* it, whenever that lay within our power. We have turned to the sun for energy to heat our houses and our water, and now Lou Swift's cell will let us draw our household electricity from the sun. We here in the West have learned terrible lessons from the nuclear catastrophe in Seattle, and our state governments now prohibit exposing us to such perils. We have recognized the fateful drain that oil imports put upon our economy, and we have taken realistic if painful steps to cut back the ruinous economic burden of the private automobile.

"These have not been easy accomplishments, and we deserve to feel proud of them. They have demanded serious commitment to a new vision of how human beings can live decently on the earth, conserving its resources and caring for it so that it can support us, and the other species we share it with, for all the generations to come.

"But how has the federal government responded to our example? By obstruction and opposition, by actions and inactions so unrealistic and self-destructive as to border on the suicidal.

"The federal government has discouraged our turn away from fossil fuel energy sources toward the inexhaustible renewable energy derived from the sun. It has persisted in the folly of further nuclear development, and now has the infinite gall to try to enforce the reopening of an obsolete nuclear plant on this coast—which is not even needed, since our conservation efforts have already caused our electric consumption to undergo a steady decline.

"Worst of all, the federal government has refused to develop a realistic policy to discourage the national addiction to the private automobile. Through the Madera case, it destroyed the most promising means of shifting our transportation system onto more efficient, less oil-dependent bases. And so the nation still uses foreign oil for almost half its consumption. You know from the news of the past few days what that policy is leading us to: an oil cut-off followed by economic chaos or war. The time has come, my friends, when we must decide between our automobiles and our lives. Those who live by the car will soon be asked to die for the car, in the deserts of Arabia or perhaps in a worldwide nuclear holocaust.

"This is the result of federal incompetence and stupidity so consistent as to verge on insanity. It is certainly non-survival behavior. A secret undeclared colonial war in Brazil is bad enough; like Vietnam, in time it alone would tear the country apart. To add to that the perils of an uncontainable war for oil is intolerable.

"We here in the West have spoken out against these tragic federal policies. We are a hopeful people who believe in reasonable solutions. We speak for life, not death. We speak for joy, not anxiety. We speak for voluntary joining together to create a new world, not for military tyranny to preserve an old one.

"But the national government has not listened to our pleas. We have spoken and argued, through television and the press and our representatives in Washington. We have pointed out that a large majority of the people in this region favor survival-oriented policies. And with the recent realignment in California politics, we can now say that the whole Northwest rejects the stubborn, unrealistic, war-bent elite that has been determining federal policies.

"My friends, we simply cannot afford to follow the road taken by the federal government. It leads to disaster and doom. We must strike out on our own new road. We must dissociate ourselves from the federal government or we will be dragged down with it.

"What can we actually do? I come before you, tonight, after many weeks and months of reflection on that question and after lengthy consultations with the wisest people our region has produced. And the conclusion we have drawn is that we must take the same step our forebears took when the policies of the British government became so intolerable that they were forced to dissociate themselves from it: we must form our own new nation, so that we can do for ourselves what the federal government refuses either to do or to allow us to do.

"Since we came to this conclusion, a few days ago, we in the Survivalist Party have begun to set up working committees—networks of people throughout the states of Washington, Oregon and Northern California—to organize our separation from the federal union.

"Our plans are already being finalized in certain areas: ways to divert tax revenues from federal to local purposes, to reorganize the

319

National Guard as the Home Guard and put it under state command, to protect our financial and economic community from reprisals by federal officials, and to begin a program of nationalization of oil corporations within the region.

"Tomorrow morning, Survivalist representatives in the three state legislatures will propose that those legislatures gather themselves into a constitutional convention for our new nation. This convention will meet here in San Francisco to work out a new federal structure for our region and to negotiate with the government in Washington toward a peaceful and constructive settling of the many difficult issues that our independence will raise.

"I am happy to report to you that there is no immediate threat of civil war. Federal troops which were stationed in Nevada with the capability of occupying our region have been withdrawn. We understand legitimate federal concerns about military security, and we have confidence that during the coming transition period solutions will be found.

"It is a rare and wonderful event when a new nation is born upon the face of the earth. I invite you to join wholeheartedly in this endeavor—the most challenging political endeavor ever seen on the West Coast of this great continent. We need each other's help. Tomorrow, your state representatives' offices will begin to hold workshops on the secession plan and how it will affect many aspects of our lives. We need your participation—it is your country. Together, we can build the new nation we must have. Together, we *can* survive. Let us begin!"

The constitutional convention, meeting in San Francisco for the following three weeks, still feared that at any moment it might be surrounded by airborne troops and locked into concentration camps. Vera Allwen and other Survivalist leaders from all three states sent repeated urgent messages to President Maynard, proposing diplomatic formulas for peaceful secession and permanent links of association, following the Canada–Quebec model. These appeals were not publicly acknowledged, but the White House did establish a secret channel of communication with the Green House. Over this line a halting exchange of proposals and counterproposals began to flow.

Meanwhile, intelligence sources reported that all troops remaining in Nevada had now departed. Raye Dutra's staff, working around the clock, produced endless drafts and briefs on assurances the new nation offered to the "mother country": uninterrupted access to the aerospace facilities of Boeing and Lockheed and to the electronics industry of Silicon Valley; unimpeded evacuation of nuclear military and research equipment; a gradual transfer of the Trident and Mare Island nuclear submarine bases to San Diego; transshipment and other economic agreements similar to those existing among European countries. Reactions to these proposals from Washington came erratically, and varied from outrage to grudging acceptance; the highest level personnel were evidently stretched to the utmost dealing with the unfolding Saudi and Brazil crises and gave fitful attention to the Ecotopian question.

In the end, tentative accords were reached. The new nation would remain within the American military orbit, but it would have no offensive forces. Instead, like the Swiss, Ecotopia would maintain a strong citizen militia with defensive armaments only.

Why the national government accepted this astonishing compromise is not fully known to this day. It may have been because confusion in Washington caused by the president's disability allowed only well-defined military issues to get top-level resolution. A cold military assessment of relative military risks and benefits may have led to the conclusion that American armed strength had to be deployed in more distant areas; the Ecotopians, after all, seemed unlikely ever to pose a hostile military threat. The administration may also have been influenced by messages sent, rumors said, by a clandestine group of militants who claimed to have planted nuclear bombs in New York and Washington, which they would detonate if military force was used against the embryonic Ecotopian government. Future historians will no doubt unravel these mysteries.

What is clear is that the constitutional convention, like its predecessor two hundred years earlier, gave creative thought to the formation of a governmental structure unprecedented on the face of the earth. The political subdivisions of the territory were redrawn on bioregional criteria—by watersheds, for the most part—into natural areas considerably larger than most counties but smaller than states, each with a natural metropolitan center. The original "No More" list drawn up in the early days of the Survivalist Party, now refined after considerable experience, was incorporated into the constitution along with the traditional civil guarantees of the Bill of Rights. The powers of the people, and of their immediate communities, were carefully safeguarded. Novel provisions were made for social experimentation with new institutions: universal two-way television as an extension of the government, a guaranteed minimum wage or "negative income tax," employee ownership of businesses, random selection of representatives in one house of district legislatures, ritual war games— many such innovations would be tried for a time in selected areas and either discontinued or expanded after practical experience with them. The emphasis was always on the biologically viable rather than the economically profitable, on small scale, on personal accountability. When the new constitution was revealed to the world it was pronounced visionary, impractical, and unrealistic, just as its predecessor had been.

But, as Vera Allwen and her Survivalist colleagues learned in coping with the many difficult economic and political problems that the establishment of the new nation posed, the constitution worked. After some drastic readjustment of import-export balances (notably the cessation of lumber export and the near cessation of automobile imports) the rich economy of the region settled down into new patterns. Breaking away from the problem-wracked "old country" liberated long unrewarded energies. For the Ecotopians everything somehow seemed possible again and there was a spirit of equality and mutual support in the air. Tax policies were greatly simplified to favor production rather than tax-avoidance investment, and new employee-owned enterprises thrived in many fields. As year followed year, the new nation took on its own special character. Children like Theo grew up unable to conceive that once upon a time people had sent compostable kitchen wastes to the dump, and lived alone in tiny studio apartments with no one else around for support and stimulation, and went places by riding in private boxes on wheels rather than walking on streets where they would encounter friends and neighbors. Gradually but steadily, in thousands of Ecotopian mini-cities and neighborhoods, people learned to live in open dependence on the sun and within the resources of the earth—seeking stable survival rather than reckless exploitation followed by decline and fall.

New hands had moved in to assume the research functions of the Ecotopia Institute, and Raye Dutra took a year's leave to do some travelling. Maggie and Henry continued as Vera's chief aides; Nick, feeling restless, decided to get out of government for a while and

322

work in the housing industry, which was entering an exciting period of building new mini-cities.

Even during moments of gravest crisis, ordinary life had continued, as it always does. Jamie McBride, who had gone into the buggy-manufacturing business with Frank Werdon, had the pleasure of see- ing their light, handsome buggies everywhere on Ecotopian streets and roads. In time Jamie got together permanently with Lucy; they had two children and moved back out to the place in the country with Jane and Mack, where no aerial spraying would ever again be permit- ted; year by year they extended Jamie's old garden a few more rows. David Vandermeer and Sharp & Natural, now quite famous, formed a record company but decided to sell records only at their concerts, so that people would have some real experience to take home with the discs.

Life continued also for those who had opposed the Ecotopian revo- lution. Omni Oil was convicted of the attempted burglary of the Swift house; this played some role in the nationalization of the energy cor- porations in the new country. The mysterious Mr. Barber seemed to have fled to parts unknown. Raussen was forced to transfer most of its operations to the Los Angeles area or Mexico, but Howard Pender- ton got quite a decent price for his personal estate; it was transformed into an agricultural research institute and training school for new methods of biological control of pests. The remnants of the Demo- cratic and Republican parties coalesced to form a new Progressive Party, dedicated to the restoration of what its members saw as a proper spirit of untrammeled free enterprise. After two years had passed, Andy and Sarah Swift returned from Chicago; they moved back into their Orinda house and Andy began working with the new department of transportation on the construction of the Ecotopian train system.

Outside the borders of the new country, ecological disasters grew ever more common and severe. Whole cities and states were some- times poisoned by chemical accidents. As nuclear plants aged and became more prone to breakdowns, evacuation drills were a routine feature of life. The war in Brazil dragged on, seeming as unwinnable as its Vietnam counterpart. American occupation of the Saudi oil fields had not led to nuclear war, but only a bloody engagement with Iraqui tanks; the situation, however, remained tense and the drain of ever-increasing military expenditures meant widespread suffering and disorder. More than a third of the American population now lived at or below the official poverty line. Women's wages had sunk to only half those of men, and token equality had reverted to blatant sex discrimination.

With Saudi oil supplies cut off, the American economy's inflation rose to unprecedented heights as oil prices soared again. The government instituted crash construction of plutonium breeder reactors and a "nuclear safety program" to safeguard them; this blind reaction was no help to the nation's basic fuels problem, but it provided the excuse for greatly increased surveillance and infiltration of dissident political groups. Some of these groups, if permitted to flourish, might have evolved coherent and positive programs to deal with the nation's ills, as the Survivalist Party had done in the West. Instead, however, government repression allowed popular unrest no orderly outlet. Food and water supplies were increasingly believed to be contaminated, but the press had been intimidated into suppressing ecological bad news, so rumors of new health threats circulated wildly. The rich, increasingly favored by government taxing and spending policies, could afford to defend themselves with filters and special foods; the poor, in their rage, sabotaged business enterprises and looted whatever could be gotten away with. In time, refugees began to flow westward, seeking to enter prosperous and healthy Ecotopia; but since a cardinal principle of the new Ecotopian regime was to bring about a slow decline in population, the borders were closed, and militia members stood guard at night on the lonely mountain passes.

When Marissa read of Eastern events in the obstreperous Ecotopian press she was horrified, and thought back to the time when Ben had shown her the border beyond which madness lay. He had exaggerated it then, she thought—but now? After Independence she had adopted the last name "Brightcloud," in remembrance of the luminous cloud at the moment of Laura's death. Now her forestry group had taken over 17,000 acres of derelict timber country north of San Francisco and was nursing it back to productive health; Marissa was a mainstay of its executive committee. Ben had reappeared after Independence, but always refused to disclose whether his bomb project had played any role in the secession crisis. However, he did seem to be quite friendly now with Vera Allwen, and sometimes Marissa felt he had mellowed a bit.

Jan's studio warehouse had been added to yet again, this time to make room for Jeffrey. Lou always found it a stimulating place to spend a few days, but she too had done some travelling after Independence—hitchhiking through a series of very small countries. Now that she lived in a nation with less than 15 million people, she thought it might be interesting to see how people managed in other small places like Holland, Denmark, Sweden, Iceland, Austria. (They managed extremely well, she found.) After her return she had worked on a few refinements to her cell, and then gone to study biology at Berkeley. After that she helped in the setting up of a small independent research lab, where she and some friends were doing genetic work that promised to persuade certain algae to secrete alcohol directly—removing the need for a fermentation process.

Lou liked to alternate city and country experiences, so sometimes she and Bert, with whom she still spent a good deal of time, would go out to Bolinas for a few days at the Swift house. Bert had become a rather controversial writer on science-politics questions, and had moved into a journalists' communal house in San Francisco, called Franklin's Cove. He too liked a change of pace, and in Bolinas he and Lou would work in the garden with Theo, clean the solar cell panels, and have long conversations with Roger and Carol and Dimmy. (The grizzlies were safe in the Sierra, and seldom seen.) Often too, they would take walks along the beach far to the north, or out over the mesa—where electric wires no longer ran.

Once, on a hot summer day, they had followed the beach back to the lagoon inlet. It seemed time for a swim, and Lou realized that the tide was just beginning to run out of the lagoon. Heated in the shallow lagoon, the outgoing water was comfortably warm until it began mixing with the frigid Pacific. "I've got something to show you!" Lou shouted, and dove into the water. "Come on," she yelled back at Bert, "it's a new kind of stable-state system! You can swim against the ebb tide and stay exactly in the same place."

Bert joined her, but he didn't have Lou's experience with the current, so he kept getting carried either out toward the sea or off toward the beaches on either side of the inlet. But Lou, feeling lithe as a sea otter, played games with the current. She swam breast stroke, head down into the tide's pull. She swam back stroke, her long strong arms rhythmically beating the water. When she saw she was losing ground, she flipped over and regained it with her crawl. And then she floated on her back and let herself be carried by the current, closing her eyes as the sun beat on her tanned face, until she began to feel icy tingles of sea water and turned to swim upstream again.

To an observer from a distant planet, the earth hung in the night sky as it had for millions of years, unflickering and serene. The evolution or extinction of creatures upon its surface, even of those as remarkable as humans, were imperceptible on a cosmic scale. From a closer viewpoint, as from a satellite in high orbit, the fertile crescent of Ecotopia could be distinguished, green with trees, along the Pacific coast. Within its boundaries the human species had recognized that it too was a part of nature, which could not indefinitely be mocked.

If that idea spread sufficiently fast and far among the other nations of earth, the heedless rush of technological exploitation might be turned back and biological disaster averted. On the whole, destruction still reigned; surrounded by desolation, Ecotopia seemed a small, precarious island of hope. But its inhabitants had lit a beacon that might yet guide other travelers home.

Keystroking: Ernest Callenbach
Scanning and typesetting: Wilsted & Taylor, Berkeley
Type: 10/12 Times Roman
Bolstering: Walt Anderson, Stewart Brand, Jackson Burgess, Alan Freeland, Robert Greensfelder, Brian Henderson, Richard Kahlenberg, Lucy Kaplan, Tony Koltz, Christine Leefeldt, Jerry Mander, Malcolm Margolin, Nick Margulis, Richard Register, Holly Sawin, Sue Somit, Karen Valenzuela, Jerry Vizenor. And special gratitude to George R. Stewart, who first led the way.